The Exodus Murders

Previous books by Trevor Negus

The Coal Killer

For Sarah

The Exodus Murders

Trevor Negus (signature)

Trevor Negus

Published by Bathwood Manor Publishing

A CIP catalogue record for this book is available from the British Library.

ISBN 978-0-9955737-3-4

Book layout by Clare Brayshaw

Prepared and printed by:

York Publishing Services Ltd
64 Hallfield Road
Layerthorpe
York YO31 7ZQ

Tel: 01904 431213

Website: www.yps-publishing.co.uk

PROLOGUE

3.00pm Friday, February 10th 1986
Worksop, Nottinghamshire

'Excuse me love, you've forgotten your change.'

The woman slowly turned and without looking up walked back to the shop counter. She reached out and the shopkeeper placed the coins into the palm of her hand. He was worried, the woman looked so fragile. He could see that her eyes were bloodshot and red rimmed, she looked as though she had recently been crying. There was nothing of her, the baggy clothes she wore hung from her slight frame, she had the appearance of a Victorian workhouse waif. Her jet-black hair was lank and unwashed. It hung down to her shoulders.

The black hair contrasted vividly against her alabaster white complexion.

'Thanks', she mumbled, before closing her hand around the cash and thrusting it into her jeans pocket.

The woman turned to leave.

Gently, the elderly shopkeeper took hold of her arm, momentarily halting her progress, 'Are you sure you're ok love?' he asked, genuine concern in his voice.

'I'm fine, really.'

The shopkeeper released his soft grip on her arm. The young woman walked slowly out of the small off licence and back onto the busy High Street. It was three o'clock in the afternoon and the street was bustling with shoppers taking advantage of the first day of sunshine, after a depressing week of rain. It was a beautiful day; the sky was bright blue and although the sun looked watery and weak, it still felt warm.

She walked with her head down, not even looking up when a coach revved loudly right at the side of her. The large vehicle belched out a dark cloud of diesel fumes from its exhaust, just as it passed by her. Wrinkling her nose at the stench of the acrid fumes, she walked on.

The woman now had everything she needed from her little shopping expedition and started to walk briskly out of the town centre. As she strode out, she could feel the handles of the small white carrier bag biting into the palms of her hand; the contents were quite heavy.

Gradually, the streets became quieter and after ten minutes of walking, she was approaching the edge of the town. Another five minutes and she would be at Farriers Wood. It was her favourite place in the small market town of Worksop. It was an oasis of calm, situated on the very edge of the Nottinghamshire market town. Farriers Wood was spread over three acres of park and woodland, she often visited to relax, unwind and raise her spirits.

As she continued to walk slowly along the quiet streets, she could hear her mother's voice echoing inside her head, 'When you get here, there will be loads of cuddles my darling, I've missed being with you so much.' Her mother's voice sounded encouraging, it was seductive and warm.

She missed her mother so much.

Then she could hear the stern voice of her father, he was shouting, talking over her mother, determined to make himself heard, 'You will stay here with me girl. It's not time for you to leave yet!'

Her father's voice was strong and dominant now. She hoped that once inside the peaceful surroundings of Farriers Wood, it would become clear to her, what she should do.

Finally, she found herself standing at the entrance to the park. She paused at the large wrought iron gates that were flung wide open, inviting her in. The park looked stunningly beautiful, the snowdrops were starting to open, urged out by the warm sun, the stark white flowers contrasting against the lush green grass and the purple hues of the bluebells.

She walked along the red cinder pathway, until she reached the first area of dense woodland. The new leaves of the trees were starting to bud, but hadn't yet begun to unfurl. She stepped off the path and made her way into the woods, it was cooler in here and the woman was grateful for the thin cardigan she wore.

For a young woman, her face bore the lines of a troubled existence and she looked older than her twenty-eight years. The trauma she had known in her short life, had diminished the natural beauty of her face, even her once bright, blue eyes, framed perfectly by her ghostly white complexion, now appeared dull and lifeless.

Walking deeper into the woods, she found a natural clearing next to a large oak tree. The sun light was streaming through the almost bare branches, it created a welcome pool of light at the bottom of the big tree.

Feeling weary, the woman sat down at the base of the tree, placing the carrier bag at the side of her. She sat quietly for several minutes, the sun's rays warming her as she listened to the sound of birdsong and the gentle breeze moving through the branches overhead.

Her mother's voice was stronger here, her syrupy, cajoling voice easily overpowered her father's angry pleadings.

Reaching into the carrier bag, she took out the large bottle of Smirnoff vodka. Unscrewing the cap, she raised the heavy bottle to her lips, took a mouthful of the fiery liquid and swallowed it greedily. She felt the harsh spirit burn her throat, then the warmth spread through her body as the alcohol seeped into every nerve ending.

She shuddered and took another mouthful, the burn in her throat was slightly less this time. Feeling light headed, she propped the bottle upright between her legs, abandoning the screwcap on the floor next to her.

The only voice she could hear now was her mother's.

In that instant, she knew exactly what she should do. Moving carefully, so she didn't disturb the vodka bottle, she reached into the carrier bag again, this time she took out four white boxes.

Each box contained a blister pack of twenty Paracetamol tablets.

Slowly and deliberately, she began to take two or three tablets at a time, washing them down with a sip of the fiery vodka.

After ten minutes both the vodka bottle and the packets of pills were empty.

The woman hurled the empty bottle into the bracken at the side of her, turned over and lay down on the warm grass. She felt a few spasms in her stomach, but the vodka she had consumed meant the pain felt dull, easily bearable.

She curled up into the foetal position, drawing her knees up to her chest and closed her eyes.

The tablets and the vodka were already killing her, as she drifted off into a sleep that she would never wake from.

The woman was finally at peace, there was a smile on her face.

She knew her mother was waiting for her.

CHAPTER I

2.00pm Friday, March 17th 1986
Mansfield Cemetery, Nottinghamshire

It was a bitterly cold day; the strong winds drove the freezing rain across the large open cemetery. The headstones and the few scattered trees offered scant protection against the inclement conditions.

For the twenty or so mourners at the open grave, the atrocious weather had turned an already desperately sad day into a horrendous ordeal.

The pall bearers, with ice cold rain dripping from their faces, slowly lowered the heavy wooden casket down into the open grave.

The vicar spoke loudly, raising his voice to be heard above the howling wind, 'Man that is born of a woman, hath but a short time to live, and is full of misery. He cometh up, and is cut down, like a flower; he fleeth as it were a shadow, and never continueth in one stay. In the midst of life, we are in death.'

Danny Flint stood at the head of the grave, flanked by his girlfriend Sue Rhodes and his best friend and work colleague Rob Buxton. As he listened to the flat, monotonous tone of the vicar, he felt his mind begin to meander away.

As the coffin was slowly lowered down into the muddy maw of the open grave, Danny became transfixed by the rain bouncing off the brass plate on the lid of the casket. His eyes bore into the name engraved on the dull, yellow metal plate, "FRANK EDWARD FLINT".

The vicar's voice cut through into his consciousness again, 'Thou knowest Lord, the secrets of our hearts; shut not thy merciful ears to our prayer; but spare us, Lord most holy, O God most mighty, O holy and merciful Saviour, thou most Judge eternal, suffer us not, at our last hour, for any pains of death to fall from thee.'

The coffin reached the bottom of the grave and the pall bearers began to remove the straps.

So, that was it, thought Danny. Both his mother and father were now dead, his father being interred in the same grave as the one his mother had occupied for the last ten years.

Danny felt numb, both physically and emotionally. He could feel the tears streaming down his face and he swallowed hard. He felt Sue's reassuring presence beside him as she squeezed his hand tightly, then another surge of overwhelming grief as he thought of his impending wedding to her, the celebration his father would not now be able to witness.

For a while, the vicar's words were lost against the strident wind; he had given up trying to talk over it. Danny could see his mouth moving but did not hear the words. Then he saw the elderly vicar turn and walk directly towards him, his bony hand carrying a small wooden box that contained soil. With his long robes being buffeted by the strong winds, the clergyman held out the box to Danny, urging him to join in the melancholy ritual.

Now the vicar was closer, he could once again hear his voice above the wind, 'For as much as it hath pleased

Almighty God of His great mercy to take unto Himself the soul of our dear brother who has departed, we therefore commit his body to the ground; earth to earth, ashes to ashes, dust to dust; in sure and certain hope of the resurrection to eternal life through our Lord Jesus Christ.'

Danny shuddered as he thrust his fingers deep into the freezing cold soil. Taking a handful of the black dirt, he stepped forward to the edge of the open grave and allowed the dirt to drop down onto the top of the coffin. Having carried out his part of the solemn ritual he stepped back and allowed the other mourners to follow suit.

The vicar completed the blessing, saying the Lord's Prayer first, then the collect, as the final act of committing Danny's father's body into the care of the Lord. The vicar then urged everybody at the graveside to take immediate shelter from the atrocious conditions.

Sue approached the vicar and invited him to join the rest of the mourners at the wake in a nearby public house.

Rob and Sue walked either side of Danny as they left the graveside and headed back to the car park. Sue slipped her arm through Danny's and tried to comfort him.

As they made the short car ride from the cemetery to the Rushley public house for the wake, Danny reflected on the previous year. It had been an emotional rollercoaster for them all.

It was almost a year ago, to the day, when he'd received the amazing telephone call from Dave Smedley in Australia. Smedley had informed Danny that Jimmy Wade, the man dubbed The Coal Killer by the nations press, was to be found at a coalmine near Sydney, where he had found employment as a face worker.

Danny had immediately arranged for the Australian police to locate and detain Wade. It had been a simple task to then arrange the extradition of Wade back to the United Kingdom. He'd felt an overwhelming sense of relief and euphoria, when he travelled with Rob Buxton to Sydney to meet the murderer he had worked so hard to bring to justice. The two detectives had then escorted the killer back to England for trial.

Wade never uttered a single word throughout the long aeroplane journey, he sat between the two detectives and maintained a stony silence, just staring straight ahead.

He even refused to acknowledge the air stewardess when she enquired as to whether or not he would like any refreshments.

After they had arrived at Heathrow, a full vehicle escort was provided to convey Wade and the detectives back to Nottinghamshire. Jimmy Wade was already considered to be one of the country's most dangerous criminals.

The killer maintained his silence throughout every interview with the detectives. When questioned at length about the atrocious murders he was suspected of committing with Police Sergeant Michael Reynolds, Wade showed no remorse. Throughout the long interviews, his bright, blue eyes stared into the middle distance and never once betrayed an inner emotion.

The fingerprint that Wade had inadvertently left on the base of the glass vase at the home of Dc Rachel Moore, proved to be the final evidential nail in his coffin. He was subsequently charged with the murders of Albert Jones, Mandy Stokes, June Hayes, Police Sergeant Michael Reynolds and the attempted murder of Detective Constable Rachel

Moore. The trial at Leicester Crown Court began in October, 1985 and had lasted for four weeks. Once again, throughout the entire duration of the trial, Wade never uttered a word; he declined to offer any evidence in his defence. It had taken the jury only three hours of deliberations to return guilty verdicts on all the charges.

Having been found guilty by a jury of his peers, His Honour Judge Winterbourne sentenced Wade to life imprisonment. Only when sentence had been passed did Wade finally show any emotion, he allowed the faintest hint of a smile to fleetingly pass over his face as he was being led down the steps.

Jimmy Wade was now held at Rampton Hospital.

As he was sentenced, the trial judge had made it clear to Wade that the maximum-security hospital would be where he would spend the rest of his life. His Honour Judge Winterbourne considered Wade to be such a danger to the public and his crimes so heinous that he ordered that the former collier should never be considered for release.

For Jimmy Wade, life imprisonment meant life imprisonment. Considered by the Court to be criminally insane, he would grow old and die in Rampton Hospital.

The immediate aftermath of the trial saw Nottinghamshire Constabulary heavily criticised over their handling of the Coal Killer murders. The public had been outraged at the lack of manpower deployed to investigate the killings.

Even at the height of the criticism of the force generally, His Honour Judge Winterbourne had commended Danny Flint and his small team of detectives for their efforts in trying to track down the serial killer. Having commended the individual detectives involved in the manhunt, the judge then laid the blame, for the fact Wade had evaded capture, squarely at the door of the Chief Constable, conveniently ignoring the constraints on manpower that the yearlong strike had forced on the Nottinghamshire Constabulary.

The Chief Constable responded to this direct criticism by forming a specialist Major Crime Investigation Unit, to undertake prolonged investigation into murder and other specified serious crime. The head of this new department would be Detective Chief Superintendent Wainwright, a well-regarded, straight talking Scot who hailed from the tough, granite city of Aberdeen.

The MCIU, as it was to be known, would consist of a Detective Chief Inspector, responsible for supervising two investigation teams, each led by a Detective Inspector. The two teams would each be made up of two Detective Sergeants and twelve detectives.

These investigation teams would be supported by dedicated scenes of crime personnel that would be drawn from both the force and civilian resources, as required.

The Chief Constable, on the forthright recommendation of Chief Superintendent Wainwright, had promoted Danny Flint to Detective Chief Inspector and Rob Buxton to Detective Inspector. Both men had then been transferred immediately to the new investigation unit. Dc Rachel Moore had also transferred onto the MCIU, but Dc Andy Wills, the last remaining member of the small team that had worked so hard to bring Jimmy Wade to justice, had been promoted to sergeant and was now working at Beeston in a uniform role.

The feeling of euphoria and satisfaction Danny had felt upon gaining promotion and being asked to head up the new unit, had quickly disappeared when his father suffered another devastating stroke. As a result of this second catastrophic stroke, his father had been hospitalised in order to receive round the clock care. The prognosis was a poor one; there was absolutely no prospect of him returning to the Pleasley nursing home, where he had been so happy.

It was during this period of emotional turmoil that Danny found himself being drawn ever closer to Sue Rhodes. It had seemed a natural progression to elevate their commitment to one another, so on Christmas Day, Danny had proposed marriage. Sue readily accepted and the couple had set their wedding day for the 7th of May 1986.

Then, on the 6th of March, just after the doctors at the hospital had noticed some tell-tale signs of a gradual recovery, Danny had received the devastating news that his beloved father had contracted pneumonia and was close to death. He'd immediately driven to the hospital to be with his father. He could still tangibly recall the feeling of helplessness that had overwhelmed him as he sat by his father's bedside holding his hand, watching him pass peacefully away.

Thinking about that moment, Danny could now feel the grief closing in around him again.

As the dark mood enveloped him, his mouth became dry and he found it difficult to swallow. Once again, he could feel the sting of new tears filling his eyes.

The car, driven by Rob, pulled into the car park of the Rushley public house.

Danny squeezed Sue's hand gently and said, 'Can you go inside with Rob? I just need a few minutes by myself, before I come in.'

Sue smiled and said, 'Of course, take as long as you need sweetheart. We'll be waiting inside when you're ready.'

Danny got out, then walked out of the car park and along Nottingham Road towards Mansfield town centre. Five minutes later, he was standing outside his father's old house on Garth Road. Danny had sold the house in November last year, after he'd moved in to live with Sue at her house, on the other side of town. The money raised from the sale of the property had originally been intended to help pay for the nursing home where his father had lived happily until the second stroke had occurred.

As he stood looking at the front of the house, Danny could already see how the new owners had altered things. The planting in the garden was different, the curtains had changed and the windows had all been replaced with brown UPVC frames.

Danny smiled to himself, turned away from the house and started to walk briskly back to the Rushley pub.

Seeing the changes to the house had helped him realise that life never stands still; it keeps moving forward relentlessly. He'd been understandably devastated at the loss of his father and that wouldn't change, but he now knew that his future with Sue would be wonderful. He felt uplifted and thankful for everything his mother and father had given him.

He was energised, the depression he had felt at his father's passing gradually diminished with each step.

He now felt eager to embrace life; he couldn't wait to marry Sue and spend the rest of his life with her. He also realised how much he was looking forward to making a success of the newly formed Major Crime Investigation Unit.

CHAPTER 2

5.00pm Monday, March 20th, 1986
Underwood, Nottinghamshire

It was the third day.

The Watcher lay motionless in the hide he'd created. Heavily camouflaged and under the cover of darkness, he'd crawled into the patch of gorse bushes three days ago. He had brought with him enough food and water to last him a week, he hoped his mission wouldn't take that long. The prickly gorse bushes provided fantastic cover, he knew from experience they would also deter any passing dogs from investigating his presence too closely. As the days passed he'd gradually refined the hide. This was natural habitat for the Watcher, a large part of his adult life had been spent in similar hides doing exactly this.

The stalking and killing of prey came naturally to him, whether that prey was animal or human, mattered not to him.

He was used to foul and inclement weather, the constant rain that had fallen and the cold nights didn't concern him. The camouflaged overalls and the head and shoulders of his ghillie suit did little to keep him warm, but he knew he could always draw on the rage burning within him, to help keep out the cold and the wet.

The roll of dark green tarpaulin he lay on, kept most of the damp from the sodden earth at bay. The tools he would need later were all in a leather grip bag that was protected from the weather by a black plastic bin liner. The bag was never more than an arm's length away.

From his position in the hide, he had an unobstructed and elevated view of the large detached bungalow that lay below. His target hadn't returned home for two nights now, but he remained totally focussed; maybe tonight would be the night.

The previous night, he'd used the time the bungalow remained unoccupied to do a complete recce of the premises. Without leaving any trace, he had forced entry into the property and had examined every room. He took great care over the alarm system, it was a simple one that utilised the telephone line. With his specialist skills, it had been an easy task to bypass the system. On the night of the operation, he wouldn't bother to bypass it, he would simply sever the telephone line. People would be aware soon enough that the property had been entered.

He'd been surprised at the opulence of the bungalow, everything inside was perfect. The appliances were all top of the range and it had been decorated throughout by somebody with exquisite taste.

The reason he had been surprised was because he knew his target lived alone, but it was as though the bungalow had been adorned with a feminine touch. He'd been particularly impressed by the low-level lighting in the kitchen, he had made a mental note to use the kitchen as the interrogation and killing room on the night of the mission. As he exited the bungalow, he'd ensured that no tell-tale signs had been left, that would give away his presence inside the property.

He was methodical and professional; these precautionary actions were second nature to him.

Patience was the key; he knew he could only strike when the time was right.

He fully understood what his mission demanded, once he had made entry to the property he would need to spend considerable time alone with his target. What he needed to do, in order to get what he required, could take a long time, he could not afford for there to be any interruptions or unexpected visitors.

As dusk fell and twilight replaced daylight, the rain finally abated and the Watcher settled down in his hide for another long night.

CHAPTER 3

5.45pm Monday, March 20th, 1986
Arnold, Nottingham City

It had been a long and tiring day.

Cavalie Naylor finally placed his pen down on the dark wood desk and stretched, he then bunched his hands and rubbed his sore, tired eyes. He had, at last, finished writing up the specifications for the next Nottinghamshire County Council building project. His father would now be able to place a tender to the council for the contract to build the new police station, planned for the village of Mansfield Woodhouse.

Cavalie was twenty-nine years of age, son and heir to the huge property development firm, Naylor Properties Ltd.

He was an intelligent, articulate, smart individual, who dressed impeccably and spent a great deal of care over his appearance. He was a slim, good-looking man who women easily found themselves attracted to. His overall appearance and demeanour, coupled with his obvious wealth and status meant he had women virtually throwing themselves at him.

The adoration and attention from women meant nothing to Cav.

He had known from a very early age that he wasn't interested in women. He was gay. Due to the pressure of outside influences, mainly his father's attitude, he hadn't yet dared to come out into the open about his sexuality.

Everything in his life, so far, had been gifted to Cavalie Naylor; his father had seen to that. He had paid for his son to receive the very best private education available, Cav had attended the Nottingham High School for Boys. From there it had been a natural progression for him to attend Nottingham University, where he'd obtained a first-class degree in Business Studies and Commerce. Cav had played rugby union at the university, in an attempt to hide his true sexuality.

He'd endured a terrible time obtaining his higher education; he was befriended by three members of the rugby team who were all loathsome individuals. The three friends, urged on by one in particular, constantly teased Cav, making reference to some of his more effeminate mannerisms. Cav found that he had been regularly encouraged into playing the part of a macho arsehole, forced to show a total disrespect for the opposite sex. On a number of occasions, urged on by his three so called friends, he'd been forced into acts with women that he found totally abhorrent.

It had been a nightmare time, and his graduation from university in 1979 had come as a massive relief. He'd been forced to remain in touch with the three men even after he had left university. This was in order to facilitate business deals for his father's company. He tolerated this situation, but made no secret of the fact that he didn't like the three individuals, and had nothing to do with them on a social basis.

He stood up, walked from behind the desk and quickly sneaked a look outside his office door to ensure that his secretary had left. Seeing that she was not at her desk, he then returned, sat back down, leaned forward in his chair and reached for the telephone on his desk.

He dialled a number from memory and spoke softly into the phone, 'Hi Chris. I've had such a shit day. Why don't I pick you up on my way home, I'll cook something nice for us and you can stay over. I'm desperately in need of a hug or two.'

There was a pause, as he waited for the other person to speak.

Cav's face lit up and he grinned broadly saying, 'That's great, you bring a nice bottle of red and I'll make a lasagne, it won't take long. I'm sure we'll find something to do while we wait for it to cook, see you in twenty, lover.'

He glanced at his watch as he replaced the telephone. It was now almost six o'clock in the evening. From Christopher's flat to his bungalow in Underwood would take about ten minutes; if he drove his Jaguar to the max he could be home by half past six.

He was excited about seeing Christopher. He hadn't seen him for over a week, as he'd been away in Glasgow on business. Cav genuinely believed that Christopher was the special person he'd been looking for.

Over the last three years Cav had been out with many men, but nobody had provided him with the same amount of pleasure and contentment as Christopher. Just being in his company gave him an enormous thrill. He didn't care that Chris was slightly older, had no money and lived in a scruffy flat in a run-down area of Hucknall. He had already decided that he could gladly spend the rest of his life with him. If it hadn't been for Cav's overbearing father, they would be living together already.

As he made his way down the stairs and out into the car park Cav smiled, he thought to himself how fantastic it was that Christopher sounded equally as pleased at the prospect of spending the night with him. Cav knew that Christopher thought the world of him, but little moments like that just reinforced it.

Exactly half an hour after putting the telephone down and having picked up an excited Christopher on the way, Cav drove his Jaguar onto the driveway of his luxurious secluded bungalow in the village of Underwood. The car engine ticked loudly as it cooled down after being driven at high speeds through the country lanes. Both men eagerly got out of the car and stepped quickly towards the main entrance of the property, which was located to one side of the bungalow.

The porch light came on as Cav excitedly fumbled for his keys. Christopher stepped forward and still holding a bottle of Chianti in each hand, he wrapped his arms around Cav's neck. Leaning in he kissed Cav passionately on the lips. Cav returned the kiss and slipped his arms around the other man's waist.

'God, I've missed you so much Chris', purred Cav.

He looked closely at Christopher, he was like a blonde-haired version of himself. They were total mirror images of each other. Cav had stylishly short dark hair and brown eyes. Christopher had blonde hair and blue eyes. They were exactly the same height and build, had the same style haircut and the same taste in clothes, which Cav always purchased for both of them from the best designer shops in Nottingham.

Christopher eventually released his arms from around Cav's neck and broke off from the passionate kiss. He put his cheek on Cav's cheek and whispered, 'Get inside that house, I think we both need to shower before dinner!'

Both men giggled and went inside the bungalow, totally unaware that their every move was being scrutinised.

Up above them, lying motionless in his gorse hide on the edge of the wooded copse, the Watcher settled down for another long night.

Maybe tomorrow night would be the night.

CHAPTER 4

10.00am Tuesday, March 21st, 1986
Nottinghamshire Police Headquarters

Danny Flint stepped along the command corridor at Nottinghamshire police headquarters and knocked on the door of Detective Chief Superintendent Wainwright's office.

A few seconds passed before he heard the familiar Scottish brogue of Bill Wainwright's voice, 'Come in!'

Danny opened the door and walked into the spacious and airy office. Wainwright was a bear of a man, he stood over six feet five and weighed close to nineteen stone. His hair was turning from the straw blonde colour it once was, to a steel grey. It was also beginning to thin and recede. Dressed in a charcoal grey business suit, crisp white shirt and a crimson paisley patterned tie, he looked like a very successful businessman.

Danny stood in front of the large mahogany desk and said quietly, 'You wanted to see me sir?'

'Aye Danny, come in, sit down. First and foremost, let me offer you my sincere condolences for your loss, are you sure you want to be back at work so soon after the funeral?'

'Yes sir, I'm fine and thank you, I appreciate both your condolences and your concern. Truth be told I feel a little better about everything when I'm at work. The last place I want to be right now is sitting around at home, on my own.'

'Well if you have a change of heart and you want some time off, just let me know, okay?'

'I will sir, thank you.'

'Look Danny, we've been working together for the last four months, I think it's time you dropped the sir and called me Bill, when it's just the two of us chatting, don't you agree?'

'That suits me fine Bill. Now what was the reason you wanted to see me?'

'You see, that's exactly what I like about you Danny, straight to the point, no beating around the bush with you, is there son?'

'No, there isn't. I know you wouldn't have called me out here just to offer me your condolences over my father's passing.'

The big Scotsman grinned, before allowing the usual dour expression to return to his face. He leaned back in his chair, steepled his fingers and said, 'I've had a meeting with the Chief Constable this morning about the future of the Major Crime Investigation Unit.'

'Do I need to be worried?'

'No Danny you don't, not at all. Quite the opposite actually, the Chief's been really impressed by the progress of the team. I know the workload has been light so far, but that was always going to be the case, Nottingham isn't exactly New York when it comes to murder cases is it?'

'Very true. So if the Chief's happy, what did you need to see me about?'

'He's asked me to provide him with a full breakdown of the man hour costings for the three murders investigated by the team so far. He's getting heaped with praise from the Home Office, at the moment. They like the initiatives he's introduced recently, the formation of the MCIU at Mansfield, and the brand new Sexual Offences Investigation Team based at Carlton in Lindrick. I think his concern is that some of the costs of these units might come back to bite him on the arse. If the budgets are seen to be too extravagant and outrageous with little end product to show, the criticism will start to drift in.'

'I can sort the breakdown on man hours out pretty quickly for you Bill. I always keep a running log on manpower costs, for every investigation. As you know, each of the three murders we've investigated so far have been domestic situations and the offenders were all arrested and processed relatively quickly. Simply because I've got a large team, I was able to keep the enquiry costs down to a minimum. Individual officers weren't racking up huge amounts of overtime, the workload could be spread. Two of the prosecution files were submitted quickly and Rob Buxton is finalising the last documents for the third. Obviously, I haven't yet factored in the hours that will be spent at Crown Court when these cases are finally listed for trial, but certainly at the moment our manpower costs have been relatively low.'

'That's good to hear Danny, how soon can you let me have the figures?'

'I'll check all the figures again today, I can draft a report tomorrow. I'll be able to let you have that completed report first thing on the 23rd.'

'That's great, thanks.'

'What about the new Sexual Offences Investigation Team? Have they been asked to provide similar costings for the enquiries they're running?'

'I don't think so Danny, they appear to have the personal backing of the Chief. He's really good friends with Maurice Dennington, the Superintendent in charge of the team. If it ever came down to a straight choice to keep one of the units, it would definitely be the MCIU that would go, regardless of results and viability.'

'I've heard of Maurice Dennington, but I've never worked with him, what's he like Bill?'

Raising his huge frame from the chair, Wainwright stood and walked to the window. With his back to Danny he said, 'I'll be kind to the man, and just say he's a career minded individual, let's leave it at that shall we.'

Danny also got to his feet, 'If that's all then Bill, I'll get back over to Mansfield and make a start on those figures.'

'Aye, you do that Danny, I think we can really make a difference with the MCIU, but we must be mindful of costings, it's not a bottomless budget, despite what noises the Chief made to the press when he set it up.'

'I get the picture, I'll keep a tight rein on the budget.'

'Thanks, and remember what I said about having some time off Danny, I know just how hard it can be when you've lost somebody close.'

Danny recalled that Bill Wainwright had lost his wife the previous August.

'I will, and thanks again for your concern Bill.'

Danny was in a reflective mood as he made his way to the car park.

The MCIU had been set up amid a glare of adverse publicity for the Nottinghamshire Constabulary. Very astutely, Chief Constable Miles Galton, had used that negativity to his advantage when negotiating budgets with the Home Office. He touted the cost of policing the pit strike as the main reason for the negative public reaction.

A sympathetic government, still grateful for the part the police had played in defeating the striking miners, had rewarded Chief Constable Galton with a substantial increase in his budget.

It was now obvious to Danny that the honeymoon was over and normal budget restraints would be applied in the very near future. He knew it would be down to him and Bill Wainwright to keep the costs of the newly formed MCIU in check, or it would very quickly be disbanded.

So much for the Chief's soundbite to the press, when he announced the formation of the new unit, "All the manpower needed, no restraint on costs. Whatever is required to investigate murder and other serious crime will be provided". The press had lapped it up.

Danny hated all the politics involved within the police force. All he'd ever wanted to do was investigate crime and lock up criminals. It was becoming apparent to him, that in the very near future, exactly which offences and how they were investigated, would be down to the cost.

The pounds, shillings and pence of each enquiry.

As he drove steadily back to Mansfield, he felt sick to the pit of his stomach.

CHAPTER 5

9.00pm Tuesday, March 21st, 1986
Underwood, Nottinghamshire

The Watcher stared down as the metallic grey Jaguar was driven slowly onto the driveway of the bungalow. It was much later than the previous night, nearly nine o'clock and already dark. He watched as his target got out of the driver's door of the sleek car. He waited patiently to see if the passenger door would open.

It didn't.

Finally, his victim was alone at the secluded property. The Watcher felt the usual rush of adrenaline course through his body, as he realised the time for action had finally arrived.

He continued to observe the man as he walked to his front door, where once again he was illuminated by the automatic porch light. No bottles of wine tonight, no lover to complicate things.

Tonight, Cavalie Naylor would pay for his sins.

The porch light went off. Seconds later the light in the lounge came on.

The Watcher knew every room of the house after his meticulous recce. With a tinge of excitement, he began to prepare the kit he would need for his night's work.

Silently, he dragged the black leather grip bag towards him and made a check of the contents. Inside the grip bag was a black day sack that contained a black woollen ski mask, surgical latex gloves, that he would wear beneath his black woollen ones, a roll of brown Gaffer tape, two long lengths of thin but very strong nylon cord, a two-inch paint brush with a red handle, a small crowbar, a tea spoon that had a long pointed bowl, clear plastic ziplock bags, the razor-sharp Sumunugashi skinning knife in its leather scabbard and finally a loaded Smith and Wesson.38 revolver with a black rubber grip.

A grim smile of satisfaction played across his lips as he felt the weight of the revolver in his hands.

Deep down he knew he wouldn't need the firearm.

It would be an easy task for him to overpower his victim, using his own massive physical strength. Although only slight in stature, the Watcher was extremely powerful and naturally strong. He carried the firearm purely as a contingency, should his meticulous plan go awry.

Finally, every light in the bungalow was switched off.

It was now after midnight. The Watcher made a last check of the hide that had been his home for four days. Nothing had been left behind. The leather grip bag now contained everything he had used in the hide. Small plastic bags containing his own excrement had been gathered up and placed in the bag. Apart from a slight indentation in the ground and some crushed vegetation, it was as if he'd never been there. The tools he needed for his mission were already in the black day sack, which he carried over his shoulder.

Stealthily, he made his way down towards the rear of the bungalow. The black ski mask had now replaced the head and shoulders of his ghillie suit, which had been carefully placed in the black leather grip bag he carried in his left hand.

When he reached the rear of the bungalow he stashed the grip bag beneath one of the rhododendron bushes that were dotted all along the rear of the property. He made his way quietly, to the small junction box that contained the telephone line. Using the skinning knife, which he had now attached to his belt, he quickly severed the telephone line.

Being careful how he placed his feet on the loose gravel, he made his way to the weak French doors that opened out from the kitchen. He'd previously identified these flimsy wooden doors as the best point of access into the bungalow. Swiftly and silently, he used the small crowbar to prise open the doors.

Having opened the doors, he crouched outside and waited.

After two minutes of silence, he stepped through the open doors and into the luxurious kitchen. Moving into the hallway, he located the alarm panel on the wall.

Satisfied that there had been no activation, the Watcher stealthily made his way through the bungalow and into the master bedroom. Cavalie Naylor was already in a deep sleep. As soon as his eyes had adjusted fully to the low levels of light in the bedroom, the Watcher stepped over to the bed and landed a single, concussive blow with the clenched fist of his right hand, directly onto the forehead of the sleeping man, instantly rendering him unconscious.

Pulling back the duvet, the Watcher removed the boxer shorts being worn by the now unconscious Naylor, then lifted the naked man from the bed. He carried him through the bungalow and back into the kitchen, where he used the two lengths of thin nylon cord to bind him securely to one of the sturdy, wooden chairs.

The Watcher then wrapped sticky brown Gaffer tape over the mouth of Naylor before standing back and waiting patiently. Confident in his planning, he closed the venetian blinds on all the windows, then flicked on the low-level lighting in the kitchen.

After almost ten minutes, Naylor finally started to stir from his unconscious state. As he slowly drifted back to full consciousness, the Watcher stared at him. He could see the fear appear in the man's eyes as the realisation of his situation, and what had happened became apparent.

Naylor was terrified, he panicked and began to struggle against his bindings. He quickly looked around the room and for the first time he saw the Watcher standing to his left.

Illuminated only by the low level, subdued lighting, the Watcher looked a terrifying sight.

Naylor could see the figure standing there was dressed from head to foot in dirty, camouflaged clothing. He wore blue latex gloves and his face was covered by a black woollen ski mask. The only parts of the face that Naylor could see, were the staring, crystal clear, blue eyes and the cruel mouth.

He was terrified by the vision and started to hyper ventilate beneath the Gaffer tape, making a wheezing, panting noise.

The Watcher stepped forward and ripped the brown tape from Naylor's mouth. He gripped the bound man's throat and growled softly, 'If you scream or make a sound, I'll kill you right now. Co-operate with me and you'll live. Do you understand?'

Frantically, Naylor nodded.

Very slowly the Watcher eased the pressure on Naylor's throat.

Finding his voice, Naylor muttered, 'Who are you? What do you want?'

In his soft Scottish accent the Watcher replied, 'What I want from you is information. Before I leave here tonight, you'll tell me the names and everything else I need to know about your three friends from Nottingham University.'

'I don't know who you mean, what friends? I've got no friends from my university days.'

Without speaking the Watcher stepped forward and immediately wrapped more brown Gaffer tape around the head of Naylor covering his mouth, but leaving his nose clear.

He stood in front of Naylor and showed him the skinning knife, holding it in front of the terrified man's eyes. The keen blade on the large, bone handled knife glinted in the subdued lighting.

'You'll soon learn that it's pointless to try and lie to me, laddie. You will give me those names and the information I want, eventually. It's entirely a matter of your own choosing how much pain you want to endure, before you do.'

The razor-sharp blade of the skinning knife was then used to expertly remove a six inch by three-inch strip of flesh from Naylor's chest. The upper layers of the skin had been peeled off with a deft hand, that was totally at ease with skinning animals. Blood started to seep from the large wound and Naylor let out an agonised, muffled scream into the Gaffer tape.

The Watcher repeated this process three more times. He very carefully laid each strip of flayed flesh over the back of another wooden chair that had been positioned so Naylor could see the strips of his own flesh.

The excruciating pain of being flayed alive, caused Naylor to lapse in and out of consciousness.

Finally, when Naylor returned to full consciousness, once again the Watcher removed the Gaffer tape from the tortured man's mouth.

Naylor panted, then started to softly whimper. Sweat began to bead on his forehead.

The Watcher moved close to his victims face and whispered gruffly, 'Are you ready to talk to me now? Or have I got to remove more of your worthless skin?'

Naylor sobbed, 'Please, no more. I'll give you their names, but they're not my friends, I don't know what they've done to you, but whatever it is, it's nothing to do with me.'

'Boy, just give me their names, NOW!'

Naylor blurted out the three names and then mumbled a response to each of the Watchers questions. When the questioning had been exhausted, more Gaffer tape was placed over Naylor's mouth. Even though his body was racked with pain he started to struggle against the nylon cord and grunted into the Gaffer tape, his eyes now wide with fear.

The Watcher reached into the breast pocket of his camouflaged overalls and took out a small laminated photograph which he held out directly in front of Naylor's face, forcing him to look at it.

As he looked at the photograph, Naylor's eyes suddenly widened with fear, he began to weep and tears streamed down his face, his body convulsed, racked with sobs. Naylor now knew exactly why this was happening to him. Through the Gaffer tape he tried to scream the words, 'I'm sorry!'

The noise that emerged from his mouth behind the tape was unintelligible.

The Watcher wasn't there for apologies.

He took the pointed tea spoon out of the day sack, holding it in his left hand he pressed it hard into the side of Naylor's right eye socket. He exerted pressure on the back of Naylor's head with his right hand until the metal of the spoon slid in and behind the eyeball. With a deft flick of the spoon, the Watcher popped Naylor's right eyeball out of its socket and on to his cheek.

The pain was overwhelming and Naylor again blacked out.

He quickly regained consciousness, but was now totally disorientated. His right eyeball was lying on his right cheek bone and faced down towards the floor, Naylor could still see the images through the eye but they were no longer aligned with the images being seen by his left eye.

The Watcher stepped forward and used the keen blade of the skinning knife to slice through the optic nerve of the right eye. He held the severed eyeball by the stringy nerve and dangled it in front of Naylor growling with contempt, 'Now you're truly sorry laddie.'

Frantically Naylor nodded in agreement, whimpering behind the tape.

The pointed spoon was then used in exactly the same way to remove the left eyeball from its socket. Naylor experienced another brief moment of disorientation as he continued to see the world through the eye that was lying on his cheek.

The Watcher quickly sliced through the optic nerve of the left eye, Naylor was suddenly and instantly plunged into a sightless darkness. Beneath the gag, he started to mutter the word, 'No' repeatedly.

Having dropped both of the severed eyes into a clear plastic zip lock bag, he then placed the small clear bag into the day sack.

Moving silently, the Watcher manoeuvred around Naylor until he stood directly behind him. Naylor was numb with shock, his body convulsed as he sobbed behind the cloying gag.

With his left hand, the Watcher grabbed a handful of Naylor's hair, he pulled his head sharply back, and savagely sliced the skinning knife across the exposed throat. The razor-sharp knife easily sliced through windpipe, tendons, muscles, nerves and arteries.

The blood loss from the gaping wound was massive.

Still bound to the wooden chair, Naylor was quickly surrounded by a pool of his own blood, the dark liquid spread slowly out across the polished white marble floor tiles.

For Cavalie Naylor, death came quickly as he bled out.

The Watcher surveyed the scene of carnage and smiled.

He felt satisfied that the first part of his pilgrimage was now complete. He stretched his arms out in front of him, raised his blood-soaked palms to the sky and said a quiet prayer, thanking the Lord God Almighty for guiding his hand.

Methodically, he moved around the kitchen, gathered all the tools he'd used and placed them back into the day sack. Finally, he took the two-inch paintbrush out of the day sack. There was one last thing that needed to be done, before he could leave the bungalow.

Bending forward, he dipped the paintbrush into the already congealing, pool of Cavalie Naylor's blood.

CHAPTER 6

4.45am Wednesday, March 22nd, 1986
Clumber Park, Nottinghamshire

The caravan site, situated in Clumber Park, had served as his base of operation since the start of his pilgrimage. It suited his purpose perfectly. The small caravan he had rented was cheap and easily big enough for his needs. The site itself was very secluded and only a couple of the other caravans on site were occupied. The shower block was still in good working order and provided hot and cold running water.

He'd arrived at the site a week ago, on March 17th, and had told the owner he would only need a short-term rental for a month. The story he had given to the owner was that he was on holiday for the next four weeks and wanted to use the caravan as a base for a walking expedition he had planned in the nearby Derbyshire Dales. He'd explained to the owner that he wanted to experience a different walk each day, so would often be away from the site.

On his arrival that first day, he'd promptly stowed all his gear in the caravan then set off that evening to establish the hide at Underwood. Once he'd found a suitable location that overlooked the bungalow, he'd prepared the hide and stashed everything he would need for both the observations and the operation itself. Only when everything had been taken care of did he return to the caravan park to rest.

The next day, he'd driven the battered olive green Land Rover Defender he was using to Jacksdale. Geographically, it was the closest village to Underwood. He'd visited a local newsagent in the village, where he saw a hand-written notice in the window, advertising a single garage to rent.

He removed the advertisement card from the window and drove to the address. The garage was at the side of a private house. The Watcher checked the address carefully. The external paintwork was shabby and the garden was overgrown. He saw there was a handrail at the side of the front door. All the indications were that it was an elderly person who lived there.

As daylight was turning to dusk, he knocked on the front door of the decaying house. The door was eventually opened by an incredibly frail looking old lady. The Watcher explained to her that he was interested in renting the garage for a week. The old lady explained that her husband had passed away six months ago, and she no longer had any use for the garage. The woman agreed to rent the garage to him for one week, at a cost of ten pounds.

Taking the black leather grip bag that contained everything he would need, that wasn't already stashed at the hide, he locked the Land Rover in the garage at Jacksdale.

Ensuring there were no prying eyes watching him, he then set off on foot, under the cover of darkness, across the fields to the neighbouring village of Underwood.

With the Land Rover safely tucked away out of sight and under lock and key, he could now concentrate solely on the observations at the bungalow.

Two days prior to him taking up residence at the caravan, the Watcher had established where Cavalie Naylor lived by following him from his workplace to his home address. The only information he had at the beginning of his pilgrimage, was the name Cavalie Naylor and the name of the company he owned and worked for.

It had been an easy task for him, firstly to locate the company in the Arnold district of Nottingham, then secondly to establish that the Jaguar car parked in the bay marked Managing Director belonged to Cavalie Naylor.

The first time he saw Naylor, he'd had to resist the strong urge he felt to slaughter him, and his boyfriend, there and then. Before he dispatched him to Hell, he needed answers. He knew that he needed information from him to help identify the other three demons who needed to pay before God, for their sins.

With the Lord's help, he had managed to stay his hand that day, he had demonstrated the patience required. This patience had been rewarded and the Almighty had delivered unto him the first of the demons.

He had carried out the Lord's bidding perfectly, he felt at peace.

The first part of his mission had taken four long days with hardly any sleep and very little sustenance. It was nothing to him. He'd spent far longer periods in hides when it had been required.

The Watcher had been trained by the best, he was a total professional. Stalking and killing were his stock in trade, he was a cold-blooded assassin who revelled in his work.

Having killed Naylor, he had walked in the pitch black, back across the farmland to Jacksdale. It had been almost three o'clock in the morning, when he stealthily stalked through the deserted streets of the small village, until he came to the rented garage. The roads of the village had few street lights and were dimly lit, he hadn't seen a soul. He had felt an overwhelming sense, that once again, the Lord was protecting him. He retrieved the Land Rover from the garage and left the padlock with a ten pound note stuffed beneath it outside the old lady's front door.

Having arrived back at the caravan site in the early hours of the morning, he had utilised the rudimentary washing facilities in the deserted shower block, to wash his kit before the few other caravaners on the site were awake. The only thing he didn't wash, was the head and shoulders of his ghillie suit.

He then returned to his caravan and placed the ziplock bag that contained Naylor's eyes, into the small fridge.

He made himself a cup of coffee, and buttered two slices of toast.

As he sipped his black coffee and ate the hot toast, he scribbled down the information he had extracted from Naylor. He now had sufficient information about the three other demons, that God had ordered him to despatch back to hell. Naylor had readily given over the names, occupations, brief descriptions and other useful information as he writhed in agony, cruelly flayed alive by the Watcher.

Now as he ate his toast, he pondered his next move and studied the ordnance survey map he'd picked up from a local garage, when he'd filled up the Land Rover with diesel. The map gave detailed information of the area surrounding Clumber Park.

Carefully scanning the detailed map, he soon found the nearest public telephone box. Glancing at his watch, he saw that the time was now five o'clock in the morning. He would sleep until eight thirty, then drive to the telephone box.

All it required was a simple phone call to the operator, he would then be able to establish the exact location of his next target. As soon as he discovered that location, then he would be in position to proceed with his grim pilgrimage.

He'd changed into grey jogging bottoms and a navy-blue fleece top as soon as he'd arrived back so that he could wash out the blood-soaked, mud stained, camouflage overalls.

He finished his coffee and toast.

Suddenly, tiredness overwhelmed him, he didn't bother to undress, he just climbed straight into the sleeping bag on the small bench that constituted his bed.

Within minutes the Watcher was fast asleep.

CHAPTER 7

8.30am Wednesday, March 22nd, 1986
Major Crime Investigation Unit, Mansfield

Danny Flint sat in his office staring at the rows of paperwork in front of him. Laid out on the desk were reams of overtime sheets submitted by the detectives on his team. They were in three distinct piles, one for each of the murder enquiries that had been investigated by the newly formed unit.

He glanced up at the clock on the wall, it was still only half past eight in the morning. He had been the first to arrive at work that morning, getting in just after seven o'clock. He still found it difficult to believe that these plush new offices were his. They had been fitted with state of the art computers, he was now trying to enter the data for the costings of the three cases on to a rudimentary spread sheet.

He made a mental note to himself, to get himself enrolled on a basic computer skills course as soon as possible.

There was a knock on the door.

'Come in!' shouted Danny.

Rob Buxton walked in carrying two steaming mugs of coffee, he was followed into the room by Brian Hopkirk, the other Detective Inspector on the MCIU. Rob gave one of the mugs of coffee to Danny, Brian was carrying his own.

Danny had specifically requested that Rob be promoted and join him on the unit. He was equally happy to have Brian Hopkirk to lead the other team of detectives.

Brian was forty three years of age, still extremely fit and very smart in appearance. As well as being a hard man, he was a talented detective who had a sharp brain and possessed a real talent for interviewing. He'd worked the city of Nottingham all his career, so was the perfect foil to Rob Buxton who'd only ever worked the north of the County. Rob and Brian had hit it off immediately, which made life for Danny, as their immediate supervisor, a lot easier.

Brian was a keen rugby union fan and had played to a high level when he was younger. Rob was a diehard rugby league man. The two men regularly engaged in very harsh banter, but they formed a very tight team and drove their respective halves of the unit professionally and with great skill and tenacity.

Danny had realised very quickly that his own role on the MCIU, would inevitably become more political in nature. More of a management and administrative role, rather than the cut and thrust of every day detective work. He still missed following up lines of enquiry, making arrests and interviewing suspects.

Both men sat down opposite Danny.

It was Brian who spoke first, 'You wanted to see us boss?'

'I did, I wanted to keep you both up to speed on the meeting I had with Bill Wainwright yesterday. It looks like the honeymoon is well and truly over, as regards the budget for the unit. From now on, I'll need you both to run everything by me that has a cost implication. I know, I was the world's worst for hammering the overtime budget when I was a Dc and a Ds, but the simple truth is, if we don't treat the budget responsibly this unit could be very short lived. We're competing for cash, with other newly formed units, so we've got to be a bit careful, is that understood?'

Brian sipped his coffee, then said, 'Understood boss, it's no bother. Obviously, we all love a bit of overtime, but we've both got plenty of manpower, so we shouldn't need to be spending a fortune on overtime to get results.'

Rob nodded his head in agreement, then said, 'Neither of us have ripped the arse out of the overtime on the jobs we've had so far, and they were all done and dusted pretty quickly.'

'I can see that Rob, I've spent most of yesterday and this morning doing the costings for the three cases we've had so far, they're all well within target. My only worry is, how would we fare with a protracted enquiry? Another Jimmy Wade scenario, when things aren't quite so clear cut.'

'I know what you're saying boss, but don't forget, on that enquiry from start to finish we had hardly any manpower to work with, but a budget where overtime was no object'.

'That's very true Rob. I just wanted to keep you both informed as to where we stand, before the next enquiry came in.'

'Personally speaking, I'll be glad when something does come in', said Rob. This time it was Brian who nodded in agreement.

Rob continued, 'We could do with a really interesting, protracted case to test the mettle of the unit, to see if it can function as well as we all think it can.'

'Yeah? I think, maybe you two should be very careful what you wish for. That's all gents, thanks. Rob, keep me posted on how that last court file is progressing please.'

'Will do boss, I've just got to plough my way through all the contemporaneous notes of the interviews'

Both men got up and left Danny to his three piles of paperwork.

He picked up the first overtime sheet, but his mind wandered and for a split second he recalled how he'd felt when Jimmy Wade and Michael Reynolds were killing women and leaving no clues in their wake.

He inwardly shuddered and muttered aloud, 'Be very careful what you wish for gentlemen.'

CHAPTER 8

8.30am Wednesday, March 22nd, 1986
Ollerton, Nottinghamshire

The Watcher parked the Land Rover in the car park of the Snooty Fox public house in Old Ollerton. After looking around, checking the area, he got out of the vehicle, crossed the road and stepped inside the red telephone box.

It was still quite early and the street was deserted. He was relieved to see the telephone box hadn't been vandalised and the telephone itself was still in good working order.

He phoned directory enquiries and asked the operator for the number of the Grosvenor Hotel in Nottingham. He scribbled down the number when the automated voice recited it.

Wasting no time he dialled the number and waited for the beeps, he stuffed loose change into the coin slot and heard a voice say, 'Grosvenor Hotel, Vicky speaking, how can I help you?'

Calmly he replied, 'Good morning Vicky, I was contacted by a friend in Nottingham yesterday, she asked me to meet her in the foyer of your hotel later today. Like an idiot, I didn't ask her precisely where your hotel is located in Nottingham.'

Vicky chuckled pleasantly before saying, 'That's no problem sir, we're by far the biggest hotel in Nottingham, I'm sure you would've found us anyway. We're located on

Maid Marian Way, right in the city centre. Is there anything else I can help you with this morning, sir?'

'No, thank you Vicky, that's great. Thanks for your help.'

He walked back across the road to the Land Rover, then made the short ten-minute drive back to the deserted caravan site.

Once inside his caravan, he went to a large suitcase on the floor and removed a dark blue business suit, white shirt and dark tie. From a holdall, he took out a pair of smart black brogues.

He knew he needed a totally different method, in order to get close to the second devil.

Having hung up the smart clothes on hangers, he settled down with a cup of coffee and his copy of the Old Testament. He'd neglected his study of the bible while he was in the hide. He yearned to spend some time communicating with the Lord, while he contemplated his next move.

CHAPTER 9

8.45am Wednesday, March 22nd, 1986
Arnold, Nottingham

Geoff Naylor scowled as he drove his dark blue Jaguar into the car park of Naylor Properties Ltd. The first thing he had noticed was that the grey Jaguar, used by his son Cavalie, was not in the car park.

He parked his own car and glanced down at his Rolex watch. It was almost nine o'clock in the morning, his son should have started work at eight.

Naylor got out of his car and stretched. He grunted at the effort, then bent forward, leaned back inside the car and grabbed his black briefcase from the front passenger seat.

He slammed the car door and strode purposefully towards the front door, he was already in a foul temper.

Geoff Naylor, at fifty-three years of age, was a self-made millionaire. He'd started his property development company in the mid-fifties, after being demobbed from the army. His National Service had started in January 1951, not long after the conflict between North and South Korea had begun. After completing his basic infantry training, he was quickly sent overseas as part of the ten thousand strong military presence, sent by Great Britain to support their allies the United States.

As soon as he arrived in Korea, he had been sent to the Imjin River. Naylor's regiment, the Glosters, were involved in heavy fighting at Imjin River, repelling North Korean troops, supported by the Chinese Red Army, as they tried to cross the river. Casualties were heavy on both sides. During the fierce fighting, an exploding mortar shell had landed alongside Naylor's shallow foxhole and his left leg was lacerated by flying shrapnel. He was evacuated from the front line by helicopter, his wounds were so severe that he subsequently didn't see any further action. As a result of his injuries he was flown back to the UK, where after making a partial recovery, he spent the rest of his National Service at Bicester Camp in Oxfordshire.

In January 1953, his national service complete, Geoff Naylor was demobbed from the army.

His big business breakthrough came in 1964, when his firm was awarded its first contract from Nottinghamshire County Council. After attaining that first contract, he found himself in the enviable position of being able to effectively control all new developments, commissioned by the County Council. As a result, his business had gone from strength to strength. His company now employed over one thousand people, but the one person he desperately needed to show more interest in the business, was his feckless son, Cavalie.

Geoff Naylor had become a father when he was twenty-four years old.

As soon as he discovered that his girlfriend Jean was pregnant, he had quickly proposed and the couple were married immediately. Cavalie was born seven months after the wedding, causing a few raised eyebrows at the time. The business was still in its infancy then, and Geoff hardly ever saw his young son. This was one of the reasons why, as soon as the business took off, he'd spend a lot of time and money on his only son.

His wife Jean, had died from a brain tumour, eight years ago, and this sudden and unexpected bereavement had made the bond between father and son even closer. It was a real source of frustration for Geoff, that although extremely competent and capable, Cavalie appeared reluctant to fully embrace the family business. Indeed, right at this moment, it appeared to Geoff Naylor that his son had no interest whatsoever, in taking the company forward.

He walked into the foyer of the building and took the lift to the third floor where his office was located. His son's office was immediately next door to his.

The lift door opened and Geoff Naylor stepped out.

He walked directly over to the desk situated outside his son's office door and said angrily to his son's personal assistant, 'Iris, has that idiot son of mine not turned in for work yet?'

The PA was shocked by the tone in the normally affable older man's voice.

'I'm sorry sir, Cavalie hasn't been in yet.'

'Well has he left any bloody messages, that would explain his absence?'

'No sir, I've been at my desk since eight o'clock this morning and there haven't been any calls from him. It's strange though, I was expecting him in this morning. Yesterday, he asked me to stay late, so I could have these figures ready for him first thing this morning.'

The personal assistant indicated a large manila folder on the edge of the desk.

'Are they the costings for the Mansfield Woodhouse project?'

'Yes sir, he wanted to go through them with you first thing today.'

Snatching up the folder, Naylor furrowed his brow and growled, 'Obviously, my son's idea of first thing and mine are very different. If he does eventually wander in, tell him I want to see him straight away.'

'Will do sir.'

The comment from Iris was aimed towards Naylor's back, as he was already striding towards his own office. Without looking back or acknowledging the PA's comment, he slammed the door behind him.

A stunned Iris turned to Sarah, Geoff Naylor's own PA, who occupied the desk in the same area as her own. The two women were stationed like sentinels, immediately outside each of the office doors.

Iris and Sarah had worked for the Naylor's for many years and were good friends as well as colleagues.

Iris took a deep breath and said, 'Bloody hell Sarah! Have you ever seen Geoff so angry?'

'No I haven't. I think Cav's finally pushed him too far. Geoff needs to be careful though, getting that wound up over Cav will set off his heart trouble again.'

Twelve months previously, Geoff Naylor had been diagnosed with acute angina and now regularly took medication to keep the symptoms at bay. He'd been advised to lose about three stone in weight. He knew he was still probably two stone overweight, the result of too many rich business lunches and a desk bound existence with very little exercise. The business took up all his time, he couldn't afford to spend hours at a gym to get fit, the pills would keep him right.

Geoff Naylor was a heart attack waiting to happen.

Having sat down at his desk, Naylor couldn't settle, he was still fuming. He picked up the telephone and pressed the internal speaker so he could talk to Sarah.

'Sarah, get me Cavalie on the telephone right now!'

Sarah immediately dialled the number and as soon as it started ringing she transferred it back through to Geoff Naylor.

The telephone continued to ring.

No answer.

After two minutes, Naylor hung up.

His mood worsened and he muttered under his breath, 'I bet the little shit has fucked off on holiday with that prick Christopher again.'

He pressed the intercom and bellowed at his PA, 'Keep trying his house number Sarah, if he picks up, put it through straightaway!'

'Will do sir.'

Naylor then picked up the manila file and began to go through the figures.

The work was excellent, Cav had done a fantastic job on the new project, there was no way they wouldn't be offered the contract to build the new police station at Mansfield Woodhouse.

Finally, his mood began to improve and he calmed down. Taking a last look at the figures he wondered why his son couldn't be as professional all the time?

In response to his own thoughts, he muttered out loud, 'Bloody Christopher, that's why.'

Geoff Naylor hated the sycophantic bastard, with a passion. Why couldn't Cavalie see that the effeminate, pouting Christopher was clearly a homosexual and was only out to fleece him for whatever he could get.

What his son saw in the man was beyond him.

As far as Geoff was concerned, the sooner Cav settled down with a good woman and started popping out grandkids, the happier he would be.

He stood up from behind the desk and stretched again, his back was really hurting today. There were still two small fragments of metal from the Chinese mortar shell, just above his left knee. The constant pain from the shrapnel caused him to limp, which in turn caused his lower back to ache. Even with the pain, if it hadn't been for the fact that he had two days of meetings in London and had a train to catch, he would have driven over to Underwood right then to sort out his feckless son, once and for all.

Instead he grabbed his briefcase and left the office.

Turning to Sarah he said, 'Don't bother calling Cavalie anymore today Sarah, I've got to get the train down to London now for the meetings at Franklin and Sons. I need to try and hammer out a better deal than they're offering for the supply of internal electrical cabling. I'll have words with my idiot son when I get back.'

The old man's mood had mellowed a little and his thoughts were now focused on the two days of upcoming meetings in London. He hated spending time in the capital, he found the vast metropolis too noisy and far too hectic for his taste.

As he drove to Nottingham's Midland Railway Station, his thoughts turned back to his errant son and he pondered on what would be the best way to deal with the problem of Christopher Baker.

CHAPTER 10

9.45am Wednesday 22nd March 1986
Grosvenor Hotel, Nottingham

The Watcher made his way in through the glass revolving doors and stepped inside the plush foyer of the Grosvenor Hotel. He paused for a second, quickly assessing his surroundings, then walked briskly up to the reception desk. He was now dressed in a smart, navy blue, two-piece business suit, white shirt and dark blue tie. His black brogue shoes were highly polished. He was clean shaven and his grey hair was slicked back and neat. He gave the appearance of being a successful businessman.

Smiling broadly, he engaged the pretty female receptionist saying, 'I'm so sorry to be a bother. I've arranged to meet a business contact here this morning who's travelling into Nottingham on the ten o'clock train from Birmingham. Would you mind if I wait here in the foyer, until he arrives?'

Immediately taken by the stranger's soft voice and the distinctive Scottish accent, the receptionist smiled and replied politely, 'Of course not sir, please feel free to wait in any one of the seats in the foyer.'

With a wave of her perfectly manicured hand, she indicated the four cream leather settees that were situated across the foyer, at the furthest point away from the reception desk.

'Thank you so much, I'll make sure I keep out of your way.'

The young receptionist smiled, 'Don't worry sir, it's no trouble. We often have people arrange business meetings in our foyer, especially if the clients are from out of town and are staying with us. Can I get you a cup of tea or coffee while you wait?'

With a smile, the Watcher shook his head and declined the offer of a hot drink. He was being very particular about which surfaces he touched, he'd also ensured that at all times, his back was facing the security camera that was situated in the foyer.

He stepped across the slick, cream coloured marble floor of the foyer and occupied a seat that gave him a clear view of the revolving door that formed the main entrance to the hotel. It was also the only seat in the foyer that allowed him to remain out of sight from the security camera.

No other guests or business people were waiting in the foyer, so he settled down on the soft leather of the cream settee. Inwardly, he hoped his target would make himself known soon, so that he wouldn't have to wait there too long.

At exactly five minutes past ten, the revolving glass doors flew round and a harassed looking individual strode into the foyer. He was a very smart looking man, dressed in a single breasted, black jacket and grey pin stripe trousers. His hair was jet black and parted down the centre in quite a fashionable style, that was probably just a little young for a man in his late twenties to early thirties. He had a copy of the Daily Telegraph, folded and tucked, under his left arm and he carried a small black leather briefcase in his right hand. After the man had breezed into the reception area, the Watcher detected a very strong smell of expensive aftershave.

As the man in the black jacket approached the reception desk, the young woman who had been so accommodating to the Watcher smiled and said, 'Good morning Mr Hall, is everything ok?'

The response was terse and belied a certain arrogance, 'No it bloody well isn't, Amanda. The bloody train was late again, some bullshit excuse about leaves on the line, its March for Christs sake! There aren't any bloody leaves on the trees, let alone on the line!'

The receptionist looked suitably horrified and said, 'Oh no, that's terrible sir!'

Almost instantly, an easy affable charm replaced the now supressed anger and the man smiled a greasy, almost lecherous smile towards the young woman, 'Oh well, I'm here now Amanda. This place won't run itself, will it? I've got a stack of work to do today and I've got to get the early two o'clock train back to Beeston.'

Oblivious to the Watchers presence in the foyer, the man leaned forward now, resting his brief case on the counter. He reached forward with his left hand and began to caress the young receptionist's long blonde hair, twirling it between his fingers. The young woman remained stony faced, obviously not enjoying the close attention. He leered at her full breasts, and in a breathy whisper said, 'Unfortunately, it's Vanessa's bridge night at the Ladies Rotary Club. So, it's down to me to pick the brats up from school and put them to bed. Once they're tucked up in bed though Amanda, I'll be all on my lonesome for the rest of the night.'

Amanda took a strategic pace backwards, standing just far enough away to be out of the man's reach, and in a very business-like tone said, 'That's too bad Mr Hall.'

Hall immediately straightened up, sniffed loudly and began to stride away. As he walked away from the reception desk he shouted over his shoulder, 'I'll be in my office if anybody needs me. A cup of coffee, no sugar would be perfect. Thanks Amanda!'

The Watcher had seen enough and walked slowly over to the reception desk. It was now almost ten fifteen.

Smiling at the now slightly flushed Amanda, he said, 'Well, it looks like my client must have encountered a problem. He hasn't shown up for our meeting. He should've been here by now, so I'm going to head off back to my office where I can make a few calls and find out what's happened. Thank you so much for letting me wait.'

She smiled a genuinely warm smile back and said, 'No problem sir, any time.'

'I thought that was him coming in just now, but I'm guessing that was your boss, right?'

'Yes, that's Mr Edward Hall. He's been my boss for the last three years, he's a lovely guy.'

The Watcher admired the young girl's loyalty. It was obvious from her body language that she despised her boss, but she was far too professional to say as much to a stranger. He smiled at the young woman and nodded before walking out, again conscious not to show his face to the security camera.

CHAPTER 11

1.45pm Wednesday 22nd March 1986
Midland Railway Station, Nottingham

The Watcher shifted uncomfortably on the hard bench. It was a relic from Victorian times and had been made from wrought iron and wood. He'd waited patiently for the arrival of the two o'clock train, that ran from Nottingham to Beeston. He'd filled the time spent on the platform, by sipping two large, hot, frothy cappuccino coffees and reading a copy of the Daily Mirror that he'd purchased from the small coffee shop at the entrance to the station.

He had read almost every word that had been printed in the newspaper, as he waited. He looked around, admiring the architecture of the splendid Victorian platform, there were now no more than ten other passengers waiting for trains.

While he had waited, numerous other trains had pulled into and then out of the busy station. One of his favourite pastimes was people watching. He was fascinated, as he observed passengers of all ages alighting from the various trains, he wondered what stories lay behind some of the anguished expressions on their faces.

He glanced along the station platform, there was still no sign of the reason he was waiting here so patiently. He knew he'd overheard the hotel manager, Edward Hall, say to the receptionist that he was catching the two o'clock train home.

Just as he began to wonder if there had been a problem that necessitated Hall's presence at the hotel, right on cue, he saw a red faced and flustered Edward Hall racing down the stairs onto the platform. He reached Platform 2, at exactly the same time as the train destined for Beeston came to a stop. The service to Beeston only consisted of two carriages, half a dozen passengers got off the train and made their way along the platform towards the station exit.

The Watcher stood up, threw the two empty coffee cups into the nearest waste bin and tucked the newspaper under his arm. He waited until Edward Hall got onto the train, before boarding himself. He got into the same carriage and occupied a seat three rows behind the breathless hotel manager.

He reached into his jacket pocket, found the return ticket he'd purchased, then began to scan the newspaper. He wasn't reading it, just using it as a prop to conceal his face in case Hall turned around.

The train pulled out of the station, and began to sway gently as it picked up speed heading for the open countryside between Nottingham and Beeston.

'Tickets please!' shouted the portly conductor as he lurched along the carriage towards Hall's seat.

The Watcher saw Hall disdainfully hold out his ticket towards the conductor without even looking up at the man. The uniformed man took his ticket and scribbled on it before returning it and moving along the carriage.

'Any more tickets? Please', he said again. A note of boredom could now clearly be heard in his voice.

The Watcher held out his return ticket and made eye contact with the conductor.

The conductor took the ticket and nodded in a gesture of thanks. Once again, the ticket was taken, scribbled on and returned.

As he moved further along the carriage he shouted, 'Your next stop is Beeston. Beeston is your next stop!'

The entire journey had only taken fifteen minutes at the most.

The train slowed, then crawled slowly alongside the platform at the very small Beeston station. Edward Hall jumped up clutching his briefcase to his chest and made his way to the automatic doors. The train finally came to a complete stop and the doors opened. Hall jumped from the train carriage and onto the platform.

As soon as Hall was on the platform, the Watcher stood and also made his way off the train, he loitered on the platform behind Hall and was able to avoid any eye contact with the hotel manager. Three other passengers had also got off the train at Beeston, the Watcher used these people to screen himself from Hall as he followed him out of the station.

Hall walked out of the station building and into the car park.

Immediately a slim and very attractive brunette, wearing a red winter coat and black slacks got out of a gun metal grey, BMW estate car. The car had been parked in the space nearest to the station entrance. The Watcher loitered in the entrance, remaining close enough to hear the conversation between Hall and the young woman.

Hall leaned forward and pecked a kiss on the cheek of the woman, 'Hello darling. What a day I've had. It's been a bloody nightmare; the train was late this morning. I was waiting on this bloody platform for forty five minutes after you dropped me off!'

The woman turned away brusquely not returning the kiss, 'Well you're back now. Come on darling, do hurry up. You know it's my bridge night, and I've still got stacks to do before I can even think about getting ready.'

'Ok sweetheart, let's get home.'

The woman handed the car keys to Hall who immediately opened the driver's door. They both got into the BMW and as soon as both doors were slammed shut, it was driven off at speed out of the car park.

The Watcher smiled, made a mental note of the car and its registration number, before turning around and striding back into the small station ready to catch the next train back to Nottingham.

Both the platform and the station were now empty.

He had no idea when the next train was due to arrive, so once again he sat down on a cold, hard bench and waited. Sitting quietly, he closed his eyes, opened his palms to heaven and muttered a quiet prayer of thanks to God.

CHAPTER 12

7.30am Thursday 23rd March 1986
Beeston railway station

The battered green Land Rover was driven slowly into the car park at Beeston railway station. The Watcher parked the vehicle as near to the station entrance as he could and then glanced at his wristwatch, it was now almost seven thirty in the morning.

He'd arrived at the small railway station early, he didn't want to risk missing Hall, if his target decided to catch an earlier train.

The previous day, when he'd arrived back at Nottingham Midland Station he had purchased a train timetable, that included the times of the service that ran from Beeston to Nottingham. After examining the timetable, he knew that there were trains scheduled to leave Beeston at seven forty-five, eight fifteen and eight forty-five that morning.

He'd waited patiently for almost three quarters of an hour yesterday before the train had arrived that took him from Beeston back into Nottingham City. He'd used that time and the rest of the day, researching and planning how he was going to deal with Edward Hall.

He was satisfied with his plan.

It felt good inside, knowing that at some time within the next twenty-four hours Edward Hall would have answered to God for his sins.

The Watcher would personally see to that.

Once again, he was dressed appropriately for his chosen course of action. He was now wearing a pair of old olive green combat trousers, a black woollen crew neck sweater and a pair of black trainers, that had been meticulously washed clean of Cavalie Naylor's blood.

Passengers began to arrive for the seven forty-five train and very soon the car park began to fill. There was no sign of Edward Hall's grey BMW.

The Watcher heard the seven forty-five train arrive in a screech of air brakes. He then saw the carriages lurch forward, pick up speed slowly and leave the station. The car park became quiet again. To pass the time before the next train arrived, he reached over and checked the contents of the black grip bag that was lying on the passenger seat next to him.

Everything he would need for his mission was in the bag, methodically, he checked the items.

The loaded Smith & Wesson revolver, the freshly honed Sumunugashi skinning knife, four separate metre long lengths of nylon cord, two pairs of blue latex surgical gloves, a two-inch paint brush, a roll of brown Gaffer tape, a black woollen ski mask, clear plastic zip lock bags, a pair of sturdy pliers, a small crowbar and a mini Maglite torch. It had been instilled into him during his training to check and then recheck his kit.

Cars started pulling into the car park again, the Watcher glanced at his watch. It was now almost ten minutes past eight.

Just when he began to think that Edward Hall must be catching the later train at eight forty-five, he suddenly saw the sleek, grey BMW estate sweep into the car park.

Hall's car had barely stopped before the two front doors flew open and both Edward Hall and his wife jumped out, leaving two children in the back of the car. He had been driving the car and his wife had been the front seat passenger. Having exited the vehicle, they left the doors wide open and theatrically ran around to the front of the car, where they embraced.

The Watcher wound down the driver's door window of the Land Rover an inch or two, so he could now listen in on the couple's conversation.

Edward Hall quickly kissed his wife. She returned his kiss and said, 'Have a good day sweetheart, I'll be here at five o'clock. I'll bring the children with me so we can nip into town and have pizza for tea.'

The two children in the back of the car squealed loudly at the prospect of pizza for tea.

Hall again kissed his wife on the cheek, before saying, 'That'll be perfect darling, pizza it is kids!'

He waved to the two children in the back of the car, then strode off purposefully towards the station to catch the eight fifteen train.

Vanessa Hall waved before getting into the driver's side of the BMW. She reached across and closed the passenger door before driving out of the car park. The Watcher started the Land Rover and began to discretely follow the unsuspecting Vanessa Hall.

As he followed the sleek estate, the Watcher was troubled.

He hadn't factored small children into his plan, he needed to think.

After a ten minute drive the BMW came to a stop, outside the entrance to a very exclusive private school. Instantly, the two back doors were flung open and two very excited children dressed in smart red and black school uniforms jumped out. The children were quickly followed by their mother. All three walked through the school gates and made their way inside the school building.

The Watcher estimated that Edward Hall's daughter was probably seven years old, maybe eight. The boy looked to be even younger, six years old at the most.

Having delivered the children into school, Vanessa Hall came back to the car and quickly drove off. The Watcher followed her, maintaining a discreet distance behind in the Land Rover.

Five minutes later and both vehicles were being driven along a very nice, tree lined street in Beeston Fields, a very upmarket suburb of Beeston. The houses here were all very grand, detached properties with large, well established gardens. The Watcher smiled as he saw the BMW turn into the driveway of a particularly large detached house. The front garden of the property was very big and the house itself was set back, quite a distance from the road.

He parked the Land Rover directly opposite the property, got out and walked over to the large privet hedge that surrounded the garden. Peering through the hedge, he was just in time to see Vanessa Hall using a key to access the front door of the large house.

The Watcher walked slowly back to the Land Rover, got in and shut the door. He closed his eyes and said aloud, 'Oh Lord, please steel my heart and strengthen my hand, enable me to carry out your will tonight. Amen.'

He then started the vehicle and drove away from the large property. He already knew the time Vanessa Hall would be picking up her husband and he was confident that he could do what needed to be done in the window of opportunity that had been created by the Halls' plans to take the children into town for pizza.

There was no point in him waiting around on this affluent street, where a nosy neighbour could very easily notice a scruffy old Land Rover parked up outside the Halls' family home.

Instead he headed into Beeston town centre and parked the Land Rover in a multi storey car park. Ensuring that his grip bag was now out of sight in the back of the vehicle, he secured the vehicle and walked into the pedestrianised area of the town centre, where he soon found a small café.

As soon as he walked in to the café he could smell the delicious aroma of fried bacon and sausage.

Suddenly, he became aware of just how ravenously hungry he was, he ordered a full English breakfast and a mug of tea. The young waitress brought the breakfast and the mug of tea to his table promptly. Hungrily, he wolfed the food down quickly. Once he'd finished the breakfast he ordered a second mug of tea and enquired with the waitress if there was a library in the town centre.

The waitress served him a second mug of strong tea and provided directions to the public library.

The Watcher heaped two teaspoons full of sugar into the tea and gave it a good stir. He always liked something sweet, after eating a fatty fry up. He paid for the breakfast and left a good, but not over generous tip, he didn't want to do anything that would cause the young waitress to remember him.

Walking out of the café, he wandered through the pedestrianised town centre, following the directions he had been given. He needed time to think and refine his plan, there were a couple of things he could do, while he waited for Edward Hall to return home.

CHAPTER 13

9.30am Thursday 23rd March 1986
South Lodge, Retford

Stewart Ainsworth sat in his car and flicked through the paperwork he'd brought with him from Rampton Hospital. The first thing he saw was the unsmiling face of Jimmy Wade, those piercing, hypnotic, blue eyes stared back at him out of the photograph.

Ainsworth was twenty-four years old and a newly qualified social worker, he'd been employed at Rampton for just over six months. His role was to support the patients incarcerated at the high security hospital, his main job was to look after their welfare.

He had been given the dossier on Wade, by his supervisor the night before. It was now his responsibility to personally visit the woman, who had become a regular visitor to Wade in the maximum-security hospital. As he read the paperwork, it soon became apparent to him that his supervisor had some concerns over this particular visitor.

Wade had been incarcerated at the hospital for just over four months, in that time Melissa Braithwaite had visited him on no less than six occasions. Staff supervising the visits in the Main Hall, had noticed that the woman was becoming very close to Wade. Their conversations were held in secretive, hushed tones and they had been observed holding hands across the table, staring into each other's eyes.

It was a routine part of his role, to make enquiries about the motives of any person visiting someone considered to be as dangerous as Wade.

Ainsworth had already undertaken enquiries similar to this, on a number of occasions in relation to other long term patients. He had visited sad lonely women, who had become fixated over a misconstrued perception of glamour surrounding murderers.

The young social worker had studied the report that detailed the crimes Jimmy Wade had been convicted of, the night before. He wasn't easily spooked, but he'd been disturbed by the ruthless and sadistic nature of the offences.

He finished reading the scant information he'd brought with him and closed the folder.

He intended to talk to Braithwaite and try to gauge her motivation for the visits. He would then make an informed decision, whether or not to recommend that the top security hospital refuse further Visiting Order requests. At the moment Rampton Hospital were showing no more than a general concern over the volume of visits. Apart from the fact that Braithwaite was obviously getting very close to Wade, there was nothing he could see in the report that would specifically warrant a ban on any further visits. It would be down to him to make the final judgement.

Ainsworth had driven his small car along the pot holed dirt track, that led to the secluded property in the middle of dense woodland on the outskirts of Retford. He drove his vehicle directly behind a dark blue Ford Sierra saloon that was parked outside the property. This Sierra was also shown in the file as belonging to Braithwaite, it was the same vehicle she had parked at Rampton Hospital when visiting Wade.

He stepped out of his own Fiat Uno, not bothering to lock the door.

Although the small stone house was surrounded on all sides by thick forest, Ainsworth felt the cold wind bite, straight away. He hadn't brought a coat with him, so he pulled the jacket of his cheap, light grey suit tighter around him and walked up the short garden path to the front door of the house. The wind whipped his long dark hair around his face and he frantically tried to smooth it down as he approached the house.

He rang the doorbell and made a quick visual inspection of the property.

The house was a very old, stone built lodge, that had at one time been a gate house for the nearby Retford Hall estate. There was a neat well-cared for front garden. The small lawn was well trimmed and the borders were all weed free. There were clean net curtains at the windows and the window frames and front door were all freshly painted. There were four stone outbuildings within the grounds of the property. They had probably been used in the past as store houses of some description. They were crumbling now and had obviously been neglected over the years. At the rear of the property he could see a stream running across the bottom of the lawn that made up most of the larger back garden.

He pressed the ornate doorbell a second time.

This time there was a reply from inside, he heard a woman's voice shout, 'Just a minute!'

He could now hear footsteps coming towards the door, so he reached into his pocket for his identification badge.

The front door was flung open, he instantly caught the aroma of fresh ground coffee and toast. Standing in front of him was a woman in her mid-thirties, with blonde hair that had been cut in a neat bob. She wore full make up and had a very pretty, open face with large blue eyes. She was wearing a pink vest top and grey jogging pants, with the word "pineapple" in pink letters stretching from hip to toe on the right leg.

Ainsworth held up his identification badge and said, 'Sorry to disturb you, my name's Stewart Ainsworth, I'm a social worker employed at Rampton Hospital. Can I speak to Melissa Braithwaite please?'

Only now did Stewart realise just how petite the woman was. She was barely five feet tall, very slim, but curvaceous at the same time. He noticed she wasn't wearing a bra beneath the tight vest top.

'I'm Melissa Braithwaite, how can I help you?'

'I need to talk about your regular visits to see James Wade at Rampton Hospital.'

Suddenly, Melissa Braithwaite let out a yell, 'Bloody hell!'

She turned and sprinted off down the hallway, shouting behind her, 'Come in Mr Ainsworth and close the door behind you, my bloody toast's burning!'

Stewart chuckled, stepped inside the hallway and quietly closed the door.

A few minutes later and a now calm Melissa, returned to the hallway, 'Sorry about that Mr Ainsworth. I very nearly had to call the fire brigade out, the bloody toaster's playing up. It doesn't stop cooking when the toast's done. I have to stand there and watch the bloody thing. Please come through into the lounge, can I get you a coffee or a cup of tea?'

'A cup of coffee would be lovely, thanks.'

'How do you take it?'

'White no sugar, thank you.'

'Be two ticks, grab a seat, please make yourself comfortable.'

Stewart eased his tall, skinny frame down into one of the two large arm chairs that dominated the living room. He looked around the room and noted that it had been very well decorated, and contained some very nice pieces of furniture. Obviously, money wasn't a problem for Melissa Braithwaite.

On the wall, above the fireplace, he could see a framed photograph of her in a black mortar cap and gown being presented with a scroll. Next to this photograph was a framed certificate. A first-class degree in Psychology, awarded by the University of Sheffield.

Braithwaite came back into the room, carrying a tray that held two steaming hot mugs of coffee. She handed the milky one to Stewart and took the black one herself. She sat cross legged in the other arm chair, took a sip of her coffee and said, 'Right Mr Ainsworth, you said you wanted to talk to me about my visits to Jimmy Wade. Can I ask why the Social Services are so interested in me visiting Jimmy? Is there a problem?'

'Please, call me Stewart and thanks for the coffee by the way, it's delicious. There's no problem Mrs Braithwaite, it's a routine enquiry we carry out whenever a patient like Wade has a regular visitor. Before we talk about your visits to Wade, I need to establish a few things about you, if I may?'

'No problem Stewart, ask away?'

He indicated the framed certificate on the wall and said, 'I noticed you have a degree in psychology. Are you currently working as a psychologist?'

'Not at the moment. I went to university quite late in life. After my parents died in a car crash five years ago, they left me a substantial amount of money. I decided to quit my job as a secretary, return to school and try to better myself. I've always been interested in psychology, in particular the psychology of violent criminals.'

'When did you graduate?'

'I graduated just over a year ago, I'm currently working on my Masters. Hence my regular visits to see Jimmy Wade.'

'I see. Is there any particular reason you chose Wade, to be the subject of your Masters?'

'Not really, there wasn't any single particular reason at all, it was just coincidence. When I started to think about what I should base my research on, the Coal Killer case, and Jimmy Wade in particular, was very topical. His crimes were being reported widely in all the newspapers and all over the media. Then there was the extradition from Australia, and the subsequent trial. It was all perfect timing for me. As soon as he'd been found guilty and sentenced, I immediately made enquiries with Rampton Hospital, to see if I could get access to interview him for the final part of my work.'

'Does Wade know that the only reason you're visiting him is for research? So you can achieve a Master's degree?'

'I thought it only fair that I told him the reason for my visits. So, the short answer is, yes he does know.'

'What was his reaction?'

'He was fine with it Stewart. Jimmy is a highly intelligent man, I think he finds our conversations quite stimulating.'

'The staff, supervising your visits, have witnessed the two of you holding hands on a couple of occasions. Why did you feel that level of intimacy was necessary, Mrs Braithwaite?'

'It's Ms Braithwaite, I've never been married. Please, just call me Melissa, whenever I hear Mrs Braithwaite it reminds me of my mother.'

'Okay Melissa, why was it necessary to have that level of intimacy, that close physical contact?'

'I would hardly describe it as intimacy. It's only happened on the last couple of visits, when I was asking him about his earliest crime.'

'You mean the drowning of seven-year-old Billy Daines.'

'Yes, the death of that poor unfortunate child.'

'Wade's never admitted his involvement in the child's death. In fact, he's never spoken one word to the police, about that incident or any of his other crimes. Do you have open discussions with him about his crimes? Has he made any admissions to you Melissa?'

'God no! We do speak freely, but he's never made any admissions at all. Just for the record, I genuinely believe that he wasn't in any way responsible for Billy Daines' death. Apart, that is, from being unfortunate enough to be there at the time the boy fell into the pond and drowned. It must have been a thoroughly traumatic thing for a young child to witness. On the two occasions, we spoke about the death of the young boy, Jimmy became really agitated and upset. I held his hand purely on a human level, to both calm him and reassure him, that's all.'

'How many more visits to the hospital do you think you'll need in order to complete your research, Melissa?'

'I think one more visit should suffice, two at the most.'

'Okay, I think that's all I need to know for now. Thank you for your time this morning and I'm so sorry for ruining your toast. I'll let my supervisors at the hospital know the reason for your visits, and that you'll only require one or two more visits to complete your research. I'm sure there won't be a problem about you gaining access to see Wade for that number of visits.'

'Thank you so much Stewart. Can I ask you something, strictly off the record, while you're here?'

'Of course, you can.'

'Speaking as someone who has contact with him on an almost daily basis, what's your own personal opinion of Jimmy Wade?'

'You said off the record so don't quote me on this in your work Melissa, you need to understand that this is purely my own personal opinion of him. In my view, Wade should never be allowed out from behind those walls ever again. He is without doubt the coldest, most calculating and dangerous individual, I've ever met.'

'Thank you, Stewart. It's good to get your perspective, as I've only ever seen the perfectly charming and polite side to his nature.'

Stewart thought back to the detailed files of Wade's crimes, he'd studied the previous night and said, 'Trust me Melissa, you never, ever want to see the other side of Wade's nature.'

He stood up and stretched his tall frame before walking out of the lounge, followed by Melissa Braithwaite.

She opened the front door and held out her right hand.

He shook her hand gently, made eye contact and said, 'Good luck with your research Melissa, I hope it all goes well and you achieve your Masters. Just do me one favour and always remember, exactly what Wade is.'

It was now her turn to meet the gaze of the young, inexperienced social worker.

'And what exactly is that, Stewart?'

'Wade is a pure psychopath, a monster. I've got no psychology degree and I'm not researching for a Masters, but trust me Melissa, that's exactly what he is. Take care.'

'You too Stewart.'

She watched the young social worker walk back to his little car and waved to him as he drove off, back down the secluded lane. She closed the front door and returned to the lounge, sitting down heavily in the arm chair.

Inside she was raging.

How dare that young upstart talk about her soul mate in such disparaging terms! Not once had he referred to Jimmy by his Christian name.

They were all wrong.

Only she knew his true nature, his kindness, the way he'd reached out to her when she was in the depths of despair. He was the only person who had cared, the only one who'd been there for her.

Her parents hadn't died five years ago, they had been killed just over nine months ago, soon after she had graduated from Sheffield. She had felt totally lost after the only two people she'd ever loved, were wiped out in a split second of madness. The car they were travelling in had been hit head on by a car being driven dangerously by a young joy rider. A police patrol car had been in pursuit of the car thief driving at high speeds, and this had obviously contributed to the subsequent collision.

Why were the police so stupid?

In the depths of her grief, she had seen the reports about the trial of Jimmy Wade, the man the nations press had dubbed The Coal Killer. Impulsively, she had decided to travel to the Crown Court at Leicester, to watch the proceedings.

To this day, she didn't understand why she had gone to the court building, but as soon as she saw Jimmy Wade, she knew instantly he was the man destined to be her soul mate. They had spent the entire trial, staring intently across the packed court room at each other.

While ever she was in his presence, she no longer felt the sharp pain of her loss. She'd been completely devastated when he was found guilty and sentenced to be detained indefinitely at Rampton Hospital. As far as she was concerned, there was absolutely no proof that Jimmy had committed those horrendous crimes, or that he was in some way mentally deranged.

Melissa Braithwaite had convinced herself, that the police and the justice system wanted a scapegoat, to deflect from the fact that the real murderer, Police Sergeant Michael Reynolds, was one of their own. It was convenient for the establishment to blame Jimmy as Sgt Reynolds had avoided trial by killing himself in Newstead Abbey woods.

She had been a regular visitor to Wade while he was on remand at Wakefield prison, and had visited him on a number of occasions giving an acquaintances name and details on the Visiting Order. It was only after the trial when she started visiting Wade at Rampton that she had given her own details.

During her most recent visit to the high security hospital at Rampton, Wade had warned her that before long somebody would contact her and ask questions about the regular visits she was making. Between them, they had discussed at length how she should react, and what she would say, should such a visit happen.

Now that the idiotic, wet behind the ears social worker had left, she felt pleased that she had remembered everything Jimmy had told her to say. She knew that her inquisitive, but inexperienced visitor had swallowed every word of it.

The only thing she hadn't lied to Ainsworth about, was the fact that she only intended making one more visit to the hospital.

It would only take one more visit, to set in motion the chain of events that would eventually lead to the new life she dreamed of.

That new life would be spent with her soul mate, Jimmy Wade.

CHAPTER 14

11.00am Thursday 23rd March 1986
Beeston Public Library, Beeston

It had been the Watcher's intention to spend the day researching the names he had obtained from the gruesome torture of Cavalie Naylor. Now as he stood outside the library, he felt desperately disappointed; for a town the size of Beeston, the library was pathetic.

He walked inside the red brick building, that resembled a large residential bungalow, and spoke to the librarian. She was a shrew like woman in her sixties, with scraped back grey hair and thin, mean looking lips. She was dressed from head to toe in black garments, in what would best be described as widow's weeds.

'Do you have any sort of reference section I could make use of please?' he asked politely.

The woman looked up at him, she grimaced and forced a weak smile, 'Is there anything in particular that you're trying to research? Our facilities are spread over different areas of the library.'

'It's local news really, that sort of thing.'

Without acknowledging his request verbally, she stepped from behind the counter and beckoned him with a bony, claw like hand, to follow her.

He dutifully followed the old woman into a secluded corner of the empty library.

She indicated a rack of wooden shelves in the corner, and said in a high pitched, reedy voice, 'There are copies of the three local papers that serve this area, but they only go as far back as twelve months. There are also telephone directories, that cover the main towns of Nottinghamshire and Derbyshire. If you need anything else, young man, you'll have to come back and see me at the desk.'

Without waiting for a response, the old woman walked off and left the Watcher alone.

With the facilities on offer, he knew that he wouldn't be able to accomplish too much research into the names he'd got from Naylor, but at least the library was empty and warm. It was as good a place as any to wait, until the time came for him to return to the Hall's residence.

From a pocket in his combat trousers, he took out a small piece of paper that contained the list of names he'd extracted from Naylor by using his own barbaric grisly methods.

As he scanned the names, he knew that the last name on the list would not be a problem. Thanks to the precious newspaper clipping and photograph, he had taken from the old copy of the Worksop Advertiser, he knew exactly where he would find him. The clipping itself was safe in a plastic poly pocket back at the caravan. Happy that he would be able to get to the last name easily, the Watcher instead turned his attention to the second name that had been provided by Naylor.

Frederick Reece was a business lawyer. He was the person responsible for facilitating contracts between Naylor's business and various public bodies. It was his interventions that always resulted in Naylor Properties Ltd being awarded contracts after they had submitted tenders.

Reece was totally dishonest, he greased the wheels of commerce by way of bribes and other corrupt practices.

Geoffrey Naylor was unaware that the contracts were achieved in this way; he naively believed it was down to his son's business acumen and contacts. While ever business was so good, he wasn't going to be asking too many questions.

Cavalie Naylor had first met Frederick Reece at Nottingham University. After both had graduated, Reece insisted that Naylor use his fledgling law firm to facilitate his company's business dealings. Because of their history and events that had happened at the University he'd felt powerless to refuse. In effect, Reece had, in a very subtle way, blackmailed Cav Naylor into using his newly established law firm. Due entirely to the corrupt practices employed by Reece to obtain new public service contracts, both men had steadily grown very wealthy.

Naylor soon forgot the feeling of duress he'd felt at the beginning of their business relationship, instead he enjoyed the fruits of their dishonest dealings with the local authority.

As the Watcher had slowly flayed the skin from Naylor's body, the businessman had readily informed him, that Freddie Reece had been one of the main instigators of the disgusting event that happened when they were both students at the university. He also quickly gave the Watcher the name of Reece's law firm.

Richmond Legal Enterprise Limited had offices in the town of Southwell in Nottinghamshire.

The Watcher scanned the long rows of business phone directories on the shelving and quickly found the one that related to the minster town of Southwell. He removed the directory from the shelf and sat down at one of the two small tables. Thumbing through the pages, he soon found the entry for Richmond Legal Enterprise Limited. Scanning across the page from the telephone number, he saw the address for the business. Richmond Legal Enterprise Limited could be found at 31, Spittle Row, Southwell, Nottinghamshire.

Smiling, the Watcher glanced over his shoulder before tearing the entire page out of the book.

He was aware that this third name on the list of devils, Frederick Reece, would prove the most challenging to get close to, but obtaining the business address was a great start.

He glanced at his watch, it was now almost time to leave the library. He used the toilet facilities before leaving. As he made his way out of the library he said goodbye to the librarian, the old woman didn't even glance up from the book she was reading.

He walked back along the pedestrianised town centre and called in at the first newsagent's shop he saw. He purchased a small bottle of water and two Galaxy chocolate bars to sustain him overnight, then made his way back to the multi storey car park where he had left the Land Rover.

It would soon be time for Vanessa Hall to deliver her husband Edward, to him. The next demon on his list would soon have to answer for his sins before God.

CHAPTER 15

4.45pm Thursday 23rd March 1986
Beeston Fields, Beeston

The Watcher loitered by the hedge of a neighbouring house and from a distance of almost fifty yards he saw the grey BMW emerge from the long driveway. He could see Vanessa Hall behind the wheel of the car and that there was nobody else in the car with her. She drove off at speed, in the direction of the railway station.

He felt the weight of the day sack, that he'd retrieved from the Land Rover earlier, and smiled.

Carefully, he looked around in all directions to make sure he wasn't being observed, then he began to slowly walk towards the open gates of the large house set back from the road.

He knew there were failings in his plan and that it was by no means perfect, but with God's will, everything would be fine.

That was with God's will, and every ounce of skill and professionalism he'd acquired and mastered over the last twenty or so years.

For his plan to succeed, he would need to become a ghost, an undetected phantom. His powers of self-discipline would be tested to the maximum, he knew he would need to remain undiscovered and invisible for many hours.

The light was now beginning to diminish, as daylight faded into twilight. There wasn't a breath of wind, but he could still detect the pleasant smell of wood smoke, as a neighbour burned garden waste on a bonfire some distance away.

He was now dressed head to toe in dark, drab camouflage clothing. He wore black training shoes and a black benny hat, that doubled as a ski mask with holes for the eyes and mouth.

He moved stealthily down the long driveway towards the Hall's beautiful home. He stayed close to the neatly trimmed, privet hedge. The ground underfoot was dry, which would help later. He couldn't afford to leave muddy footprints, that would betray his presence inside the house.

He made his way to the rear of the property. The large house was not overlooked by any other properties at the back.

The Watcher was free to do as he wanted, without the risk of any interference.

He put on a pair of blue latex gloves, then took out a small aerosol can from the daysack. With the aerosol can, that contained builder's foam, tucked inside his jacket, he climbed up a drainpipe towards the bright yellow, alarm box. He sprayed the foam inside the alarm box. The foam quickly set like stone, rendering the alarm box useless.

After sliding back down the drainpipe, he returned the can of foam to the day sack before taking out a small blue crowbar. Using the breaking tool, he quickly forced open a transom window that led into the kitchen. He gained access easily and without causing major damage to the window frame.

It was vital to the success of his plan, that any damage he caused was easily repairable.

He pushed the black nylon daysack through the forced window and climbed in after it.

Once inside the house, he squatted down on his haunches and waited for two minutes, without making a sound. He slackened his jaw and allowed his mouth to remain slightly open, as an aid to his already acute hearing, he wanted to be sure there were no unexpected visitors inside the property.

Satisfied he was alone in the house, he made his way to the hallway where he found the alarm box. Dropping the panel to examine the system, he smiled when he saw that the intruder alarm hadn't even been set.

From the hallway, he made his way up the stairs. At the top of the staircase he saw a loft hatch positioned in the ceiling directly above the stairs. Quickly, he climbed on to the bannister rail and checked the hatch. It was loose, he applied pressure and the hatch raised easily, it hadn't been painted over and wasn't sealed.

Climbing back down from the bannister rail, he checked that he hadn't left any tell-tale foot marks on the cream painted hand rail.

He looked at his watch, it was time to stage the burglary.

He began by moving items of value from around the house, down to the rear door that led from the kitchen out onto the back garden. He removed a video recorder and video tapes from the lounge, and some costume jewellery from the master bedroom. He then placed all the items in a neat stack next to the back door. He then opened the door from inside and left it ajar.

He picked up the daysack and made his way back up the stairs. He walked around each of the rooms upstairs, he quickly identified the master bedroom and the two bedrooms used by the children. Leaving no signs of his presence, he moved around the rooms until he was completely familiar with the layout.

The Watcher moved the loft hatch to one side, he stood on the bannister rail and pushed the day sack into the loft before pulling himself up. Once inside the loft he looked down at the bannister rail, satisfying himself once again that he'd left no scuff marks that would betray his hiding place.

He allowed a second for his eyes to adjust to the gloom of the roomy loft space, then he flicked on the mini Maglite and began to move items that could easily be disturbed, or that could possibly make a noise. The last thing he wanted, was for an accidental noise to give him away.

Finally, satisfied that nothing could be unwittingly disturbed, he took out a pair of heavy pliers. He used the steel head of the pliers to gently tap the two clout nails, he had removed from his pocket, into the reverse side of the loft hatch. He then carefully placed it back into position. He would use the nails to lift the hatch later, when the time was right.

He had been meticulous in his preparations, it was now time for him to become a phantom.

He settled down to await the arrival of the Hall family, using the Maglite to illuminate his watch he saw it was now six o'clock. There would be at least a couple more hours to wait before the family returned home, he would use the time to get totally into stealth mode.

From now on his movements would be kept down to the absolute minimum, everything he might need had been placed at arm's length and was within easy reach.

He scanned the Mini Maglite around the loft and made one last inspection of his makeshift lair. The loft space had a slightly musty smell, it was obviously used to store what the family no longer needed.

It smelled quite badly of damp and mould.

The thin beam from the torch picked out myriads of dust particles that had been disturbed by his presence.

As he settled down to wait, he could only hear two sounds, the rhythmic tick tock of a faraway clock and the slow, steady thump of his own heartbeat.

CHAPTER 16

6.00pm Thursday 23rd March 1986
Major Crime Investigation Unit, Mansfield

It had been a long day for Rob Buxton.

He walked into the office, slumped down in the chair at his desk and flicked on the desktop lamp. The only other light in the large open plan office, emanated from Danny Flint's office. He threw his old pocket books into the drawer of the desk, wearily stood up again, walked over to Danny's office and knocked on the closed door.

'Come in!' shouted Danny.

Rob walked in and was surprised to see Brian Hopkirk, the other Detective Inspector on the team, already in the office.

'Sorry boss, I didn't mean to disturb you.'

'Don't be daft Rob, you're not disturbing anything. Brian and I were just going over the interview records for the Grayson murder enquiry. How was your day at Crown Court?'

'It went ok, I hate getting called to court on the hurry up like that. I'd only just arrived here, when I got the call to get my arse down to court. I'd had no prior court warning or any other notice. Apparently, they'd got through a couple of the witnesses quicker than they had anticipated. I wouldn't mind, but I still had to wait around for three hours, before I was called to give my evidence. Trial's going well though, our barrister doesn't foresee any problems, it should be the second successful murder conviction for the team.'

'That's great news Rob, have you got other stuff you need to do this evening?'

'No, I'm done for the day boss. Do you need a hand with anything here?'

'No thanks Rob, we're fine, just get yourself off home, you look knackered. See you tomorrow.'

'Thanks boss, I'm shattered. It's surprising how tired you can get, just sitting on your arse, doing nothing all day.'

He laughed and said, 'Goodnight gents, see you both tomorrow.'

'Night Rob', said Brian.

Rob closed the door and heard the two men starting to go through the interviews once more. Grabbing his coat, he headed for the door, then suddenly realised just how hungry he was. He paused, picked up the nearest phone and called home.

'Hello sweetheart, I'm just leaving now. Do you want me to pick up some fish and chips for you and the kids on the way home?'

There was a pause.

'Loads of salt and vinegar, no problem, see you in twenty minutes, love you.'

Rob replaced the phone and strode out of the office, he could almost taste the fish and chips already.

CHAPTER 17

8.15pm Thursday 23rd March 1986
Beeston Fields, Beeston

The grey BMW estate purred onto the driveway, the large tyres crunching along the gravel. No sooner had it come to a halt than the two children piled out of the back doors. They squealed happily, their little bellies full of pizza and coca cola.

'Come on kids, stop messing about, I want you straight in the house and upstairs ready for bed. It's way past your bed time and it's a school day tomorrow', shouted Vanessa Hall.

Edward Hall gently touched his wife's arm and said, 'Ease off the kids love, they've had a good night, they're bound to be excited. I'll take them upstairs and get them ready for bed, you put the kettle on and make us a nice coffee. I'm gagging for a brew.'

He opened the front door and made his way to the alarm box, he tutted when he saw that it hadn't been set.

He shouted at the kids, 'Up the stairs kids, get into bed, I'll come and tuck you in shortly. Don't forget to clean your teeth, I'll be checking.'

'Okay dad', squealed the daughter.

As soon as the kids were out of earshot, Hall rounded angrily on his wife and whispered menacingly through gritted teeth, 'What's the point of having a fucking state of the art burglar alarm, if you don't set the fucking thing when we're out!'

Vanessa rolled her eyes and said nonchalantly, 'Sorry darling, I was in a rush to get the kids, I must've forgotten.'

Hall shook his head in a resigned manner and began to trudge up the stairs to tuck in the two children, ready for bed. As he climbed the stairs he shouted, 'I'm coming! I hope you're both in bed. Sorry kids, no story time tonight, it's way too late.'

Up above in the loft space, the Watcher could clearly hear the conversations of the Hall family below.

Now that the children were in bed, there was a momentary silence, then suddenly the air was split by a piercing scream from Vanessa Hall. The Watcher smiled as he realised she had discovered the staged break in. He heard heavy footsteps directly beneath him, as Edward Hall raced down the stairs to see what had caused his wife to scream.

In the loft, the Watcher concentrated even harder not to move a muscle, not to make a sound. This was the dangerous time, they had found the burglary. Would they call the police?

Having rushed downstairs, Hall found his wife in floods of tears in the kitchen, shakily she pointed at the wide open back door. He could see the pile of videos and the video recorder on the floor near to the back door. He looked around the kitchen and saw the splintered wood of the forced transom window.

'Bastards!' he said angrily, before turning on his wife, 'Now do you see why you should always set the fucking alarm!'

Vanessa Hall nodded and started to cry even more. He relented a little, moved towards her and put his arms around her. She had obviously been very shaken by the discovery.

He cuddled her and said reassuringly, 'Don't worry sweetheart, we must've disturbed them as we drove up the drive way. I'll check the bedrooms and make sure nothing's missing.'

He made his way back up the stairs, and made a quick check of the bedrooms. He couldn't see anything obviously missing, everything still looked in place. Vanessa had followed her husband upstairs, she was still sobbing and pointed to a jewellery box that was open.

He slid his arm around her waist and said reassuringly, 'Look sweetheart, whoever was here, has long gone. I can easily repair the damaged kitchen window tonight. It looks as though nothing of any value has been taken, the costume jewellery that was in that box is now piled up by the backdoor, so don't worry. It's getting late, the kids are tired and have got to be up for school in the morning. Dry your eyes, then go in and settle the kids down. They'll have heard you scream. I'll call the cops in the morning to report the break in, there's no point getting them out here tonight.'

She wiped her face, nodded slowly then walked into her young son's bedroom.

Above them in the loft the Watcher smiled, he raised his palms to heaven and mouthed a silent prayer thanking the Lord. He'd clearly heard Edward Hall's comment that he would call the police in the morning. He listened as Vanessa spoke soothingly to the two small children and then heard her footsteps on the stairs. Now he could faintly hear the conversation between her and Edward downstairs.

Edward walked out of the back door and across the patio to the garage, he grabbed a hammer and a handful of nails. As he walked back from the garage he muttered angrily to himself, 'Maybe now, the silly cow will take the time to set the alarm.'

In the loft the Watcher heard the nails being hammered into the damaged window frame.

He hoped Edward Hall left the hammer in the kitchen when he'd finished the repair, he might find a better use for it himself, later.

CHAPTER 18

3.00am Friday 24th March 1986
Beeston Fields, Beeston

The Watcher flicked on the Mini Maglite and glanced at his watch.

It was now almost three o'clock in the morning.

Immediately below his position, he could hear loud rhythmic snoring emanating up from the master bedroom. He knew it was the master bedroom from the recce he'd carried out earlier that day.

After the shock of finding the burglary, Edward Hall had initially comforted his wife, reassuring her that the burglars had long gone. Slowly Vanessa had regained her composure. As soon as he finished repairing the damaged window frame, the couple had retired to their bedroom.

The Watcher had listened as Vanessa made a quick check on the two young children. He heard her return to the master bedroom where Edward continued to comfort her. Eventually his comforting became more passionate, as he and Vanessa became aroused.

Above them, in the loft space, the Watcher listened intently as the couple began to make love.

The couple made love passionately, for over an hour. He had heard their cries as they both climaxed, then waited patiently for them both to drift off to sleep.

At half past one in the morning, he'd heard somebody half wake from their slumbers and slowly get out of bed. He listened carefully, from the sound of the footsteps as they crossed the landing directly beneath the hatch he knew it was Edward Hall who was awake. He heard the footsteps head into the family bathroom. There was the sound of the light switch being flicked on, then Hall urinating. The stream eventually abated and the light was flicked off again. The footsteps padded back to the bedroom, then he heard the bedsprings sag as Hall got back into bed.

There had been no noise at all, from either of the bedrooms occupied by the two small children.

It was now three o'clock in the morning, time for him to move.

The early hours of the morning are widely regarded as the time when the human body is in its deepest unconscious state. It is the time of deep sleep, which eventually transforms into the dream sleep state.

The Watcher made no sound as he used the pliers to grip the nails that he had knocked into the loft hatch earlier. Silently, he lifted out the piece of wood and carefully placed it to one side, before slipping the nylon day sack around his neck. Before he moved, he ensured that none of its contents knocked against each other.

Using his powerful, muscular arms he slowly lowered himself down from the loft until he felt his feet gently come to rest on the bannister rail.

With great agility, he got down silently from the bannister rail.

His movements were fluid, he made no sound, the years of training hadn't been in vain. He moved across the landing like a phantom, a fleeting shadow in the moonlight.

He slowly opened the door to the master bedroom and saw the couple fast asleep. Vanessa was lying on her side facing away from her husband who was lying flat on his back. It was he who was snoring loudly.

The Halls' hadn't closed the bedroom curtains, the room was illuminated by the bright moonlight flooding in from outside. He breathed in deeply through his nose, he could still detect the scent of their earlier lovemaking.

Stealthily, he crept to the side of the bed where Edward lay. He rolled down the black hat he was wearing, turning it into a black ski mask. The mask left only his eyes and mouth still visible.

Drawing back his left hand he bunched it into a massive fist, then smashed it down onto the forehead of the sleeping Hall, instantly knocking him out.

The Watcher stepped onto the bed and knelt across the sleeping woman, effectively pinning her beneath the duvet. As she began to stir, he flipped her over roughly, so she lay on her back. As she awoke and her senses returned, he clamped his gloved hand across her mouth. The first thing she saw was the Watcher's masked face, illuminated by the white moonlight. Her eyes widened in sheer terror, she began to writhe beneath the duvet, but was pinned. She tried to scream but the noise was muffled under the gloved hand.

Finally, her energy spent, she stopped struggling.

The Watcher leaned forward and whispered menacingly, 'If you scream, or make any noise at all, I will kill your daughter, then I will kill your son and you will watch them die.'

He saw her terrified eyes dart to the left, as she looked to her husband for help.

'Your husband's not going to help you, he's unconscious. I don't want to hurt either you or your children, but if you leave me with no other choice, I'll kill you all in a heartbeat. Do you understand me?'

Vanessa Hall nodded frantically.

'Are you going to behave, Mrs Hall?'

She was shocked that he'd used her surname, the shock panicked her even more.

Again, she nodded but this time she made eye contact with her attacker. All she wanted was for her children to be spared this horror.

Very slowly he removed his hand, she made no sound. He reached into the day sack on his shoulders and grabbed the roll of Gaffer tape, deftly he wrapped the sticky brown tape twice around her head, covering her mouth but leaving her nostrils clear, allowing her to breathe.

He moved off the bed and pulled the duvet onto the floor. Instinctively Vanessa drew her knees to her chest to cover her naked body. The Watcher wasn't interested in her sexually, he grabbed her arms and roughly turned her over until she was face down on the bed. He used nylon cord from the daysack, to bind the naked woman's hands behind her back, then left her face down on the bed.

Turning his attention to the still unconscious Edward Hall, he repeated the process binding him with cord then using Gaffer tape to gag him.

He reached down to his waist and removed the razor-sharp Sumunugashi skinning knife from the scabbard on his belt, holding it in his right hand. Using his left hand, he roughly turned Vanessa over on the bed, until she was lying on her back facing him. Any thoughts of protecting her modesty were now forgotten.

Holding the knife in front of her eyes, he allowed the stark, white light of the moon to glint off the honed blade.

He leaned forward and whispered, 'We're going to your children's bedrooms now, if you do exactly as I say and cooperate with me, then your children will see the sun come up tomorrow. If you try to resist me, or cause any other sort of problem, I'll slaughter your son and daughter before your eyes, then I'll gut you like the devil worshipping scum you are and leave you to die slowly. Do you understand me, Mrs Hall?'

The horrified woman nodded vigorously, she would do exactly what this maniac wanted. She would do whatever it took to protect her children.

The Watcher grabbed Vanessa and pulled her up off the bed until she was standing. Her legs felt weak and she very nearly collapsed. The Watcher held her upright until she nodded that she was okay. He then pushed her out onto the landing and into her daughter's bedroom. Swiftly and without fuss, he dragged the terrified young girl from her bed, then bound and gagged her without speaking. He then pushed Vanessa into the boy's bedroom, where he quickly repeated the process, binding and gagging the boy. The small boy was then dragged with his mother back into the daughter's bedroom. The Watcher then used more cord to tie all three to the bed post of the young girl's bed.

Closing the door, he then stalked back across the landing to the master bedroom. Using his great strength, he lifted the unconscious, naked Edward Hall from the double bed and carried him down the stairs into the large kitchen. He pulled out one of the heavy pine chairs from beneath the large breakfast table, and tied Hall to it using more of the cord.

Moonlight flooded into the kitchen, the room was covered in lines of shadow, caused by the half-closed venetian blinds.

Edward Hall was still unconscious and was slumped forward; the only reason he remained upright, was due to the cord that bound him to the wooden chair.

The Watcher needed Hall to be awake.

He grabbed a Pyrex measuring jug from the draining board, filled it from the cold tap, then threw the cold water into Hall's face. The shock of the cold water immediately caused Hall to stir, after a few more minutes he fully regained his senses.

As the fog in his brain cleared, he could finally focus on the terrifying figure of the Watcher. His eyes widened with fear as he took in the sight before him, a squat, powerful man standing in lined shadow, dressed in stained camouflage clothing and a black ski mask.

Hall instantly focussed on the object being held in the man's right hand, his eyes were fixated on the glinting metal blade of the large skinning knife.

In a state of panic, Hall began to struggle against his bindings and shouted muffled threats.

Holding the lethal knife out in front of him the Watcher slowly walked towards Hall. He leaned in close to Hall's face and said in a menacing whisper, 'I haven't touched your wife and kids yet, you piece of shit. If you atone for what you've done right now, then the good Lord will allow them to live beyond today.'

The Watcher reached into his pocket and retrieved a small laminated photograph, which he held in front of Hall's horrified face. He angled the photograph, so Hall could clearly see it, as it was illuminated by the moonlight.

'Do you repent your sins Edward Hall?'

After seeing the photograph, Hall instantly knew exactly which sin he was being asked to repent, tears streamed down his face and he nodded wildly, screaming 'Yes', from beneath the Gaffer tape.

'The Lord will show mercy and accept your repentance; the innocents will live on after tonight. For you, Edward Hall, it's too late, you're beyond the point of forgiveness; the scriptures in the Old Testament have instructed me clearly what needs to be done.'

Bowing his head, the Watcher whispered aloud, 'Forgive me Lord, as I do your bidding, thank you for allowing me to spare the innocents. I know you watch over me. Amen.'

He then walked slowly past Hall whose eyes strained wildly to see where he was going.

The last thing Edward Hall saw was the flash of the gleaming blade, as it slipped in front of his eyes, down towards his throat. He then felt his hair being grabbed roughly from behind, his head was yanked backwards until he was looking directly up at the ceiling of his kitchen. His neck felt taught, then it suddenly slackened as the vicious blade sliced deep into his throat. Hall felt the warmth of his own blood as it gushed from the gaping wound in his throat onto his chest.

Within a minute, he had bled out and was dead on the chair. He sat in an ever-widening pool of his own blood.

The Watcher retrieved the heavy pliers from the day sack, ripped the brown Gaffer tape from around Hall's head and began to systematically remove every single tooth from his mouth.

Each tooth was dropped into a clear plastic zip lock bag. After removing all of Hall's teeth he sealed the zip lock bag and placed it back into the daysack. There was still one last thing to do before he left the house. He took the two-inch paintbrush from the daysack and dipped it into the dark pool of Hall's blood.

Having finished his macabre ritual, he made one last check of the kitchen to make sure he'd left nothing behind, then returned to the lounge. From the large teak wall unit, he removed a single framed photograph. There were dozens of photographs on the unit, but this particular photograph of four men, interested the Watcher. Having placed the framed photograph into his daysack, he stepped out through the front door of the house and into the bright moonlight.

The street was quiet and still, the only noise he could hear was the distant hoot of an owl, away in the distance. Stealthily, he crouched low and moved across the lawn at the front of the house. The heavy dew on the grass soaked his training shoes and washed Hall's blood from the soles and welts.

Moving carefully and sticking to the shadows, the Watcher slipped unseen through the deserted streets, back to the multi storey car park. He started the engine of the Land Rover and drove out of the car park. He didn't see another vehicle until he'd been driving fifteen minutes.

The vehicle he saw was one of the bread delivery wagons that race around the streets during the early hours of the morning. The drivers with nothing on their mind, except the next delivery point where they could drop off their freshly baked bread.

After an uneventful drive from Beeston, he eventually steered the Land Rover onto the near deserted caravan site at Clumber Park.

Everywhere was still and in complete darkness.

He utilised the quiet time to wash and clean his gear in the deserted shower block before retiring to his caravan. He opened the small fridge and placed the zip lock bag containing Hall's teeth, next to the bag that contained Naylor's eyes. He then took out a carton of long life milk and a tub of Lurpak butter.

He put the kettle on, put two slices of toast under the grill of the tiny cooker and dropped a tea bag into a mug.

When the kettle had boiled, he poured the hot water into the mug and buttered the toast.

Sitting on the step of the caravan he sipped his tea and ate his toast, as he watched the sun slip over the horizon, heralding the start of a new day.

CHAPTER 19

8.45am Friday 24th March 1986
Beeston Fields, Beeston

The house had been quiet for hours now

Vanessa Hall was stark naked and freezing cold, although the heating was on in the house, her entire body was starting to ache with the cold. Her two young children were snuggled together trying to keep warm. They had stopped sobbing beneath their sticky, smelly gags now, but they continually glanced at their mother with scared confused eyes.

Truth be told, she was as confused and scared as her children. She had racked her brain but still had no answers to the questions that kept forcing their way into her mind.

Who was that madman?

How did he know her name?

What had she done to be visited by such a creature?

Where was her husband, Eddie?

Vanessa continued to try and loosen the thin cord that bound her daughter's hands. She had been trying for well over an hour, but with freezing cold fingers the thin, slippery cord was almost impossible to grip.

Suddenly, there was the slightest give in the cord, frantically she began to work harder, trying to untie the knot she'd loosened. Her hands and fingers ached with the effort. She leaned forward towards her daughter, and mumbled in her ear. She desperately hoped the young girl would understand the garbled message spluttered from beneath the cloying brown tape, 'When mummy unties you, take the brown tape from mummy's mouth. Do not go out of this room. Do you understand?'

The young girl stared, the fear even more evident in her eyes now.

Finally, she nodded.

'Becky, are you sure you know what mummy wants you to do?'

The young girl nodded again, a little more vigorously this time.

Vanessa unravelled the final knot in her daughter's bindings. The girl's hands were now free. Instantly the youngster began to pull at the brown tape around her mother's face. The pain was intense as the girl slowly peeled away the sticky tape, inch by inch. Eventually, the tape was pulled completely off, Vanessa gulped in air.

'Well done sweetie, now I'm going to turn around and I want you to try and untie mummy, can you do that?'

The girl nodded enthusiastically, pleased that her mum was happy with what she had achieved so far.

It took a further twenty minutes for the young girl to loosen Vanessa's bonds enough for her to shake them free. The girl's smaller fingers had fared much better with the thin nylon cord than her mother's.

Once free of the cord that had bound her wrists, Vanessa quickly untied her feet and then undid the remaining ties on the children. Lastly, remembering the pain she had experienced, she carefully removed the brown tape from around their small mouths.

When they were all finally free from their bonds, Vanessa pulled the children close into her, cuddling them both tightly.

Vanessa now had a big decision to make. She needed to summon help, the only way to do that was to venture out of the room and hope that the maniac had gone.

She plucked up all her courage and shouted loudly, 'Eddie, help us!'

No response, not a sound in the house.

She shouted again.

Nothing.

She looked at her frightened children, 'I want you both to stay here, you must be very, very quiet. Mummy's going outside to find Daddy, I won't be two ticks. Whatever you hear, you must stay here and wait for Mummy to come back for you. Becky, will you look after Hugo for me?'

The young girl nodded and pulled her young brother closer to her.

Vanessa stood up and put her index finger to her lips as she looked into the eyes of her terrified children. The kids knew that signal and both did the same back, placing tiny index fingers over their own lips.

She then tiptoed out of the room and closed the bedroom door carefully behind her.

Silently, she crept across the landing, noticing immediately that the loft hatch was no longer in place. A wave of fear crashed over her and she felt her legs weaken. Remembering her children, she steeled herself, picked up a heavy glass vase that stood on the window sill at the top of the stairs and moved forward.

Moving slowly, she checked all the other upstairs rooms. There was no sign of Eddie.

Calling on the last reserves of her courage, she made her way carefully down the stairs, still clutching the heavy vase. As she made her way down the carpeted stairs she saw that the front door was wide open.

Suddenly she felt elated, a sense of relief washed over her, the monster had gone. All she had to do now was find her husband, untie him and get the kids out of there.

Carefully, she stepped by the open front door, walked along the hallway and into the L shaped kitchen. As she stepped onto the kitchen tiles, she suddenly felt something sticky on her bare feet. This part of the kitchen was little more than a corridor and the light was poor. She looked down at her feet and could make out something dark on the floor tiles.

There was a strange metallic odour in the room.

She turned the corner into the main part of the kitchen and flicked the light on as she did so.

The sight that confronted her was like a scene from the worst kind of horror movie.

Her husband sat naked on one of the wooden chairs. He had been secured to the chair by thin nylon cord. His head was back, his throat had been cut virtually from ear to ear.

The huge wound caused his neck to gape open in some macabre smile.

The floor tiles around the chair were an inch deep in dark brown jelly.

Suddenly, Vanessa realised that the jelly she stood in, was actually her husband's congealing blood. She let out a gasp and felt her legs buckle beneath her, the heavy vase slipped from her grasp and shattered as she fell.

Falling to the floor, she desperately began trying to shuffle backwards out of the kitchen, away from her slaughtered husband. As she slipped around in the blood, she could feel the panic rising in her.

Finally, she gained some purchase from the floor, scrambled to her feet and bolted out of the kitchen.

Her adrenalin fuelled panic caused her to run straight out of the front door. She sprinted down the driveway, not feeling the sharp gravel as it cut into her bare feet.

Vanessa had totally forgotten she was stark naked, she'd also forgotten that her two young children were still in the house, she was in flight mode and just wanted to get as far away from the horror as she could.

It was daylight now and her neighbours from the house directly opposite, were sitting in their car on the driveway about to drive onto the road, when suddenly they saw the naked Vanessa Hall covered in blood, sprint down her driveway away from her house.

The neighbour, Mr Hughes, immediately stopped his car, jumped out and intercepted Vanessa just as she reached the road.

He tried to grab her by the arms.

She began to lash out at the old man, catching him with a glancing blow just beneath his left eye. He gamely held on and shouted, 'Vanessa, calm down! It's me, Bill Hughes. Calm down!'

All the fight suddenly evaporated from Vanessa and once again she felt her legs buckle. Mrs Hughes joined her husband and hurriedly placed her own coat around a now shivering Vanessa.

A shaken Bill Hughes, turned to his wife and said, 'I've got her Muriel, I'll bring her up to the house. You go ahead and call the police, something terrible has happened, she's covered in blood.'

The old lady shuffled ahead to call the police, while Bill slowly helped Vanessa back to his house. As he reached the front door of the house Bill whispered, 'What on earth's happened, Vanessa? Where are the children?'

Suddenly the shock became too much for her and Vanessa Hall completely passed out.

Bill Hughes carried her the final couple of steps into his house and laid her down on a sofa.

He turned to his wife and said, 'I'm going over there.'

'No, you're bloody not, you old fool! The police are on their way, they can deal with it. You said yourself she's covered in blood.'

'But the children might still be in danger!'

'And what can you do, old man? Except maybe get yourself killed.'

In the distance, they could hear the sound of sirens approaching.

'They'll be here in a moment', said Muriel. 'You just wait here.'

'Alright, alright. I'll stay here woman, but God forbid something awful's happened to those two beautiful children.'

CHAPTER 20

9.00am Friday 24th March 1986
Arnold, Nottingham

Geoff Naylor was in a foul mood.

He had spent the last two days in London, the important business meetings he'd attended, had not gone well.

As he parked the car outside his office, he reflected on the arguments he'd become embroiled in with Malcolm Franklin.

Malcolm was the youngest son of Gregg Franklin, the owner of Franklin & Sons, he had only just joined his father's company and was fresh out of some dishwater university, down south. The gobby little shit thought he was God's gift to commerce. What an arrogant jumped up prick he was, trying to tell him how he could make massive savings, if he would only run his company in a more modern fashion. Never mind the fact that he had built his company by himself, from scratch, and had probably forgotten more about running a business than Malcolm would ever learn.

After the first clash and the heated exchanges that followed, Geoff had lost all interest in closing the deal. The result being, that he'd come away from London late yesterday evening having told Gregg Franklin and his cockney dickhead son Malcolm exactly where they could stick their very competitively priced electrical cabling.

The consequence of this rash act meant he would have to start ringing round other suppliers for the cabling urgently. Geoff knew in his heart that he'd behaved unprofessionally, and that his anger and spur of the moment decision to pull the plug on the deal, would end up costing Naylor Properties Limited a great deal of money. He was now worried that it might even affect the costings for the pending contract with Notts County Council to build the new Mansfield Woodhouse Police Station.

He slammed his car door, and with an air of defiance he said aloud, 'Who gives a fuck! It will cost that prick Franklin far more than it will cost me!'

He chuckled briefly, but the smile evaporated immediately when he noticed that his son's car was not in the car park.

He stormed into the building and walked straight into his office. He ignored the two personal assistants that sat outside the office. Their greetings, made in unison, of 'Good morning Mr Naylor', fell on deaf ears today.

He sat down heavily in his leather chair and hurled his briefcase onto the settee that was positioned the other side of the desk. He felt a familiar heaviness begin to spread across his chest. He knew that particular feeling of tightness only too well.

Reaching into his jacket pocket he took out a small, solid silver pill box. He flicked open the lid and took out a single black pill which he popped into his mouth. He allowed the pill to dissolve beneath his tongue then closed his eyes and willed himself to calm down.

After a few minutes the feeling of tightness in his chest passed.

Feeling calmer, he picked up the telephone and dialled the number for his son's home. It just rang and rang, there was no answer. Naylor slammed the phone down and picked up his car keys. He'd made his mind up, he was going to drive over to Underwood, confront Cavalie and get this sorted once and for all.

Either he got rid of that useless, grasping piece of shit, Christopher, or he could leave the company. He wasn't going to be pissed about or disrespected like this anymore.

No sooner had he grabbed the car keys than the phone on his desk began to ring. That would be typical of Cavalie, he thought, to call right at the point of confrontation.

Still feeling angry he picked up the phone, 'What?'

He instantly recognised the soft, effeminate, lisping voice. It was the detestable Christopher on the phone, 'I'm sorry to bother you at work Mr Naylor, but has Cavalie had to go away on business again?'

'No, he hasn't, why?'

'I've been away for a few days on a sketching course in Cornwall, we were supposed to be going out for drinks tomorrow evening, but he's not returning my calls. I've phoned him every night since I arrived in Cornwall on Tuesday, he hasn't returned a single call or left any messages. I'll be honest with you Mr Naylor, I'm beginning to get worried.'

Geoff Naylor detested every fibre of the man who was on the phone. Just the sound of his voice made his flesh crawl. Then the enormity of what he was hearing Christopher say, began to worm its way into his brain, bypassing his foul mood and circling around his hatred for the loathsome man.

A question began to scream through his brain, where was Cavalie?

He just dropped the telephone on his desk, ignoring Christopher's cries, 'Mr Naylor, are you there? Mr Naylor?'

He walked straight out of his office and growled at his PA, 'Hold my calls Sarah, I'm driving over to Cav's house at Underwood.'

CHAPTER 21

9.00am Friday 24th March 1986
Beeston Fields, Beeston

The two police patrol cars arrived virtually together, they screeched to a stop outside the home of Bill Hughes.

A young constable jumped out of the first car and ran down the driveway to the front door of the Hughes residence. Bill Hughes was waiting on the doorstep and immediately began to explain to the officer what had happened. He described how he'd seen his heavily bloodstained neighbour running from her driveway totally naked and in a state of panic.

'Where's your neighbour now sir?'

'She's in the house, resting. I'm afraid she's passed out officer.'

'What's her name?'

'Hall, her name's Vanessa Hall.'

The sergeant who'd been driving the second patrol car, joined them on the doorstep just as the old man said, 'We don't know what's happened to her children though.'

The sergeant echoing the old man asked, 'The children?'

'Mr and Mrs Hall have two young children, a girl and a boy. We can't find out from Vanessa if they're ok.'

The sergeant turned to the young officer and said, 'Jim, stay here with Mrs Hall. Get an ambulance travelling, by the sound of it she's going to need medical attention. I'll go across the road and see what's happened.'

Bill Hughes was listening to the conversation and said, 'I'll come over with you sergeant, you may need some help.'

'Thank you, sir, but that won't be necessary. I'd appreciate it, if you stayed here with Pc Thorne. It will be good for your neighbour to see a friendly face when she comes round again.'

A crestfallen Bill Hughes nodded his head and showed the young constable inside his home.

Sergeant Andy Wills then sprinted back down the driveway, crossed the road and approached the Hall residence.

He immediately saw that the front door to the house was open. He quickly put on his black leather gloves and drew his wooden truncheon, gripping it in his right hand. Using the back of his left hand he opened the heavy front door as wide as it would go. He saw the smears of blood all along the walls of the hallway. There were no bloody marks on the walls of the stairs, all the blood marks appeared to be on the ground floor. There were bloody footprints leading from the kitchen along the hallway towards the front door. The sergeant could clearly see the bare footprints of Vanessa Hall and also a larger boot print. Both sets of footprints were leading out of the front door.

Quietly, he made his way through the house, holding his truncheon out in front of him ready to engage any threat he may face. After checking the lounge and the dining room he made his way towards the kitchen. He could see the blood that had pooled on the floor tiles. He avoided the blood and stepped into the kitchen.

As soon as he entered the kitchen, he fully understood the reason why Vanessa Hall had fled her own house in such a state of sheer panic.

Sgt Wills could see the dead body of a naked male, still tied to a heavy wooden chair with a massive wound across his neck that had severed both arteries. The blood loss had been quick and catastrophic. He looked down at the pool of blood on the floor, he could see the small footprints that had been made by Mrs Hall. He could also see scuff marks in the congealed blood where she had fallen.

There was nothing more to be done for the victim.

Sgt Andy Wills knew everything about scene preservation. Very carefully, he retraced his steps out of the kitchen not touching or disturbing anything. Ordinarily he would have sealed the house off immediately, but he still had a problem, somewhere in this charnel house were two small children.

They must be upstairs.

With a feeling of utter dread at what he may be about to find, Andy Wills began to climb the stairs, one at a time. He ensured his weight remained on the sides of the treads, so they didn't creak and betray his approach. He was still acutely aware that whoever had slaughtered the man downstairs, could still be in the house.

He got to the top of the stairs and saw that the loft hatch was open.

The doors on the landing were all closed, he had to check the loft space before he went any further. The offender could still be hiding there.

He looked for any obvious footmarks on the bannister rail and saw none.

Quickly, he put his truncheon back in his trouser pocket, reached up and hauled himself up into the loft. He scanned each corner of the loft and saw nobody. He jumped down out of the loft, took out his truncheon again and began to check the bedrooms.

The first room he entered was obviously the master bedroom, he checked under the bed and the wardrobes, it was empty. The second room he checked appeared to be the young boys room, pictures of Thomas the Tank Engine and Postman Pat adorned the walls, again he checked beneath the bed and the single wardrobe, finding nothing.

The next door he opened led into the family bathroom, Andy checked inside, nothing.

There was one room left to check and the door remained closed.

It had a small nameplate on the door, that declared in baby pink letters "Becky's Room".

Andy gripped his truncheon a little tighter, this was the last room, the children had to be in here. He pushed down on the door handle with his left hand and opened the door.

As soon as he entered the small bedroom, he heard what sounded like a soft whimper and saw movement beneath the flowery duvet cover. He quickly checked below the bed and looked inside the single wardrobe. Nothing.

There was no obvious threat now, so Andy slipped the truncheon back into his pocket.

In a very soft voice he said, 'Kids, are you in here? I'm a policeman. You can come out now, it's safe. There's nothing to scare you anymore. Your mum's next door with your neighbours.'

He knelt down at the side of the small, single bed and said quietly, 'Come on Becky, are you under here? I need to get you and your brother back to your mum.'

Slowly the duvet cover shifted a few inches, Andy could now see two pairs of very frightened eyes staring back at him.

'Is that you Becky? My name's Andy. Becky, can you see the silver buttons on my jacket? I'm a policeman, I've come to get you out of here and take you to your mum. Is that your brother with you under there?'

He saw the girl nod.

'Come on then sweetheart, let's get you and your brother back to your mum.'

Nothing moved, then he heard a tiny voice say, 'Has the horrid man gone?'

'Yes, he's gone. It's just me here now and I'm your friend, Becky. Shall we go and see your mum?'

Slowly, the traumatised children moved the quilt cover and for the first-time Andy could see exactly how totally, shell shocked they were. He picked up the small boy, held the young girls hand and walked them down the stairs and out of the house of horrors, that had once been their home.

As he walked across the road with the children, the first ambulance was pulling up outside the Hughes house. Another police car arrived with two female officers on board.

Andy began to organise his staff; his heart had stopped racing now. After the tension of the house search he'd started to calm down again.

He sent Pc Thorne across the road to begin and maintain the crime scene log. Then he tasked one of the women police officers to stay with Mr and Mrs Hughes and start taking their first account. The other policewoman was instructed to follow the ambulance containing Vanessa Hall and her two young children to the hospital. They all needed to be checked over after their horrific ordeal.

Having organised his small team Andy quickly drove back to Beeston police station and rang the contact number for the recently formed Major Crime Investigation Unit.

The phone rang twice before it was answered, 'MCIU, Detective Inspector Buxton, how can I help you?'

'Hello Rob, it's me, Andy.'

'Andy, good to hear from you. How's life as a uniformed sergeant treating you?'

'It's all good thanks Rob. I'm calling you with a referral though, we've had a murder in Beeston overnight.'

'Right, I see. Ok Andy, exactly what have we got?'

Andy then painstakingly relayed every detail of what he'd encountered at the house.

Having listened to the detailed briefing, Rob said, 'Get back up to the scene Andy, keep it tight, you know the drill. I'll arrange for a Scenes of Crime team and a Home Office pathologist to be travelling to your location. I'll give Danny a courtesy call to let him know what's happening, then I'll be hot footing it up there with my team. I should be with you in less than an hour. It'll be like the old days Andy, when we were all chasing The Coal Killer.'

'Wait until you've seen inside the house, it certainly looks like you've got another maniac to catch. I'll see you soon Rob.'

CHAPTER 22

9.45am Friday 24th March 1986
Underwood, Nottinghamshire

In the time, it took him to drive from his offices in Arnold out to the small village of Underwood, Geoff Naylor's mood had gone from angry to extremely worried. He'd assumed that his son Cavalie, was off galivanting somewhere with that grasping friend of his.

The telephone call he'd received from Christopher, just before he left his office, had put paid to that idea. If he wasn't on holiday abroad somewhere with his friend, where was he? What was he playing at? Why hadn't he been in to work?

Geoff had driven his car at crazy speeds along the country lanes that led to his son's bungalow.

Finally, the modern property came into view and he slowed his vehicle. He let out an audible gasp when he saw his son's Jaguar still parked on the driveway. There was an icy dread beginning to creep slowly over him. He had an intuition, only shared between a father and child, that something was dreadfully wrong. Horrific thoughts began to gnaw into his mind.

He drove onto the driveway and parked his own Jaguar immediately behind his son's.

His eyes were locked onto the car in front of him, he sat there staring, almost in disbelief, that the car was there.

Frantically, he began searching the glove compartment of his own car, for the spare set of keys to Cavalie's bungalow. He found them and got out of the car, a hundred different scenarios now played through his mind.

Whenever an innocent explanation came to mind, it was quickly replaced with the idea that some dreadful harm had befallen his only child. His legs felt weak, his heart was pounding in his chest, with a feeling of real trepidation he slowly made his way to the front door.

He listened at the wooden door, then peered through the stained glass at each side of the door. He couldn't hear a thing, but he noticed several large, black house flies on the inside of the glass panes.

He banged on the heavy door with his fist and shouted, 'Cav, are you in there, son?'

The silence was deafening.

He lifted the heavy brass letter box in the middle of the door, then leaned forward intending to shout his son's name again.

The shout never came.

As he lifted the letterbox to shout his son's name, he instantly gagged on the smell emanating from within the bungalow.

It was a smell he knew, he remembered it well from his days as a soldier in the Korean war. It was the sickly-sweet, cloying smell of death and it was coming from inside his son's bungalow.

He felt his chest tighten, his hands shook as he fumbled with the front door key.

At last the Yale key slipped into the lock, he gave it the half turn needed to open the door. The bungalow still appeared neat and tidy, but was full of large flies. The stench was overpowering, he fought hard against an overwhelming urge to vomit.

As he walked through the bungalow, he knew exactly what he was going to find.

Even though he was expecting it, the shock of what he saw as he walked into the kitchen made him almost keel over. He grabbed hold of the granite worktop to prevent himself from collapsing completely.

He began to sob quietly as he saw his beloved son bound and gagged in a chair in the centre of the kitchen.

His son's throat had been cut from ear to ear.

Dried crusty blood covered his naked torso, a large pool of blood had congealed beneath the chair. Maggots crawled in and around the deep slash wound across the throat. The creamy white larvae stood out against the black of the dried blood.

He couldn't bear to see the horrendous image any longer and looked away. He was immediately confronted with another hideous sight, large strips of human skin had been laid over the back of one of the other chairs, the edges were beginning to curl in now that the flesh had dried.

He looked back at his sons mutilated body and saw that the lengths of skin had been flayed from his chest. There were four lengths of skin in all, whoever had killed his son had tortured him first.

Regaining some of the composure of a veteran soldier, who'd seen horrendous wounds and countless mutilated bodies in the heat of battle, he steeled himself and looked closer at the body of his dead son.

He could now see that both his son's eyes were missing.

The sockets were now gaping black holes. The maggots danced in and out of the voids created, as they searched desperately to find a way into the dead man's skull.

Geoff Naylor looked down on the floor below the chair, expecting to see the eyes. There was nothing lying in the congealed pool of blood.

The eyes were nowhere to be seen.

From the moment, he had first walked into the kitchen that now resembled a slaughter house, Naylor had remained motionless. Finally, he found the strength in his legs to move, he turned away and now faced the far kitchen wall.

As soon as he turned away from his dead son, he was confronted with another image that chilled his blood again.

Painted on the cream wall of the kitchen, in letters ten inches high, were a series of numbers and letters. They had been brushed onto the wall using his sons blood, there were streak marks down the wall where the blood had run, the dried rivulets made the whole scene even more macabre.

Geoff Naylor could take no more, he stumbled backwards out of the bungalow and onto the York stone driveway. He bent forward, placed his hands on his knees and ejected his recently consumed breakfast all over the yellow coloured flagstones.

The action of vomiting strained his stomach, he felt a familiar dull pain start to throb in his left armpit, this pain grew steadily until it shot like a lightning bolt, down the length of his left arm.

He staggered back to his car, frantically he grabbed for his suit jacket that he'd left on the passenger seat, from the pocket of the jacket he retrieved the small pill case, quickly slipping a black pill beneath his tongue. He picked up the small bottle of water that was on the front seat, then slumped down beside the car.

He sipped the water slowly and waited for the pounding in his temples to calm down.

Gradually, the heavy ache in his chest subsided and the shooting pains in his left arm stopped altogether.

After ten minutes, he got onto his hands and knees and crawled back towards the front door of the bungalow. It was too soon to risk standing, but he needed to raise the alarm. He knew if he wasn't careful, he would be as dead as his son long before any help arrived.

Progress across the driveway was painfully slow, eventually he crawled back into the bungalow. The telephone was on an antique wall unit in the hallway, not far from the front door.

Not far to go now.

He lifted the handset of the cream coloured telephone and dialled three nines.

Nothing.

He held the phone close to his ear, he couldn't hear a dialling tone.

The line was dead.

He slumped from his hands and knees and lay face down on the floor.

Using the last reserves of his energy, he rolled onto his back, his eyes felt heavy now. He knew, deep down, if he went to sleep now, he would never wake up. Just as he was losing the battle to keep his eyelids open, he heard a knock on the front door, then a man's voice called out, 'Hello, anybody in?'

Naylor saw a man's head look around the heavy door, he saw the man's eyes widen as he saw him lying on the floor in the hallway.

The man rushed into the hallway, bent down at the side of Naylor and said, 'Bloody hell mate, are you alright? You look like shit.'

Naylor recognised the uniform of the Post Office, it was the postman.

In a voice that was little more than a croaky whisper he gasped, 'Call the police. It's my son, he's been murdered. The phone line here's dead. Go and get help for God's sake.'

'I'll go to the next house and call the police mate. Are you gonna be ok? You look terrible.'

'I've got my heart pills with me, I'll be fine. Go and call the police, now!'

The postman stood up and raced back out of the bungalow.

Feeling hopeful now, with a great effort Naylor propped himself up against the wall, next to the telephone table and took another sip of water. He felt the shooting pain down his left arm again. It was getting worse, he fumbled for his pill box and took another of the tiny black pills, letting it dissolve below his tongue, he hadn't felt this bad for ages.

The agonising pain in his arm gradually subsided, replaced by a feeling of heaviness across his chest. It felt as though a man was standing on his chest.

His breathing was shallow, he panted in an effort to get more oxygen in. He closed his eyes, attempted to shut out the pain and concentrated on trying to remain calm.

Finally, in the distance, he could hear the sound of sirens approaching.

CHAPTER 23

10.15am Friday 24th March 1986
Beeston Fields, Beeston

Danny Flint stood outside the front door of the Hall's house in Beeston, he was flanked on either side by Brian Hopkirk and Rob Buxton. He had his arms folded across his chest and was deep in thought.

Upon his arrival at the scene earlier, Rob had made the decision to call out the second enquiry team, led by Brian Hopkirk. It had been immediately obvious to Rob, that there would be a lot of house to house enquiries to undertake.

'Right Rob, who's the victim?' asked Danny.

'Dead man's name is Edward Hall.'

'What do we know about Edward Hall?'

'Hall is, sorry was, the manager of the prestigious Grosvenor Hotel in Nottingham city centre. He lived here with his wife Vanessa and their two young children.'

Rob glanced down at his notebook, then continued, 'The daughter, Rebecca, is seven and the son, Hugo, is five.'

'Any physical injuries to the wife and children?'

'They were all bound and gagged for a lengthy period of time, they're all at the hospital being checked over. Physically, they're pretty much unscathed, God only knows what the damage is mentally. Luckily, as far as we know, the children haven't seen the state of their father. This is a bad one Danny. It's like a slaughter house in the kitchen, there's blood everywhere.'

'I'll go and have a look for myself in a second, what's been organised so far?'

'Seamus Carter's the on-call home office pathologist, he's been here about five minutes and is already inside examining the body. I called Brian straight away and asked him to mobilise his team to help with the house to house enquiries. This is a large residential area and the house to house alone will be a massive undertaking. I've also arranged for a scenes of crime team to attend, they're currently on their way.'

'What's the bloody hold up with them? I've managed to get here from Mansfield, where are they?'

'Vehicle trouble boss. Apparently, the van they were originally in, has broken down, they've had to wait for the workshops to attend. They couldn't get it going, so they've had to return to headquarters and get another vehicle. They should be here in ten minutes.'

'Brian, you wait outside, there's no point in us all going in and disturbing the scene. Come on Rob, show me what we've got.'

The two men signed into the scene log, then walked into the house protected by forensic suits, gloves and overshoes.

As they walked along the hallway towards the kitchen, Danny could hear the distinctive Irish brogue of Seamus Carter as he rumbled into his Dictaphone.

Danny let out a low whistle as he surveyed the scene of carnage for the first time.

'Good morning detective, how are you today?' asked Seamus.

'I'm fine and dandy Seamus, what have we got?'

'Early days, but the obvious cause of death is the massive wound to the throat, blood loss was catastrophic, he would have bled out very quickly, dead within a minute or two.'

'Weapon?' asked Danny.

'Not sure exactly what was used, but whatever it was, it's incredibly sharp. Almost scalpel like. Not a scalpel though, it's a much broader blade. I'll maybe know more when it comes to the post mortem.'

'Can you give me an estimated time of death?'

'I'd say sometime after three this morning, between three and four thirty, that's a ball park figure.'

'Any other injuries, apart from the wound to the neck?'

'After the victim's throat was cut and he'd bled out, the killer has then very crudely extracted all the dead man's teeth. No care was taken, they've literally been ripped out of his mouth. I can't see any of the teeth here, which means the killer has taken them with him.'

'Trophies?'

'Possibly.'

'Ok Seamus, anything else?'

'Only what's scrawled on the wall.'

The pathologist indicated the wall that was to Danny's right, just out of his line of sight.

Danny took a step to his left, he could now clearly see the series of random letters and numbers that had been painted on the wall. The killer had used blood to write on the wall, in letters ten inches high, EC21V2425.

'Jesus Christ! What's all that about Seamus?'

The huge shoulders of the pathologist shrugged, 'Not sure what it means Danny. What I can tell you is that the message, whatever it is, has been painted on the wall using our victims blood. If you look closely you can see that there are brush marks, so I'm guessing a small paint brush was used. There's no paintbrush to be found here, which makes me think this was all done in order to leave that message.'

'So, you're thinking that whoever did this, came prepared to leave this message.'

'Exactly that.'

'Thanks Seamus, Rob's going to be in charge of the scene, let him know if you need anything.'

'Will do Danny, we must catch up over a pint soon.'

'That we must my friend, that we must.'

Danny made his way out of the house, followed by Rob.

Waiting outside was a uniform sergeant standing next to Brian Hopkirk.

Danny recognised the sergeant and said, 'Andy, how are you? Rob told me you were first on the scene.'

'I'm good thanks boss, I'd only just come on duty when this call came in. The control room have just contacted me, they are trying to get hold of you, there's been another murder reported this morning at Underwood. The force control room have received a request from Division, that the MCIU attend.'

'Bloody hell boss, they're like London buses, nothing for weeks then two come along together', said Rob.

'Thanks Andy', said Danny, before continuing, 'Right Rob I want you to gather your team and get across to Underwood, you know that area. Brian, you stay here, sort out this scene and get the enquiries underway here, again you know this area much better than Rob. It makes sense for you to work the areas you're familiar with, get onto the control room and arrange for a section of the Special Operations Unit to help out with the house to house enquiries here.'

'Ok boss, I'm on it', said Brian.

'Rob, get your team travelling over to Underwood immediately. Anybody who's been into the scene here will need to go via our office and get a change of clothing. That goes for you and me too, I don't want to risk any cross contamination of the scenes.'

'I'm the only one who's been inside boss. If it's okay, I'll travel back to Mansfield with you to get a change of clothes, that'll save tying up one of our motors?'

'No problem. Is there anything else you need Brian?'

'A Scenes of Crime team would be nice, boss.'

Right on cue, the large white van containing the Scenes of Crime team and equipment turned into the street.

'There you go Brian, as requested. I want you to get a landline set up here so we can remain in contact between the two scenes. Call the office at three o'clock this afternoon and let me have an update. I'll be back in the office by then.'

'Will do boss.'

Danny and Rob walked down the driveway of the house back towards their car, followed by Andy Wills.

At the car, Danny turned to Andy Wills and said, 'Andy get onto your control room for me and find out exactly where this incident in Underwood is, I want to get Rob's team straight over there.'

'Will do boss.'

'Thanks Andy. When are you going to transfer over onto the Major Crime team?'

Andy smiled, 'As soon as you like boss, I've done six months in uniform now, I could do with getting a suit on again, the shift pattern is killing me. We've done a week of day shifts and because it's the last shift we're working a split today. I've got to work from nine this morning until one o'clock this afternoon, then go home for a few hours and come back for an evening shift tonight. I start later at ten o'clock tonight and work through until two in the morning, then we get three rest days. Its diabolical, everybody spends the first rest day in bed.'

'Leave it with me Andy. I've got a vacancy on Rob's team coming up in a couple of months' time. It's yours if you want it.'

Andy grinned and said, 'Can I wait for a vacancy on Brian's team boss?'

'Cheeky bugger!' said Rob grinning.

'Seriously, that would be great boss. I'm ready to get back doing some detective work', smiled Andy.

'I'll sort it Andy, it'll be good to have you back on the team. Now, what's that address at Underwood?'

CHAPTER 24

1.00pm Friday 24th March 1986
Underwood, Nottinghamshire

As Danny and Rob pulled up outside the bungalow at Underwood, it was already a hive of police activity.

Danny parked the car behind the two large white vans that were being used by the scenes of crime team and the Special Operations Unit. A little further down the quiet lane, an ambulance was parked up near to several dark coloured cars, that were being used by the team of detectives from the MCIU.

A uniformed constable stood outside the front door of the bungalow, clipboard in hand, guardian of the all-important scene log.

Detective Constable Rachel Moore came out of the crime scene wearing a pale blue forensic suit and overshoes, carrying a clipboard. Pulling off her latex gloves, she waved at Danny and Rob as they approached her.

'Hello boss. DS Mayhew phoned in sick this morning, so I've been into the scene to take notes from the home office pathologist.'

'That's fine Rachel, what have we got?'

Rachel glanced down at the clipboard and said, 'Our victim is Cavalie Naylor, twenty-nine years of age, company director of Naylor Properties Ltd. He lives here alone and was found by his father, Geoff Naylor.'

Rachel pointed down the lane and indicated an ashen faced man who sat on the rear step of the ambulance parked a short distance away. He still had an oxygen mask on his face and was being attended to by one of the ambulance crew.

'Is he okay Rach?' asked Rob.

'The first officer who got here, thought he was having a heart attack, so he called for an ambulance. Turns out he's on medication for acute angina, so it was a good shout by the cop. He's recovering now, but the ambulance crew still want to take him to the hospital, but he's refusing to leave his son.'

'Who's the pathologist?' asked Danny.

Rachel again glanced at the clipboard, 'It's Ms Sarah Appleby. I've not met her before, she normally covers North Lincolnshire but as Seamus Carter had already been called out to the scene at Beeston, she was the next name on the call out list. She's a very nice lady, and extremely thorough.'

'Is the cause of death obvious?'

'The victim has had his throat cut boss, there's an awful lot of blood everywhere, looks like he's bled out. There's something very bizarre in there as well, the killer has left us a message.'

'A message', echoed Rob.

'Some sort of coded message has been written on the wall.'

Danny and Rob exchanged a meaningful glance, then Danny said, 'Come on then Rob, let's get booted and suited and have a look inside the bungalow. Thanks for holding the fort Rachel, I want you to go and have a chat with Geoff Naylor. I want to know exactly what he found when he got here, please. Clear it with the ambulance people first, make sure you don't push him too hard, I don't want him keeling over. I'll have a look at what we've got inside first, then I'll come and introduce myself to him. Go gently with him Rach.'

'Will do boss.'

Rachel removed her protective clothing, then made her way over to the ambulance. The two senior detectives donned the forensic suits, overshoes and gloves, then walked along the driveway towards the front door. As he walked along the drive, Danny could see the team of Special Ops officers doing a thorough search of the extensive gardens at the rear of the bungalow.

Both detectives gave their names to the officer maintaining the log, then walked inside. Scenes of Crime officers were already busily working inside the hallway, they had placed two strips of yellow adhesive tape on the floor. From behind his face mask, Tim Donnelly, the scenes of crime team leader said, 'Make sure you stay between the lines of tape gents, we've already checked there for fibres and stains.'

'Thanks Tim', said Danny before continuing, 'Is there much forensic evidence?'

'Early days' yet boss. We haven't really started on the scene itself yet. It's through there in the kitchen, we're just waiting for the pathologist to finish up. We've taken all the photographs we need so far, but we'll be getting more when the body's eventually moved.'

'Okay, keep at it Tim.'

Danny and Rob followed the tape trail until they reached the kitchen, both men stood and stared at the scene of horror before them.

Cavalie Naylor's mutilated body had been tied to a chair, his throat sliced open and both his eye sockets were now just hollow holes. Painted on the far wall, behind the body of the victim, was a series of letters and numbers that had been daubed in blood.

The letters and numbers were ten inches' high, the message read EC21V2425

Standing to one side of the body, with her back turned towards them, was a middle-aged woman wearing a forensic suit. She turned to face the detectives and said, 'Good afternoon gentlemen. I hope that you're either the Senior Investigating Officers, or that you've got a bloody good reason for being in my crime scene.'

'I'm Detective Chief Inspector Flint and this is Detective Inspector Buxton. I'm the SIO on this investigation, you must be Sarah Appleby.'

'I am Sarah Appleby, you've obviously been well briefed detective, quite a bizarre scene, I think you'd agree?'

'Until a few hours ago, I would have agreed with you, but I've just come from a murder scene in Beeston that's a mirror image of this one, including the message on the wall. Any idea what that means?'

'Sorry Chief Inspector, I've no idea what that message is all about, coded messages aren't in my remit I'm afraid. What I can tell you, is that your victim has died as a result of massive blood loss after having his throat cut. The wound is huge and has severed both of the major blood vessels in the neck. He would have bled out very quickly.'

'Any idea what type of weapon has been used Ms Appleby?' asked Rob.

'Please call me Sarah, won't you? In answer to your question, it will have been some kind of large, broad bladed instrument, that's extremely sharp. That's all I can tell you at the moment, I might have a better idea at the post mortem examination.'

Danny stepped forward to look closer at the gaping wound and the deep holes of the eye sockets, 'What's happened to his eyes Sarah?'

'That's what I was examining when I heard you come in. It appears that his eyes have been put out.'

'What do you mean "put out"? asked Rob.

'The eye can be popped out of the socket using a surgical instrument, so it rests on the cheek. It's how ophthalmic surgeons can operate on the back of the eye. The optic nerve is quite robust and will stretch a little without causing damage. In a mature adult, its roughly the thickness of a shoe lace. It would appear that the killer has used some sort of instrument to crudely put out the eyes, before severing the optic nerves and removing them altogether.'

'Bloody hell', whispered Danny, 'You mean the poor sod was alive, when his eyes were cut out?'

'It would appear so detective. I'll know for certain when I can examine the eye sockets and what's left of the optic nerve at the post mortem. He was also very much alive when those strips of skin were flayed from his chest. The strips of removed skin have been laid over the back of that chair and would have been visible to the victim after they had been removed.'

'Would he have been able to stand that level of pain without blacking out?'

'Almost certainly. He would have been in agony, but I doubt it was enough to cause him to pass out.'

'The strips of skin have been left behind, is there any sign of the eyes anywhere?'

'No, they've been removed and taken away.'

'Like the bloody teeth', whispered Rob.

'Exactly', said Danny, 'Our boy likes to take trophies it would seem.'

Putting her hands on her hips, Sarah Appleby pursed her lips and said, 'Am I missing something here, Chief Inspector? What bloody teeth?'

'Sorry Sarah, the other scene I mentioned. There was a murder at Beeston last night, the killer left exactly the same message on a wall there, using the blood from his victim. The victim had all his teeth extracted, they're missing from the scene so it would appear the killer has taken them away with him. The pathologist at that scene is Seamus Carter, it's going to be imperative that after you've both concluded your scene examinations and the post mortem examinations, of the respective victims, that you liaise fully. Do you and Seamus Carter know each other?'

'I know Seamus very well, we trained together.'

'That's good news, this is obviously the work of the same individual. Looking at the level of decomposition and infestation, I would think Mr Naylor here, has been dead for at least a couple of days.'

Sarah Appleby nodded in agreement and said, 'My best estimate would be that he was killed three days ago, so this poor unfortunate man would have been the first victim of your killer.'

'It would appear so Sarah, I'll leave you to your work. What time do you think you'll be in a position to start the post mortem examination?'

She glanced at her watch, 'I think if we aim for five o'clock this evening, that should be about right.'

'Okay, Rob will be staying here at the scene, so if you need anything else just give him a shout.'

Danny retraced his steps out of the kitchen and made his way outside, Rob carefully followed in his footsteps.

As they stepped outside the front door, they signed out of the scene.

Danny turned to Rob and said, 'Get a land line established here first priority, I want to be able to liaise with you and Brian. I want to know every similarity you find. It's obvious these two murders are heavily linked, and look like the work of the same killer. I don't want to start shouting serial killer just yet, but we need to be ready for that possibility.'

There was a shout from the rear garden of the bungalow.

A detective came rushing down from the raised garden and waved to Danny, 'Over here boss!'

Danny and Rob walked over to the breathless detective who said, 'The Special Ops lads have found what appears to be the remnants of a hide, that looks down over the property.'

'Okay Rob, get it all photographed and then get the Special Ops lads to fingertip search it. If it's been used by the killer and he's left something behind, I don't want us to miss it.'

'I'm on it boss.'

Rob walked off, following the detective who'd been with the Special Ops team.

Danny got out of the now bloodstained forensic suit and overshoes. He took off the gloves and placed them in the bin bag at the front door. A note was made in the scene log that the protective garments he was wearing had been discarded correctly.

He then walked over to the ambulance.

In the back of the ambulance he saw Rachel talking gently to Geoff Naylor. The old man now looked much better and had a little colour in his face.

Rachel said, 'Mr Naylor, this is my boss, Detective Chief Inspector Flint.'

Danny said, 'Mr Naylor, I'm very sorry for your loss.'

'Are you going to catch whoever did that to my beautiful boy, Chief Inspector?'

'I'll do everything in my power to find whoever's responsible. Have you any idea who might have a reason to want to harm your son?'

'None at all, Cav wouldn't hurt a fly.'

'Does the writing on the kitchen wall inside, mean anything to you?'

'I'm afraid not, I don't understand that at all.'

'I know your son was a director of your company, have there been any problems with the business that you're aware of?'

'Nothing at all. Obviously, I'm also a director of the company. I know for a fact, there are no problems with the business. I can talk to you about every business deal we've ever had and everyone that's currently ongoing. There are no issues with our business.'

'Have you had any problems with recently laid off staff?'

'No nothing, we've got a very settled workforce, we haven't had any redundancies or dismissals for years.'

'Was Cavalie having any problems privately, that you're aware of?'

'You need to have a look at his friend, Christopher Baker.'

The old man virtually spat the name out, contempt heavy in his voice.

'What's the problem with Mr Baker?'

'There's something very strange about Christopher 'bloody' Baker! He's really got his claws into Cav. He's a grasping bastard and I wouldn't trust him as far as I could throw him. He'll have some involvement in this, you mark my words. He's been hanging around our Cav like a bad smell for months. I just don't trust him, he's weird.'

'Where can we find Mr Baker?'

'He lives over in Nottingham, Hucknall way I think, his address will be in Cav's office somewhere.'

'Okay Mr Naylor, thank you. I want you to do something for me now, I want you to go with the ambulance and get checked over at the hospital. You've had the worst imaginable, kind of shock today. I know you don't want to leave Cavalie, but we're here to look after things now.'

'I'll do as you ask and go to the hospital Mr Flint, I do feel like shit. Get hold of that bastard, Christopher Baker. I guarantee the answer to this horror show won't be far from him.'

Danny and Rachel stepped out of the ambulance and Danny spoke to the ambulance crew, 'He's ready to go to the hospital now, thanks for your patience.'

He then turned to Rachel and said, 'Rachel, go with him and stay with him. I want you to find out everything you can about this Christopher Baker character. He looks like being our starter for ten.'

'Will do boss.'

Danny walked back over to the bungalow and sought out Rob.

He found him organising the fingertip search of the hide at the very top of the rear garden. He said, 'I'm going back to the office now, Rob. I need to be able to liaise with both you and Brian. I want you to attend the post mortem at five o'clock, hopefully I can get the post mortem for Edward Hall organised for the same time. I'll try and arrange for both bodies to be taken to the Nottingham City Hospital mortuary. There's no reason why both examinations can't be done at the same time. It's certainly big enough at the hospital and that way we'll be able to flag up any similarities straight away. I'll talk to Seamus and see if there's any problem with doing that. I know there are individually sealed examination rooms, adjacent to each other, so cross contamination shouldn't be an issue. Once I've arranged it all, I'll phone you here, so you can inform Sarah Appleby of the arrangements. I want both teams back at our offices by nine o'clock tonight. We need to drive this enquiry forward quickly. This could quite easily turn out to be the first two murders of a series. I need to know exactly what those messages mean by tonight as well, so tell everybody to get their bloody thinking caps on.'

'No problem, I'll push it on here boss. I'll also talk to Sarah about the post mortem arrangements, just let me know the time and the venue as soon as it's arranged.'

Danny nodded and walked back to his car.

CHAPTER 25

5.00pm Friday 24th March 1986
Nottingham City Hospital Mortuary,
Nottingham

The two examination rooms were separated by a thick, glass partition wall.

Originally, the rooms had been designed to be used by students learning the techniques employed during post mortem examinations, there was a large viewing gallery that overlooked both of the rooms.

Speakers mounted on the front wall of the viewing area, allowed students to hear every word uttered by the examining pathologists.

Standing in the viewing area, looking down on both the examination rooms, were Danny Flint and Detective Chief Superintendent Bill Wainwright. Both men were dressed in dark business suits. Standing behind them, with a large notepad at the ready, was Police Sergeant Tina Prowse.

Tina Prowse was a recent addition to the unit. She was a highly ambitious young woman, very slight in stature, with blonde hair that she wore in a ponytail style. As a graduate entry, she had already taken and passed her sergeants promotion exam with just over three years' service. After completing her two-year probationary period and passing the qualifying exam she had been promoted to Sergeant immediately. She had since undertaken and passed her

Inspectors exam and was awaiting the next available accelerated promotion course at Bramshill Police College. On completion of the course she would be promoted to Inspector.

The graduate entry scheme also allowed participating officers the opportunity to serve with specialist departments. Although Tina had never been on a CID course, Danny considered her to be a great asset to the unit. Her intellect was beyond doubt and she combined that with a very good work ethic. No one doubted that Tina Prowse was destined for the very top.

Below them, on stainless steel examination tables were the naked, mutilated bodies of Edward Hall and Cavalie Naylor. It was obvious which of the two men had been killed first. The level of decomposition and putrefaction of the body in the right-hand examination room was far higher. The viewing gallery was air conditioned, so none of the associated smells and odours of death were apparent to the three spectators.

There were no such pleasantries within the examination rooms, Rob Buxton and Brian Hopkirk stood alongside the two exhibits officers, who were poised ready to label and bag any exhibits that were recovered during the post mortems.

Seamus Carter and Sarah Appleby began the post mortem examinations by issuing instructions to their assistants to photograph anything they deemed relevant. Once the photographs had been taken, each pathologist made their own visual study of the cadavers laid out in front of them.

The pathologists took it in turns to speak aloud their observations. Dc Tina Prowse scribbled furiously in her note pad, recording their spoken findings. Dictaphones were being used in the actual examination rooms, the tapes would be used later by each pathologist to prepare their individual written reports for the investigation team.

Particular attention was paid to the necks of both victims, in order to establish whether the same, or a similar weapon had been used to cause the damage.

Interestingly, a very small area of bruising was found on each of the victims' foreheads. The bruises showed very distinctive knuckle marks. It looked as though both men had been initially incapacitated by a single punch to the forehead.

The bindings that had been used to tie the victims, were then carefully removed from the wrists of the dead men and examined. The cord appeared identical in make-up and colour. Forensic examination would later determine whether or not the cord was scientifically identical.

While Sarah Appleby spent time examining the wounds around the eye sockets of Cavalie Naylor, Seamus Carter busied himself examining the gaping maw of Edward Hall. Both pathologists endeavoured to establish what instruments had been used to sever and remove the eyes of Naylor, and extract the teeth of Hall. Tests carried out by Sarah Appleby confirmed that Naylor had been very much alive when his eyes had been removed.

The large gaping wound of the neck on each man was then minutely examined.

By scrutinising the angle of the large cut, they established that in both cases, the sharp bladed instrument had been held in the assailant's right hand.

The weapon used to make both wounds, was believed to be a heavy, large bladed, razor sharp hunting knife. Seamus Carter offered the opinion, that it could be a knife similar to ones regularly used by hunters to gut and skin their prey.

Sarah Appleby then examined the wounds on the chest of Naylor, that had been caused by the removal of the skin. She voiced her opinion that the flayed skin had been very carefully removed; she believed the person who had removed it was very skilled in the removal of skin or hide. She based this opinion on the fact that the outer skin had been removed without causing massive damage to the underlying flesh. It was her opinion, that the blade used to flay the skin from the body was also razor sharp. A final test determined that the strips of skin had been removed from Naylor while he was still alive.

Both pathologists worked intently, after another forty minutes, they had completed their examinations. All the exhibits taken had been labelled, signed and bagged. Danny pressed the intercom switch so he could talk to the occupants of both examination rooms, 'Thank you Sarah and thank you Seamus. How soon can you let me have your full reports, please?'

'Mine will be with you by tomorrow afternoon', said Seamus.

'I can have mine ready for then as well', said Sarah.

'Thank you both, I appreciate that. Brian, Rob make sure everything is recorded and the exhibits are stored appropriately. I want everybody back at Mansfield for a debrief at nine o'clock.'

Both detectives nodded and began tidying everything away.

'Seamus, Sarah thank you very much for your efforts, I know you've both had a long day.'

The pathologists both acknowledged with a wave, before leaving the examination rooms to the mortuary attendants, who would ensure the remains of Edward Hall and Cavalie Naylor were returned to the refrigerated drawers in the main part of the mortuary. As they were both the victims of foul play, they would be placed in deep freeze drawers, in case there was a need for a further examination in the future.

Danny turned to Bill Wainwright and said, 'Are you coming back for the debrief sir?'

'No Danny, it's your enquiry, you run it how you see fit. I'll need to speak with you first thing in the morning though, to discuss what we're going to give out as a press release. I'm going back to headquarters now, to give the Chief Constable a call. I think it's right I inform him, that there's every likelihood we've got a serial killer on the loose.'

'I don't envy you that phone call, sir.'

'That's exactly what I'm here for Danny, to keep that kind of headache away from you. If I can deal with all that side of things, it leaves you free to get on with the task of catching this warped bastard.'

Bill Wainwright smiled and said, 'See you in the morning Danny, bright and breezy.'

CHAPTER 26

9.00pm Friday 24th March 1986
Major Crime Investigation Unit, Mansfield

A thick pall of blue smoke hung in the air of the briefing room at the Major Crime Investigation Unit. Both teams had returned from their respective duties at the murder scenes in Beeston and Underwood.

It was time for a de-brief, to establish exactly what similarities there were at each of the scenes. It was also the time for Danny, Rob and Brian to listen to the progress that had been made, then to determine the new lines of enquiry that would take the investigation forward.

There was the soft murmur of voices as the teams of detectives discussed, amongst themselves, various aspects of the two cases.

The door to the briefing room opened and Danny walked in, clutching his blue hardback notebook. Any developments and all the enquiries to be carried out, would be noted in this book, that way Danny would have an up to date record on the progress being made in each of the two cases. He had made no cast iron decision, whether to treat the two cases as separate or to acknowledge the fact they were inextricably linked, and almost certainly the work of the same offender.

The large briefing room fell silent, Danny addressed the gathered detectives, 'Right, I know it's been a long day for all of us, but let's not skimp on any of the detail during this debrief. It's vitally important that everyone in this room, is fully aware of every development in both of these cases. That's the only way we'll be able to function as a coherent team, it's also the best way to get this thing cracked as quickly as possible. Brian, I'd like to start with your scene at Beeston please.'

'Right boss. The deceased is Edward Hall. He was the manager of the Grosvenor Hotel in Nottingham city centre. Married to Vanessa. There are two children from the marriage, Rebecca aged seven and Hugo aged five. It would appear that our offender gained entry to the property via a rear window. The property is a large detached dwelling, set back from the road, in a very affluent area of Beeston. The search of the property has revealed, that the offender spent a considerable amount of time hidden in the loft of the property, before he attacked the family during the early hours of the morning. Vanessa and the two children were all bound and gagged, before being placed in the young girl's bedroom. The offender has then at some stage, moved Edward Hall from the master bedroom to the kitchen where he tied him to a wooden chair. While Hall was tied to the chair his throat was cut, causing him to bleed to death. Anomalies at the scene, all of Hall's teeth have been crudely extracted, then removed from the scene. The following message EC21V2425 has been painted on the kitchen wall using our victims blood. Hall's wife and children were not physically harmed in any way, although God only knows what this traumatic episode will do to them mentally. This means it's likely that the attack was personal, targeted specifically at Edward Hall.'

'Thanks Brian. Would you now brief everyone, about the findings from the post mortem examination of Edward Hall?'

'The post mortem was carried out earlier this evening at the City Hospital, we'll get the full written report from the pathologist tomorrow. The cause of death, as I've already said, was a large wound to the neck that severed both arteries. Blood loss would have been enormous and catastrophic. We have to assume that there's every chance our offender would have been heavily bloodstained after the attack. The weapon used to cause the wound to the victim's neck, is believed to be a razor sharp, broad bladed instrument, possibly a hunting knife of some description. Apart from the later extraction of the teeth, the only other injury found on the body was bruising to the forehead, believed to have been caused by a single punch. There are visible bruises, that can be identified as knuckle marks which are normally associated with injuries caused by punching. The pathologist confirmed that the teeth were all extracted post mortem. We are still waiting on the toxicology reports.'

'Thanks Brian, who's been tasked with organising the house to house enquiries at Beeston?'

Dc Jeff Williams spoke up, 'I have boss, I've completed the mastering of all the surrounding streets and I've already briefed a section of the Special Operations Unit so they can continue the house to house first thing tomorrow. I've asked them to complete personal descriptive forms for every one they speak to. Immediately prior to this briefing, I phoned the Sergeant in charge of the Special Ops team to see if there was anything noteworthy to report from today's enquiries. They're well into the task, but as yet there's nothing to report. They've just finished for the day, it's getting dark and policy dictates we don't carry out house to house enquiries after the hours of darkness.'

'Thanks Jeff, you've done a great job. I want you to stay on it, I'd like to get all the house to house enquiries completed by tomorrow, if at all possible.'

'Will do boss.'

'Who interviewed Vanessa Hall?'

Sergeant Tina Prowse spoke up, 'Vanessa Hall is currently on a ward at the City Hospital under sedation. I've been at the hospital waiting to speak to her most of the day boss. Unfortunately, she's so traumatised by the events of last night, doctors have kept her sedated. They wouldn't allow me to speak to her at all today. Dr Phoebe Gillender, who's in charge of her care, has assured me that I'll be able to talk to her briefly tomorrow morning.'

'Okay Tina, thank you for taking the notes at the post mortems, they're very comprehensive. I want you to stick with Vanessa Hall, be at the hospital first thing in the morning, anything she can tell us about the events of last night will be invaluable. I want you to get an account from her as soon as possible. It's a priority enquiry, explain that to Dr Gillender, she may give you a little leeway.'

'Will do boss.'

'What about the two children, who's been looking after that enquiry?'

Dc Lyn Harris answered, 'I've been trying to get access to the two children, they're currently staying with Vanessa's sister and her family. I'm afraid it's a similar scenario to Tina's. Neither of the children are in any fit state to be questioned yet, however gently. They are totally traumatised.'

'Have you managed to get anything?', asked Danny

'Nothing from the boy, he doesn't want to talk at all. The girl keeps sobbing and asking if the horrible man is going to come back. So apart from the fact that it would appear to be one man acting alone, we've learned nothing. I daren't push it boss, they are both so young and are already traumatised.'

'Don't worry Lyn, I totally understand, just stick with it please. If either of them volunteers any information, to you or their auntie, I want to know about it straight away, okay?'

'Of course, boss.'

'Scenes of Crime, what have we got?'

A very short, stocky man with a full beard and crew cut hair spoke up, 'Hello sir, we haven't met, my name's Stephen Brewer, Senior Scenes of Crime Officer, I've just transferred down from the Durham force.'

'Welcome to the MCIU Stephen. Forensically, what have we got?'

'There's quite a lot going on sir. My team have recovered plenty of glove marks from all over the house. It looks like the offender spent quite a long time inside the house. We've also recovered a lot of fibres from the loft, where he's pulled himself in through the hatch. I understand that Sgt Wills also pulled himself up through the hatch to check the loft, so I'll need his tunic for fibre comparison.'

'Brian, can you make a note of that please, arrange for Sgt Wills to submit his tunic asap.'

'Will do boss.'

'What else have you got, Stephen?'

'There's a single boot print found in the blood on the kitchen floor, we believe that boot mark to be from the offender, it's the wrong size for Sgt Wills. No fingerprints anywhere, I'm afraid. Everything at the scene has been photographed by Dave Mitchell, he's a civilian who is currently seconded to our team. He's assured me he'll have the first album of photographs ready by tomorrow morning. I've already submitted the fibres recovered from the loft to the forensic lab, I'll keep you posted of any updates.'

'Thanks Stephen, make sure I get those scene photographs, and the photographs from the post mortem tomorrow morning, first thing.'

'Will do sir.'

'Has anybody got anything else from Beeston, before I move on to the Underwood enquiry team?'

Dc Simon Paine spoke up, 'Yes sir, I've spent the day with Bill and Muriel Hughes, the neighbours who initially called the incident in. I've taken statements from them both. The interesting thing is this boss, Mrs Hughes recalls seeing a battered old Land Rover Defender, she saw it driving along the street a couple of days ago, she's never seen it before. Unfortunately, she can't remember any of the registration number, all she can say with any certainty is that it was a dark green colour and very dirty. She said the only reason it stuck in her mind was because whoever was driving it, was travelling really slowly, it just looked out of place.'

'How sure is Mrs Hughes that it was a Land Rover Defender?' asked Danny.

'She's adamant boss, she grew up on farms apparently, her family always had Land Rovers.'

'Ok, tomorrow morning I want you to check any CCTV you can find in the area, let's see if we can find this vehicle.'

'Will do boss.'

'Right then, if there's nothing else from anybody, we'll move onto the Underwood scene.'

There was a brief silence, then Danny spoke again, 'Okay Rob, give us all an overview please.'

Rob Buxton spoke slowly, allowing the gathered detectives time to take down any notes they wanted.

'The deceased is Cavalie Naylor, 29 years, a single man who lived alone. He was one of the two Company Directors of Naylor Properties Ltd. He was found dead at his home address, a large detached bungalow, set on the edge of the rural community of Underwood. The offender gained entry by forcing wooden French doors situated at the rear of the property. The phone lines were cut, prior to entry taking place. It would appear that the victim was overpowered in his bedroom, then taken to the kitchen of the property. Once in the kitchen, he was bound to a chair, then subsequently killed by having his throat cut. Like the Beeston scene the blood loss was enormous, he would have quickly bled out. Nothing's been stolen from the property. Anomalies at the scene, there are the remains of a hide in the rear garden, it appears that the offender spent a period of time there, prior to the offence. Police dogs managed to briefly follow a track towards the neighbouring village of Jacksdale. The track was quickly lost, so doesn't really take us any further on. The victim had both of his eyes removed and these are missing from the scene. Again, like the Beeston scene, the offender painted the message EC21V2425 on the kitchen wall using the victim's blood. The deceased was discovered by his father this morning, after not being seen for a few days. From the state of decomposition, it's likely he was killed approximately three days ago, so if this is a series, Naylor is our first victim. It's very likely he was tortured before he was killed.

Found draped over the back of a chair in the kitchen were four strips of skin, flayed from his torso while he was still alive. It would also appear that both of his eyes were removed, while he was still alive. The eyes are nowhere to be found at the scene.

That's everything from the scene, so I'll move onto the post mortem findings. Like I said earlier the cause of death was the severed throat and massive blood loss. Other injuries found, are the four strips of skin flayed from the torso, the severing of the optic nerves of both eyes and bruising to the forehead. Similar to the Beeston victim, this bruising is conducive with a single punch. The weapon used to cause the wound to the throat is again believed to be a razor sharp, large bladed weapon. It's likely that this weapon was also used to remove the strips of skin from the victim. The pathologist is of the opinion that it's possibly a large hunting knife. As I've already pointed out, there are several striking similarities to the murder at Beeston.'

'Thanks Rob. Rachel, you've spent the day with Geoff Naylor, the victim's father. What can he tell us?'

Dc Rachel Moore glanced at her notebook before speaking, 'I've taken a full statement from Geoff Naylor. He used a duplicate key to gain access to his son's house this morning, where he found the horrific scene, as described by DI Buxton. He tried to phone for help, but discovered the phone was dead, he then enlisted the help of a postman making a delivery, to call the emergency services. By that time, Mr Naylor was suffering with his heart condition, he has episodes of acute angina. He's adamant that one of Cavalie's close friends, Christopher Baker, will in some way be involved in his son's death. However, he's got nothing concrete to base this theory on and there appears to be a real antipathy between him and Baker. I've spent most of the day with him going over recent business deals that his son has been involved in. There's nothing of note that could prove to be a motive for this attack.'

'Did you find out where Christopher Baker lives?'

'Yes boss, he lives in a small flat on the Brindle estate at Hucknall. His address is 32 Byron Court.'

'Thanks Rachel. I want you to do all the background checks on Baker, with a view to preparing an operational order ready to arrest him first thing tomorrow morning. Let's get him in and get an account from him. Contact the Special Operations Unit and arrange for them to affect the arrest and search his flat. Will you need any help to arrange all that by tomorrow morning?'

'No boss, I'm on it, I've already started doing the checks on Baker. Do you have a preference for an interview team once he's in custody?'

'I want DI Buxton and Dc Lorimar to carry out the interviews once he's in. When you're doing the background checks on Baker, see if you can ascertain any links between him, Cavalie Naylor and Edward Hall. If there is something linking the three of them, that could prove interesting.'

'Will do boss.'

'Tim Donnelly, what have Scenes of Crime got from Underwood?'

'We've taken casts of a couple of boot marks found at the rear of the property, which I'll be comparing with the boot mark found by Stephen's team at Beeston. Nothing of any value was found in and around the hide. Whoever was in there left it extremely sterile, which suggests to me, some kind of military training. There were glove marks at the point of entry, as well as inside the property. We've also recovered quite a few fibres at various points within the property, which suggests our offender isn't all that forensically aware. Again, we'll be running comparisons to the fibres found at Beeston. I can let you have all the photographs both of the scene and the post mortem by tomorrow morning.'

'Thanks Tim.'

Danny took a minute or so to digest all the information he'd been given.

'Right everyone listen up. I think it's fair to say that the similarities we have highlighted so far, mean it would be remiss of me not to officially link these two murders. I expect the fibre evidence and the footmarks to confirm this once the comparison tests have been completed. As a matter of urgency, we need to establish the meaning of the message left on the wall at both scenes. I want you all to concentrate on establishing a link between our two victims, I can virtually guarantee there will be one somewhere. I think it's highly unlikely that our killer has targeted two random individuals. The torture of the first victim could be highly relevant, it could mean that as well as the second victim, Edward Hall, other people could be in danger from this man. Find the meaning of the message and find the link between the two victims and we'll be getting somewhere. The following are to be considered as urgent enquiries; Rob, I want you and your team to concentrate on the arrest and interview of Christopher Baker. I'm aware there's not a lot of house to house enquiries to be done around the Underwood scene, finish what there is, then deploy the house to house team to look deeper into the business dealings of Naylor Properties Ltd. We need to try and establish a motive as soon as possible.'

'Ok boss, no problem', said Rob.

Danny continued, 'Brian, I want your team to concentrate on following up the enquiries with Vanessa Hall, we need a statement from her as soon as possible. Follow up the CCTV enquiries, let's see if we can spot this Land Rover anywhere and continue with the house to house enquiries. I also want a full search of the office used by Edward Hall at the Grosvenor Hotel. I want all the staff at the hotel interviewed to see if Hall has upset anybody recently, a disgruntled guest, a previous employee, you know what I'm looking for.'

'Right you are, boss.'

'Ok everybody, finish up what you've got to do tonight and then get off home. I want everyone back on duty at six o' clock tomorrow morning. I'll stress once again, I need two things as a matter of urgency. I need a link between our two victims and I need to know what that bloody message means! See you all in the morning.'

CHAPTER 27

11.30pm Friday 24th March 1986
Beeston Police Station

Sgt Andy Wills sat in his office at Beeston Police Station, it was his last shift of a very eventful week. The week of day shifts always ended with a split shift which meant that he and his shift would not be going off duty until two o'clock on Saturday morning.

Because of events at the Hall's house in Beeston Fields, none of his shift had been allowed to go off duty until two thirty that afternoon. He had gone home, grabbed a couple of hours' sleep, got ready and returned to work. He'd paraded his shift back on duty at ten o'clock that night.

He made himself a cup of tea and was just about to start clearing his desk of all the urgent outstanding paperwork ready for his impending rest days, when there was a quiet, almost timid knock on the door.

Andy shouted, 'Come in!'

The door opened to reveal a very nervous looking, Pc Gerry Standish.

Gerry was the newest member of the shift, he'd only been at Beeston Police Station for four months, having recently completed his training at Dishforth Police Training Centre.

He was an accomplished footballer, who had joined the police force quite late in life after a brief spell in the professional ranks of the game. He was slightly built, but very fit and strong. He was nearing thirty and had a mature air about everything he did. He was almost three months out from working with a tutor constable and was keen to take on anything new. Andy had been impressed by what he had seen of him so far.

'Come in Gerry, what's the problem?'

'Sorry to disturb you sarge, I've been out on my beat and as I walked past the Man of Trent pub, a bloke stopped me and gave me some information about a crime. I know I need to act on it, but I'm not sure what I can do about it.'

'Firstly, you're not disturbing me, that's what I'm here for, grab a seat. So, who was the bloke who gave you the information?'

The young officer flipped open his pocket book and said, 'He gave his name as Freddie Cox. He told me he regularly gives information to Detective Sergeant Carlisle, but he couldn't get hold of him tonight and this needed to be sorted out urgently.'

'What exactly is it that needs sorting out?'

'There was a burglary two nights ago, at the Yeoman's Army Stores on the High Street, where a load of camping equipment was stolen. Apparently, all the stolen gear from that burglary is being stored at 26, Arkwright Road tonight, but it's being shifted first thing in the morning. If we don't get into the address tonight, we'll miss it.'

'Okay Gerry, have you done any checks on the information provided by Cox?'

'Yes, I have sarge, there was a burglary at Yeoman's two nights ago, where a load of camping gear was stolen. All the property stolen during that burglary is still outstanding. I've checked our systems in the Local Intelligence Office and the address at 26, Arkwright Road is the home address of a bloke called Davy Finch, he's got previous convictions for handling stolen goods.'

'Right, that's good, the information has merit. So, what do you think we should do Gerry?'

'Well I thought about getting a warrant under the Theft Act to search for stolen goods, but by the time the Magistrates Courts open in the morning, it will probably be too late.'

'Ordinarily, that's exactly what we would do, we'd go to the Magistrates Court and swear out a warrant before the sitting magistrates. As it's this time of night and urgent, we have to use a contingency plan. We can call a magistrate who's on the out of hours' list. If you contact the control room, they'll give you the telephone number for the next out of hours, on call magistrate.'

Andy indicated the telephone on his desk.

Pc Standish made the call to the control room and scribbled down the name, telephone number and address of the magistrate he was given.

'Right sarge, the magistrate's name is Beatrice Hayes, she lives on Oakfield Road up near the Leisure Centre.'

'Give her a call and make the arrangements to go and see her. Give yourself at least an hour to type up the warrant and the information form. Tell her, we'll be outside her house at half past midnight. When you've completed the paperwork, come back to me so I can check it, then I'll come out with you to obtain the warrant.'

'Righto sarge', said a now beaming Pc Standish.

Half an hour later, there was another knock on the door of Andy Wills office, 'I've got everything sarge, are you still good to come with me?'

Andy quickly checked over the documents, then stood up and grabbed his car keys, 'That's great Gerry, one last thing I forgot to mention, have you got a bible to swear out the information on?'

'Mrs Hayes specifically told me not to bring a bible, as she prefers to use her own.'

'Okay, let's go.'

Just before half past midnight, both officers were standing on the doorstep of Mrs Hayes' house.

Pc Standish rang the doorbell.

The door was answered almost immediately by an elderly, very frail looking, grey haired lady who was obviously well into her seventies.

'Come in, come in officers, you're letting all the cold air in.'

'Apologies for the late hour Mrs Hayes, but we need a warrant as a matter of urgency', said Andy.

'I was awake anyway sergeant, don't worry about the hour. Now what do you need from me?'

Andy indicated for Gerry to start talking and the probationer quickly gave a brief outline of the circumstances that had led to the need for a warrant. He stressed the fact that if they didn't get into the property that night, by the morning the stolen goods would have been moved on.

Mrs Hayes asked, 'Are there any small children living in the house the warrant is intended for?'

'On the checks I've made, no ma'am, there are no small children at the house.'

'That's good. Do you have a typed, Information Form for me?'

'Yes ma'am', said Gerry.

'Right, I'll get my bible, then you can take the oath before giving me the information.'

Less than a minute later, Mrs Hayes returned with a leather bound antique bible, which she gave to the officer.

Gerry held the bible in his right hand, spoke the oath and laid the Information to Mrs Hayes, who listened carefully before duly signing the Theft Act search warrant.

Andy took the leather-bound bible from Gerry, he was about to hand it back to the elderly magistrate, when he noticed a couple of yellow post it notes sticking out from the pages. Andy saw that written on some of the notes, were a series of letters and numbers that looked familiar.

'Mrs Hayes, I hope you don't mind me asking, but what do these notes of random letters and numbers refer to?'

'They're bible references Sergeant. Friends have given them to me, they highlight beautiful verses from the good book.'

Andy retrieved his own pocket book, flipped through the pages until he found the note he'd made of the message left on the wall of the Halls' house the night before.

'Mrs Hayes, what do you make of this message?'

He opened his pocket book and showed her the note he had made, EC21V2425.

'That's an easy one, Sergeant. It's a reference to one of the most well-known sections of the Old Testament. It refers to the book of Exodus, Chapter 21. Verse 24 to 25.'

The old lady quickly thumbed through the Old Testament of her bible, then opened the book on the relevant page.

'There you are Sergeant, see for yourself.'

The old lady held out the bible and said, 'An eye for an eye and a tooth for a tooth. Like I said, it's probably one of the most well-known phrases from the bible. What most people don't know, is that the passage goes on to say, "an arm for an arm and a foot for a foot, burning for burning, wound for wound, stripe for stripe".

Andy quickly made a note of what he had been told before saying, 'Thank you so much Mrs Hayes, we won't take up any more of your time. We need to execute this warrant immediately. That's a beautiful old bible, by the way.'

'You're more than welcome Sergeant, I hope you're both successful with the warrant. The bible is very valuable, its been in my family for generations. It's the King James 1st version, I absolutely adore it.'

The old lady clutched the leather-bound bible to her chest and closed the door.

Andy was deep in thought as he walked back to the police car. He now fully understood the motive for Hall's killing, he would need to contact Detective Chief Inspector Flint as soon as possible, but first he had a warrant to execute and a load of stolen camping gear to recover.

CHAPTER 28

4.30am Saturday 25th March 1986
Beeston Police Station

Sgt Andy Wills was dog tired.

He looked at his watch, it was now half past four in the morning. The warrant had been a massive success, every item of camping equipment stolen from Yeoman's shop had been recovered. Pc Gerry Standish was beaming like a Cheshire cat as he filled in the register for the recovered property. Andy had helped him complete the handover for the arrest of Davy Finch. Detective Sergeant Carlisle was on duty in the morning, so he would be able to continue the enquiry.

The arrest of Finch together with the recovery of all the outstanding stolen property, would go a long way towards helping the young officer become a valued member of his shift, it would also help him to get through his probationary period.

Andy was in a quandary, it was so late, but he knew he needed to pass on the information he'd learned from the magistrate, Mrs Hayes, as soon as possible.

He yawned, picked up the telephone on his desk and dialled Danny Flint's home number.

After four rings, a half awake Sue Rhodes answered the phone, 'Hello, who's this?'

'Sue, it's Andy Wills. I'm so sorry to call at this time of night, but I need to speak to Danny urgently, is he there?'

'He's fast asleep Andy, he's got to be up at six, can't it wait 'til then?'

'I'm really sorry Sue, but this is vitally important. Danny needs to hear this right now.'

'Okay Andy, just a minute.'

A few seconds passed before Andy heard Danny's voice on the phone. 'Andy, what's the problem? Don't tell me there's been another murder?'

'No boss, there hasn't, but I had to call you. I've cracked the message left on the wall at the Beeston murder scene, I know what it means.'

A now fully awake and attentive Danny said, 'Go on, Andy.'

'It's a bible reference. It relates to the Book of Exodus from the Old Testament. It refers to the passage that states "an eye for an eye and a tooth for a tooth".

'That all makes sense Andy. What you don't know, is that the victim at the Underwood murder had both of his eyes gouged out. They had subsequently been removed from the scene. He was killed before Edward Hall so it makes sense. It also clearly demonstrates that revenge is probably the motive for both murders.'

'Boss, what you also need to know, is that the verses stipulated in the message, also refer to, an arm for an arm and a leg for a leg, burning for burning, wound for wound, stripe for stripe.'

'You think our killer could be stalking more victims?'

'It's got to be a distinct possibility, that's why I needed to call you at this ungodly hour.'

'Don't worry about the time, you were right to call me. Listen Andy, Detective Sergeant Mayhew on Rob's team phoned in long term sick yesterday, he's got a slipped disc and won't be coming back to work anytime soon. I can't afford to be a man down at this time, with everything that's currently going on. If I can arrange it with Detective Chief Superintendent Wainwright, this morning, is there anything preventing you transferring on to the Major Crime Investigation Unit sooner rather than later?'

'No I'm clear, boss. If you can smooth it over with my gaffers at Beeston, I'd love to join the MCIU and get back in a suit.'

'Okay, I'll call you at three o clock this afternoon to let you know one way or the other. If I can arrange it, I'll need you to be back at work this evening, so it will mean you missing your rest days.'

'Just like old times then boss, I'll wait for your call.'

'Nice work Andy, you can tell me later how you sussed it out, I hadn't got you down as a religious man.'

'It was easy boss, although I did have a little help from a lovely old lady and a King James 1st bible.'

CHAPTER 29

6.30am Saturday 25th March 1986
Hucknall, Nottinghamshire

Rob Buxton sat in a car outside the entrance to Byron Court.

A run down, seedy looking block of flats, Byron Court was situated on the Brindle estate in Hucknall. The flats had been built in the late fifties and were already coming close to being considered slums. The walkways and stairs leading to the first-floor flats, were covered in graffiti and smelled strongly of urine. Fortunately, number 32 was on the ground floor, so there would be no stairs to climb.

Sitting in the car with Rob, was Detective Constable Glen Lorimar, a veteran detective with a flair for interviewing. Danny had specifically chosen him for the job of questioning Christopher Baker, as he considered him to be the most accomplished interviewer on the MCIU. If there was anything amiss with Baker's account, Danny trusted Glen Lorimar to find it out.

A little further down the road, a plain white Ford Transit van waited with the engine ticking over. This vehicle contained a section of the Special Operations Unit, led by Sgt Archer. Following the arrest of Baker, he and his team would carry out a meticulous search of the flat.

Rob glanced at his watch, it was now almost six thirty, he picked up his personal radio and spoke to the SOU sergeant, 'Are your men in position at the back of the flat?'

'We're good to go sir', came the reply.

'We're not expecting any trouble from the arrest itself, so you and your men remain in position, we'll go and knock on the front door.'

'Received sir, I'll wait for your update.'

The two detectives got out of the vehicle and started to walk towards the block of flats.

As they approached Baker's flat, Rob could see there was a light on inside, the window was covered by venetian blinds, but the tell-tale chinks of light could be seen between the slats of the blinds.

Glen Lorimar stepped forward and using his balled-up fist, he banged loudly on the flimsy door of the flat.

Almost immediately there was movement inside the flat.

Glen Lorimar continued to hammer on the door.

'Alright, alright I'm coming. Who's banging?'

'Christopher Baker, it's the police. Open the door right now, or I'm going to put it in!'

No sooner had Glen finished speaking, than there was the sound of a key being turned in the lock. The door opened but only a fraction, it remained closed, held by a security chain.

Both detectives held out their warrant cards, so the clearly frightened Baker could see that they were police officers.

Glen Lorimar said loudly, 'Open the door, Mr Baker!'

Quickly, Baker removed the security chain from the door. Glen Lorimar pushed the door open and stepped inside the hallway of the small flat.

It was immediately obvious to the detective that Baker had been awake all night, his eyes were blood shot and red rimmed, his blonde hair dishevelled. He was dressed in a creased white T shirt, that had a red Levi's emblem across the chest, stone washed blue denim jeans that were baggy and drawn in at the waist with a brown leather belt, he wore no socks but had dark blue, canvas boat shoes on.

An exhausted Baker said, 'Come through to the living room.'

The two detectives followed him along the narrow hallway. Rob noticed a small suitcase and three cardboard tubes dumped near the front door.

'Are you going somewhere Mr Baker?' he asked.

'No, just the opposite. I only got back from a trip late last night. I just dumped the case there when I walked in.'

The three men walked into the small, smoke filled, living room. The light, Rob had seen from outside the flat, was a dim table lamp. It sat on a coffee table in front of a threadbare settee. Next to the table lamp were three half full coffee mugs, the contents were stone cold. Alongside the mugs, was an ashtray, full to overflowing with cigarette butts.

It looked like Baker had been drinking coffee and chain smoking all night.

In a weary voice Baker asked, 'You said you were from the police, are you hear about Cavalie?'

It was Rob who answered the question with one of his own, 'Yes Mr Baker, we're here about Cavalie Naylor. Why did you assume that was the reason for our visit?'

'Because I've not heard from him for days, then I had a strange conversation over the phone with his dad yesterday. His dad suddenly hung up the phone on me, then wouldn't answer when I tried to call him back. I just figured something wasn't right. Is Cav okay?'

'Mr Baker, Cavalie Naylor was found murdered in his home at Underwood yesterday morning.'

It was said matter of factly and both detectives studied Baker's face to see exactly what his reaction to the news would be.

The reaction was one of stunned silence.

A look of bewilderment crossed his features, then he shook his head slowly and allowed his legs to buckle beneath him, slumping heavily onto the settee.

After two minutes of silence, Baker said softly, 'I don't understand, Cav's the gentlest, sweetest man you'll ever meet. Why would anybody want to hurt him?

'When did you last see Mr Naylor?' asked Rob.

'I saw him last Tuesday, the 21st, he dropped me off here, why?'

Rob nodded towards Glen Lorimar.

Glen stepped forward, 'Christopher Baker, I'm arresting you on suspicion of the murder of Cavalie Naylor.'

He took hold of Baker firmly and placed his wrists in handcuffs.

Baker started to protest, 'What the fuck are you doing? You don't think I had anything to do with it, do you?'

The detective maintained a calm presence and in an emotionless voice cautioned Baker.

Baker replied angrily, 'You've got to be kidding me, this is some kind of sick joke, right! My best friend's been killed and you lot think I did it? You're all off your fucking heads!'

Rob spoke on his personal radio, 'Sgt Archer, we've detained Baker, get your men in here to start searching the flat.'

The room was filled with static from the radio, before the reply came, 'On our way sir.'

As soon as the SOU search team came into the flat, Dc Lorimar walked Baker outside to the CID car. Baker was now calm and said, 'Detective, can I take my smokes with me please?'

Without replying Rob turned and went back inside the flat, where he retrieved a packet of Embassy cigarettes. He walked back outside and tossed the cigarette packet to Glen.

He turned to Sgt Archer, who remained on the doorstep of the flat, 'I want a full search doing sarge, you know what we're looking for. I'm taking Baker to Hucknall nick, I'll see you back there at nine thirty. I'll want an update on the result of the search by then, so we can prepare for interview.

'No problem sir.'

Rob joined Glen and a now very subdued Baker, in the CID car. The short drive to Hucknall Police Station was made in stony silence.

As they walked to the cell block, Baker turned to Rob and said quietly, 'You've got this completely wrong detective. You've no idea what's going on between me and Cav. I bet it's his old man that's set me up to be fucking arrested, am I right?'

'Save it for the interview Christopher, you'll get your chance to tell me exactly how everything is. You look like you need to rest, before we have a little chat.'

Baker stepped into the holding cell and Rob slammed the heavy steel door shut.

CHAPTER 30

9.00am Saturday 25th March 1986
Southwell Town Centre, Nottinghamshire

The Watcher expected that the police would have discovered at least one of the bodies by the morning of Saturday. He'd spent most of Friday planning his next move, he knew he needed to act quickly on the information extracted from his first victim.

He'd risen early and after a good breakfast he had showered, shaved and then dressed in the same business suit he'd worn at the Grosvenor Hotel, when he was stalking Edward Hall.

His plan today demanded he be dressed in a similar fashion. He checked the information one last time, then studied his ordnance survey map to plan his route from Clumber Park to the Minster town of Southwell.

As he walked out of the caravan he picked up his black daysack that contained a single roll of Gaffer tape, a small bag of black plastic cable ties, a Smith and Wesson .38 revolver, a box of .38 ammunition and the small, silver framed photograph he'd taken from the home of Edward Hall.

As before, when he had dispatched Cav Naylor, he knew that if everything went to plan, he wouldn't need the weapon, it was there simply as a contingency. His military background and training always made him plan for the worst-case scenario.

After a twenty-minute drive, he parked his vehicle on a side street in the centre of Southwell, not far from the famous Minster. He walked to a nearby newsagents, where he purchased a street map of the town. He scanned the street map and soon found the location he was searching for.

He took a minute to get his bearings, tucked the street map into the black document case he was carrying, then set off on foot, walking across town towards Spittle Row. He walked into the shopping area of the town centre, passing the Saracens Head public house. Spittle Row was little more than a yard, situated just off the main road. Walking into the yard, he saw it contained three small shops. On one side was a craft shop and an artisan bakery. The other side contained a single office that displayed a navy-blue sign above a plate glass window. In gold lettering on the dark blue background the sign read, Richmond Legal Enterprises Limited.

The Watcher glanced through the window into the small office and saw a young woman sat at a desk. There appeared to be no one else in the office.

He checked his appearance in one of the neighbouring shop windows, smoothed down his short, steel grey hair, straightened his tie then confidently opened the door into the small office.

The young secretary smiled, 'Can I help you sir?'

The Watcher returned her smile and said amiably, 'Is Freddie about?'

'Not today sir. I'm very sorry, but Mr Reece never works on a Saturday. Is there anything I can help you with?'

'I'm afraid not, I've got the legal papers that he needs urgently. He was chasing me for them all yesterday and asked me to pop them in to the office today, so he could sign them. Would you contact him for me, let him know that I'm here and that I have the papers ready for his signature.'

'I'm so sorry, I'm not being deliberately obstructive but I can't do that; Mr Reece never answers his telephone at the weekend, especially on Saturdays. It's the one day of the week he has the opportunity to visit his mother in the nursing home at Edingley. He has always given me strict instructions that I'm never to disturb him on a Saturday, for any reason.'

The young girl leaned forward and said in a conspiratorial whisper, 'His mother has Parkinson's Disease, bless her.'

'Look miss, I can see that you're not going to break his rule, but this situation is serious, if Freddie doesn't get to sign these documents today, he stands to lose an awful lot of money. If you give me the name of the nursing home, where he's visiting his mother, I could drive over there and wait for him to come outside. I won't need to disturb him, I can just catch him when he comes out after he's visited his mum. He won't lose a small fortune, and you won't get into trouble for disturbing him.'

'I really don't know if I should, that's private information you're asking me to divulge.'

'The amount of money I'm talking about, he really won't mind just this once. Trust me.'

The young secretary looked thoughtful, then said, 'Okay, I don't suppose it will cause any harm. The nursing home is called the Belle Vue, it's a specialist nursing home for Parkinson's sufferers. Just a second, I've got the address here.'

She reached for the Rolodex on her desk, grabbed a card and said, 'Here it is, The Belle Vue Nursing Home, Whipgate Street, Edingley.'

'That's great, thank you so much for your help. I won't let on you gave me the address, I'll just say I knew the place. It'll be our little secret; I'm sorry Miss, I didn't catch your name?'

The young girl blushed slightly, then said coyly, 'It's Donna.'

'Well Donna, you've been a star, thank you so much. I'll see you again soon.'

He winked at her then walked out of the office.

As he walked back to his car, the Watcher passed the magnificent Southwell Minster. He paused outside the distinctive twin steeples, held his palms open, looked up towards the sky and muttered a quiet prayer of thanks, before walking on.

As he reached his parked car, he got inside, shut the door and said aloud, 'You truly are directing me heavenly Father, please don't allow me to fail you.'

CHAPTER 31

9.30am Saturday 25th March 1986
Hucknall, Nottinghamshire

The two detectives waited patiently in the CID office at Hucknall Police Station. They had spent the morning since the arrest of Baker, discussing at length, exactly how they were going to tackle the prisoner's interview.

At exactly nine thirty, Sergeant Archer from the Special Operations Unit walked into the CID office, with a resigned air he said, 'Right sir, the search of the flat hasn't yielded much at all I'm afraid.'

'Bollocks! Have we got anything?', asked Rob.

'Nothing that would be of any relevance to the murder scene at Underwood, no weapons, blood stained clothing, eye balls etc. What we have recovered that might be of interest, are a load of personal letters, sent by Cavalie Naylor to Baker, some of them are quite explicit in content. We've recovered bank statements, from Baker's Nat West current account. There's nothing of any interest in them really, no massive sums being transferred in. Basically, it would appear that Christopher Baker doesn't have a pot to piss in.'

'What was in the suitcase and the cardboard tubes I saw in the hallway?'

'Dirty washing in the suitcase, rolled up charcoal drawings in the tubes.'

'So, it looks like he was telling the truth, when he told me he'd just come back from somewhere, rather than just going?'

'Definitely boss. There was also a pamphlet in the case, extolling the virtues of a place called, The Tranquil Waters Retreat for Artists. The Retreat is a farmhouse in Cornwall, located just outside the town of Bude. It offers residential courses to budding artists, who want to improve on their sketching and painting skills.'

'Have you recovered the pamphlet?' asked Glen Lorimar.

'We have, we thought it would be relevant, if that's where he's just come back from.'

'Nice one. Anything else that might be useful?'

'No that's it I'm afraid. The flat's very spartan. The living area has a settee, a television and a coffee table. The bedroom's tiny, there's just a wardrobe and a double bed in there. The clothes in the wardrobe are fashionable and smart, but there's not many of them. The kitchen has a cooker, a fridge, a washing machine and a small table and two chairs, it's extremely basic. The spare bedroom's done out like some half-arsed, artist's studio, it has an easel, oil paints and a load of shit paintings scattered on the walls and all over the floor.'

'That's a bit harsh Sergeant. Remember, art is always in the eye of the beholder', grinned Rob.

'I take your point boss, but this stuff is really crap. Unless you consider paintings of dismembered bodies and body parts in general as art. It's all just a bit too fucking weird!'

'Interesting, do any of the paintings depict bodies lacking eyes or teeth?' asked Glen.

'No, when I first saw the paintings, that thought did occur to me. These are dismembered bodies, arms and legs missing, that kind of thing.'

Rob asked, 'Has everything you've recovered been bagged up and exhibited properly? Have all the labels been signed?'

'Everything's been done correctly sir; the guys are downstairs finishing off their statements now. I'll leave the search log with you. The letters, bank statements and other documents have already been booked into the property store.'

'Thanks for a good job this morning, Sergeant.'

'No problem sir, I'll bring the statements up to you as soon as they're finished.'

Sgt Archer left the office to re-join his men and Glen Lorimar walked down to the property store to retrieve the recovered documents.

Half an hour had passed before Sgt Archer returned to the CID office with the completed statements from his team. He found Rob and Glen busy reading the pile of letters that had been sent from Cavalie to Chris. Rather than disturb the two detectives studying the content of the letters, Sgt Archer quietly placed the statements on the desk in front of them and left the office.

CHAPTER 32

10.00am Saturday 25th March 1986
Edingley, Nottinghamshire

The Watcher raced through the winding country lanes on the short journey from Southwell to Edingley.

Edingley was a small village, it consisted of two large farms, a row of houses each side of the main road, a white washed pub called The Plough Inn and a small shop. Just through the village, on the road to Farnsfield, stood a magnificent red brick building. This two storey building was set back from the road in its own pretty grounds. The property had previously been the country house of the local squire, it was now The Belle Vue Nursing Home.

The home was quite isolated, surrounded by open fields. The road that ran past the front of the building was little more than a country lane.

As the Watcher drove by, he saw a small car park, located to one side of the building. He stopped his vehicle on the lane, then looked over his shoulder to get a clearer look at the cars parked in the car park. There were six vehicles in total, two battered Ford Escorts, a rusting Fiat, a two-tone Vauxhall Viva, a sporty little Peugeot 206 that had seen better days and a gleaming, one year old, black Range Rover. He knew instantly which car would belong to Frederick Reece.

He parked his Land Rover on the grass verge, a little further down the lane from the main entrance to the nursing home. From his location, he still had an unobstructed view of the large oak front doors of the nursing home and also the small car park.

Placing the small framed photograph he'd stolen from Edward Hall's house onto the front passenger seat, he settled down for what he knew might be a lengthy wait.

Almost two hours had passed slowly by, when his attention was drawn to movement near the front doors of the nursing home. A balding, middle aged man stepped outside onto the doorstep and lit up a cigarette. As he drew hard on the cigarette, he was joined by a young woman. She looked to be in her late teens, her auburn hair tied back in a ponytail. She wore black trousers and a thin, cream coloured jacket over her care assistant's uniform.

The young woman also lit up a cigarette, took a long drag then spoke to the balding man. Both smokers moved away from the main entrance, to a wooden bench and sat down next to each other. The bench, surrounded by shrubbery, could not be seen by anyone inside the home, but was still within the view of the Watcher.

The two smokers talked quite animatedly, gesturing with their hands. They both pulled hard on their cigarettes, exhaling the last of the smoke, before throwing the butts to the floor and grinding them out with their shoes. Suddenly the man reached out and grabbed the young woman by the hair. He pulled her violently towards him. The woman did not resist, instead she placed her hand around the back of the man's neck, then kissed him hard on the mouth.

Somewhat surprised, the Watcher continued to observe.

The man slid his hand between the legs of the woman. She squirmed, pulled the man's hand from between her legs, then placed her own hand on the man's crotch. Expertly, she unzipped his trousers, exposed his erect penis and began masturbating him. It took a couple of minutes for the man to climax, just as deftly, the woman then replaced the balding man's penis back inside his trousers and did up the zip. They separated and sat each end of the bench before lighting up more cigarettes.

The man took a long pull on his cigarette before getting out a wallet from his jacket pocket. He handed the girl several banknotes, which she quickly stuffed into the pocket of her jacket.

Having finished her cigarette, the young girl stood up, pecked the balding man on the cheek and walked away, going back inside the nursing home.

The balding man leaned back on the wooden bench, looked up to the sky and exhaled the last of the blue smoke from his cigarette.

Glancing down at the photograph on the passenger seat, the Watcher compared the balding man's features to the four men in the photograph. The man sitting on the bench was definitely in the photograph. He was unmistakeable, he had the same podgy, fat build now as he did then, when he was smiling for the camera, in his black graduation gown.

The hair that had already started to recede when he was at university, had now gone completely. It was definitely Frederick Reece. He was a man ageing before his time, due to poor diet, sloth and excessive drinking.

The Watcher smiled as he saw Reece stand up and walk back inside the nursing home.

He watched him go back inside and said aloud, 'Playing the dutiful son who visits his sick mother every week? Your visits are all about paying that poor young woman to pleasure you every week. Reece, you're an ungodly devil, the time for you to be dispatched back to Hell is almost here.'

Another hour slowly passed; he checked his watch, it was now almost one o'clock in the afternoon.

Suddenly, there was again movement at the large wooden doors of the home. Frederick Reece stepped out of the doorway, then turned to speak to an elderly woman who had followed him outside. The woman wore the dark navy blue uniform of a Matron. There was a brief conversation, then he shook hands with her briskly and walked off towards the car park.

He walked straight to the black Range Rover, opened the driver's door, got in and started the engine.

The Watcher started up his Land Rover and waited.

As the Range Rover turned out of the car park and onto Whipgate Street, the Watcher pulled out and followed behind the sleek black vehicle at a discreet distance.

The Range Rover was being driven towards the village of Farnsfield.

The fact that Reece obviously had no intention of going back to his office in Southwell suited the Watcher. He continued to follow the Range Rover, as it was driven slowly through the village of Farnsfield. The black vehicle accelerated as it left the village and headed back out into the countryside.

Less than half a mile out of Farnsfield, the road once again turned into little more than a country lane, with very little traffic.

It was the perfect location for the Watcher.

He mouthed a silent prayer of thanks to the Lord, then began flashing the headlights of the Land Rover, trying to get the attention of Reece in the Range Rover.

Immediately, the Watcher saw brake lights illuminated on the black vehicle in front, the Range Rover was driven off the road and came to a stop in a small layby. The Watcher followed and parked the Land Rover directly behind the Range Rover. The layby was barely big enough to accommodate both vehicles.

With an anxious expression on his face, the Watcher jumped out of his vehicle and walked towards the Range Rover.

Reece wound down the driver's window, leaned out, scowled, then shouted back towards the approaching Watcher, 'What the hell's the matter man?'

'Thank goodness you've stopped; the back bumper of your motor's virtually hanging off. I reckon it'll drop off completely if you go much further.'

'Don't be ridiculous, what on earth are you talking about?'

'Seriously, I'm surprised you can't hear it dragging along the road, have a look for yourself.'

With an air of impatience, Reece got out of the Range Rover with a face like thunder and stomped round to the back of the vehicle.

The Watcher quickly checked around for any approaching vehicles, he decided against a physical attack and instead reached for the .38 Smith & Wesson revolver in his jacket pocket.

Reece had by now reached the back of the Range Rover, when he saw there was no damage he was incandescent with rage and spun round to face the Watcher, 'Are you completely fucking insane man! There's nothing wrong with the bumper!'

He was so angry, it was only as he finished his rant, that he realised he was staring down the black barrel of a handgun.

Undeterred and losing none of his arrogant bluster, he demanded, 'What the hell do you think you're doing man?'

The Watcher pointed the handgun directly at the face of Reece and said quietly, 'Listen to me very carefully. If you say one more word, I'll pull the trigger and spread your brains across this lane. Do you understand me?'

The menace in the voice of the Watcher made it clear to Reece, that he needed to do exactly as he was told.

'Walk to the back of my Land Rover, now.'

Reece did as he was instructed.

Still pointing the handgun at Reece, the Watcher undid the back door of the Land Rover.

He gestured with the handgun and said, 'Get in.'

Reece started to protest, 'You won't get away with this! The Range Rover's fitted with a tracker, you fucking moron!'

'I won't tell you again. Get in!'

Slowly, Reece climbed into the rear of the Land Rover. Once he was inside, the Watcher stepped forward and using the pistol grip of the handgun dealt him a crushing blow on the back of the head. The force of the blow instantly rendered Reece unconscious.

The Watcher quickly bound him with cable ties, then gagged him using Gaffer tape. He searched Reece, found the keys for the Range Rover in his jacket pocket, then covered him with old blankets.

He walked to the Range Rover and locked it before returning to his own Land Rover. He started the engine and drove off steadily, back in the direction of Farnsfield. Once he was in the small village, he quickly found the only public car park which was located at the rear of the Co-op general store.

The car park was fairly busy and several other vehicles were already parked.

He parked the Land Rover in the very far corner of the car park, away from the other vehicles. He got out and checked in the back of the vehicle, Reece was still out cold. He replaced the old blankets over Reece and locked the rear door.

Keeping his head down and avoiding other people using the car park, the Watcher then walked briskly out of the village. As soon as he reached the country lane at the edge of the village he broke into a run. His work kept him extremely fit and active and it took him less than ten minutes to reach the black Range Rover parked in the lay-by.

He intended to drive the Range Rover back to Farnsfield, park it in the Coop car park and effectively hide it in plain sight.

Just as he reached the Range Rover, he heard a car approaching from behind, he looked over his shoulder and saw a marked police car approaching. He stood at the side of the Range Rover, the police traffic patrol car came to a stop alongside him.

He noted with a smile that the police vehicle was single crewed.

The male officer leaned over, opened the passenger door window of the police car and said, 'Is everything all right sir? You don't look too good.'

'I'm fine officer, everything's good thanks.'

'Is your vehicle alright?'

'It's okay, I was just having a breather.'

'Are you sure everything's okay, you're sweating?'

'Look, I clipped a fox or something as I was driving, when I looked back I could see it lying in the road. I jumped out to see if it was okay, but every time I get near it the bloody thing runs off. I've been chasing it around, that's why I'm sweating.'

The policeman switched off the engine and got out of the police car.

The Watcher noted that the police officer was a big man, probably over six feet three inches tall, very broad and powerful. He looked to be around twenty-five years old and obviously worked out regularly at the gym. The Watcher realised if things got physical, he would have a problem overpowering the officer.

The policeman started to examine the Range Rover.

'Is the vehicle registered to you sir?'

'No, it belongs to a friend of mine, I'm just borrowing it.'

'I hope his insurance covers you. Exactly where did this fox hit the vehicle sir? I'm struggling to see any damage.'

The policeman then looked squarely at the Watcher, sizing him up, 'This business about hitting a fox is all bullshit, isn't it? Why don't you stop pissing about and tell me what's really going on here?'

The Watcher realised he could bluff no more and for the second time that day he produced the black handgun from his jacket pocket.

In a flat emotionless voice, he said, 'Do exactly as I tell you and you won't get hurt. Do not make the mistake of thinking I won't use this. The last thing I want to do is kill you, but if you leave me no option, I'll do it in a heartbeat. Do you understand me?'

The policeman nodded, never taking his eyes from the armed stranger.

The Watcher raised the gun a little higher, pointed at the officer's eyes and said with a growl, 'Stop fucking eyeballing me and throw your radio, car keys and handcuffs on the road behind you.'

The three objects clattered to the floor.

Maintaining eye contact with the Watcher, the officer said, 'You're making a huge mistake mate, you won't get away with this.'

'Shut up and walk, go through the layby and into the trees.'

The Watcher followed two yards behind the policeman into the trees at the side of the layby.

'Stop. Kneel down and fold your arms.'

'Don't do this mate.'

The Watcher stepped forward and smashed the butt of the hand gun onto the back of the policeman's head. The officer fell forward and the Watcher checked to see if he was unconscious.

Satisfied that the policeman was indeed unconscious, the Watcher walked back to the road where he quickly located the objects the policeman had dropped. He picked up the handcuffs and the car keys, then smashed the officer's personal radio on the floor. He returned to the unconscious policeman, seated him against the trunk of a tree and restrained him using his own handcuffs.

The last thing the Watcher had wanted to do was injure the officer, but it was a better option than killing him. He was only interested in making the four demons answer for their sins and the young police officer definitely wasn't one of them.

Having handcuffed the still unconscious policeman, he checked that the wound on the back of his head wasn't bleeding too badly. Leaving the officer in the woods he then walked to the police car. He got in and drove the vehicle about a hundred yards down the road before he turned off the lane and dropped the car into a ditch. As he walked back to the Range Rover he looked back over his shoulder, the police car had dropped out of sight, was well hidden and couldn't be seen from the road.

He got in the Range Rover and using the keys he had taken from Reece he drove the vehicle back to Farnsfield. He drove into the Co-op car park and parked the vehicle next to his Land Rover. He got out and hurled the Range Rover keys into the small stream that ran alongside the car park.

The Watcher checked in the back of his Land Rover to make sure that Reece was still unconscious. Satisfied that the fat solicitor was still out for the count, he covered him with the old blankets again and this time piled old tools on top of him as well, before locking the back door. He got into the driver's seat and slowly drove the vehicle out of the car park.

As he drove out of Farnsfield, a smile played across the Watcher's face. The third of the demons was now captured. Before today's events, he had considered that the capture of Frederick Reece would prove to be the most challenging. As it turned out, apart from the unfortunate interruption by the police officer, it had been easy.

Just like Naylor and Hall before him, it would soon be time for Reece to pay for his sins.

CHAPTER 33

2.00pm Saturday 25th March 1986
Rampton Hospital, Nottinghamshire

Melissa Braithwaite drove her Ford Sierra through Woodbeck, the tiny village where Rampton High Security Hospital was located. She indicated, then took a right turn onto Fleming Drive, passing the two huge pillars that marked the entrance to the hospital.

Directly in front of her, she could see the impressive looking red brick buildings, that flanked the main entrance and reception. The large buildings housed the doctors, nurses and other staff that worked at the hospital. She parked her vehicle in the main car park situated just off Fleming Drive.

Before getting out of the car she checked her small handbag to ensure her passport was inside and then adjusted the bra she wore beneath the thick crew neck jumper. The small crochet hook she had secreted below the wiring of her bra was very uncomfortable, but she knew it wouldn't have to be in there much longer.

On her previous visits to Rampton she had experienced the pat down search that was administered to all visitors. She knew if she was patient and waited until almost the end of the queue the nurses doing the searches would be bored and tired.

The crochet hook Jimmy Wade had asked her to bring, was made of steel but covered in a plastic sheath, it was no more than five inches long. She had no reservations about helping Jimmy. The establishment, the lawyers and the police in particular, had blatantly used him as a scapegoat, to deflect the public's attention away from the horrific murders committed by Police Sergeant Reynolds.

Melissa had always genuinely believed this was the case and now, after speaking with Jimmy on several occasions, she was convinced of it. All she wanted to do was help him get out of the horrendous place, so they could then spend the rest of their lives together. On her previous visits, they had spoken at length about how this could be achieved. Everything they had planned was now in place, if everything went well, today would be her final visit to this awful prison.

She got out of the car and put on a thick woollen overcoat, it was a nice Spring day and the sun was shining, but the wind was strong and had a cold edge.

Melissa walked along Fleming Drive, between the two residential blocks, then down the slope towards the main reception. She booked in at the desk, produced the visiting order and her passport as identification, then handed her small handbag to the staff on reception for safekeeping. No bags or containers of any description were allowed in the main hall during visits.

There was already a long queue of men and women, waiting patiently to visit their loved ones. The weekend visiting times were always the most popular. Patients from all over the country were detained at the hospital and Saturday was by far the easiest day for friends and relatives to make the sometimes, long journey into the isolated hospital.

The queue of people slowly began filing along the long corridor, being directed towards the main hall by a member of the nursing staff.

Once outside the main hall, there was a further delay as the pat down searches began. Melissa positioned herself towards the rear of the queue, estimating there were probably a dozen women and a similar number of men in front of her.

By the time, she reached the front of the queue, the female nurse responsible for carrying out the searches looked suitably bored.

Although referred to as nurses, the staff all wore uniforms similar to those worn by the prison service, the uniforms made the feeling of overbearing security, even more acute. As far as Melissa was concerned, Rampton was a high security prison and nothing like a hospital.

The young nurse doing the searches looked blankly at Melissa and said, 'Take off your coat.'

Melissa did as she had been instructed and removed the thick coat.

The nurse continued in a monotone voice, 'Hold your arms out and spread your legs a little please.'

As soon as Melissa adopted the position, the nurse began the pat down search. Her hands swiftly ran along each of Melissa's arms over the top of the thick jumper, then down each side of her body and across the front and back of her torso. The sturdy bra she was wearing gave away no sign of the crochet hook beneath it. The nurse then swiftly ran her hands down each of Melissa's legs, over the top of her tight corduroy jeans.

Finally, she ran her hands over the coat Melissa had been wearing before handing the garment back and waving her through.

As she entered the main hall, Melissa could see Jimmy Wade already sitting at a table near the centre of the hall.

He smiled when he saw her and waved her over. There were twenty or thirty visitors, being supervised by eight members of staff.

The staff nurse supervising the visits stood at the front of the hall, other staff were positioned at intervals around the hall looking in towards the area of tables and chairs that had been set out for the visit. A male nurse stood outside the gent's toilet, which was located at the side of the main hall. It was his job to supervise any trips to the lavatory made by visitors or patients. A female nurse had a similar role outside the ladies' toilets.

Melissa sat down opposite Jimmy and smiled, she never tired of gazing into those beautiful, clear blue eyes.

Jimmy reached over the small table, held Melissa's hand and whispered, 'How's your aunties crochet coming along?'

'It's beautiful sweetheart, can't you tell I'm wearing it?'

Jimmy smiled, 'I'm getting on really well in here now and as a reward for being a good little boy, I've been listed to go on a working party at the concrete plant this coming Monday.'

'That's fantastic news, sweetheart. It just so happens that I'm going to have a drive out in my car on Monday. I'm going to take a picnic with me to a lovely place I've seen not far from here. You might have heard of it, Jimmy, it's called Haggnook Farm.'

'I don't think I've heard of that farm sweetheart.'

'It's not far from here, just outside the village, between here and Retford. I'm going to have my picnic there, probably around half past three.'

'I wish I could join you there, who knows maybe one day.'

'Not one day, Monday', smiled Melissa.

Both of them enjoyed talking in riddles, it was a game to them. The message was clear. If everything went to plan Jimmy would be out on Monday, he would then meet her at Haggnook Farm, where she would be waiting with her car.

When Jimmy Wade had first arrived at Rampton, two of the male nurses had brutalised him at every opportunity, leaving him bruised and battered. At first, he'd resisted the assaults and retaliated, but that just made the beatings worse. Jimmy had adapted, he had taken the decision to become totally subservient, he was submissive around the nursing staff, until they no longer troubled him. Being Jimmy Wade, he had made a mental note of the two nurses names and faces, he would bide his time and then exact his revenge.

He'd been working hard towards building up such a level of trust, that he would be allowed to go on a working party. In particular, he wanted to get on the working party at the concrete plant.

There was a very simple reason for this.

The concrete plant was situated adjacent to the lowest perimeter fence at the hospital. The fencing at that location comprised of old, flimsy chain link, it was only seven feet high with two strands of barbed wire on the top. It could easily be scaled in seconds. Beyond that chain link fence was open countryside, as far as the eye could see.

The concrete working parties usually consisted of three male patients who were accompanied by six nursing staff, two of which constantly maintained a position, between the patients and the perimeter fence.

Jimmy knew he would have to get through the nursing staff, if his plan was going to be successful and that's where the crochet hook came in.

Melissa stood up and said loudly, 'I'm just nipping to the loo Jimmy, I won't be a minute.'

Jimmy smiled benignly.

She walked over to the toilets and went inside, followed by the supervising nurse.

Inside the toilets, the nurse remained outside the cubicle.

Once inside the cubicle, Melissa took off her coat and quickly removed the crochet hook from beneath her bra and slid it inside the sleeve of her thick jumper. Putting her coat back, on she flushed the toilet and walked out of the cubicle. She walked over to the sinks, watched by the supervising nurse, and thoroughly washed her hands. The door to the toilets opened and another visitor stepped inside wanting to use the toilet.

The nurse turned to the new arrival and said, 'Wait outside please! Only one visitor at a time is allowed inside the toilets.'

'That's alright, I'm all finished, thanks', said Melissa, smiling as she stepped out of the toilets.

The nurse was too preoccupied with the second visitor to pay any attention to Melissa, who walked across the hall and back to her seat opposite Jimmy.

Once again Jimmy reached across the table and held Melissa's hand. Very slowly his fingers felt for the crochet hook, hidden beneath the sleeve of her sweater. Keeping a watchful eye on the supervising nurses, almost imperceptibly he eased the crochet hook from Melissa's sleeve. In one fluid movement, he slid the hook beneath the sleeve of his own grey, V neck sweater.

Jimmy then stood up and walked over to the gents' toilet, where he spoke to the nurse, 'I'm really sorry sir, but

I desperately need to go to the toilet, I've eaten something that's gone right through me. It's the third time I've had to go today.'

'Alright Wade, I don't need chapter and bloody verse, be quick. I don't want to stand in a toilet, listening to you having a shit!'

'Okay sir, I'll be as quick as I can, thank you sir.'

Once inside the toilet cubicle, Wade removed the crochet hook from beneath his sleeve and placed it into the lining of his left boot. It fitted perfectly, virtually undetectable behind the stiff leather of the boot.

He flushed the chain and came out of the toilet smiling at the nurse, 'Bloody hell, that's better, I needed that.'

'Wash your hands Wade!'

'Sorry sir, of course.'

Jimmy stepped over and washed his hands before walking back out into the main hall.

He walked over to Melissa sat down and smiled.

It was now time for the second part of their plan.

After a couple of minutes, she suddenly pushed her chair backwards, causing it to screech across the tiled floor. She stood up angrily and said, 'Don't you bloody dare say that to me!'

Wade looked hurt and said, 'I'm sorry Melissa, I didn't mean it!'

'Yes, you bloody did, I'm not having it!'

Melissa walked to the front of the hall, stood in front of the staff nurse and demanded, 'I want to leave right now, please.'

The staff nurse in charge signalled for one of the supervising nurses to come over, 'Escort this lady back to reception, then get Wade back to his room.'

The young nurse gently took hold of Melissa's arm and said, 'This way please, follow me.'

Melissa followed the nurse out of the main hall, she never even glanced in Jimmy Wade's direction as she walked by.

As they walked along the corridor Melissa turned to the nurse and said, 'I really don't know how you do this job, that's the last time I ever want to see Jimmy Wade. Throw away the key, will you?'

The nurse allowed a grin to play across her mouth and said, 'I wouldn't worry about that love, Jimmy Wade's key was thrown away a long time ago.'

Melissa retrieved her handbag and passport from reception, then returned to her car in the car park. As she drove along Fleming Drive, hopefully for the last time, she smiled.

For Melissa Braithwaite, Monday couldn't come quick enough.

CHAPTER 34

3.30pm Saturday 25th March 1986
Hucknall, Nottinghamshire

The two detectives had deliberately taken their time, first reading all the letters, then studying the bank statements before finally going through the other documentation recovered from Christopher Baker's flat.

Now, as they sat with Baker in a small interview room at Hucknall Police Station, they could see he was nearing exhaustion.

Rob opened his packet of Benson and Hedges cigarettes, offered one to Baker and said, 'Christopher, are you sure you don't want a solicitor present for this interview?'

Baker accepted the cigarette and a light from Rob. He took a pull on the cigarette and said in his soft, distinctive, effeminate voice, 'I'm sure, thank you.'

Rob put the tapes into the recorder, switched it on, announced the time and the date before introducing both himself and the other officer present. He then invited Christopher to give his full name and date of birth.

Finally, he cautioned him and said, 'Christopher, you've been arrested on suspicion of the murder of Cavalie Naylor. Do you have any knowledge of the events, that led to the death of Cavalie Naylor?'

'None at all, Cav is, sorry, was, extremely special to me.'

Glen Lorimar leaned forward placed his elbows on the interview table and said, 'How long have you known Cavalie?'

'Just under a year.'

'Where did you two meet?'

'In Nottingham, at the Wimpole Art Gallery on Houndsgate.'

'How did that meeting come about then Chris?'

'I was looking at a particular painting, he stood next to me and passed a comment about it being one of his favourites, we got chatting and ended up going for a glass of wine together. We've been friends ever since.'

'You said earlier, that you believed Cav's father was responsible for your arrest today. Why do you think that is the case?'

'Because Geoff Naylor hates my guts, that's why.'

'Why does he hate you Christopher?'

'He thought I was all wrong for his precious Cavalie, he wanted him to meet some gorgeous woman, fall in love, get married and have kids, the whole nine yards.'

'Why was that such a problem?'

Christopher Baker laughed.

'What's so funny Christopher?'

'I'm amazed you still can't see it, you must have read the letters at my flat. Cav Naylor didn't need to find someone to fall in love with, he was already in love, with me. We're both gay for Christ's sake. The only problem was, he couldn't face telling his father, so consequently Geoff thought I was some terrible bastard, who was only interested in fleecing his son for everything he'd got.'

'And were you?'

'Was I what?'

'Trying to fleece Cav for everything he'd got?'

'No, I wasn't. Listen detective, I know it's hard for you to understand this, but I genuinely love, loved, Cav. I know we're from completely different backgrounds, but we could have been really happy together.'

Tears had never been far away from Christopher's blue eyes, now as he spoke, he blinked and teardrops spilled from his eyes and rolled slowly down each cheek. With a tremor in his soft voice he said, 'I really loved that man, detective.'

Glen Lorimar pressed on, 'What happened the last time you saw Cav?'

'He picked me up from my flat on Monday after work, we drove out to his bungalow at Underwood. We had a nice meal, drank a bit of wine and chatted about my charcoal drawing course.'

'Did you stay with him all night?'

'Of course I did. We were lovers, it's what lovers do detective.'

'How did Cav seem to you that evening?'

'Perfectly normal, we had a lovely night.'

'And the next morning?'

'Everything was fine, we had a bit of breakfast, then he dropped me back at my flat, so I could get my things, ready to travel down to Cornwall.'

'Let's talk about Cornwall, tell me about Tranquil Waters Retreat for Artists?'

'I saw the place advertised in a magazine, I'm currently into drawing with charcoal, they were advertising a residential course on that very subject at Tranquil Waters. I mentioned it to Cav some time ago, unbeknown to me he paid for the course and booked me on it as a surprise gift. Yes, before you ask detective, he also paid for my train fare there and back. Cav was an extremely generous man, which is something else that always pissed his old man off.'

'When did you travel to the Retreat?'

'Tuesday morning, I caught the ten o'clock train from Nottingham to St Pancras, where I changed trains. I had a half hour wait at St Pancras before getting the train down to Bude, in Cornwall. I arrived at the Retreat, around three o'clock in the afternoon.'

'Who can verify your time of arrival Chris?'

'The guy who runs Tranquil Waters Retreat is a very nice old man called Teddy Blake, he's quite a well renowned artist. He booked me into my room at that time, it was him who actually taught the class I attended.'

'When did you arrive back in Nottingham?'

'I wasn't due to come back until this morning, but after the strange phone call with Geoff on Friday morning, I decided to come home early and caught the late train on Friday. So, in answer to your question, I arrived back in Nottingham around midnight on Friday.'

'What was it about the phone call with Geoff, that made you change your plans?'

'It was the last straw, that's all. When I arrived in Bude on Tuesday, I was knackered so I didn't bother calling Cav, I just went to bed. The next morning, Wednesday, I called Cav first thing, but couldn't get through. It sounded as though his phone was constantly engaged. I just thought Cav had somehow knocked the phone off the hook, without realising it.

Anyway, by Friday morning I'd had enough of the engaged tone at his house, so I rang his office, that's when I spoke to his father, Geoff. I asked him if Cav was there and the ignorant old bastard hung up on me. I decided something definitely wasn't right, so I caught the late train on Friday. I intended going over to Underwood to see what was going on this morning, but you guys arrested me.'

'Christopher, are you aware of any enemies Cav might have?'

'Not a single one, Cav was the gentlest, kindest, most loving person you could ever hope to meet.'

'Have you two ever discussed Cav's business interests?'

'No, we didn't, I was never bothered about his business, Cav never talked about work after a hard day, all he wanted to do was unwind.'

Glen Lorimar turned to Rob Buxton and said, 'Is there anything you want to ask sir?'

'Do you know a man by the name of Edward Hall?' asked Rob.

'No.'

'Has Cav ever mentioned that name to you?'

'No, he hasn't.'

'Have either of you stayed at the Grosvenor Hotel in Nottingham recently?'

'Well I certainly haven't, it's well out of my price range, I can't say whether Cav has or hasn't, but I don't recall him mentioning anything to me about staying there.'

Rob then glanced at his watch, said the time out loud and terminated the interview.

All three men stood up and walked out of the interview room.

Rob turned to Glen and said, 'Make the phone calls to the Retreat, verify Christopher's story, especially the timings. Confirm the exact date when the course was booked and who paid for it. If everything checks out, bail him for two weeks, I need to get back over to Mansfield and liaise with the boss.'

'No problem sir, I'm on it.'

Glen watched Rob walk out of the cell block then turned to Christopher and said, 'Come on Chris, let's get you back to your cell while I make these phone calls. Do you want a cup of tea or coffee?'

'Coffee, two sugars would be great, thanks detective. I really did love Cav, you do know, that, don't you?'

'I know you did Chris, I know you did.'

CHAPTER 35

8.30pm Saturday 25th March 1986
Major Crime Investigation Unit, Mansfield

One by one, the weary detectives trailed into the main office of the Major Crime Investigation Unit.

It was time to de brief the day's enquiries. Each detective had been tasked with their own individual enquiries to try and move the investigation along, it was now time for them to brief the entire team how their particular enquiry had gone and whether or not they had learned anything useful.

As soon as everyone was in attendance, Danny addressed them collectively, 'I know you've all been on duty since early this morning, so I won't drag this out. I want you debriefed and away home, ready for another early start tomorrow morning. Before we start the debrief, I want to introduce you to Detective Sergeant Andy Wills, who will be working on DI Buxton's team. Andy's already known to most of you, he'll be replacing Ds Mayhew who has unfortunately slipped a disc and will be off for a while. Andy, you can start the briefing by enlightening everyone about the exact meaning of the messages found on the walls at the murder scenes.'

'Okay boss. The series of numbers and letters written on the walls, is actually a bible reference. It refers to a passage from the Book of Exodus, found in the Old Testament and is a very well-known quote from the bible. The particular passage it refers to states, "an eye for an eye and a tooth for a tooth." Everybody in this room, has probably heard that expression sometime in their life. What you may not know is, the scripture in the reference then goes on to state, "hand for hand, foot for foot, burning for burning, wound for wound, stripe for stripe." The two victims so far, have lost their eyes and their teeth respectively. It seems pretty clear that the motive for the killings is vengeance. If the killer is following the scripture to the letter, it could mean there's potential for several further victims.'

'Thanks Andy.'

Danny then turned to Rob Buxton, 'Rob, how did the arrest and interview of Christopher Baker go?'

'We arrested him at home this morning without a hitch, he's been interviewed at length and has a cast iron alibi for both murders. At the time of the murders Baker was attending a residential painting by numbers course in Bude, Cornwall. I've released him on bail, Dc Lorimar is still with him, obtaining as much background information on our victim, Cav Naylor, as possible. It's true, there was no love lost between Christopher Baker and Geoff Naylor and it turns out there's a very simple reason for this. Christopher's gay and was in a relationship with Cavalie, who in turn, couldn't face coming out as it would have meant telling his father of his true feelings for Christopher.'

'Thanks Rob, is there any suggestion either Christopher Baker or Cavalie Naylor knew Edward Hall?'

'Definitely not as far as Christopher's concerned boss, he'd never heard the name Edward Hall.'

There was a pause which was filled with the voice of a woman, 'There is a link between Hall and Naylor though sir.'

The voice belonged to Sergeant Tina Prowse.

'Go on Tina', said Danny.

'After I finished getting the statement from Vanessa Hall this morning, I was tasked with doing background checks on Edward Hall. I started by doing comparisons between the two victims. Both men were of a similar age, both were in professional occupations, so I started thinking about the qualifications they would have needed to achieve their respective positions of employment. Sure enough, I found Edward Hall had attended Nottingham University, I did a quick cross check and found that Cavalie Naylor had also attended Nottingham University at the same time. I don't know if the two men knew each other at university, but it's definitely common ground and perhaps worthy of a bit more digging.'

Detective Inspector Brian Hopkirk said, 'I think it's a bit more than common ground, Tina.'

He turned and addressed his comments to Danny, 'Sir, this afternoon I was tasked with searching the office used by Edward Hall at The Grosvenor Hotel, one of the items recovered was a small framed photograph of four men on their graduation day. One of the men in the photograph was obviously Edward Hall and I'm pretty sure that one of the other three was Cavalie Naylor. I telephoned Vanessa Hall and asked her if she knew who the other two men in the photograph were, but she couldn't say. Vanessa asked me if I'd taken the photo from her home as it was identical to one they kept in the lounge at their house. I've checked the search logs and no such photo was recovered by the search teams at the Beeston scene. For my own peace of mind, I drove over to the Halls' house and had a look to see if it had been missed by the search teams. There was no sign of any photograph anywhere, identical or even similar to the one I recovered from Hall's office. That means either Hall took the photograph from home to the office, or there were two photographs and one is now missing. Either way, the photograph proves Tina's link, and demonstrates that our two murder victims were at the very least acquaintances at university.'

'That's great work both of you. As a top priority enquiry, tomorrow morning I want Tina and Rachel to go to Nottingham University. As a matter of urgency, I want you to establish who the other two men in the photograph are. Brian, I want you to start researching incidents that occurred at Nottingham University at the time our two victims were there. It appears likely that the killers motive is revenge, if the only link we can find for the two victims is their time spent together at university, it's not a vast stretch of the imagination to think that their murders are in direct revenge for something that happened when they were there. Tina, how did you get on with Vanessa Hall this morning?'

'She was much better today sir, I took a full statement from her but there's not too much detail. I think the shock of seeing her husband like that has clouded her memory, she could remember very little about the assailant, but one thing she does recall quite vividly, is seeing what she describes as a huge hunting knife being held in front of her face by the intruder. Dr Gillender informed me that after such a traumatic experience the memory can become vague, but that it does sometimes improve after a period of time. I think it would be prudent to revisit Vanessa Hall at a later date to see if any further memory has come back to her.'

'I'll make a note of that Tina, at least we now have some idea of the kind of weapon used, sounds like Seamus Carter's opinion wasn't too far off the mark.'

The debrief continued for another half hour, but nothing else of any major importance was revealed.

When every detective had reported their findings, Danny turned to the team and said, 'Good work everyone, we're starting to make progress, but there's still plenty more to be done, so I want everybody back here at six o'clock tomorrow morning. Before you all go home, there's something else you all need to be aware of. Just before we started the debrief this evening, I was informed by the control room that a police officer has gone missing whilst on duty. Pc 212 Colin Moreton was working a day shift at Southwell, he should have gone off duty at six o'clock. Both he and his vehicle have been missing since around three o'clock this afternoon. I asked the control room if they wanted us to stay on duty to help locate the officer. The duty Inspector told me that he had all the manpower needed to search the area tonight and that there was a real possibility that staff from the MCIU might be required tomorrow morning. So get off home, but be aware that tomorrow, in all probability, some of you will be seconded from this enquiry to assist with enquiries into the disappearance of your colleague. Let's wait and see what the night brings. I'll see you all in the morning.'

The news brought murmurings of concern for their colleague from the detectives as they made their way out of the briefing room. It was an extremely unusual occurrence and one that almost always didn't have a good outcome. Most of the officers were already fearing the worst for their missing colleague.

CHAPTER 36

9.00pm Saturday 25th March 1986
Teversal Manor, Cotgrave, Nottinghamshire

Paul Fencham pushed hard on the button and rang the ornate doorbell again.

This time a light came on in the hallway of the grand house. He had parked his small Datsun car on the road outside the house, then walked up the gravel driveway. He'd been amazed at the size of the palatial residence. Since leaving the army, Geoff Naylor had really done well for himself.

Fencham had been stunned, when out of the blue he had received the telephone call from Naylor. Of course he had already heard about the murder of Geoff Naylor's son, Cavalie Naylor, from the news desk. As a crime reporter for the Nottingham Evening Standard, it was his job to know about any major enquiries being undertaken by the police.

The telephone call had still surprised him though; he didn't understand why Naylor, the successful businessman, had called him to say he had information for a story.

He hadn't seen Geoff since they were demobbed from the army back in the fifties, both men had served in the same regiment during the Korean War. They had been close during their time in the service, but as is normal for people, they had drifted apart once they left the army. He hadn't seen Geoff Naylor at any of the Korea Veterans reunions he'd attended over the ensuing years.

He'd been shocked that Naylor even knew he was a reporter.

Paul Fencham was realistic enough to understand that at his time of life he was never going to get that lucky break. He knew that the one big story that would set him up, enabling him to become a top reporter for a national, Fleet Street paper, was never going to happen. He was now the wrong side of fifty and had started drinking heavily after his divorce five years ago. He was a short, squat man at least three stone overweight.

He couldn't afford to buy a suit, so he wore a tatty tweed jacket with leather patches on the elbows, a grimy blue shirt, a garish mustard coloured tie and scruffy, stain ridden, black trousers. His brown brogues were scuffed and devoid of any polish. He had a permanent five o clock shadow, his once blonde hair was now grey and receding rapidly.

All in all, Paul Fencham was a mess and more tellingly, he knew he was a mess.

He could now hear footsteps from inside the house, approaching the double front doors.

A lock was turned from within and the right-side door opened, Geoff Naylor stood there with a cut-glass tumbler, full of whisky in his hand. Involuntarily, Fencham licked his lips at the sight of the amber coloured liquor.

'Well don't just stand there Fenchers, come inside', said a clearly tipsy Naylor.

Fencham stepped inside the grandiose hallway, Naylor closed the door and said in a slurred voice, 'This way old friend, follow me.'

Fencham followed him down the hallway and into a huge lounge.

'Grab a seat Fenchers, can I get you a drink?'

It was the second time Naylor had referred to him by his old army nickname.

'I'll have the same as you please Geoff.'

'Yeah, course you will, good man.'

Naylor poured a huge measure of single malt whisky into a tumbler and handed it to the newspaper reporter.

Fencham took a huge gulp of the fiery liquid, smacked his lips and said, 'Ah, that's better! I was really sorry to hear about your son, Geoff. Is that why you've asked me to come over? Is it something to do with his death?'

'The fucking police aren't taking me seriously, I've told them who's done it, virtually handed them the case on a fucking plate and they're still not interested. That bastard, Christopher Baker, killed him. The cops arrested him this morning, then just before I called you I heard that the useless fuckers have already let him go again. I don't understand what's going on, I want to know what the fuck they're playing at.'

'If the cops have questioned and released this Christopher Baker already, I'm sure they've got their reasons, Geoff. Perhaps they've let him out on bail until they get more evidence.'

'Yeah, that could be it. He's a devious, clever bastard alright, killing that poor fucker over in Beeston just to cover his tracks.'

Fencham was aware of the other murder in Beeston, but there had been no suggestion anywhere that the two murders were linked.

Naylor stood up on shaky legs, poured himself another huge measure from the dark green Glen Fiddich bottle and said, 'Want another one Fenchers, my old mate?'

Fencham quickly gulped down the remaining whisky in his glass then handed it to Naylor, who promptly filled it to the top again. He took the glass back from Naylor and took another big mouthful, he could feel his cheeks starting to flush as the whisky raced into his system.

'Geoff, why exactly do you think your boy was murdered by this bloke Baker?'

'Because I know he was after Cav's money, pure and simple. The police are saying nothing about the murders to your lot, are they? They haven't even told you about the message left on the wall, have they?'

Fencham thought Naylor had finally lost it, he was obviously pissed and was making no sense. Then the old habits of the reporter kicked in, Fencham put his drink down on the coffee table, he needed to think clearly.

'What writing, on what wall, Geoff?'

'That bastard had written a message on the kitchen wall in Cav's house, using my precious boys blood.'

'What was the message?'

'It didn't make any sense, it was just numbers and letters, gobbledegook to throw the cops off the scent. I overheard one of the cops, saying that the same message had been written on a wall at the Beeston murder. That's got to prove that evil little fucker Baker did them both. Am I right Fenchers?'

'You're dead right Geoff. What else did Baker do at both the murders?'

'I don't know mate. I want you to talk to the cops for me, make them see sense, can you do that?'

Naylor was now slurring his words so badly that it was hard for Fencham to understand clearly what he was saying.

'Of course, I can Geoff, but I think you should have a rest now mate. Get your head down and sleep off some of that whisky, I'll see myself out.'

Geoff Naylor lay down on one of the plush settees, within seconds he was snoring loudly.

Fencham was now deep in thought. Leaving Naylor snoring loudly in the lounge, he walked back out into the hallway. He spotted a telephone on an antique occasional table, picking up the phone he quickly dialled a number from memory.

'Hello mate, it's Paul Fencham. How would you like to earn yourself fifty quid?'

There was a pause before Fencham spoke again, 'It's easy money Dave. Just answer me one question, were you working on that murder at Beeston the other day?'

Another pause.

'You were, that's brilliant. Listen, I know you take photographs of everything on them jobs, a little bird tells me something was written on the wall. What was it?'

A longer pause.

'Come on Dave, it's the easiest money you'll ever make, let's say seventy-five quid.'

Fencham then exploded down the phone, 'Fuck off, I'm not paying you a hundred quid you grasping shit!'

Quickly the reporter spoke again, 'Don't be too hasty Dave, alright a hundred nicker it is, but for that money, I want to know exactly what was written on the wall.'

A broad smile spread across the reporters features, he grabbed the small note pad and pencil that was always in his jacket pocket.

He quickly scribbled on the paper before repeating it back.

'EC21V2425. Are you sure, that's all it was? What the fuck's that supposed to mean?'

There was another pause while Fencham listened to his informant talking.

'What do you think Dave? I'll post you the cash as normal. You haven't moved house have you? No, well stop fucking panicking, you'll get your money. I've never let you down, before, have I?'

Fencham put the phone down, picked it straight back up and called his news desk, 'I've got something I need you to look at, I've got a series of random letters and numbers, EC21V2425. I want to know exactly what they mean, get on it. I'm coming back to the office now, I want to know by the time I get back.'

Fencham walked back into the lounge where Naylor was now fast asleep, the snoring had subsided a little and had changed into the slow rhythmic breathing of a deep sleep. He finished his whisky, then poured himself another large one.

He swallowed the fiery liquid in one go, raised the glass and said, 'Cheers Geoff, I don't know who the fuck Christopher Baker is mate, but thank you so much for the tip off about the serial killer.'

He walked out of the house, along the gravel driveway and back to his car. He had a warm glow, he couldn't tell if it was the effects of the single malt whisky or the fact that he'd just been handed the biggest opportunity of his newspaper career.

All he had to do was figure out the meaning of the message on the walls, then he could make some serious money selling the story to the red tops.

CHAPTER 37

4.00am Sunday 26th March 1986
Farnsfield, Nottinghamshire

Pc Colin Moreton was shivering cold.

He was grateful it had stayed dry, but the flip side of being dry was the way the temperature had plummeted overnight, beneath a clear sky. He was also thankful that he'd decided to put a jumper on beneath his tunic, before he went on patrol yesterday.

As the first light of dawn began to creep over the horizon and the birds started to sing, he glanced down at his wristwatch. It was awkward to see the watch face clearly, his wrists were twisted at a strange angle because of the handcuffs. Eventually he could make out the time; it was just after four o'clock, which meant he had been propped against this tree for over twelve hours. It was time to try and get moving.

His head still ached from the blow, but at least he no longer felt like he would pass out if he tried to move. He was grateful that he'd only been knocked unconscious. When he had been forced to kneel down, with his back facing that nutter with the gun, he'd been convinced he was about to be shot and killed.

The worst thing about the whole incident, was the fact he still had absolutely no idea what the hell it was all about. Initially he thought the bloke had broken down, then he noticed that he was sweating profusely and breathing hard as though he had been running. The last thing he had expected when he got out of the police car, was to be confronted with a handgun.

His head ached a little more as he tried to work it all out.

It was time to stop thinking about what had happened, time to try and do something, he'd been sat down too long.

He forced his back into the trunk of the tree, then tried to lever himself off the floor by pushing with his legs. It was difficult because of the handcuffs and the uneven ground, but eventually he managed to get to his feet. He moved his head from side to side and his neck felt sticky, he could feel that his shirt collar was damp. The wound to his head must have bled badly for his shirt to feel that wet. It was slowly getting lighter now and he could just about make out the layby through the branches of the trees.

Very gingerly he took a couple of steps, he fully expected a new wave of nausea to rush over him and cause him to collapse again.

Nothing happened.

He gave a triumphant little grin as he took another step, then another.

Eventually, he stepped onto the tarmac of the lane, just as the first rays of the sun crept over the horizon. He knew it was psychological, but just feeling that weak sunlight on his face, made him automatically feel warmer.

He looked both ways along the lane, there was no sign of the black Range Rover or his police car. Had there been two offenders all the time? Had he completely missed an accomplice?

From where he now stood on the lane, he couldn't see his police car lying in the ditch, where it had been abandoned by the Watcher.

A glint of sunlight reflecting off a metal object on the road, caught his eye. He shuffled slowly over to the object and saw that it was the smashed remnants of his personal radio.

After a few minutes, he got his bearings and remembered exactly where he was. Gingerly, he started to walk in the direction of Farnsfield, trying to ignore the throbbing pain that was building in his head.

He had staggered along for a distance of about fifty yards, when he suddenly felt dizzy and nauseous. He stopped for a rest and looked along the lane.

Away in the distance, he could just make out a vehicle being driven very slowly in his direction. Now that the sun was creeping ever higher, the vehicle only had its side lights on. As the car slowly approached and got closer, his face suddenly creased into a wide grin. He could now clearly see the blue light bar on the roof of the white vehicle; he realised it was a Traffic patrol car.

They must be out searching for me, that's why it's going so slowly, he thought.

Raising his manacled hands above his head, he tried to attract the attention of the officers in the approaching Traffic patrol car.

The action of raising his arms brought on another dizzy spell, this time it was enough to make him slump to the ground. He didn't have the energy or strength to try and stand again, so he remained sitting, cross legged at the side of the lane as he willed the aching pain in his head to stop.

Suddenly, he heard the roar of the patrol car's engine as the officers finally spotted him sitting on the side of the lane, the driver of the car accelerated along the lane to reach him.

The car screeched to a halt, the officers jumped out and ran towards him.

Pc Moreton muttered out loud, 'Thank fuck for that!'

CHAPTER 38

4.30am Sunday 26th March 1986
Mansfield, Nottinghamshire

Danny Flint stood in the kitchen of his home, he was just about to pour the hot water from the kettle onto a tea bag, when he heard the key slide into the Yale lock of the front door.

He pushed open the door that led from the kitchen into the hallway, just in time to see his fiancée, Sue, walking in through the open front door.

Danny instinctively glanced at his watch, it was now four thirty in the morning, Sue's shift at the Casualty Department of Kings Mill Hospital should have finished at two o'clock.

'You're late sweetheart, been busy?' he asked.

'There's been a bad accident on the motorway, three cars and a lorry. We had four serious casualties brought into our department just after one o' clock. They're all stable and on the wards now though, thank goodness. No fatalities this time, why people insist on driving so fast, never ceases to amaze me.'

'The kettle's just boiled, do you want a cuppa? Or do you want to get straight off to bed?'

'Ooh! A cup of tea would be lovely, thanks sweetheart.'

Danny finished making both cups of tea, then joined Sue sitting at the breakfast table in the kitchen.

Sue held the mug in both hands and took a sip of her hot tea, 'That's bloody lovely, just what the doctor ordered.'

'Yeah, literally', laughed Danny.

'Anyway detective, why are you up so early?'

'It's hectic at the minute, we had two murders come in on Friday. They appear to be linked, even though they were at different ends of the county. It looks like we've got another nutter on the loose, it could be like Jimmy Wade all over again.'

'That sounds awful, have you any idea at all who you're looking for?'

'It's early days yet, but at this moment in time, very little. On top of that, just before I left work last night, I was informed that one of our uniformed cops was missing on duty. I don't know if he's been located yet, or if something nasty has happened to him.'

'So, it looks like being a long day for you?'

'More than likely, why?'

'Had you forgotten about our little appointment with the vicar this evening at six o'clock?'

'Bugger! I'm so sorry Sue, I'd totally forgotten. I might be able to slip away for a little while, even if I can't make it, you can still go, can't you?'

Sue smiled and said, 'Of course I can, but I think the idea of the vicar wanting to see the bride and the groom, was so he could talk to both of us about the sanctity of marriage.'

Danny smiled back and said, 'He already knows we've both been married before, what do you think he's going to try and tell us?'

'Oh, I don't know Danny, maybe, better luck this time!'

They both giggled and sipped their tea.

'Seriously sweetheart, don't worry if you can't make it tonight, I'll let you know what the vicar said later, but you and your best man had both better be at that church on May 7th.'

'I'll definitely be there sweetheart, I don't know if Rob will be able to get time off from work though, apparently, the bloke he works for is a complete knob!'

'Funny, I'd heard that too. Shouldn't you be at work by now, Chief Inspector?', Sue replied dryly.

Danny grabbed his suit jacket from the back of the chair, took a last drink of tea and made for the front door.

He stopped half way, spun around and walked back into the kitchen where he kissed Sue hard on the mouth.

She responded to the kiss before saying, 'I should think so too.'

Danny smiled, 'See you later sweetheart, say hello to the vicar for me.'

'Get to work Danny, before I change my mind!'

CHAPTER 39

4.30am Sunday 26th March 1986
Rampton Hospital, Nottinghamshire

Jimmy Wade lay on top of the hard bed in his cell at the high security hospital, he was wide awake and staring at the ceiling.

It amused him, how the staff all referred to the cells as rooms. Who were they trying to fool? Rampton Hospital had the highest security he'd encountered since his arrest, that included the maximum-security prison in New South Wales, where he'd been held while the British police arranged to take him back to the UK to stand trial.

Wade still cursed his luck every day. He still didn't understand how he had failed to spot that spineless twat, Dave Smedley, at the Beltana mine. He lay in the dark and replayed in his mind the moment the Australian detectives had arrested him in the pit canteen after his shift. He had literally taken one bite from his sandwich, when three of the biggest and strongest men he'd ever seen, grabbed him and threw him to the floor, before handcuffing and arresting him.

Everything after that initial moment of capture had been a blur.

He hadn't said a word to Detective Inspector Flint or his sidekick Detective Sergeant Buxton throughout the entire journey from New South Wales back to England. He refused to speak to them during the hours of interviews as well.

He knew he was fucked and that he just had to accept the inevitable.

That feeling of inevitability, changed at Leicester Crown Court, when he had first seen Melissa Braithwaite in the public gallery. He'd been mesmerised by her, it wasn't the old urges he felt when he looked into her beautiful, soulful eyes that already held so much pain. He wanted to be with her, he found her attractive and beautiful, he had no inclination or urge to snuff out her very existence.

Ever since her first visit at Wakefield prison, while he was on remand, he'd been totally besotted. He was amazed at her loyalty. In the face of overwhelming evidence, she always maintained, that he was innocent and that the real guilty party was Sergeant Michael Reynolds.

He hadn't wanted to burst her bubble, so he played along with her theory and insisted she was right. He really was an innocent man.

He'd been delighted when after his conviction and subsequent life sentence, she had continued to visit him at Rampton Hospital. Throughout the many visits, their special bond and friendship had grown stronger.

When he'd first mentioned his plan about the concrete unit working party and the possibility of him getting out, she had been overjoyed and promised to help.

She had definitely fulfilled that promise, today.

He got up from the hard bed and made his way over to the small sink in his room. Kneeling on the floor, he reached up behind the sink, fingers searching. Hidden right at the back, in the small recess between the sink and the wall, his straining fingers found the crochet hook.

Having retrieved the hook, he started to work on the thin sheath of plastic that surrounded the metal. Using his teeth, he stripped away the plastic, until he was left with a metal rod the same diameter as a knitting needle, but only half the length.

The unpainted bricks near the tiny window of his cell were very rough in texture. He spat on one of the bricks, then began to draw the metal rod back and forth through the spit over the rough brick. There was a scraping sound, but it wasn't too loud. Unless somebody was actually standing directly outside the cell door, he was in no danger of the noise being heard outside his cell.

He walked over to the locked door, straining to see as far as he could along the corridor. His view was limited, as the window was merely a slit in the heavy metal door, but he could see that no lights were on.

He returned to the window and began working the crochet hook on the rough brick.

After half an hour, the harmless crochet hook had been turned into a lethal, metal spike with a sharpened point. He then used folded toilet paper to put a pad on the blunt end of the crochet hook before nestling it into the palm of his hand, leaving the sharpened spike protruding five inches between his middle and ring fingers. He bunched his fist around the makeshift weapon, then punched the spike into the pillow on his bed.

The sharpened spike penetrated the pillow easily and the padding on the blunt end meant there was very little discomfort in the palm of his hand.

Having satisfied himself of the effectiveness of the home-made weapon, he again secreted it in the same place behind the sink.

He lay back down on the top of his bed, interlaced his fingers, placed both hands behind his head and smiled.

As he lay in the darkness, he thought of all the people he would visit when he finally got out. Some people had to pay for the way they had treated him, or for the way they had deceived him.

First on his list were the two sadistic nurses, who had regularly beaten him when he first arrived at Rampton. He'd taken great pains to establish their names and identities, he was now aware that they were both single men. Fred Barnes, the older of the two, lived in Retford and Jack Williams lived in the small village of Dunham. They would both pay, heavily, for the way they had treated him. Lying in the darkness, he stared at the ceiling and played out their deaths in his mind over and over again. They would both suffer horribly, he would see to that.

Next on the list was that mealy-mouthed, skinny bastard, the social worker Stewart Ainsworth. He'd told him countless times about the beatings and he hadn't done a thing. Not once had he tried to help him. As far as Wade was concerned, by his inaction Ainsworth was complicit in the beatings. The weak social worker had been more interested in taking Melissa to task, over visiting him. Well, he would pay for his ineptitude and cowardice, he had something very special lined up for Stewart Ainsworth, he too would suffer and would soon realise that he had crossed the wrong person.

Revenge would be sweet.

Finally, there was Rachel Moore, the beautiful, enigmatic detective, who cheated death at his hands and who had then provided the final clinching evidence to secure his conviction.

It would soon be time for her to pay, he would make sure that this time, there would be no escape.

He closed his eyes and thought of tomorrow's events, playing out various scenarios in his mind.

Monday could not come quick enough.

CHAPTER 40

4.30am Sunday 26th March 1986
Farndon, Nottinghamshire

The sound of dripping water began to seep into the consciousness of Frederick Reece.

As he began to come around, he realised just how freezing cold he was. He had no idea where he was, and felt totally disorientated. He tried to stand, but realised immediately that he'd been bound in such a way that he was prevented from being able to physically stand.

He also quickly realised that he'd been gagged.

Using his tongue and teeth, he tried to move the sticky brown tape, that covered his mouth. Despite his best efforts, it was useless, he couldn't shift it. Thankfully he could still breathe easily through his nose.

He tried to shout out, but the gag stifled his cries.

His hands had been bound tightly behind his back, his wrists and shoulders ached because of the strained, unnatural way his arms had been pinned. He rolled his head from side to side, then up and down, trying to alleviate the ache in his shoulders.

There was no blindfold and now as dawn broke and light started to filter into the building, he was able to look around the place, that was in effect, his prison.

He was being held in what appeared to be some decrepit, disused building. The concrete walls were a drab grey, discoloured in places by various water marks, stains and random obscene graffiti. The building looked as though it had once been used as some sort of industrial unit, possibly agricultural judging by the smell.

He wrinkled his nose, what was that smell?

It was like rotting rancid flesh, he'd never smelled anything quite like it, it was disgusting and made him want to vomit. He fought the urge to be sick, he knew vomiting behind the gag would be catastrophic, he didn't want to die choking on his own sick.

He strained his ears.

Above the constant drip of the water, every once in a while, he could hear a rumbling noise in the distance. Suddenly, he realised what the sound was. There must be a road fairly close by, the rumbling noise was being caused by heavy goods vehicles being driven at speed.

The realisation that he was still close to civilization, raised his spirits briefly, but that brief euphoric feeling quickly disappeared when Reece realised he desperately needed to urinate.

He couldn't hold it any longer, suddenly he felt a warmth envelop his lower waist and thighs as he urinated. He screwed up his face in disgust, both at the smell and the thought of wetting himself. The warmth he initially felt disappeared almost immediately, as his urine soaked trousers and underpants instantly went cold.

Feeling totally helpless, he felt tears start to burn his eyes, he felt them trickle down his cheeks until they reached the tape that covered his mouth. He cried out in anger and frustration, the noise a strangled, muffled plea.

Questions raced through his mind.

Who was that maniac? Why had he brought him here? Why was this happening to him?

Unfortunately, for Frederick Reece, the answers would come soon enough.

CHAPTER 41

5.30am Sunday 26th March 1986
Clumber Park Caravan Site, Nottinghamshire

The Watcher felt good.

It was Sunday, the Lord's Day, a day of rest.

He filled the kettle with water, then placed it on the small stove in the caravan. He lit the gas, then popped a tea bag and a spoonful of sugar into a mug. As he waited for the kettle to boil, he opened the caravan door and drew in huge lungsful of the cool, crisp morning air.

Reaching skyward, he stretched his arms, scratched his head and wondered at the beauty of the sunrise. The sun was now rising steadily, the early morning light looked eerily beautiful, diffused by the tree branches.

He held his hands out in front of him, palms facing up and said quietly, 'Defend me, your humble servant in all assaults of my enemies: That I, surely trusting in thy defence, may not fear the power of my adversaries, through the might of Jesus Christ, our Lord. Amen.'

Just as he finished his prayer, he heard the whistle from the kettle as the water boiled. He stepped back inside the caravan, poured the boiling water into the mug, splashed in some long-life milk, stirred the sugar and took a sip of the hot, sweet tea.

He placed the mug on the table next to the ordnance survey map. He studied the map and soon found what he was looking for. Just outside the small town of Farndon he could see the map symbol for a chapel. He knew he would be a stranger in the congregation, but it didn't matter, everyone was welcome in the house of the Lord.

As he sipped the hot sweet tea, he formulated his actions for the day.

He would go to church first thing this morning, then on the way back he would drop into the disused maggot farm and check on the captive Frederick Reece. He chuckled as he thought how apt it was, that Reece was incarcerated in an old maggot farm. He considered him to be no better than a filthy maggot, one that he would soon crush.

But not today, the Watcher refused to work on the Lords day.

Today, he would just check on Reece, to ensure he was still securely bound, so he could answer for his sins tomorrow morning.

He finished the mug of tea, grabbed his small toiletries bag, stepped out of the caravan and made his way to the toilet block. If he was going to chapel, he needed to have a shower, a shave and make himself look presentable.

CHAPTER 42

5.30am Sunday 26th March 1986
Major Crime Investigation Unit, Mansfield

Danny Flint stood and addressed his team, 'Good morning, thanks for getting here early, we've got another very busy day in front of us. The first thing you all need to know is that Pc Moreton has been found. He's alive and although injured is expected to make a full recovery. He was located by a Traffic patrol car, just over an hour ago. I've only got sketchy details from the control room so far, but it appears he was attacked by an armed man after he stopped to check what appeared to be a broken-down Range Rover, just outside Farnsfield, yesterday.'

There was a murmured approval that the officer had been found, a voice from the back of the room asked, 'Was he badly injured boss?'

'His injuries are considered serious, unfortunately he was hit over the head with a handgun and knocked unconscious. He was then handcuffed using his own cuffs, propped against a tree and left for dead. Again, I only have sketchy details, but it would appear the wound to the back of his head was very nasty and Pc Moreton lost a lot of blood overnight. From what the doctors at the hospital are telling us, Pc Moreton's very lucky to be alive. The enquiry into this assault, quite rightly, looks to be heading our way. The Chief Constable has insisted that the attack on Pc Moreton will be treated as an attempted murder, which means the MCIU will commence the investigation, on top of our two current murder enquiries.'

There was more murmuring around the room. Danny raised his hands for silence, then continued, 'Rob, I want you and DS Wills to get across to Kings Mill Hospital, first thing this morning. I want you to get a first account from Pc Moreton, establish exactly what happened to him. I understand he's conscious, I know he'll be resting after his ordeal, but as soon as you can, I want you to speak with him.'

'Ok boss', said Rob.

'In the meantime, I want as much information as possible from Nottingham University. I know it's a Sunday morning, but their security teams will still be on the campus. Dc Moore and Sergeant Prowse, I want you to get over to the university this morning and liaise with their Head of Security, Jim Cronin. He's a retired detective, a first-rate man, who'll assist you wherever he can. Don't be shy, call out anybody you think may be able to help you. If it means bothering the Vice Chancellor on a Sunday morning, then bother him. Your priority is to establish the identities of the other two men in the photograph, but while you're there I also want you to find out if there were any incidents of note, that occurred at the university while Naylor and Hall were students there. Don't forget the probable motive for these two murders is revenge. We need to try and establish exactly what it is, that's being avenged by the killer, so keep a very open mind please ladies. See if Jim Cronin can shed any light on what Naylor and Hall were like while they were at the university. We now know Naylor was gay, be subtle, but try and ascertain if there was any sign of that while he was a student.'

Rachel and Tina both nodded, Rachel said, 'Understood boss.'

Danny now turned to Brian Hopkirk, the other Detective Inspector on the team, 'Brian, I want you to organise the teams that are left, to look at the rest of the outstanding enquiries. I want a team to concentrate solely on the personal life of Edward Hall, was he a ladies man etc.? You know the stuff I'm looking for. I want another team to look deeper into the business dealings of Naylor and anything else that came out of the interview with Christopher Baker yesterday.'

'No problem boss. Just picking up on what you said to Rachel and Tina, I'd like a couple of detectives to remain here to research any sexual assaults that happened in and around Nottingham University, at the time Hall and Naylor were students. Nothing fuels the thirst for revenge like sexual assault.'

'That's a good call Brian, I'll leave you to organise the teams for each of the outlined enquiries. I've got to work on the details of the press release this morning, it's due to go out at eleven o'clock today.'

'It's all in hand boss, I'll get everything sorted.'

'Thanks Brian. Finally, I want everybody back here at two o'clock this afternoon, for an update. Thanks.'

Danny walked into his office, closed the door and started making notes for the press release.

CHAPTER 43

7.00am Sunday 26th March 1986
Kings Mill Hospital, Mansfield.

Dr Anil Paratha was not budging.

'I'm very sorry Detective Inspector Buxton, but your colleague needs rest. He's suffered a major trauma to his skull, that resulted in a wound requiring twelve stiches, concussion and heavy blood loss. If you couple the trauma involved with those injuries, plus the fact he spent the night out in the cold and was borderline hypothermic when he was found, your man's extremely lucky to be alive.'

Rob Buxton was not easily put off, he replied, 'Doctor, I fully understand everything you're telling me and I really appreciate the fact that you're caring for my colleague so well. Will he be in any physical danger, if we talk to him for just five minutes? I have to balance the fact that my colleague needs to recuperate, with the fact that there's a gun wielding maniac out there who's already shown he's a danger to members of the police force as well as the general public. All I'm asking for, is a quick five minute chat.'

Dr Paratha looked at his watch, 'Very well Inspector, you've got five minutes, and I mean five minutes. I'll be back then and I will insist that you leave, so your colleague can rest.'

'Thank you doctor, I really appreciate it.'

Rob and Andy walked in to the small side room on the admissions ward.

Pc Moreton was awake. He was sitting up in bed, his head heavily bandaged, sipping sweet, tepid tea from a plastic beaker, through a straw.

'It's the CID, I wondered how long it would be before you guys got here', grinned Pc Moreton.

'Colin, I'm Detective Inspector Rob Buxton, this is Detective Sergeant Andy Wills. We're from the Major Crime Investigation Unit, I know you want to rest, but we need to know exactly what happened to you yesterday, so we can set about catching this lunatic before he hurts anyone else. First and foremost, how are you feeling? Are you up to answering a few questions?'

'My head aches sir, but apart from that I'm fine, so fire away.'

'Exactly what can you remember about yesterday?'

'I'd just resumed mobile patrol after taking my meal break at Southwell nick. I drove over to Farnsfield. The town was quiet, then as I drove out of Farnsfield, I saw a black Range Rover parked in a small layby. I'm sorry sir, I never made a note of the registration number, all I can tell you is that it looked fairly new. I remember seeing a bloke standing in the road, at the side of the Range Rover. My first thought was that he'd broken down or something, so I stopped to see if he needed any help.'

'You're doing great Colin, go on', encouraged Rob.

Pc Moreton took another sip of the lukewarm tea, then said, 'There was something weird about the bloke, he looked totally out of place. He was smartly dressed, wearing a dark suit, white shirt and dark blue tie, I think. The weird thing was, he was sweating like fuck, like he'd been running.'

'Can you remember anything else about his appearance?'

'He was late forties, early fifties, quite short and stocky, he looked very strong. Not like a body builder, but naturally powerful. I remember he had piercing blue eyes. His hair was a steel grey colour, it was thick and brushed back and he had a ruddy complexion.'

'Anything else?'

'Yes, he was Scottish. Well, he spoke with a Scottish accent anyway. The accent was more Sean Connery than Billy Connolly, if you know what I mean.'

'That's great Colin. What can you tell me about the weapon he had?'

'It was a black handgun, a revolver I think.'

'Did he say anything to you?'

'When I first stopped, he gave me some bullshit story about hitting a fox or something, but when I got out of the car, he went quiet. It was like he was appraising me, sussing me out almost. This guy knew exactly what he was doing. He pointed the gun at me and said, if I did as I was told he wouldn't hurt me. He also said, he'd kill me in a heartbeat if I messed him about. I looked into his eyes, I knew he meant it. He marched me off the road into the woods, made me kneel down with my back to him, then belted me. That's the last thing I remember until I came around again. He'd handcuffed me with my own cuffs and propped me against a tree.'

The door to the room opened and Dr Paratha walked back in, 'Time's up detectives, I'm sorry but that's all for now, your colleague needs to rest.'

Rob turned to the doctor, 'Thank you doctor, it's been a massive help.'

As the two detectives started to walk out of the room, Pc Moreton spoke again, 'One other thing you should know sir, this wasn't a new situation for this guy. He was totally at ease with what he was doing, almost professional. It was matter of fact for him.'

'Thanks Colin, now do as the doctor says, get some rest, we'll chat again when you're feeling better. Well done out there, it sounds like you handled the situation just right.'

'I didn't handle anything sir, that nutter was in control at all times. The only reason I'm still alive is because it didn't suit him to kill me.'

'Thanks Colin, get some rest.'

As soon as they left the room Rob turned to Andy, 'Find a telephone, ring the control room, get the description of the Range Rover and the suspect circulated asap. Make sure you tell them that this vehicle or the suspect is not to be approached under any circumstances. From what Pc Moreton's just told us this is one very dangerous individual. I don't want some young probationer getting shot, going after this nutter.'

'I'll nip down to the medical secretary's office and use one of their phones.'

'Thanks Andy, I just want to have a quick chat with Dr Paratha to establish what the prognosis is for Colin and how soon we'll be able to get a written statement from him. I'll see you back at the car park.'

Chapter 44

8.30am Sunday 26th March 1986
Farnsfield, Nottinghamshire

Pc Jim Miller and Pc Damian Cox were on mobile patrol in Southwell. They were on the early shift and had started work at six o'clock. Pc Miller was a veteran of twenty-three years' service. He was tutoring the very young and inexperienced Pc Cox, who two weeks ago had turned up for his first ever shift, as a probationary Police Constable, after completing his training at the Police Training School in Dishforth, North Yorkshire.

All the talk at that mornings briefing had been about the assault on their colleague, Pc Colin Moreton. It had been discussed, at length, how the Traffic patrol car had found him badly injured on a country lane, just outside Farnsfield. Pc Miller had often worked alongside Colin Moreton, he was inwardly seething at the news of the assault. Pc Cox was understandably feeling very nervous, nobody at training school had ever mentioned anything about maniacs with guns.

It was just after seven o'clock, when they received the radio message from the control room, giving the description of the suspect wanted for the attack on Pc Moreton. At the same time, they were given the description of a new black

Range Rover that was believed to be being used by the suspect. The descriptions of the suspect and the vehicle were issued with a warning not to approach either. Should the suspect or the vehicle be seen, the instruction was to call in the sighting and wait for armed back up.

Jim Miller glanced at his watch, it was now almost eight thirty. There was still half an hour to go before they were scheduled to go into Southwell Police Station, to take their refreshments.

He turned to his young probationer and said, 'Let's have a steady ride back to the nick Damian, we'll go through Farnsfield and check all the car parks. You never know, we might spot the bastard that's had a go at Col.'

Trying to maintain a confident note in his voice, Damian replied, 'That's a great idea Jim.'

The young officer smiled at his tutor constable, but inside he was feeling scared and vulnerable. What would they do, if they did happen to stumble across this nutter with a gun?

Twenty minutes later, Jim Miller drove the Panda car slowly into the car park, at the rear of the Co-op store in Farnsfield. The entrance to the car park was through an old archway, unless you knew the village, it would be easy to miss the car park behind the store.

'Jim, look over there, in the far corner', said Damian.

Sure enough, parked on its own in the far corner of the car park was a fairly new, black, Range Rover.

'What do you think Damian, can you see anybody inside it?'

'Not through the tinted glass.'

'Let's have a quick look, shall we?'

'I don't know Jim, control said this bloke's armed. Shouldn't we wait for back up?'

If Jim Miller had been alone, there was no way he would have waited, he was still seething about the attack on his friend and colleague. He wanted to catch the bastard responsible for putting his mate in hospital, but he had his probationer to think about, so he slowly reversed the Panda car into the archway, until it effectively blocked the entrance to the car park.

'You're right Damian, we'll wait for armed back up, did you manage to see the registration number?'

'Yeah, its 440 FDR.'

'Right, get on the radio, tell control that we've sighted what could be the suspect vehicle in the car park behind the Co-op store in Farnsfield. Ask them to do a vehicle check on the PNC, let's see who its registered to, shall we?'

The young Pc used the radio as instructed.

The reply from control was immediate, 'Maintain your position, under no circumstances approach the vehicle, an armed response vehicle is travelling to your location from Southwell. ETA ten minutes, control out.'

Jim Miller acknowledged the call and asked, 'Received that, thanks. Who's the registered keeper, is it somebody local?'

'Negative, the keeper on PNC is shown as being Frederick Reece, home address is Mayflower Cottage, Rankin Lane at Beckingham, control out.'

'Beckingham, near Newark?'

'That's the one, why?'

'It doesn't appear as though anyone's still with this vehicle. Are you sending an armed team to the keepers address as well?'

'Stand by.'

There was a brief pause, then the control room operator spoke again, 'Control to Pc Miller, affirmative. An armed team from the Special Operations Unit are travelling to the address at Beckingham right now, control out.'

'Thanks control, out.'

With his eyes fixed firmly on the Range Rover, Jim Miller smiled, then said to his young probationer, 'Well Damian what do you reckon, does Reece sound like a Scottish name to you mate?'

'Could be Jim, could be. Where the fuck is this armed car?'

'Relax young un, the offender's long gone. We're looking at a harmless chunk of metal.'

A few minutes later, two traffic patrol cars came to a stop behind them in the archway. Pc Miller got out of the Panda, walked over and spoke to the Traffic officers, leaving Pc Cox staring at the Range Rover.

From metal boxes within the traffic cars, the four officers removed weapons and ammunition; having donned their Kevlar vests, they quickly formulated a plan to best approach the vehicle.

Approaching on foot was dangerous, but allowed an element of surprise. It could be that the suspect was asleep inside the vehicle. The problem for the armed officers was the tinted glass, they had no view inside the vehicle. They moved forward tactically, two officers had their weapons trained on the vehicle at all times, as the other two moved forward. They alternated this action, until they were literally on top of the suspect vehicle.

One of the officers went forward, staying low beneath the tinted windows. As the other officers trained their weapons on the vehicle, their colleague reached up and opened the rear door. Nobody was lying on the rear seat. The process was repeated with the front door, then finally the boot.

It had taken the armed team ten minutes to clear the Range Rover. There was nobody inside the vehicle. The vehicle had been unlocked, there were no keys in the ignition.

One of the armed traffic officers contacted the control room, he requested a full lift for the Range Rover, so it could be removed to the forensic bay at police headquarters for examination.

While they waited for the vehicle examiners to attend and remove the vehicle, the officers chatted in the car park.

Jim Miller said, 'Is there anything known about this Frederick Reece character?'

One of the traffic officers replied, 'As we were travelling here, we got a message saying there was no record of him on any of our systems, so it looks like he's never come into contact with the police. It's a bit strange, to go from nothing to assaulting a cop with a gun, but stranger things have happened.'

Jim nodded, 'You're right, it does seem a little strange. I expect it will all become clearer, once the SOU lads have raided his house and got him in custody.'

CHAPTER 45

9.30am Sunday 26th March 1986
Beckingham, Nottinghamshire

When news of the Range Rover sighting had first come through to the MCIU, Det Insp Brian Hopkirk had readied a team to travel to Farnsfield, but then Danny made the decision that the Det Insp and his team should instead travel to the keeper's home address at Beckingham, ready to take the owner of the vehicle, Frederick Reece, into custody.

Brian and his team of three detectives now sat in their car on Rankin Lane, well back from the small thatched building that was Mayflower Cottage. The detectives watched as the men from the Special Operations Unit prepared to raid the cottage.

Dressed entirely in black, the armed officers approached the front door of the cottage behind a ballistic shield, while their colleagues trained weapons on the windows of the building and covered the door at the rear.

A team of officers forced the front door and stormed in.

Brian could hear shouts of 'Clear!' emanating from within the cottage.

Within a minute, a message came over the radio being held by Brian, 'The building's clear Inspector, you and your men are safe to approach now. There's no sign of Frederick Reece, the cottage is empty.'

Brian turned to the detective behind the wheel of the car, 'Let's go.'

The CID car pulled up outside the cottage, just as the SOU sergeant stepped out of the front door.

The sergeant held a bundle of documents in his hand, 'You need to see this sir. Frederick Reece is a solicitor, he's got office premises on Spittle Row at Southwell.'

Brian reached for the radio in the car, he immediately passed that information to the control room.

After a brief pause, the radio crackled into life, 'From control, instruct the SOU team you are with to re-deploy to the office premises at Southwell. They are to search the offices and arrest Reece if he is at that location, control out.'

Brian acknowledged the instructions from the control room then turned to the SOU sergeant, 'Right Sarge, I need your team to regroup, then travel with me to the office address in Southwell. You and your team are to raid the office premises, search for Reece and detain him if he's there.'

Immediately the sergeant barked instructions at his men, they scurried with equipment back to their vans.

Brian turned to his own team of detectives, 'Right, Phil and Martin, you stay here and start a search of the cottage, I'll arrange for someone at the office to drive up here with exhibit bags and labels, they can assist you with the search and be transport for you when you've finished. Nigel, as you're driving, you can come with me down to Southwell. We'll keep the exhibits kit in the car with us, in case we need it down there. Phil, if you find anything here that's important, contact me via the control room, ok?'

'No worries, sir.'

The SOU sergeant shouted over, 'We're ready to resume, if you're good to go sir?'

'Ok sarge, we're ready, let's go.'

The two SOU vans sped off down the country lane, followed by the CID car.

CHAPTER 46

10.00am Sunday 26th March 1986
Southwell, Nottinghamshire

Once again Brian Hopkirk was sitting in the car watching the men from the Special Operations Unit, as they prepared to raid the office premises of Richmond Legal Enterprises Limited in Southwell town centre.

Brian's radio burst into life, 'Control to Det Insp Hopkirk, over.'

'Go ahead control, over.'

'Sir, I've a message from Dc Harper. The message is as follows, they've found several photographs of Frederick Reece in the cottage at Beckingham. He states that there's no possibility that Reece is the man who attacked Pc Moreton. The photographs bear no resemblance to the description of the offender provided by Pc Moreton, over.'

'Thanks control. For your information, the office here at Southwell is locked up. SOU are about to raid it now. Would you inform Dc Harper that Dc Helen Bailey is travelling to his location at Beckingham with a vehicle and an exhibits kit, she shouldn't be long.'

'Okay sir, control out.'

Once again, the team from the Special Operations Unit deployed. Using the same method, they approached the premises behind the cover of a ballistic shield then forced entry through the front door. The premises were small, they consisted of a main office, a small kitchenette and a toilet. It took less than a minute for the premises to be cleared by the armed officers.

Having received the all clear from the SOU sergeant, Brian walked into the small office. Immediately, his eyes were drawn to a framed photograph on one of the two desks.

The photograph depicted four men smiling at the camera, from beneath their mortar boards. All four men were dressed in black graduation robes. Brian had seen the photograph before, it was identical to the one he'd recovered from the office at The Grosvenor Hotel.

Brian immediately picked up a telephone in the office and dialled a number from memory.

Danny Flint answered the phone on the first ring, 'Hello, Detective Chief Inspector Flint.'

'Boss its Brian, we've just raided the office of Frederick Reece. Reece isn't here, but there's a photograph on his desk that's identical to the one I recovered from Edward Hall's office at the Grosvenor Hotel. I think the attack on Pc Moreton and our two murders are all connected. The control room have already arranged for Reece's secretary to attend to secure the office as she's a listed keyholder. If the secretary confirms that Frederick Reece is one of the men on this photograph, then I reckon it's fair to say he's just become our third victim and the man who attacked Pc Moreton, is probably our killer.'

'That's great work Brian, let me know straight away if the secretary does identify Reece on the photograph. I'll contact Nottingham University, speak to Rachel and Tina and let them know that we may have already identified one of the other men in the photograph. It makes it even more imperative that we identify the fourth man as a matter of urgency.'

'It looks like we're on the right lines, with the link from university sir, we just need to establish what it is these men are supposed to have done while they were there.'

'That's exactly right, the team you set up here, researching sexual offences around that time, have already come up with a number of interesting possibilities. Keep me posted on the secretary. I'll circulate Frederick Reece as a missing person, then chase up Scenes of Crime, I want the Range Rover forensically examined, as soon as possible.'

'One other thought sir, has anybody established whether the description given by Pc Moreton is similar to that given by Vanessa Hall? Has she been asked about her attacker's voice? Moreton described a strong Scottish accent. I just wondered if that question had been asked of Vanessa Hall?'

'It's a good point Brian, I know it was difficult to get anything from Vanessa Hall initially. I know that Rob and Andy are stymied at the hospital at the moment, the doctors won't let them take a statement from Pc Moreton. I'll instruct Andy Wills to travel to Beeston, speak with Vanessa Hall and ask those questions. Let me know when you've got a definitive answer from the secretary. I've got the press conference to do at eleven o'clock, with Chief Superintendent Wainwright, if you can get it to me before then, it would be better. Great work Brian.'

'Thanks sir, I'll call you as soon as I've got the answer from Reece's secretary.'

CHAPTER 47

10.00am Sunday 26th March 1986
Clifton, Nottinghamshire

Paul Fencham smiled at his own reflection in the mirror.

For the first time in years, he felt like a winner. The dingy, scruffy bedsit he stood in, didn't bother him today. He couldn't give a shit about the half-empty cartons of Indian and Chinese takeaway food, scattered all over the floor, or the pile of smelly, dirty washing stacked at the foot of the disgusting single bed with the stained duvet on.

After today's press conference at police headquarters, he would definitely be on the up.

It had been three o'clock that morning, when he'd finally realised the meaning of the coded message. He now fully understood, what the message painted on the walls of the murder victim's houses meant.

It had been so simple, when he finally stumbled on the answer.

After hours of racking his brains he had cried out loud in frustration, 'Oh for God's sake!'

In that instant, the answer had come to him in a blinding flash of inspiration.

That was the answer. For God's sake. God was the answer.

Suddenly, he had remembered all those long, boring Sundays as a child, when his deeply religious parents forced him to go to Sunday School, instead of allowing him to play football on the local recreation ground with his pals.

He vividly recalled the painful memory of being given a bible reference every week, that he then had to study. Ready to repeat the passage it referred to, verbatim the following Sunday.

The message scrawled on the walls was a bible reference, pure and simple.

As soon as he had added the correct punctuation, to the numbers and letters that had been written in blood, it became clear.

With punctuation in place the message now read E.C21. V24-25.

Feeling elated he grabbed the Gideon's bible he'd stolen from a hotel some years earlier. Excitedly, he had then quickly thumbed through the pages of the Old Testament.

There it was.

The Book of Exodus, Chapter 21, Verses 24 to 25.

Smiling, he had read the verses aloud, 'An eye for an eye and a tooth for a tooth, a hand for a hand and a foot for a foot. Burning for burning, wound for wound, stripe for stripe.'

He had danced around the room with joy, before another lightning bolt of inspiration had come to him. It was the Book of Exodus, the red top newspapers loved to either give the serial killer a nickname or the cluster of murders a title. He grabbed his old Olivetti typewriter, put in a clean sheet of A4 paper and began to type.

The first words he typed in capital letters were, 'THE EXODUS MURDERS'.

An hour later and the typewriter keys again fell silent. It was the best article he'd written for years, decades even.

He had spent the entire morning on the telephone, to the crime desk editors of various tabloids, trying to sell the story. The Daily Mirror had made him the best offer. They had agreed to pay him the huge amount of ten thousand pounds immediately after the press conference being held at police headquarters that morning, on the single proviso that the police didn't disregard the theory out of hand. The Mirror were going to send their top crime writer, to ask questions at the news conference, he would be the sole judge as to whether the story had credibility.

Fencham knew the story was credible, by midday he would be a wealthy man, who knows, there might even be a future for him, working for The Daily Mirror.

He splashed hot water on his face in preparation to shave. He wanted to look his best for the press conference, after all today was his big day.

He couldn't wait for the press conference to start at eleven o'clock.

CHAPTER 48

10.00am Sunday 26th March 1986
Farndon, Nottinghamshire

The Watcher had changed his mind, he'd decided to check on the huge maggot that was Frederick Reece first. He had stopped off at the disused maggot farm before he went to the chapel to celebrate the Lords day. He didn't want to be distracted in his worship by thinking about Reece. He knew if he checked on him first, he would then be able to forget about him until Monday morning.

As he drove the Land Rover down the dirt track towards the disused buildings, he constantly checked the surrounding area. Nothing had changed, there were no fresh vehicle tracks heading towards the drab concrete buildings. His training and background caused him to constantly review, to check everything and leave nothing to chance. Observational prowess was just one of his skills. It was one of many that had been instilled in him over the years, being able to kill another human being without a moment's hesitation was another.

He parked his vehicle behind the buildings, so it couldn't be seen from the main road, that ran past the farm entrance just four hundred yards away.

Taking care not to mark his suit on the filthy Land Rover, he got out and walked to the entrance of the building. The door had long gone, the entrance was now covered by a sheet of corrugated iron. The ground was quite firm underfoot, but it was still a dirt path. He'd taken great pride in getting his clothes and appearance looking smart for church. He didn't want to undo all that good work by being careless where he trod now.

He pulled back the sheet of corrugated iron so he could gain access into the decrepit building. He stepped inside, paused and allowed his eyes time to adjust to the gloomy light, before walking further into the building, eventually coming to the room where he had imprisoned Reece.

Reece was awake, his eyes widened with fear when he saw the Watcher walk in.

Saying nothing to his captive, he walked over to a plastic carton that was full of water. He picked up the water and walked back to where Reece sat on the cold floor.

Reaching forward, in one decisive movement, he ripped off the brown Gaffer tape that covered Reece's mouth. He grabbed a handful of the man's receding hair and forced his head back.

He poured the water from the carton directly into his captive's open mouth, forcing him to drink. The bound solicitor, managed to swallow two big mouthfuls of the cold water before he almost choked.

Reece spluttered and coughed, as the water trickled down his windpipe.

The Watcher waited for him to stop coughing before returning the water to the other side of the room. He then picked up the roll of brown Gaffer tape, ready to gag his prisoner again.

Reece took the opportunity to speak now the gag had been removed, 'Who are you? Why are you doing this? I haven't done anything to you.'

The Watcher ignored the questions, stepped forward and reapplied the tape across the mouth of Reece. He checked that he'd left his prisoners nose clear of the tape, so he could breathe and then stood up.

He started to walk out of the room, but heard Reece screaming muffled cries at him.

He stopped, turned and reached inside his jacket pocket taking out a small laminated photograph.

The Watcher said nothing, he squatted down in front of his captive and held the photograph directly in front of the fat solicitor's face.

Suddenly, Reece turned from being angry and arrogant, into a cowering, trembling wreck.

He shook his head, then began to cry and sob into the Gaffer tape, tears now streamed from his eyes and rolled down his cheeks.

The Watcher stared straight into Reece's terrified eyes and said in a growl, 'Tomorrow you will pay.'

He then stood up and replaced the photograph in his jacket.

As he watched his captor leave the room, once again Reece could feel the warmth of his own urine around his groin as he emptied his bladder, but this time the warmth was accompanied by the disgusting stench of his own faeces as the contents of his bowel also spilled into his trousers.

CHAPTER 49

10.00am Sunday 26th March 1986
University of Nottingham, Nottinghamshire

Dc Rachel Moore and Sergeant Tina Prowse had accessed the vast campus of Nottingham University through the North Entrance, driving in from Derby Road.

Tina said, 'Aren't there any security barriers to go through?'

Rachel replied, 'No Tina, the university is an open site, anybody can come onto the campus at any time. There are security patrols twenty-four hours a day, seven days a week, but there are always quite a few problems on the campus. More so in the summer time, than now.'

'How come you know so much about the university?'

'Before I transferred to Mansfield, I was stationed at Hyson Green. Although the uni's not in the Hyson Green area, I was called over here a few times, when a policewoman was needed.'

'How did you find working at Hyson Green?'

'Honestly, I hated every minute of it. The best thing I ever did was transferring to Mansfield, working with Chief Inspector Flint is brilliant, he gives everyone a chance and treats everyone the same.'

'What was it like working on the Coal Killer enquiry?'

'At the time, it was bloody hard graft. It's something I try not to talk about too much, for obvious reasons.'

'Oh God! I'm so sorry Rachel. I totally forgot what that creep Jimmy Wade did to you. I can be such a clumsy cow at times.'

'Don't worry Tina, it's all water under the bridge now. Wade's in the best place, he's locked up in Rampton and will never set foot outside of those walls ever again. I've tried hard to move on, I try not to think too much about what happened. I refuse to let that psychopath ruin the rest of my life.'

'I'm going to embarrass you now Rachel. You were one of the main reasons I asked to spend some time on the MCIU. As soon as I realised that under the graduate entry scheme, I could cherry pick which departments I wanted to experience, I applied to come onto the MCIU as soon as I could. I don't think you're aware just how highly regarded you are by other policewomen in the force.'

'Yep, that's done it, you've officially embarrassed me Tina.'

Both women laughed, then Rachel said, 'Just work hard while you're here Tina. I know the only reason you're on the unit is because of the graduate entry scheme, but nobody resents you being here, if you can keep coming up with little gems like the link you established yesterday, you'll fit right in. Let's see if we can find Jim Cronin, shall we.'

Rachel drove onto Cripps Hill, then along Cut Through Lane, down onto East Drive before she finally parked the car outside the old Nissen hut, that served as the University Security's control building.

Before the women left Mansfield police station, Rachel had phoned ahead to the security office and established that Jim Cronin was indeed working that morning.

The two detectives walked into the hut and sitting at his desk waiting for them was Jim Cronin.

Cronin stood up to greet the two women. He was well over six feet tall and weighed over eighteen stone. He had a full head of hair, which was now snowy white. The hair was the only give away of the man's age, he was still extremely fit and strong despite his sixty plus years.

He held out a huge hand in greeting towards Rachel Moore, 'Detective Moore, how lovely to see you again, and looking so well after that dreadful business.'

It was the second reference that day, about the attack made on her by Jimmy Wade. Inside she cringed.

'It's good to see you too Jim, you look extremely fit as usual, you'll have to let us ladies have your secret, minus the white hair of course.'

Jim smiled, 'It's clean living ladies, pure and simple.'

'Jim, let me introduce you to Sergeant Tina Prowse, she's recently joined the MCIU, so I'm guessing you two haven't met.'

'Good to meet you Tina.'

The same massive hand was once again offered in greeting, then Jim said, 'Right, before we get down to the reason for your visit, I was about to make myself a coffee, so can I get you two anything to drink?

Rachel looked at Tina, 'Coffee?'

'That would be lovely, thanks.'

'Two coffees please Jim.'

'How do you take it?'

In unison, Rachel and Tina said, 'White no sugar, thanks.'

Jim laughed, 'Sounds like you two have been working together for ever!'

Five minutes later, all three were sitting at a briefing table in the same hut drinking their coffees. Rachel took out the small framed photograph of four men standing in their university robes.

'Do you know any of these men Jim?' she asked.

'Unfortunately, I know them all lass, that's the four musketeers. They were a royal pain in the arse when they were here, getting up to all sorts of mischief. They always knew just how far to push things, but they sailed very close to being expelled on a couple of occasions.'

'What was the main issue with them?' asked Tina.

'Their shameful attitude to female students and women in general was the problem. A couple of them thought they were God's gift and sometimes wouldn't take no for an answer, if you know what I mean.'

'In what way?'

'Any female student was considered fair game to them, the more attractive the better. There were numerous complaints about inappropriate sexual advances, but it was never enough to chuck them out.'

'What's their names?'

Jim Cronin took the small photograph in his huge hand, he pointed out the men as he said their names. His index finger moved across the photograph, from left to right, stopping at the different faces as he identified them.

'This first one, on the end of the photo, is Cavalie Naylor, he was the quietest of the bunch but easily led. He was doing Business Studies and got a first-class degree. Standing next to him, holding his mortar board in his hand, is Frederick Reece, he was a real pain in the arse. He was the ugliest, most unfit one of the bunch, but thought he was a proper

Casanova. Loved the ladies did that one. He studied Law, and also achieved a top degree. The next man is Edward Hall, another one who was a real smooth operator. I dealt with a lot of complaints about him. At one time, I thought he may have been dabbling in drugs, but I could never prove anything. He was another arrogant, cocky bastard who thought he could get away with anything. He was doing a degree course that was in some way related to the leisure industry. Out of the four of them, he was the only one who left with a shit degree, but he always was a lazy sod.'

Jim Cronin then tapped the photograph, his index finger drumming on the face of the last man.

'Last and most definitely least, Maurice Dennington. I'm surprised you didn't recognise him Rachel, he's in the job.'

'The only Dennington I've ever heard of on the job is a Superintendent.'

'The very same, Superintendent Maurice Dennington. I don't know what he's like now Rachel, but back then, the man was a pig. He had zero respect for women. I lost count of the amount of complaints I had to deal with, because of his arrogant attitude and the aggression he would show towards any woman who rebuffed his advances. I tried, unsuccessfully, on a number of occasions to get him chucked out, but nobody was listening. Academically, he was a brilliant student, he left here with a first in Law. For some reason, unbeknown to the rest of us, the Vice Chancellor always appeared very impressed by him.'

'Apart from Reece and Dennington, the four of them were studying for different degrees, how come they were so close? Did they all have something else in common, that pulled them together?' asked Tina.

'Apart from being a pain in the backside, you mean. The thing that brought them all together was rugby. All four played rugby union for the university team. Dennington was an outstanding fly half, at one time he was being tipped to play for England, but then he suffered a serious knee injury, which put paid to that. Even after the injury he continued to play for the university team, but any thought of international honours had gone. Now I think about it, that was probably why the Vice Chancellor let him get away with so much crap.'

'Was there a natural leader of the group?'

'Dennington was the leader. Without a doubt, he was the driving force behind most of their escapades.'

'Thanks Jim, this is all really helpful', said Rachel.

'Rachel, can I ask why you want to know so much about these four idiots?'

'It's no secret Jim, two of them, Cavalie Naylor and Edward Hall are now dead. They were murdered. Can you think of any reason, why somebody would want to kill them?'

'Not off the top of my head I can't, but while they were here these four individuals must have made a lot of enemies, they upset an awful lot of people.'

'Upset enough, for somebody to want them dead?'

'The thing is, with this four anything's possible. I can't prove anything but I genuinely believe they were involved in a lot of incidents here, that were never identified as being down to them at the time. I can think of several very serious, sexual assaults that happened around that time, that still remain undetected.'

'Any incident in particular, that sticks out for you?' asked Tina.

Jim Cronin looked troubled, he stroked his chin thoughtfully, 'There is one that sticks in my mind, a dreadful assault on a young girl, during Freshers Week in 1977.'

'Tell us about that, Jim', pressed the young sergeant.

Slowly, he stood up and walked over to a large set of grey drawers. He opened one of the drawers and thumbed through some old files. Eventually, he found the file he was looking for. He removed a mustard coloured folder from the drawer and walked back to the table.

'This won't make for pleasant listening, I'm afraid.'

'Go on Jim', urged Rachel.

Jim Cronin opened the file and began talking to the detectives as he scanned the contents, 'Freshers Week, 1977. A young student just down from Scotland, Jean Mackay, had been in Nottingham with a couple of other students, enjoying a few drinks for the Freshers celebrations. Miss Mackay had only arrived in Nottingham that week, she wasn't a drinker, so at ten thirty she decided to catch the last bus from town. The bus she caught that night travelled from the city centre along Derby Road to the university. Her friends decided to stay in town, intending to go on to a nightclub. Anyway, from the enquiries made at the time, it would appear that Jean caught the bus okay. Her journey was uneventful and she got off the bus on Derby Road, outside the North Entrance. She was staying at the Hugh Stewart halls of residence, so began walking along Cripps Hill, before turning onto Lenton Hall Drive. The poor girl never made it to the halls of residence. She was found, just after midnight, on The Downs by one of my security patrols.'

'What are The Downs?'

'The Downs is an area of open grassland that bisects the campus and runs alongside Lenton Hall Drive. Back then a lot of it was quite overgrown and was pitch black at night.'

'What had happened to Jean Mackay?' asked Rachel.

'She'd been subjected to a vicious sexual assault by four men. I know that four men were involved, because when she was examined later by the police surgeon, the doctor found four different blood groups in the swabs he took. Four different blood groups means four different semen samples which means four different men. In those days, there was no such thing as this new-fangled DNA, that you've got now.'

'What could Jean Mackay tell the police about the attack and her attackers?'

'Absolutely nothing, the poor woman couldn't speak, the attack traumatised her so badly, she just withdrew into herself and never uttered a word. Look in your police records, you'll find far more detail there than I've got. I just remember it was an awful attack. When she was found, she'd been stripped naked, subjected to a number of serious sexual assaults, been badly beaten and left for dead in pitch black darkness in the middle of a field. It was an horrendous assault, one of the worst I've seen both in my police career and my time on security here.'

'Was anybody ever charged?' asked Tina.

'No. This attack happened a few years after I came here, I'd only been left the force three years, so I still had a lot of contacts in the CID who kept me informed, on the quiet, how things were progressing with the enquiries. I know the CID did a lot of enquiries here at the time, interviewing people, getting statements, but they had very little to go on and the university authorities wanted to close down the enquiry as soon as possible. That kind of publicity wasn't what they wanted for their university.'

Tina shook her head and said, 'That's a disgusting attitude.'

'I know lass, but that's how it works here. The university relies on the fees paid by students, foreign students in particular. The publicity generated by that sort of incident would be very damaging to the precious reputation of the university, it was effectively swept under the carpet as soon as possible. Once it had all died down, I was tasked with improving the lighting around the campus and ensuring there were more security patrols around the site during the hours of darkness.'

'What about your so called 'four musketeers', were they ever questioned?' asked Rachel.

'I believe they were, your police records will confirm it. I just remember that they couldn't be connected to it at the time. Personally speaking, I wouldn't have put it past them. Back then Dennington was an arrogant, nasty piece of work and the other three would follow him like pathetic sheep and do anything he asked.'

'And what about Jean Mackay, what happened to her?' asked Tina.

'She dropped out of her course. She was here to study medicine, I believe her dream was to become a doctor. The attack affected her so badly, there was no way she could have continued on her course. Eventually, when she was well enough to be discharged from hospital, her mother took Jean back to Glasgow.'

'What about her father Jim, did he travel down as well?'

'I don't think he did, I seem to recall he was in the military and couldn't get here, but I'm not a hundred per cent sure on that. I've got mum and dads names in the file.'

'Go on.'

Jim glanced at the file in his hands and said, 'Let me see, mum's name was Glenys Mackay and dad's was Ben Mackay.'

'Thanks Jim, you said mum took her back to Glasgow, is that where she was from?'

Jim Cronin looked at the documentation in front of him again and said, 'I've got her home address in the file. It's from 1977, but it might still be relevant.'

'What's the address?'

'Number 16, Crosshill Road, Bishopton. I think Bishopton is a small town just outside Glasgow, not far from the airport.'

Tina quickly noted down the address and said, 'Thanks Jim.'

Jim replaced the folder back in the filing cabinet, turned to Rachel and said, 'Do you think the other two in the photo, Reece and Dennington, could be in danger then Rachel?'

'I really don't know, its early days yet. The murders of Naylor and Hall could be totally unconnected, this is just one of many lines of enquiry we're looking at.'

'Well, if you need anything else Rachel, just give me a ring, or better still come and see me, my doors always open. Before you leave, I'll take you over to The Downs and show you the Hugh Stewart halls of residence, just so you can get an idea of the layout of things.'

'Thanks Jim.'

Half an hour later, after seeing The Downs and the halls of residence for themselves, the two detectives were driving out of the university.

'Rachel, can I ask you something?'

'You can ask me anything you want.'

'Why did you tell Jim Cronin that we still didn't know, whether or not the murders of Naylor and Hall were connected?'

'It's a habit I've developed, you always need to play your cards close to your chest Tina. I know Jim's an ex-detective, but I also know that whatever I tell him, will be all over this campus within two days. Never tell anybody, anything that hasn't already been released to the press, if you do and it comes out later, it can seriously bite you on the arse.'

The rest of the journey back to Mansfield was made in silence.

CHAPTER 50

11.00am Sunday 26th March 1986
Nottinghamshire Police Headquarters

Danny Flint took his seat next to Detective Chief Superintendent Wainwright, he stared out at the television cameras and assembled reporters from various newspapers. He hated press conferences with a passion, but he was pragmatic enough to realise that there were occasions where the media, and the press in particular, were a huge help to the police. There were several very well documented cases where a press release had helped to drive an investigation forward.

He'd discussed, with Bill Wainwright, exactly what to provide the press with on this occasion. The two men had agreed that it was prudent, at this stage of the enquiry, not to link the two murders.

The information that Frederick Reece's secretary had identified her boss as being one of the four men in the photograph, came in just minutes before they were due to meet the press. The two senior detectives were satisfied their enquiries were being channelled in the right direction, they both believed that as soon as they established the reason behind the revenge attacks, on the four men, they would establish the identity of the killer.

Neither man could see any benefit in linking the murders at this stage, they were only too aware of the media frenzy whipped up whenever the possibility of a serial killer being on the loose was revealed.

Danny, in particular, was satisfied they were not random killings and that only the four men in the photo were at risk.

Chief Superintendent Wainwright was prepared to back his Detective Chief Inspector's judgement.

It was Wainwright who started off the press conference, by giving a brief overview of the two murders they were currently investigating. He kept detail to a minimum and made it clear to the media at the end of his presentation, that there was nothing to suggest at this time, that the two murders were linked in any way. He then made a general appeal to the public, to come forward if they had seen anything at Underwood or Beeston, that they believed to be unusual or in any way suspicious.

As he concluded his part of the presentation, he said, 'I'll now hand you over to Detective Chief Inspector Flint of the Major Crime Investigation Unit, if you have any questions please address them directly to him.'

A hand was raised at the back of the room, which Danny acknowledged.

'Sally Green from the Daily Mail. Chief Inspector Flint, how certain can you be that the two murders aren't linked? It seems a bit of a coincidence, that two murders were committed on the same day.'

'Although the murders were discovered on the same day, they had been committed on different dates.'

'Where was the first murder committed, Underwood or Beeston?'

'It would appear that the murder at Underwood was committed first.'

Another hand was raised.

'Bill Prentice, the Express. I understand you've made an arrest already. Was that person arrested in connection with the Underwood enquiry, the Beeston enquiry, or both.'

'That's true, we did make an early arrest in connection with the Underwood enquiry, that person has cooperated with us fully and is currently on bail pending further enquiries. Are there any other questions?'

A white-haired man sitting on the front row, slowly raised his hand.

Danny pointed to the man and asked, 'Yes, on the front row. What's your question?'

'Chief Inspector Flint, why haven't you released details of the identical messages, painted on the walls at both the murder scenes?'

Danny was totally shocked by the question, it showed and he remained silent.

'Chief Inspector, I can already see by the expression on your face that my information's correct. What significance do you put on the messages that were painted in blood at the scenes?'

There were gasps from the other reporters.

The white-haired man continued, now warming to his theme, 'Are you still maintaining these murders aren't linked?'

Bill Wainwright tried to intervene, 'That will be all for now, thank you. No further questions at this time, our investigation is ongoing and we'll keep you appraised of any new developments. Thank you.'

The man on the front row was not about to be put off so easily, 'Chief Inspector, The Daily Mirror newspaper, who

I represent, will be running a front-page story tomorrow morning, under the headline 'The Exodus Murders'. Do you have any comment?'

Bill Wainwright stood up, virtually pulled a stunned Danny to his feet and said in a raised voice, 'We have no further comment at this time. Thank you.'

Sitting at the back of the room, behind the assembled reporters, Paul Fencham grinned, there was no way he wouldn't get paid for his story now. He had to admire Steve Galpin, the chief crime reporter from the Daily Mirror, the way he had played the two detectives was masterful.

Away from the press conference and out of earshot of any reporters, Bill Wainwright turned on Danny, 'What the fuck was all that about Danny?'

'I don't know sir.'

'Well I fucking know! Someone in your team has been talking out of turn, somebody's talked to the fucking press and I want to know who!'

'Sir, none of my team would do that.'

'Really! Well somebody has Chief Inspector, I suggest you make it your fucking mission to find out exactly who!'

'Yes sir', said a totally crestfallen Danny.

'And while you're doing that, I'll go and see the Chief, to try and explain this fucking debacle. I've never been so fucking embarrassed in all my service! Get this fucking mess sorted Danny, now!'

Bill Wainwright stormed off leaving a shell shocked, perplexed Danny alone in the corridor.

Danny walked slowly back to his car, his mind was racing.

Mentally, he began compiling a list of the people he knew had attended both scenes. It was useless, everybody in the

MCIU knew that the messages on the wall were at both the scenes.

He had to face facts, somebody had tipped off the press and at that moment in time, Danny had no idea how he was going to discover who it was.

He dreaded reading the story in the newspaper tomorrow. His mind raced, as he speculated exactly what other details of the crimes scenes had been leaked.

Danny was worried that any leaked information would have a massive effect on the enquiry.

The reporter who had asked the embarrassing questions had stated he was from the Daily Mirror, Danny decided that the best course of action would be to call the editor of the newspaper when he got back to his office, to establish exactly what detail to expect in tomorrow's paper.

Somehow, he had to attempt a damage limitation exercise.

The last thing the enquiry needed was for details of the messages to be published, which could unleash the real possibility of copycat killers.

Maybe, he could get the editor of the Daily Mirror to delay publishing all the details, he might be satisfied with releasing a limited amount of information at this time, in return for the promise of exclusivity, once the killer had been caught.

Danny knew he had to try something; as he drove back to Mansfield, he rehearsed his planned conversation with the editor of the newspaper.

CHAPTER 51

2.00pm Sunday 26th March 1986
Major Crime Investigation Unit, Mansfield

The entire MCIU were assembled in the large office, waiting for the afternoon de brief. Brian Hopkirk's team had returned from Southwell and Beckingham having completed their searches of Frederick Reece's home and office.

Rachel and Tina had returned from the university, Rob was back from the hospital after finally being allowed by the doctors to obtain a full statement from Pc Moreton. The last one to arrive was Andy Wills, who had travelled back from Beeston after speaking to Vanessa Hall.

Danny opened his office door and shouted, 'Rob, Brian get in here!'

There was an edge to Danny's voice that everybody in the room immediately picked up on.

The two inspectors walked in to the office, Rob closed the door behind him.

'Sit down both of you, this is for your ears only. We've got a fucking mole!'

'What?' asked Rob.

'The press conference this morning was a fucking nightmare. I was totally ambushed. Somebody out there, has tipped the press off about the writing in blood on the walls at both scenes. The Daily Mirror's running a story tomorrow morning under the headline, 'The Exodus Murders'. They intend announcing to the world that we've got a serial killer on the loose here in Nottinghamshire.'

'Bloody hell sir, that's just what we don't need. Any idea who it is?' asked Brian.

'No, I haven't. You two are much closer to the people in your respective teams than I am. I want you to find out who the fuck it is, I want a name. A unit such as this can't survive if information is constantly leaked to the press. I won't tolerate it.'

Both men nodded, then Rob asked, 'How are we going to prepare for the shit storm tomorrow, when the newspaper hits the streets?'

'I've been on the phone for an hour, trying to negotiate a deal with the editor of the Daily Mirror. He's agreed to hold off releasing all the detailed information they've been given for a day, in exchange for exclusivity on the story, as and when we catch our killer. Basically, we've got another twenty-four hours to catch our man. The full details of both murder scenes will be published on Tuesday morning. Brian, for the rest of the day, I want you to concentrate on nothing else but getting to the bottom of this leak. Talk to everyone who had access to both scenes, start by talking to Geoff Naylor, he's the only civilian who's seen the writing, it's just possible he's said something to somebody as well.'

'Ok sir, I'm on it. There's another possibility though.'
'Which is?'
'The killer has spoken directly to the press himself.'

'The editor of the paper assured me the information was from a legitimate source, that he wouldn't divulge. I think he would have been overjoyed to tell the world that the killer himself had been in touch with the fucking Daily Mirror. If there's no other bright ideas, let's get the debrief started.'

It was a harsh slap down and Brian felt admonished and a little ridiculed, but didn't protest. He could see Danny was in no mood to listen to his protestations.

All three detectives walked back into the hushed briefing room.

There was still an edge to Danny's voice as he said, 'Brian, tell us about the development linking the two murders to the attack on Pc Moreton.'

'It would appear that the attack on our colleague, was carried out by the same person responsible for killing Cavalie Naylor and Edward Hall. You've all seen the photograph of the four men at Nottingham University, recovered from Edward Hall's office, well, the identical photograph has been recovered today from the office of a man called Frederick Reece. Reece has been missing since yesterday afternoon, we believe it was his Range Rover that was being checked by Pc Moreton when he was attacked. It's fair to assume that Reece is the latest victim of our killer. As we have no body as yet, we have to consider the possibility that he's still alive. Three of the four men in the photograph have now been identified. They are Cavalie Naylor, Edward Hall and Frank Reece.'

Rachel Moore spoke up, 'We've now identified the fourth man. From records at the university, we believe the fourth man is Maurice Dennington, according to the head of security at the university he is now on the job.'

Danny spoke, 'Do you mean Superintendent Maurice Dennington?'

'Yes sir', said Rachel before continuing, 'I've checked and he's recently been placed in charge of the newly formed Sexual Offences Investigation Team.'

Danny took a minute to digest that information, then said, 'Is there anything else from the university?'

'All four men were quite well known by security at the time they were there. They were all members of the university's rugby union team and were considered as being jack the lads. There were numerous complaints involving the four of them, in particular their attitudes and overtly sexual conduct to the female students. '

'Anything in particular, involving them?'

'No sir, but the head of security did recall a particularly vicious sexual assault on a young Scottish student, that happened at the time these four men were at the university. The attack couldn't be linked to them, but he strongly suspected them of being involved.'

'What was the name of the female student?'

'Her name's Jean Mackay. The effect of the attack on her was so bad, she had to leave the university and went home, abandoning her studies. The university provided me with the last address they had for her. She lives in a small town called Bishopton, near Glasgow airport.'

Danny was deep in thought.

'Right, thanks Rachel. The team researching sexual assaults for the dates Hall and Naylor were at university, have you found any details of this attack on Jean Mackay?'

Dc Fran Jeffries spoke up, 'I've been researching that very assault. It was horrific sir. Four men attacked her during Freshers Week. She'd only been at the university, just over a week when she was attacked. Her mother came down to Nottingham after the attack and as soon as the girl was well enough to be discharged from hospital, took her back to Glasgow.'

'What are the details of the attack, Fran?'

'From what I can gather from our records, it would appear that Jean was out celebrating Freshers Week in Nottingham with a couple of friends. Jean wasn't a big drinker so decided to catch the bus from town to the university gates and then walk to the Halls of Residence while her friends stayed in the city to go on to a nightclub. Jean was attacked in the grounds of the university, she was found about a hundred yards from her Halls of Residence on an area of open land called The Downs. The attack was sustained, violent and degrading. The poor woman was raped anally and vaginally, beaten and left for dead, the clothes she had been wearing were scattered all over The Downs.'

'What enquiries were done at the time?'

'It was a major enquiry at the time boss and the CID carried out a lot of enquiries, putting a great deal of time and effort in to finding her attackers, but to no avail. There was very little forensic evidence at the time and no witnesses. I've checked with property, there are no surviving samples from the attack. So, any chance of possible DNA evidence we may have had, isn't there anymore.'

'Were the four in the photograph, ever questioned at the time?'

'I checked for Naylor and Hall, they were only ever interviewed in the same way as many other male students, were questioned. I will re-check after the briefing to see if it was any different in respect of Frederick Reece and Maurice Dennington. There's no record of any arrests ever being made in connection with the attack. Certainly, the records I've seen that relate to Naylor and Hall had them giving alibis for each other. I will check for Reece and Dennington now, but I suspect it will be a similar scenario.'

'Thanks Fran, keep digging. I want you to find out everything you can about that particular attack.'

'Yes sir.'

Danny then turned to Andy Wills, 'Andy, you've been to see Vanessa Hall again, could she remember anything else about her attacker?'

'Nothing else description wise, but interestingly she did recall that when he spoke to her it was with a very distinctive Scottish accent.'

'So, that's Vanessa Hall and Pc Moreton who've said our man speaks with a Scottish accent.'

Brian Hopkirk spoke up, 'Its three people now sir, Frederick Reece's secretary told me about a visitor looking for Reece, who came into the office on Saturday. Her description of this man, is almost identical to the description given by Pc Moreton of his attacker, she also stated he spoke with a soft, Scottish accent.'

Danny furiously scribbled notes into his large notebook, then said, 'Fran, you said that Jean Mackay's mother had come to collect the daughter. Rachel, when you were at the university today, could Jim Cronin give any information about the girl's parents? In particular, anything about her father?'

'I asked him that very question this morning, from memory he thought her father was in the army or similar, that was why he wasn't available to come and see his daughter. From the university records, next of kin were recorded as being Glenys Mackay, mother and Ben Mackay, father.'

Danny was deep in thought for a while, then said, 'Rachel, I want you and Tina to go home and get an overnight bag. Contact East Midlands Airport, I want you on the next available flight to Glasgow. I'll make a call to the Special Branch office at the airport, so we can waive the normal boarding procedures. Contact the CID in Glasgow and arrange for an officer to meet you at the airport with a car. I want you to visit the address in Bishopton, interview Jean Mackay and ascertain everything you can about this horrendous assault.

I realise it will be a delicate enquiry, that runs a real risk of opening old wounds, but I think it's an enquiry that needs to be done. I want you to liaise with me regularly about any and all developments in Scotland. Fran, I'd like you to also research Glenys and Ben Mackay, I want to know everything there is to know about them. In the meantime, everybody keep doing what you're doing, things are starting to come together. Brian, you know what I want you to concentrate on. Rob, you and I need to go and speak with Superintendent Dennington.'

Danny and Rob walked back into Danny's office.

Danny sat down heavily and said quietly, 'Close the door Rob.'

Rob closed the door and sat down.

Danny said, 'Do you think I was out of order, slapping Brian down like that?'

'If I'm being honest, yes I do. Don't worry about it, Brian will just get on with the job, if anyone can find the leak it will be him, especially now he's stinging a bit, after your rebuke. He's a big boy Danny, he'll soon forget it, he'll probably admit to himself that it was a pretty stupid suggestion.'

'Okay, I'll talk to him later anyway. Thanks Rob.'

Danny picked up the telephone and dialled the number for the control room.

'Do you have the contact details for Superintendent Dennington of the Sexual Offences Investigation Team?'

There was a pause.

'Okay, I understand. Contact him at home please and tell him to contact me on this number as a matter of urgency. Thank you.'

Danny replaced the phone and said to Rob, 'It's his day off today.'

Less than two minutes later the telephone in Danny's office began to ring.

Danny picked up the phone, 'Chief Inspector Flint, can I help you?'

'Chief Inspector, It's Superintendent Dennington, I've just been asked to contact you by the control room, what's the problem?'

'Thanks for calling so promptly, I appreciate it's your day off but I need to talk to you as a matter of urgency about a delicate situation that's developing.'

'I don't appreciate you talking to me in riddles, Chief Inspector, tell me what the problem is.'

'It's not a conversation I'm prepared to have on the phone, but it is urgent and I need to speak with you today.'

'Very well. Let me make this clear, do not under any circumstances come to my home. I will meet you at my office in one hour.'

Danny hung up the phone and turned to Rob, 'He's driving over to his new offices at Carlton in Lindrick, he'll see us there. He's just told me that under no circumstances, should I go and see him at his home address. He'll be at his office in one hour. Pompous git!'

'Good of him to grant us an audience boss', grinned Rob.

Danny smiled, 'Isn't it just.'

CHAPTER 52

3.00pm Sunday 26th March 1986
Teversal Manor, Cotgrave, Nottinghamshire

Brian Hopkirk was still seething.

The more he thought about it, the more he realised it had been a dumb suggestion. He was fully aware of the guidelines editors had to adhere to when dealing with information provided by a criminal source. He knew they had an obligation to disclose any communication from a person suspected of a criminal act.

He had only been trying to help when he spoke up, if he'd been alone with Danny it wouldn't have mattered so much, but it felt wrong for him to be verbally slapped down in such a condescending manner, in front of his colleague Rob.

He wouldn't dwell on it now, he would talk to Danny about it later, in private. Right now, he needed to concentrate on having a conversation with Geoff Naylor. Brian was acutely aware that it was still a very raw time for the old man, he knew he would need to be tactful and tread carefully.

Having walked up the long gravel driveway, he pressed the ornate doorbell.

He waited a minute or so, then pressed it again, this time there was movement within and he heard a croaky voice shout, 'Just a minute!'

Brian waited patiently at the door, a few minutes passed before he heard someone approaching.

The door slowly opened, standing there looking unwashed and dishevelled in crumpled clothes, was Geoff Naylor. His skin looked ashen, his eyes were red rimmed and bloodshot, Brian could immediately smell stale whisky emanating from the grieving father. He held out his warrant card and said, 'Mr Naylor, my name's Detective Inspector Brian Hopkirk, I'm one of the officers making enquiries into the death of your son. Something has come up that I need to speak to you about, as a matter of urgency.'

Without speaking, Naylor turned and started to walk back down the beautifully decorated hallway, he waved his hand indicating the detective should follow him.

Brian followed the shuffling man into the vast kitchen.

Naylor took a pint glass from one of the cupboards and filled it with cold water from the tap. He drank a full glass, then repeated the process. He took a small pill box from his pocket and slipped a black pill under his tongue, he then sat down, opposite the standing detective.

At last Geoff Naylor spoke, 'Take a seat Inspector, what can I do for you?'

Brian sat down opposite Naylor and said quietly, 'Mr Naylor, are you okay? Is there anyone I can get, to come over and be with you?'

'My son, Inspector, can you get my son?'

'No, I can't do that for you and I'm sorry.'

'What was so urgent that you needed to see me on a Sunday?'

'There's been a development that you should know about. Unfortunately, the press have now got hold of some of the details about Cavalie's death.'

'That was always going to happen Inspector, what's that got to do with me?'

'Unfortunately, it could really hinder our investigation, they're aware of details we would have preferred to keep back.'

'Won't the press knowing everything help your enquiries Inspector?'

'Sometimes it does, but on this occasion, it can only hinder us. Has anybody asked you any questions about your son's death, Mr Naylor?'

'Look, I'll be honest with you, I'd had a few drinks the other night, I rang a friend and had a conversation with him. I can't recall too much of what was discussed. Let's just say I'd had more than a few drinks.'

'Why call that particular friend?'

'He's an old army buddy that now works for one of the local papers.'

'What was it that you needed to discuss with him?'

'I was annoyed when you lot released that bastard Christopher Baker so quickly. I didn't understand how you couldn't see that he's the person responsible for Cav's death?'

Brian could see that the old man was close to tears, he didn't want to push him too far.

'Would you mind if I had a quick word with your friend?'

'I don't see why not, his name's Paul Fencham, he works for the Nottingham Evening Standard. If you give me a minute, I've got his phone number here somewhere.'

The old man stood up and left the room, he returned a few minutes later clutching a piece of notepaper with Fencham's telephone number on.

'Are you sure I can't get somebody to come and stay with you, Mr Naylor?'

'No, I'll be fine detective, thank you. My housekeeper, Dora, will be over soon to get my evening meal ready. I'm sorry if I fucked up with Fenchers, I was only trying to help.'

'Don't worry about it Mr Naylor, it's nothing we can't fix, you take care.'

Brian walked back to his car.

As he walked he grinned and said aloud, 'Right, Paul 'bloody' Fencham, let's see what you've got to say about who our mole is, shall we?'

CHAPTER 53

3.30pm Sunday 26th March 1986
Sexual Offences Investigation Team, Carlton in Lindrick, Nottinghamshire

Rob Buxton drove the CID car through the permanently open gates and into the grounds of the newly opened Sexual Offences Investigation Team offices.

The modern, spacious development had a large car park at the front of the building. The car park was freshly marked out, the parking bays surrounded by mature shrubs and bushes. There were CCTV cameras on the perimeter of the property and on the building itself.

Carlton in Lindrick is a small village and there had been strong resistance from the villagers when the new development was first proposed. The locals had wrongly suspected that sex offenders would be being brought into the village on a regular basis, to be dealt with at the new police building.

Several open meetings had taken place, where it had been stressed to local residents that the new property was being built as a centre of excellence to help the victims of sexual offences and that no offenders would ever be brought to the facility.

In the late seventies, there had been overwhelming and justifiable criticism of the police service, over their handling of the victims of rape and other serious sexual assaults. The

SOIT, had been set up to try and improve that situation. The only people using these offices would be detectives, medical personnel, administration staff and victims of sex crimes.

The new offices had been opened with a fanfare of publicity at the beginning of February and everything still looked brand new.

Rob parked the car in the vacant bay situated next to the parking space that had been specifically marked, SUPT.

Already parked in that bay was a silver Mercedes saloon, with the registration plate MWD 651.

Rob said, 'Looks like Superintendent Dennington got here before us boss.'

'I would've been surprised if he hadn't, he only lives just down the road at Ranby. His house is a bit of a palace, by all accounts.'

'That's probably why he didn't want any South Yorkshire riff raff, like me, visiting him at home then.'

'Yeah, you're probably right Rob.'

'It's a good job I'm thick skinned!'

Danny grinned, 'Or just thick! Come on, let's go and have a word with the delightful Superintendent Dennington.'

The two detectives walked up the stone steps, that led to the front doors of the new building. Rob used his standard issue police key to enter the premises. It was Sunday, so the main reception area was closed. As they walked into the foyer of the building, Superintendent Robert Dennington was walking down the stairs to greet them.

'Chief Inspector Flint, what's this all about? What's so urgent that I had to meet you on a Sunday?'

Danny knew Dennington had used his full rank, to emphasise the fact he was a rank higher. He was also aware

Dennington had totally disregarded the presence of Rob Buxton.

'Superintendent, this is Detective Inspector Rob Buxton, I don't think you two have met. Is there somewhere we can talk?'

'We can use my office, follow me.'

Dennington led the way back up the stairs. The first door they came to had a brass plate with the name SUPT DENNINGTON on it.

The superintendent opened the unlocked door and walked into his office. Everything inside was brand new; the desk was huge with a computer terminal on one side. It had an immaculate leather desktop pad in the middle, stainless steel document holders marked IN, PENDING and OUT were on the other side.

Along the entire length of one wall was a large book shelf, that contained row after row of new, bound law books.

The chair behind the desk was made of black leather, it matched the two smaller chairs in front of the desk and the two-seater settee that took up the other wall. Dominating the office was the large picture window that overlooked the car park at the front of the building.

That explained why he was on his way down the stairs as we walked in, he was looking for us, thought Danny.

Dennington remained standing behind his desk and said, 'Sit down Chief Inspector, let's get on with this shall we, I haven't got all day.'

Danny looked around the office and remained standing, 'Nice office sir. I need to ask you a few questions about some associates of yours from your days as a student at Nottingham University.'

'I knew a lot of people at university Chief Inspector, who exactly are you referring to?'

'Cavalie Naylor, Edward Hall and Frederick Reece.'

'Yes, I knew them, we all played in the university rugby union team, what's the problem?'

'The problem sir, is that Cavalie Naylor and Edward Hall have been murdered. Frank Reece is now missing, he's believed to have been abducted by the killer of the other two.'

Dennington never batted an eyelid.

'Obviously, I'm sorry to hear that, but what exactly has that got to do with me?'

'One line of enquiry we're looking into at the moment is whether or not anyone would have a motive for these murders, in revenge for something that happened to them, while they were also at university.'

'I see. I knew the three men you've named, but I wouldn't say we were particularly close. Yes, we played rugby together, but that's about it.'

Dennington had tried hard not to show it, but Danny could see the Superintendent had been disturbed by what he'd been told. He remained arrogant and haughty, trying to dismiss the matter out of hand.

Danny was having none of it, 'How was university for you, Superintendent?'

'What sort of question is that?'

'One that requires an answer, sir.'

'If you must know, I thoroughly enjoyed my time at university.'

'Did you achieve a good degree?'

'Well let's see Chief Inspector, it was good enough for me to get on the accelerated promotion course at Bramshill, good enough for me to be a Superintendent at thirty years of age. So, I'd say, yeah it was pretty good. What's your point?'

'Did you get into many scrapes while you were there?'

'None that I recall.'

'Any issues with the security staff?'

'No.'

'I know what some of you students can be like?'

Danny grinned, he was deliberately goading Dennington.

'Listen to me Chief Inspector, I haven't come here on my day off to stand here and listen to you asking inane questions about my time at university. Say what you've come to say, or this meeting is over.'

Danny ignored the overbearing tone and said, 'Have you stayed in touch with any of the men who were your friends at university, I'm referring to Naylor, Hall and Reece in particular?'

'No I haven't, we all went our separate ways when we left.'

'When was the last time you saw any of them?'

With an air of boredom, Dennington replied, 'I really can't remember.'

Rob pointed to a small photograph on the wall of the office, 'This photograph of you and three other men in your university robes is that a picture of you, Naylor, Hall and Reece on your graduation?'

'Yes, it is.'

'Coincidentally, the very same photograph was found at the offices of both Edward Hall and Frederick Reece.'

'How thrilling for you Inspector.'

'If you weren't that close, why have you all still got the same photograph?'

'Inspector, look around the office and you'll see there are a lot of photographs. They are all memories of different times, different places, different people. I really think you both need to look at an alternative theory, I can assure you nothing happened at university, involving the four of us, that would cause somebody to want to kill these men.'

Danny stared hard at Dennington, 'The thing is Maurice, if the reason for their murder and abduction is because of something that happened back then, you could be in serious danger. Let's not beat about the bush here, your life could be at risk.'

'Chief Inspector, off duty or not, I don't recall giving you permission to address me by my Christian name. The rank I have achieved is Superintendent, use that or address me as sir, as you wish. I've already told you nothing happened at university. I know I've got absolutely nothing to be worried about. Your whole theory is ridiculous, borderline insane.'

Danny continued to stare at Dennington, he ignored his reply and continued. 'I suggest immediate twenty-four hour, round the clock surveillance on you, purely for your own protection you understand.'

'Out of the question. I won't hear of anything so preposterous. Like I've already said, on two occasions now Chief Inspector, you're wasting your time and resources continuing to look down this line of enquiry. Maybe I should have a word with your line manager and let him know my views on the subject.'

Danny walked towards the door, 'Feel free to do whatever you like Maurice. I'm running the investigation into these two murders and I'll be recommending full surveillance on you. I would hate for anything nasty to happen to you.'

'I meant what I said Flint, there will be no surveillance!'

Danny and Rob left the office, they made their way back outside to the car park. As they reached the car, both men glanced back towards the building and saw Dennington standing at the window, staring at them.

Rob said, 'Look at the arrogance of the man. Standing there with his hands on his hips, like some Lord of the Manor.'

'I know what you mean Rob, he's a piece of work alright. He's sweating though, something's definitely wrong there. I'm even more convinced that this is all to do with something that happened at the university. All we need to do is find out exactly what. We do that, we find our killer.'

'What do you want to do about Superintendent Dennington?'

'Get a surveillance team on him anyway, I don't give a shit what he says. The man's an arrogant prick.'

CHAPTER 54

5.00pm Sunday 26th March 1986
Clifton, Nottinghamshire

The drive from Cotgrave to Clifton had only taken twenty-five minutes, but for Brian Hopkirk, it seemed as though he'd travelled to a different country.

He had gone from standing outside a palatial country manor house, to standing outside a stinking two-bedroomed flat, on one of the worst estates in Nottinghamshire.

It had taken a quick check with the control room to obtain the address from a reverse telephone directory. Using the fleshy part of his bunched fist, he hammered on the door. Just as he thought nobody was in, the door suddenly flew open. Standing in the doorway was a short, overweight man with a pot belly and receding hairline. He was wearing an ill-fitting jacket, beige coloured trousers and scruffy brown brogues. On the floor of the hallway, immediately behind the man, Brian could see a suitcase.

'Paul Fencham?' asked Brian.

'Who wants to know?'

Producing his warrant card, Brian said, 'Police, I think you and I need a little chat mate.'

Brian stepped into the hallway and closed the door behind him.

'Police or not, you can't just walk in here like you own the place. Come on get out, I've got a plane to catch.'

Brian turned to face Fencham and snarled, 'How about we have this conversation down the nick, that way I make sure you miss your fucking plane!'

'Alright, alright! There's no need to get all heavy. What's this all about anyway?'

'Please, don't waste my time Fencham, you know exactly why I'm here. I want to know who gave you the information about the murder scenes, that you've since sold to the Daily Mirror? I presume you've sold the story, where else would you get the cash for an overseas trip?'

'Look, selling a story to another newspaper isn't illegal, that's my job. I'm a news reporter, I get paid to sniff out a story.'

'I'll ask you again, where did you get that information?'

'I got a phone call from a mate, just somebody I knew from when I was in the army.'

'Leave your suitcase where it is, we're going to the nick, I'm not pissing about with you all day.'

'Don't be hasty, I swear I'm telling the truth. Look, the mate is Geoff Naylor, I went to see him, after he phoned me the other night.'

'And what information did Naylor give you?'

'He told me about the writing on the wall at his son's house, then he said he'd overheard one of you lot say it was exactly the same as the writing on the wall at Beeston.'

'Fine, but who gave you the information about the content of the writing, because we both know that wasn't Geoff Naylor?'

'I don't have to give you my source.'

'No, you don't, but I'll make life so uncomfortable for you, that within a week you'll wish you had. We can start today, right now if you like! Paul Fencham, I'm arresting you for attempting to pervert the course of justice and for police obstruction. Come on let's go!'

'Wait a minute detective, let me think about this.'

Fencham stepped back, away from the angry looking detective.

His mind was in overdrive. He hadn't yet paid Dave Mitchell the hundred pounds he'd promised him. If he gave his name, he wouldn't have to pay him. He didn't have to tell the detective that he'd offered him money, he could just say he owed him a favour. Mitchell couldn't say any other, or he'd be even deeper in the shit.

A sly smile flashed across his features and he held his hands up towards the detective, in a gesture of appeasement, then said, 'Alright detective, it's no big deal anyway. The guy who gave me the info owed me a favour, it was a one off.'

'Just give me the name, Fencham!'

'Alright, alright. It's a bloke I know who works as a photographer on your Scenes of Crime teams. His name's Dave Mitchell. I did a favour for him ages ago, he owed me.'

'Exactly what information did he give you?'

'He confirmed what Geoff Naylor had told me about the writing on the wall, he also told me that it was at both murder scenes and that it had been written in blood. He told me the message written was EC21V2425. I worked out what it meant by myself though, I was the one who realised it was a bible reference, that's the truth.'

'Has any money changed hands between you and Mitchell?'

'No, definitely not.' At least that's the truth, thought Fencham.

He looked shiftily at the detective, 'Am I still under arrest, or can I go and catch my plane?'

'You were never under arrest, you shit head! Just out of interest Fencham, how much did you get paid by the Mirror for the story?'

Fencham allowed himself a greasy smile, 'I got ten grand. It's sangria, sun and sex all the way for me now, detective.'

Brian Hopkirk stepped out of the stinking flat, followed by Fencham clutching his suitcase.

After Fencham locked the flat door, Brian grabbed the fat reporter by the lapels of his jacket and pushed him backwards into the wall, 'Enjoy your holiday Fencham, but get this into your thick head, if I ever hear about you putting the squeeze on any of our people again, I'll make your life a misery. Do you understand me?'

'Honestly detective, it was a one off, there was no squeeze. I fully understand, I'm thinking about trying to find work in Tenerife, while I'm over there.'

'Now that's the best news I've heard all day', said Brian as he released the lapels of Fencham's coat.

Grabbing his suitcase, Fencham scuttled off along the walkway of the flats, constantly glancing behind him to see if the big detective was following him.

Brian took out his cigarettes and lit one. He took a deep drag and exhaled, before slowly walking back to his car. He glanced at his watch, it was now almost six o'clock in the evening.

Danny had tasked him with finding the mole at two o'clock, four hours later he knew it was Dave Mitchell, a Scenes of Crime photographer. Even Danny would have to admit, that was pretty quick work.

He smiled, took another long drag from the cigarette, then tossed it away as he exhaled the smoke.

As he got back into his car, he felt relieved that the leak hadn't come from one of the detectives on the MCIU. He smiled as he thought, how much he was going to enjoy telling Danny Flint exactly who the mole on the department was.

CHAPTER 55

6.00pm Sunday 26th March 1986
16, Crosshill Road, Bishopton near Glasgow

Rachel Moore and Tina Prowse had been lucky. They had managed to book seats on a flight that left at four o'clock from East Midlands airport and which had arrived at Glasgow airport at quarter past five that day.

A telephone call made from Danny to the Special Branch office at the airport had meant the two detectives could forego the normal stringent checks and were allowed to board the aircraft quickly.

Another phone call to the CID in Glasgow had meant the two women had been met by a detective with a vehicle at Glasgow Airport.

Everything had gone to plan and as Rachel and Tina emerged from Glasgow Airport, they had been met by Detective Constable Davy Sinclair.

He had introduced himself and said, 'What's the address you're going to ladies?'

Rachel introduced herself and Tina, smiled and said, 'We need to get to 16, Crosshill Road at Bishopton, thanks. Have you been waiting long?'

'Nah, ten minutes max. This time of night we should be in Bishopton for just after six o'clock. Is it something interesting you're dealing with?'

'A double murder back in Nottingham', said Tina.

'Ah! The Malky!'

'The what?'

'Malky! It's a slang term we Scots use for murder.'

Davy was pleasant company, as he drove through the countryside between the airport and Bishopton. He kept the conversation light and never enquired about the details of the murder investigation.

He drove into the small town of Bishopton, quickly found Crosshill Road and parked the car outside number sixteen.

He turned to Rachel and said, 'My instructions are to wait for you here. Do you need any help with your enquiry, or do you want me to stay with the car?'

'We'll be fine, thanks Davy. I don't know how long this might take though, we might be a couple of hours or we might be back in a couple of minutes.'

'Well anything you need Rachel, I'll be right here. I hope you're successful.'

Rachel and Tina walked up the short garden path to the front door of the white painted, semi-detached house. It was a pleasant enough street, the gardens and houses all looked neat and tidy.

Bishopton appeared to be quite a nice little town.

There were lights on in the house, but the curtains were already drawn against the darkening skies. There was a strong smell of soot in the air, looking up Rachel could see smoke coming from the chimney of the house.

Tina used the heavy, black knocker on the red door, to let the occupants of the house know they were there.

A young woman's voice called out, 'Just a minute, I'll be two ticks!'

Rachel glanced over her shoulder and smiled at Davy sitting in the car, giving him the thumbs up. He smiled back and wound up the window of the car.

The door was opened by a young woman in her thirties. Her hair was blonde, tied back in a ponytail, she wore no make-up and had clear, bright blue eyes. She was wearing an apron over a dark blue skirt and a knitted top that was a similar colour blue.

She smiled at the two detectives and said, 'Can I help you ladies?'

Rachel and Tina held out their warrant cards and Rachel said, 'I'm sorry to disturb you, we're police officers from Nottinghamshire, we were hoping to speak to Jean Mackay.'

'I'm sorry, but you've had a wasted trip, Jean and her mother don't live here anymore.'

'Did you know Jean?'

'Aye, I did, I knew her and her family well enough. Look where are my manners, why don't you step inside so we can talk properly.'

'Thank you, that's very kind, I'm sorry I didn't catch your name.'

'My name's Nichola, Nichola Brown. Please officers, step in out of the cold.'

Nichola showed the two detectives into the living room, where there was a blazing fire in the hearth. The room was well decorated, clean and tidy. Rachel and Tina sat on the comfortable settee and Nichola sat in one of the two armchairs.

'Can I get you a cup of tea or something?'

Tina answered, 'No, we're fine thanks, we don't want to take up your time, you look busy.'

'Oh, the apron, I was just fixing my fellas' tea, he works at the airport down the road. He should be home in about half an hour.'

'What can you tell me about Jean?' asked Rachel.

'I went to school with her, when we were younger. She was such a clever, beautiful girl none of us were the least bit surprised when she got offered a place at university. She was always brilliant at science and wanted to be a doctor. I saw her just after she came back from Nottingham, she was never the same girl, after those animals attacked her. My husband and I bought the house from Jean's mum Glenys, after I found out they were moving back down to England.'

'Why would they want to go back down to England, after what happened?'

'Glenys was very poorly, some sort of cancer I think. All I know is, she wanted to go and stay with her sister, so if anything happened to her, she knew her sister would be there to take care of Jean.'

'How long ago was that?'

'We've lived here for two years now.'

'Just a second, I'm sure I've still got an address for Glenys's sister back here somewhere.'

Nichola walked out of the living room, then returned a couple of minutes later carrying a red and black address book.

'It's here, the sister is Maggie Fraser, her address is 45, Gateford Road, Worksop, Notts.'

Rachel made a note of the address and said, 'Thanks, Nichola. Have you heard from Jean or her mother since they moved back down south?'

'No, not a thing, people just move on, don't they? It was such a shame what happened to Jean, those animals were never caught, were they?'

'No, they weren't. Did you see much of Jean's parents when you were kids?'

'I saw her mum loads, Glenys is a lovely woman. Never saw much of her dad though, he was in the army or something. He was always away somewhere, I know Jean really missed him.'

'Anything else you can tell us about Jean?'

'No not really, that's about it. Like I say, I haven't seen her for at least a couple of years.'

The two detectives stood up, Rachel said, 'Thanks Nichola, that's been really helpful.'

'Can I ask why you want to speak to Jean? Have you found those bastards that attacked her?'

'We're working on it Nichola, we're working on it. Thanks again for your time.'

Rachel and Tina walked back to the car.

'That was pretty quick, how did it go, Rachel?' asked Davy.

'Bit of a wasted trip really, the woman we wanted to see left the address two years ago, but we know where she's moved to, so it hasn't been an entirely wasted journey. Davy, would you drive us straight back to the airport, we need to be on the next flight south?'

'No problem, buckle up.'

Three quarters of an hour later, they had said their goodbyes to Davy, and were booked on the nine o'clock flight back to East Midlands airport.

Rachel found a telephone at the airport and dialled the number for Danny's office.

It was now almost seven thirty at night.

The phone was answered immediately.

'Boss, it's Rachel. I'm afraid it was a dead end here in Glasgow. We went to the address but Jean Mackay and her mother had sold the property two years ago. We got lucky though, the woman who lives at the house now, knew the Mackay family well, she went to school with Jean. Anyway, it seems that Jean and her mother moved back down to Worksop a couple of years ago, so they could stay with Jeans aunt, after the mother was diagnosed with cancer.'

Danny asked, 'Have you got the aunt's name and an address in Worksop?'

'Yes, we have, her name's Maggie Fraser, she lives at 45, Gateford Road, Worksop.'

'Good work Rachel, have you managed to book a flight back tomorrow?'

'I can do better than that boss, we're on the nine o'clock flight tonight. We should be landing at East Midlands at a quarter past ten.'

'That's great, I'll make sure someone's there to pick you up. Tomorrow morning I want you and Tina to swerve the briefing and go directly to the address in Worksop. I want you knocking on Maggie Fraser's door at six thirty tomorrow morning. Okay?'

'No problem boss, talk to you tomorrow.'

'That's great work Rachel, pass on my thanks to Tina as well please.'

'Will do boss.'

CHAPTER 56

8.00pm Sunday 26th March 1986
Major Crime Investigation Unit, Mansfield

Danny saw Brian sitting on his own in the briefing room, he glanced at his watch, it was now seven thirty, there was still half an hour to go before the de-brief. He'd got time to have a quick word with his Detective Inspector, he wanted to apologise for his abrasive manner and the comments he'd made to him earlier in the day.

Danny had been rattled after the press conference, but he knew it had been unfair to take it out on one of his team, there was no excuse.

He stuck his head around his office door and shouted, 'Brian, can I have a word please?'

Brian stood up, walked across the briefing room and stepped inside Danny's office.

'Close the door and grab a seat.'

Brian quietly closed the door and sat down.

'Brian, I wanted to apologise to you for lashing out earlier. It was a reaction to the shit press conference, but I shouldn't have taken it out on you, it was unfair.'

'Thanks boss, but there's no apology needed, as soon as I made the comment I realised how stupid it was. Anyway, the good news is I've managed to find our mole. I know exactly who leaked the information to the press.'

A sense of real trepidation passed over Danny and he said quietly, 'Okay, what's the news Brian?'

'Well the good news first, it's none of the lads and lasses on the unit, nobody has talked out of line. The bad news is, it was a civilian photographer employed by our Scenes of Crime department.'

A huge sense of relief washed over Danny, he had been dreading being told it was one of the detectives on the new unit. After an audible sigh, he said, 'That's great work, how did you find out so quickly?'

'As you suggested, I started by going to see Geoff Naylor. It turns out that he'd spoken to one of his old army buddies, who now works as a reporter for one of the local papers. Anyway, I tracked down this reporter, a bloke called Paul Fencham, to a shitty little flat over at Clifton. I was ever so slightly unpleasant and we quickly came to an understanding. Apparently, the information was leaked by a bloke called Dave Michell, he's a civilian who occasionally works with our Scenes of Crime teams. I've checked the logs, he took the photographs at the Beeston murder scene. He passed over the coded message that had been left on the wall at Beeston. After his conversation with Geoff Naylor, Fencham already knew that the same message had been left at Underwood. Somehow, he's worked out that the message was a bible reference, then put two and two together, after reading the passage from the Book of Exodus that it referred to.'

'Has any money changed hands between Paul Fencham and Dave Mitchell.'

'Fencham says not, but that's probably bullshit. He's been paid ten grand for selling the story to the Daily Mirror, he's now on his way to the airport ready for a break in Tenerife.

After our conversation today, he's under no illusion what will happen to him if he ever approaches any more of our staff.'

'That's great work Brian, I'll talk to Chief Superintendent Wainwright, he can deal with Dave Mitchell. I haven't got either the time or the inclination to start going after him. I'm just so relieved it's none of our staff, the thought that someone on the unit couldn't be trusted was really depressing, I don't need those sorts of problems on top of everything else.'

'Have I missed anything while I've been chasing down our mole?'

'I haven't spoken to the teams yet, but it looks as though everyone's back now, let's start the debrief and find out exactly where we are.'

The two men walked into the main briefing room where the various enquiry teams had gathered.

Danny spoke, 'Okay everyone, let's have a bit of hush. I'll give you all a quick update first from Rachel and Tina who are still up in Glasgow. They've visited the last known address for Jean Mackay, unfortunately Jean and her mother Glenys Mackay left that address two years ago, and moved down to Worksop to stay with Jean's aunt, a woman by the name of Maggie Fraser. I've already tasked Rachel and Tina to visit the address in Worksop where hopefully they can speak to Jean and her mother.'

'I'm afraid that's not going to be possible sir.'

The voice was that of Dc Fran Jefferies.

'Go on Fran, what's the problem?'

'After researching the assault on Jean Mackay as you requested, the natural progression for me was to research Jean and her family. There are some very interesting findings.'

'Go on.'

'Sadly, Jean Mackay's dead, sir. Her body was found in woods near Worksop eight weeks ago, she had taken her own life. I've read the coroners file that was prepared for the inquest. It appears that Jean Mackay drank a full bottle of vodka to wash down four large packets of Paracetamol. The next of kin at that time was shown as her aunt Maggie Fraser. The funeral was held at Worksop, six weeks ago.'

'Why was Maggie Fraser shown as next of kin? What about her mum and dad?'

'The research I've carried out shows that Glenys Mackay passed away shortly after moving down to Maggie Fraser's address. I can't find out why her father wasn't shown as the next of kin, there's no death certificate in existence so he's definitely still alive, I can find no record of him passing away. The father's full name is Ben Fitzgerald Mackay, the last record I could find of him was his military service. He was in the Royal Marines Mountain and Arctic Warfare Cadre, a trained sniper and an expert on escape and evasion techniques. I couldn't ascertain whether or not he ever worked with the Special Boat Service or the Special Air Service, the person I spoke to at Naval Intelligence was quite evasive. Reading between the lines, it seems that Ben Mackay was probably involved in any number of deniable operations, overseas.'

'That would explain why he was never around the family home, that's good work Fran. When did Ben Mackay leave the service?'

'According to the records, he left the service in 1980. He seems to have slipped off the radar since then. I still need to do some more digging on that.'

'Keep at it Fran, I want to know everything there is to know about Ben Mackay. After what you've told me about Jean's suicide, he is definitely a person of interest.'

Danny turned to Rob Buxton, 'Rob, I want an up to date photograph of Ben Mackay as soon as possible and see if we can obtain his fingerprint records from the military. I'd like to get them compared, as quickly as possible, with any marks found at the murder scenes or the Range Rover recovered from Farnsfield.'

'Will do boss.'

Danny went through the rest of the teams, taking their information and making notes of anything relevant, at the conclusion of the debrief he said, 'Well done everybody, I think we need to concentrate on Ben Mackay as a priority. I want him traced, interviewed and eliminated from this enquiry as soon as possible. I want you to finish up anything you have left to do this evening, we shall reconvene at six o'clock tomorrow morning. I know it's another early start, but we're making excellent progress. I want Ben Mackay traced by tomorrow evening at the latest, if he is our man and he's got Frederick Reece stashed away somewhere, it's vital we find him sooner rather than later.'

Danny looked over towards Rob Buxton and indicated for him to follow him into his office.

Rob walked in and sat down.

'Quick question Rob, how did you get on with the surveillance team on Dennington?'

'They've been on him since he left his office at Carlton in Lindrick earlier. No issues at the moment, he's now at home and the surveillance team are outside.'

'Good stuff, I want him watched twenty-four seven. I've got a bad feeling about this. If Ben Mackay's our killer, with his military background and training, if he does go after Dennington we're going to have our work cut out in trying to stop him.'

'Before I go home, I'll contact the surveillance team to let them know what we could be dealing with. If nothing else it will keep them alert and on their toes.'

'Thanks Rob.'

CHAPTER 57

10.30pm Sunday 26th March 1986
East Midlands Airport, Castle Donnington, Leicestershire

It had been a long day.

As he waited patiently at the airport arrivals hall, Danny sipped a cappuccino in the coffee bar next to the flight side entrance door.

He glanced up at the information board and noticed that the status of the Glasgow flight had changed. It was now flashing, 'Bags in Hall'.

He knew Rachel and Tina had only taken hand luggage, so he expected them to be first through the automatic doors. Sure enough, the first person to come through was Tina quickly followed by Rachel.

Rachel smiled and said, 'Hello boss, when you said you'd make sure someone was here to pick us up, I didn't expect it to be you.'

'Well consider yourself honoured, I'm going to be in big trouble when I get home, I should have gone with Sue to a meeting with the vicar this evening, to discuss our wedding.'

'She's going to kill you', laughed Rachel.

'Probably, although I did phone her to let her know I wasn't going to be able to make it.'

'I bet that went down well boss.'

'She always says the same thing, "Just make sure you're there on the 7th May".'

'Oh, the joys of a relationship with a cop', laughed Tina.

'Anyway, enough of my domestic bliss. I didn't pick you up because you're my favourite two officers, I needed to give you an urgent update, before you go and see Maggie Fraser in Worksop tomorrow morning. I'll tell you all about it in the car, where there's no chance of anyone overhearing our conversation.'

Ten minutes later and the three detectives were in the CID car as it pulled out from the airport car park and headed for the M1 motorway.

Once they were cruising along the motorway, Danny said, 'Right, before you go to Mrs Fraser's address in the morning you need to know that both Jean Mackay and her mother Glenys are both dead. Glenys died, shortly after arriving in Worksop a couple of years ago and Jean committed suicide eight weeks ago, in woods near the aunt's home in Worksop.'

'Exactly how did Jean take her own life, boss?' asked Rachel.

'She took an overdose of paracetamol, washed down with vodka.'

There was silence in the car, as Rachel and Tina absorbed the information they had been given.

Eventually, Danny broke the silence, 'I still want you to go and see Maggie Fraser tomorrow morning. I want you to find out everything you can about the circumstances surrounding the suicide. I want you to try and establish what triggered it? Whether she'd tried to kill herself before? It's also imperative that you find out from Mrs Fraser, everything you can about Jean's father. We know his name's

Ben Mackay and that he has a military background. I want a recent photograph of Ben Mackay, if Mrs Fraser has one. I want to know if he attended his daughter's funeral? What the relationship was like between Jean and her father? Most importantly I want to know where Ben Mackay is now?'

Rachel looked thoughtful and asked, 'Do you think Jean's father could be our killer?'

'It's certainly a possibility.'

'What if we turn up at Mrs Fraser's house in the morning and Ben Mackay is there?'

'That's a good point Rachel.'

Danny was quiet and thoughtful for a moment, then he said, 'If that's the case and Ben Mackay is at the address, I want you to tell Mrs Fraser that the reason for your visit, is purely and simply to check on her welfare. Tell her that it's normal practice, following the suicide of a loved one. Do a few welfare questions then make your excuses and get out. I don't want either of you taking any risks with Ben Mackay. If he's our man, remember how ruthless he was with Pc Moreton, just get out of the house and arrange for back up. Is that clear?'

'Crystal clear, boss.'

'I've called the briefing for six o'clock tomorrow morning. I want you two to get a car, then get straight up to Worksop. Be knocking on Mrs Frasers' door by six thirty at the latest. I want an update from you at seven thirty, this is important. If I haven't had a verbal update from you by seven thirty, I'll be sending an armed response unit to the address, so make sure you call in, even if you have to do it from a phone box.'

'I'll call boss, don't worry', said Rachel.

CHAPTER 58

5.30am Monday, March 27th, 1986
Clumber Park, Nottinghamshire

The early morning mist drifted slowly across the heather covered slopes, caressed into movement by the slightest breeze.

At a distance of one hundred and fifty yards, standing upwind and on the opposite slope across the valley, was a handsome fifteen pointer stag.

There wasn't a sound, the air was perfectly still.

The sun emerged briefly from behind the still threatening rainclouds, it was higher in the sky now, rising slowly above the distant hills. It had rained heavily earlier, bringing a freshness to the air. The clean cold air, mixed with the subtle scent of heather, made a heady combination.

The two men that stalked the stag were dressed from head to toe in camouflage clothing. They paused and lay stock still, just below the brow of the hill. The younger of the two men, had a rifle with a telescopic sight at his side.

The stag lowered his huge head to the floor hoping to find another tasty morsel to eat. The young shoots of heather were covered in the fresh rain and early morning dew.

The younger man fidgeted with his rifle, causing an almost inaudible click.

Immediately, the stag reared its huge antlered head and looked across the valley, in the direction of the two men.

In a voice less than a whisper, the older man breathed, 'Be still your Highness.'

A minute passed, before the stag looked back over his shoulder away from the camouflaged men.

Satisfied he was alone on the slopes, the animal resumed eating.

In the same whispered tones, the younger man said, 'Is it time ghillie?'

'Yes, your Highness it's time, but move like a phantom, the slightest noise will spook the beast.'

Painfully slowly, inch by inch, the young man manoeuvred the rifle towards him.

Finally, the rifle was in position and the Prince allowed the butt to nestle comfortably in his shoulder. He lowered his head into position so he had a natural line of sight through the telescopic sight.

Through the magnification of the scope the stag suddenly appeared close enough to touch. The young royal could see the individual hairs that made up the distinctive red fur, the dew glistening on the snout of the animal and the moisture sparkling in the animal's huge dark brown eyes.

The ghillie whispered, 'He's yours now your Highness, remember to aim where I taught you, just behind the shoulder, the bullet will pass directly through the animal's heart and it won't suffer.'

Again, the stag raised his head from the heather. This time he snorted, tilted his head back and roared. The ghillie smiled, he knew this was a good sign, the stag was totally unaware of the hunter's presence.

'Breathe as I taught you your Highness, be one with the rifle and take the shot.'

There was total silence in the glen.

Suddenly the big rifle barked into life, the stag dropped like a stone, its legs crumpled beneath its body.

A clean kill.

The ghillie jumped to his feet, whooping with delight.

'That was a fantastic shot your Highness! A perfect kill! You're a natural shot, so much better than your father.'

The young man got to his feet and pulled off the hood revealing his short blonde hair.

'I've had a bit more practice than my father recently ghillie, it's not that long ago I was in a war myself, fighting the Argies.'

'Aye that's very true sir, but it was still a wonderful shot', beamed the ghillie.

'Thank you ghillie, you tracked him like a master. What do we do now?'

'You can leave the rest to me, your Highness, I'll arrange for the stag to be brought down from the hills. Let's get down to the house and tell the Duke your good news, then you can celebrate with your folks properly.'

The clouds above blotted out the sunshine and the rain started to fall again, very soon the far slope of the valley was no longer visible.

The rainfall got progressively harder and harder, the rain pounding into the peaty soil.

The sound of the rain on the earth slowly merged into the noise of the heavy rain pounding on the roof of the caravan.

Suddenly, the Watcher was dragged back from his dream, back to reality.

He sat up in his sleeping bag, rubbed his eyes and glanced at his watch. It was almost half past five, it would soon be time for Frederick Reece to answer for his sins. Only when that had been achieved, would it be time for him to snare the main architect of the evil deed that had precipitated this mission.

From a small table at the side of his sleeping bag, he picked up his Maglite torch and a photograph. He switched on the torch, illuminating the photo and whispered quietly, 'Not long to wait now sweetheart. With the grace of God, your tormentors will all soon be banished back to the Hell they came from, then I'll be free to see you and your mother again.'

CHAPTER 59

6.30am Monday 27th March 1986
Farndon, Nottinghamshire

The Land Rover bumped its way along the pot holed dirt track.

The heavy rain that had fallen earlier had turned the dusty track into a muddy, sodden, quagmire. At least now that it was starting to get light, the water filled pot holes were easy to see. The vehicle was built for just such atrocious conditions and ploughed through the mud with ease. The Watcher had engaged the four-wheel drive of the vehicle as soon as he had turned off the tarmac road and onto the track.

Once again, he parked the vehicle at the rear of the disused buildings. The grey walls looked even bleaker and darker, saturated from the heavy rain.

The rain had stopped briefly, but the Watcher still allowed himself a smile, he knew the threat of more inclement weather that morning meant there was very little chance of him being disturbed at the derelict buildings.

Having parked the Land Rover, he pulled the hood of his camouflaged jacket over his head, and moved quickly to the rear of the vehicle where he removed a black bag and a large axe.

The Watcher moved the sheet of corrugated iron to one side and made his way into the crumbling, single storey building.

The stench of the buildings previous use, was still very evident even after the torrential rain of the previous night. The building itself was now a crescendo of dripping noises, as the leaks in the roof of the abandoned building were found out by the rainfall.

He made his way through the warren of drab concrete walls until he came to the room where he'd left Frederick Reece bound and gagged.

He could see Reece in the dim light, the solicitor was shivering with cold and his eyes were half closed.

The Watcher walked over and slapped the prisoners face, hard.

Instantly, Reece was wide awake, his face stinging from the brutal slap.

He opened his eyes and saw the Watcher in front of him, his eyes widened with fear and he started mumbling beneath the brown Gaffer tape.

Reaching forward, the Watcher ripped the tape from the face of Reece. As soon as the tape had been removed the fat solicitor started to beg and plead for his life, 'I'm so sorry, please show me some mercy.'

'Maybe I should show you the same mercy you showed my daughter?'

'Please, I'm begging you, there's no need for you to do this.'

'You know exactly what you did back then and today you will finally pay for your sins.'

The Watcher bunched his huge fist and punched Reece hard on the forehead.

The force of the concussive punch was enough to knock Reece unconscious and he slumped forward.

The Watcher moved quickly now; he untied Reece's hands, then walked across the room and picked up four large breeze blocks.

He carried the four blocks over to Reece and put them down at the side of the unconscious solicitor. He grabbed Reece and turned him onto his back, then extended his arms away from his body until he was in the crucifix position.

He used the brown Gaffer tape to position the breeze blocks, one each side of the arm at the elbow joint.

Once the blocks were taped into position the arms could no longer be moved, the weight of the blocks was far too much, for an already weakened Reece, to lift. He started to come round and tried gamely to move his arms, but he was powerless to lift the heavy breeze blocks, he quickly realised he was trapped in that position and gave up trying to move.

He could see the Watcher standing over him with the large axe resting on his shoulder.

The Watcher saw Reece was fully awake and placed the axe on the floor.

For a second or two, Reece entertained the idea that the maniac standing in front of him had changed his mind about killing him. That scant hope of a reprieve evaporated when he saw his captor reach into the black bag and take out a small blow torch.

Using a disposable lighter, the Watcher lit the blow torch and adjusted it until the flame was showing as a small stream of white hot gas. He placed the blow torch on the floor and lifted the huge axe above his head.

He looked into the eyes of Reece and shouted, 'The scriptures have taught us through the Book of Exodus, that revenge shall only be complete with an eye for an eye, a tooth for a tooth, a hand for a hand and a leg for a leg!'

The large axe was brought down forcefully, it instantly severed Reece's right hand before biting into the dusty concrete floor.

Reece screamed in pain, but was powerless as he watched the man step over him and repeat the chopping motion down onto his left hand with the same devastating result.

A second agonised scream pierced the silence of the dingy concrete space.

The Watcher dropped the axe, letting it clatter to the floor. He then picked up the blow torch and used the white-hot heat to cauterise both stumps. The raw, exposed flesh sizzled under the enormous heat of the blow torch, the open blood vessels were seared shut and the bleeding instantly stopped. The agonising pain caused by the hot flame of the blow torch screamed through Reece's body and mercifully he passed out.

Smoke hung in the air of the small room, the cramped space filled with the stench of burnt flesh.

The Watcher turned off the blow torch and placed it on the floor to cool. From within the black bag, he removed two large ziplock bags. He picked up the two severed hands, that were still twitching on the floor, then dropped each one into a separate bag.

The index finger on one of the severed hands continued to contract and extend, it was as though the hand had developed a life of its own. Eventually, the nerves died too and the twitching stopped. The Watcher sealed the two bags and dropped them into the larger black bag. He then waited for the blow torch to cool down completely, before he placed it in the same black bag.

Casually, he walked back over to the unconscious Reece and began to peel away the Gaffer tape from the breeze blocks. Once the tape had been removed he moved the four blocks away from the stinking, blackened stumps.

Having removed the breeze blocks, the Watcher dragged Reece upright and propped him against the wall. He squatted down on the floor opposite Reece and waited patiently for him to recover consciousness.

Half an hour passed, during which time the Watcher's eyes never left the fat solicitor.

Finally, Reece began to stir, a low mournful moan emanating through gritted teeth was the first sign he was regaining consciousness. Another five minutes passed, before Reece finally opened his eyes fully. The realisation of his situation was instantly apparent, he began to sob.

The sobbing turned to crying, which changed to howling, then finally transformed into a single, long, piercing scream as the pain from his scorched, mutilated arms wracked through his body.

'You can scream as loud as you like, there's no one to hear your pitiful wailing.'

'Why are you doing this?' screamed Reece.

'You know why Reece. The only question you have left to answer is this, do you want to repent your sin before God?'

Reece slowly nodded his head, 'I'll do whatever you want me to do. You don't have to kill me. Have mercy, you've already maimed me.'

'Have mercy? Don't you understand that this is the only mercy I'm prepared to show you? I will mercifully allow you this one opportunity to repent before the Lord, before I deliver justice.'

'You have to understand, none of what happened to that girl was my fault, it was all Dennington's idea. He made us do it, he made us attack her, he said it was her fault, that she deserved it! We didn't kill her, she didn't die, you can let me live, please let me live.'

He was babbling now.

'Yes, you did. You don't know it, but you and your friends have killed her', said the Watcher flatly, he then stepped behind Reece and used the lethal blade of the Sumunugashi knife to slit his throat. As the fat solicitor bled out over the dirty floor of the disused maggot farm, the Watcher took a step back, away from the rapidly spreading pool of blood.

He gathered up his tools and placed them in the black bag.

Finally, he took out the two-inch paint brush which he dipped it into the steaming pool of Reece's blood and painted the same bible reference on to one of the cold, grey concrete walls.

Picking up his bag and the axe, he said softly, 'Defend me, your humble servant in all assaults of my enemies: That I, surely trusting in thy defence, may not fear the power of my adversaries, through the might of Jesus Christ, our Lord. Amen.'

With Reece dispatched, the Watcher finally allowed another name to enter his thoughts.

Maurice Dennington.

Just the thought of the name repulsed the Watcher, but thanks to the newspaper clipping left for him by his daughter, he knew exactly where he would find that particular demon.

As he walked out of the maggot farm and back to his vehicle, he salivated at the prospect of finally being able to deliver justice to the hypocritical pig.

Superintendent Maurice Dennington of the Sexual Offences Investigation Team, would soon pay the ultimate price for his own cruelty and deviance.

CHAPTER 60

6.30am Monday 27th March 1986
Gateford Road, Worksop, Nottinghamshire

Rachel Moore rubbed the sleep from her eyes, then rapped the car keys on the small glass window pane in the front door of 45 Gateford Road, Worksop.

She had hardly slept last night, worrying about visiting this address. Her mind was racing now, try as she might, she was struggling to push the tangible fear she felt, to the back of her mind. Usually, she could mask it very well at work, but ever since Jimmy Wade had attacked her in her own home, she had lost a great deal of self-confidence. She couldn't get past the fact that without the intervention of her brother, Wade would have killed her.

Tina Prowse had picked up on Rachel's anxious mood, 'Rachel, are you okay?'

'I'm fine Tina, thanks.'

'Why don't I handle things this morning, you try and relax a little.'

Rachel nodded, tightened her lips a little, then rapped a little harder on the glass pane.

Suddenly, a light appeared from an upstairs window. Although, dawn was breaking and it was starting to get light, the sky was still gloomy and threatening rain.

The window opened, a woman leaned out and said, 'Who's there?'

Tina stepped back away from the door and looked up at the woman, 'We're police officers. I'm really sorry it's so early, but we need to speak to Mrs Fraser, is she home?'

'I'm Mrs Fraser, just a second, I'll come down.'

There was a short delay before Tina and Rachel heard the key being turned in the lock of the front door. The door was opened by Maggie Fraser, dressed in a cream coloured towelling bath robe, her greying, blonde hair still in tight curlers. A plump woman, she stood only five feet tall and looked to be approaching her sixties.

'You said you're from the police, is something wrong?'

Tina held out her warrant card to reinforce the fact that they were indeed police officers, then said cleverly, 'I'm so sorry to disturb you and your family Mrs Fraser, but we need to have a chat with you about your niece, Jean.'

'There's nobody else in the house lass, just me. You do know my niece is dead, don't you?'

It was like a ton weight had been lifted from Rachel, she now knew Ben Mackay wasn't in the house.

'Yes, I did know that Mrs Fraser and I'm very sorry for your loss. Would you mind if we came inside for a few minutes? We do need to ask you a few questions, as a matter of urgency.'

Maggie Fraser was intrigued, 'Come in, come in, you'll have to excuse me though, it's so early I've still got my bloody curlers in!'

'I'm sorry it's so early, but like I said it's urgent.'

Maggie directed the two detectives into the front room of her little terraced house, there was a dark green settee and a matching armchair, arranged so they all faced the television in the opposite corner. There was a sideboard, that had a number of photographs placed at intervals along the top and a small coffee table between the settee and the gas fire. Maggie walked over and turned on the gas fire, the room still held the night's chill.

She gestured for the two detectives to sit on the settee, then said, 'I don't care how urgent it is, I can't function without a cup of tea in the morning, would you ladies like a drink?'

Rachel said, 'I'd love a cup of coffee please, white no sugar, thanks.'

Tina said, 'A cup of tea, no sugar, would be lovely, thank you.'

Maggie shuffled out of the room to go and make the drinks, Tina took the opportunity of her absence to turn to Rachel and whisper, 'Well at least we know Ben Mackay isn't still here.'

Rachel replied, 'So she says, stay alert Tina.'

Tina nodded.

Minutes later, Maggie returned to the small lounge carrying the three hot drinks on a tray. She passed the two detectives their mugs of tea and coffee, who in turn put them down on the coffee table in front of them. Her own drink was in a bone china cup and saucer.

Sitting down in the armchair, still holding the cup and saucer Maggie said, 'I know what you're both thinking, a cup and saucer, really? I just can't get used to drinking out of a big pot mug, I like my dainty little tea cup.'

She took a sip of the hot tea from the bone china cup, her little finger was raised, as though she were sipping tea at a Royal garden party.

She faced Tina and said matter of factly, 'You said it was urgent about our Jean, lass. What can be so important now the poor wee girl's dead?'

'We're investigating a number of incidents, that may or may not be connected to what happened to your niece when she was a student at Nottingham University, we need to ask you a few questions about that.'

'Well ask away.'

'After the horrendous attack Jean suffered when she lived in Nottingham before, why did her mother bring her back down to Nottinghamshire to live?'

'After she was attacked by those bastards, our Jean was never the same, she became totally withdrawn, refused to speak and would hardly eat. It was as though she'd completely given up on life and just wanted to die. My sister Glenys, looked after her twenty-four seven, and gradually Jean started to recover slightly.'

'So why bring her back down here? Closer to where the attack happened?'

'Just when things were starting to improve a little with Jean, my sister was diagnosed with cancer. The doctors informed her she had Stage 4 pancreatic cancer. The prognosis they gave her, was that she only had months, rather than years to live.

Glenys immediately sold everything in Scotland and brought Jean down here to live with me, so I could continue to take care of her, after her mother passed away.'

'Why couldn't Jean's father take care of her?' asked Rachel.

'Glenys had been separated from her husband Ben, for a number of years, so that was never going to happen. Glenys knew I'd recently lost my husband Eric, she thought that Jean would be good company for me too. You see, Jean and I always got on really well, she's a lovely girl.'

A tear formed in the older woman's eye, 'Was a lovely girl, sorry.'

'So, when did Glenys and Jean come down here to live with you?' asked Tina.

'They sold their house and came down to stay with me a couple of years ago. My sister's condition deteriorated quickly and she passed away less than a month after they had arrived here. It was a really hard time, Jean regressed a little after her mum's death, but over the last eighteen months she'd really started to improve again. I began to see glimpses of the old Jean, how she was before the attack. She looked healthy, smiled a lot and was eating properly. Like I said before, Jean and I always got on really well, we were having a good time, things were going well.'

'How was Jean's relationship with her father?'

'Her father is a good man. Ben is very religious, some might say devout. Although he was estranged from Glenys, he never, ever stopped loving Jean. The only reason Ben and our Glenys separated was because of his work, he was some sort of specialist soldier, always away from home. In the end, Glenys couldn't take the long absences anymore and they separated permanently.'

'What do you mean, "specialist soldier", Mrs Fraser?' asked Rachel.

'Please, call me Maggie. I'm not sure really. I know he was in the Royal Marines and that he was a brilliant shot, but then he joined something different and was forever being sent overseas at a moment's notice. He would be gone for months sometimes and there was never any contact back to Glenys, she never had any idea where he was, or what he was doing. Twice he came back wounded, but as soon as his wounds healed, he would be sent away again. Even when he was home he could never talk to Glenys about where he'd been or what he'd been doing, I think it was that silence that caused them to split up in the end. The separation hit my brother in law really hard, he was absolutely devoted to Jean, he worshipped his daughter. He even left his beloved job in the army to try and win Glenys back, but it was too late.'

'What did Ben do when he came out of the army?'

'He got a job working for the Royal Family as a ghillie, a stag hunter. He still works up at Balmoral, he's very well regarded up there.'

'Do you have any photographs of Ben?' asked Tina.

'I've got some here somewhere.'

Maggie stood and stepped over to the sideboard, she opened one of the drawers and took out a black photo album. She placed the album on the coffee table and turned the pages. There were a couple of photographs of Ben in his Royal Marine dress uniform and also one of him in a ghillie suit.

Finally, she found the most recent photograph.

Ben Mackay was standing outside a chapel with a sombre expression on his face, dressed in a black suit, white shirt and black tie.

'This one's the most recent, it was taken at Jean's funeral about six weeks ago.'

'Do you mind if I borrow this photograph Maggie?'

'Of course, I don't mind, but can I ask why?'

'I'm really sorry, but I can't say at the moment. I can let

you have it back tomorrow and I'll tell you then, if that's okay?'

Without saying a word, she handed over the photograph to Tina, closed the album, returned it to the sideboard and sat back down.

'Thank you, Maggie, I really appreciate it', smiled Tina.

'Maggie, you said earlier that Jean was doing well, what caused the change in her, why did she do what she did?' asked Rachel.

'I've thought about that so much and I'm convinced it was that bloody newspaper article that caused her to go backwards. After seeing that report in the paper, it was as though she had regressed right back to the day after the attack.'

'What newspaper article?'

'I've still got a copy of the newspaper, I'll fetch it and show you.'

Once again, she stood up from her armchair and left the room. She returned a couple of minutes later, clutching an old copy of the Worksop Chronicle. She placed the newspaper on the coffee table, then opened it on the pages that held the article.

There was a full-page story, reporting on the opening of the new Sexual Offences Investigation Team offices at Carlton in Lindrick.

In the very centre of the page was a photograph of Cavalie Naylor, he stood shaking hands with Superintendent Maurice Dennington, both men smiled into the camera. The article outlined how it was Naylor Properties Limited that had built the new state of the art offices and how Superintendent Dennington had been selected to lead the dedicated new team.

Maggie pointed at the article, 'It was as though reading about the type of offences that would be investigated there, tipped our Jean right back over the edge. I found her sobbing her heart out just staring at the article. I tried to talk to her, but she wouldn't or couldn't speak again. She took herself off to her room and stayed in there crying for a long time. She must have dropped off to sleep eventually, because the crying stopped.'

After a couple of hours, I went upstairs to her room and told her that I had to go out that afternoon. I had to go to the dentist, but I needed to go over to Mansfield and see a specialist about my wisdom teeth. I still to this day, blame myself for what happened; if I hadn't gone to see that bloody dentist, our Jean would still be alive.'

Once again Maggie started to get upset, Rachel walked over to the armchair to comfort her, she put an arm around the old woman's shoulders and asked gently, 'What happened Maggie?'

'When I got home from the dentist, I found a note from Jean on the dining table. It just said, "I need to think, gone to the woods for a walk". I knew she meant Farriers Wood, it's a large wood that's quite close to here, there's a path that runs through the middle of it. It's a beautiful spot, well it was a beautiful spot. I went straight to the woods, I had a feeling that something was dreadfully wrong. I found Jean lying under an oak tree, just off the path, there was an empty vodka bottle at her side. At first I thought the poor wee girl was drunk, but then as I tried to rouse her, I saw the empty packets of paracetamol all around her. I couldn't wake her, I knew she was dead. I went as fast as I could, to the nearest phone box and called the police.'

She was sobbing steadily now.

'I'm sorry Maggie, I know this is still very painful for you.'

'It's like it happened yesterday lass, I still cry every night. It was all so needless, if only she had talked to me, we could've worked through it.'

'What about her father, Ben? When did you inform him?' asked Tina.

'That evening, I phoned Ben's work and left a message. He came straight down that night and stayed with me until after the funeral. He was very quiet after the service, so I thought it would be a good time to give him the letter Jean had left for him.'

'What letter?'

'When I was sorting through Jean's things in her room, I found a sealed envelope addressed to her dad. I can tell you detective, I've never seen such a tough man break down so badly, Ben cried like a wee bairn as he read the letter. He wouldn't let me see it, he just folded the letter, put it in his jacket pocket and asked me to show him the newspaper article.'

'This newspaper article?'

'Yes. That's a different copy, I bought this newspaper afterwards, for the inquest. Ben kept the original one, the one Jean had read.'

'You've got no idea what was in the letter from Jean to her father?'

'No, he wouldn't show it to me, he stayed until the funeral, then left the next day and went back up to Scotland.'

'Didn't he stay for the Coroner's Inquest?'

'No, he didn't want to, he did say something very strange before he left, though.'

'What was that?'

'He said that he didn't need a Coroner to pass judgement on what had happened; that the Lord God had made a judgement already. He said to me, that God had told him exactly what had happened to Jean and what needed to happen now. I didn't really understand what he was saying I just put it down to his grief.'

Rachel glanced at her watch, it was now almost twenty past seven, she had to make contact with Danny before seven thirty.

'Maggie, Tina's going to stay here with you, she's going to take a statement from you. I've got to nip over to the police station in Worksop, then I'll be back. Are you going to be okay?'

'Aye lass, it's still very upsetting, that's all, Jean was such a lovely wee girl.'

Rachel took the photograph of Ben Mackay from Tina, put it in her pocket and left the house.

CHAPTER 61

7.30am Monday 27th March 1986
Ranby Village, Nottinghamshire

'Come here you silly cow and see for yourself! Look, they're out there on the lane!'

The woman slowly got out of bed, and joined her husband standing at the bedroom window.

'I can't see anything', she said sleepily.

Maurice Dennington grabbed a handful of his wife's long auburn hair and pushed her face against the cold glass of the window. With his other hand, he punched her hard in the kidneys, then screamed in her ear, 'What's that red Fiesta down there then? Fucking scotch mist!'

He pulled her back away from the window, punched her on the back of the head and threw her back onto the bed.

Liz Dennington curled up on the bed, she drew her knees up to her chest gasping for breath, she was still winded from the blow to her kidneys. She fully expected the beating to continue as her enraged husband stomped around their luxurious bedroom.

He was muttering to himself, she could just make out the words, Flint and surveillance, but that was all. She desperately wanted to cry, but she knew from bitter experience, if she attracted any attention to herself, her brute of a husband would definitely continue the physical assault.

So, like she had done many times before, she buried her face into the pillow and remained silent.

Liz Dennington had met her husband just before he was due to go to Bramshill Police College. At that time he was charm personified and a very good-looking man. When she had first seen him, he was walking through West Bridgford in his uniform, she had thought he looked amazing.

Liz Dennington was still a very attractive woman, but back then she had been stunning, with long auburn hair and bright, sparkling green eyes. At that time, she had a figure to die for, so when she began chatting to the handsome sergeant he had been only too pleased to engage in conversation with her.

It was truly a whirlwind romance, they had married six weeks after that first meeting. Liz was an only child and at the time they had met she still lived with and cared for her elderly mother, her father had passed away when she was still a toddler. Her mother warned her she was moving too fast in the relationship, but Liz thought she knew better and had ignored her mother's advice.

It was on the night of his promotion party to Inspector, six weeks after they had married, that the veneer of normality finally slipped away from her husband.

As soon as they returned home from the celebration, for no apparent reason, he launched into a vicious verbal tirade which was quickly followed by a physical assault. He was very clever and calculating during the assault and had only punched her where the bruises wouldn't show. She had considered going to the police the next morning to report it, but had decided against it, fearing no one would believe her.

From that day on, the beatings had become a regular occurrence. Liz felt as though she was living with two different men; whenever they were in company he was perfectly charming, when they were alone together he was a brutal, depraved monster.

The assaults were not only confined to physical beatings, he regularly abused her sexually. He would force her to commit gross, disgusting, painful acts at the threat of another beating. He often left her defiled and bloodied on their marital bed, the same bed she was now curled up on, trying her hardest to disappear.

Finally, Dennington stalked out of the bedroom, stormed down the stairs and picked up the telephone in the hallway.

Liz crept from the bed and listened in on the call.

The house they shared was a palace, it was decorated beautifully and was set at the top of a hill looking down over a sloping garden towards the lane. There were ornate metal gates that opened onto the York stone, paved driveway.

For Liz, the house had always been nothing more than a gilded cage.

She listened to her angry husband, 'Good morning sir, its Maurice Dennington, sorry it's so early.'

There was a pause.

'I'll tell you what's so urgent sir, it's that snide fucker, Danny Flint. Against my strict instructions he's placed a twenty-four-hour surveillance team on me. He's got his goons watching my every move. I won't stand for it sir, you need to speak to him today and get this surveillance off my back, it's bloody ludicrous.'

There was a longer pause.

'There's absolutely no reason for it, sir. Flint's a jealous little fucker, who resents the fact that I went to Bramshill and that I'm ahead of him in the game. He's just trying to score points against me and my department.'

Another pause.

'Well, I'm sure you do think he's a good detective sir, but I won't stand for it and I'm going to put a stop to it right now. You need to speak to Flint this morning, sir, or I'll be making a direct complaint about his conduct to the Chief Constable.'

Dennington rammed the phone back on its cradle.

He grabbed his coat, document case and car keys, stormed out of the house and slammed the front door. He used the fob on his car keys to remotely open the electric metal gates, then walked down the lane to the red Fiesta.

As he approached the car he could see it had two occupants, both male.

Tapping on the driver's window, he indicated for the detective to wind the window down.

It had now started to rain; a heavy drizzle was falling.

The driver of the car lowered the window a fraction and Dennington launched into a tirade, 'What the fuck do you two idiots think you're doing?'

'We've been ordered to keep an eye on you, make sure you're safe and everything's okay sir.'

'On whose orders?'

'Our gaffer, Chief Inspector Flint, he told us there was a strong possibility that your life could be in danger.'

'My life in danger, I've never heard anything so preposterous. If I see either of you two again any time today, I'll have your fucking jobs, is that clear?'

'But sir, our orders are to stay with you at all times.'

'I don't give a flying fuck about your orders detective! I've just telephoned Chief Superintendent Wainwright and put Danny Flint's bollocks in the mangle, for setting up this surveillance. If you two don't want to be the subject of a formal complaint yourselves, you'd better disappear right now, is that clear?'

'If you say so, sir.'

The detective started the car and drove off along the lane, away from Dennington's house.

Dennington stalked back up the drive and got into his Mercedes.

As he drove out of the driveway he cursed out loud, 'Fucking Danny Flint, I'll crucify the little wanker!'

He turned right along the lane, heading for his office at Carlton in Lindrick.

From the bedroom window, Liz Dennington had watched the drama unfold. As she watched her pig of a husband drive away, a feeling of despair and helplessness overwhelmed her, she felt her legs buckle beneath her.

She sat on the bedroom floor and sobbed softly.

CHAPTER 62

7.30am Monday 27th March 1986
Worksop Police Station, Nottinghamshire

Rachel walked into the deserted CID office at Worksop police station. She grabbed the nearest telephone and dialled the number for Danny Flint's office.

It was answered on the first ring, 'Chief Inspector Flint.'

'Sir, it's Rachel, everything's okay at the Gateford Road address, Ben Mackay isn't there. I think we're definitely on the right lines though, boss.'

'What do you mean?'

'Ben Mackay could easily be our man, it seems that Jean Mackay committed suicide soon after seeing a newspaper article about the opening of the offices for the new Sexual Offences Investigation Team. The article had a big picture of Cavalie Naylor shaking hands with Superintendent Dennington. The aunt thinks, it was reading about the types of offences that would be investigated there, that caused her niece to go downhill so quickly, but what if it was because she recognised the two men in the photograph? The aunt also said her niece had been perfectly fine before she saw the article and was almost back to being her old self, back to how she was before the attack.'

'What about Ben Mackay? What can Mrs Fraser tell us about him?'

'From how she describes it, I'd say he was definitely in some sort of Special Forces set up, before he left the military.'

'Where is he now?'

'According to the aunt he returned to Scotland, straight after the funeral.'

'What's he doing in Scotland?'

'You're going to love this boss, he now works as a ghillie, hunting stags with the rich and famous on the Queen's estate at Balmoral.'

'Bloody hell!'

'One other thing you need to hear, Mrs Fraser told me that Ben Mackay said something weird before he left after the funeral. Just a second boss, I made a note of it.'

Having found the note in her pocket book, Rachel continued, 'He told her that, he didn't need a Coroner to pass judgement on what had happened. The Lord God had made a judgement already, and that God had told him exactly what had happened to Jean and what needed to happen now.'

'Has Mrs Fraser seen him since the funeral?'

'No boss.'

'Anything else Rachel?'

'Yes, I've managed to get a recent photograph of Ben Mackay. It was taken six weeks ago at his daughter's funeral.'

'Fantastic, I'll get onto the Royal household at Balmoral and see what they can tell us about Ben Mackay. I want you to go straight to Kings Mill Hospital and show that photograph to Pc Moreton, you can collect Tina from Gateford Road later. This is now the top priority Rachel, I need to know if Pc Moreton can identify Ben Mackay as being the man who assaulted him.'

'Ok boss, I'm on my way.'

CHAPTER 63

7.45am Monday 27th March 1986
Major Crime Investigation Unit, Mansfield

Danny had just put the telephone down after the call from Rachel Moore when it immediately began to ring again.

He picked it up straight away, 'Chief Inspector Flint.'

'Boss, its Dc Lorimar, I'm calling you from Ranby nick, we've just been ordered off the surveillance of Superintendent Dennington.'

'What do you mean ordered off? Who by?'

'Superintendent bloody Dennington, that's who, he's given us both a right bollocking and said he'd spoken to the Chief Super. He said we were to stop the surveillance straightaway, or he would make a formal complaint about our conduct.'

'So, let me get this straight, you're at Ranby nick and nobody is watching Dennington?'

'The Superintendent was mad as hell. I'm sorry boss we had no choice.'

'Alright Glen, you and Wayne stay put at Ranby. I'll speak to the Chief Superintendent and try and get to the bottom of this. Hopefully, I'll have you two back on the surveillance as soon as possible. It's not your fault, you had no choice but to back off, stay in the CID office at Ranby nick and wait for my call.'

Danny replaced the phone, picked it up straightaway and dialled the number for the switchboard, 'Good morning, its Detective Chief Inspector Flint at the MCIU, I need you to find me the phone number for the Balmoral Estates at Ballater, Aberdeenshire. If possible I'd like a direct line number for the Secretary of the Royal Household.'

There was a pause.

'Okay, I'll wait for you to call back, thanks.

Less than two minutes later the phone rang and Danny answered, 'Chief Inspector Flint.'

It was the operator on the switchboard, Danny picked up a pen and scribbled the telephone number down on his blotter.

'Thanks, that's excellent.'

Danny finished the call then dialled the number he'd just been given. The call was answered very promptly, 'Good morning, the Balmoral Estate, Sir Jarvis Eccles speaking.'

'Good morning Sir Jarvis, my name's Detective Chief Inspector Danny Flint from the Nottinghamshire Constabulary. I was hoping to speak with a ghillie who works on the estate, a Mr Ben Mackay.'

'I'm afraid that's out of the question Chief Inspector, Mackay is currently on leave following a recent bereavement in his family.'

'I see, can you tell me when he started his leave, please?'

'Just a second, I'll grab the paperwork.'

Danny heard a filing cabinet open and close, then papers being shuffled.

'Chief Inspector, Mackay started his leave on March 15th, we're expecting him back on March 29th. Is there a problem? Mackay's an absolutely brilliant ghillie, he came to us highly recommended when he left the military. He served in the Royal Marines then with distinction in the Special Boat Service, he's extremely well liked by both Her Majesty and Prince Philip.'

'I don't know yet, Sir Jarvis. Does your paperwork say where he intended to go during his leave?'

'No, it doesn't, but I talked to Mackay before he left, he requested the use of one of the Land Rovers from the estate. He told me then he was going down south, to Derbyshire I think. He wanted to finalise some issues that remained outstanding after his daughter's death. I believe he may have mentioned that he wanted to spend some time walking in the Derbyshire Dales.'

'Did you allow him to take the vehicle?'

'I thought it would have been churlish to refuse the man, bearing in mind the recent loss of his daughter. The poor chap was obviously suffering, he told me he needed it for his mission, not his holiday. I put the fact he used military jargon down as a slip caused by his grief. So, the answer to your question is, yes he's got one of our vehicles.'

'Can you let me have details of the vehicle he's using please, Sir Jarvis?'

'Yes, I've made a note of that on the paperwork, he's got one of the old vehicles, it's a bit battered I'm afraid. It's a Land Rover Defender, registered number FJH 591.'

'What colour's the vehicle?'

'My dear boy, all the vehicles here are the same colour, its British Racing green of course.'

'Have you had any contact with Mr Mackay since he left Balmoral?'

'None whatsoever. Is the chap in some sort of trouble? I'd like to be kept informed please, Chief Inspector. Like I said earlier, Mackay is one of the Royal Family's favourites.'

'As soon as I have any more information Sir Jarvis, I'll let you know straightaway. In the meantime, if Mr Mackay returns to Balmoral, or contacts you, would you please give me a call at Nottinghamshire Police headquarters as a matter of urgency?'

'Of course, Chief Inspector. If there's anything else I can do for you, please don't hesitate to call.'

Danny put the phone down, his mind was racing.

Ben Mackay had all the skills needed to have carried out the murders and now it had also been confirmed that he was back in England at the time they were committed, albeit his employers thought he was in Derbyshire. He had transport and more importantly he had a genuine motive to commit the murders.

He just needed Pc Moreton to identify Ben Mackay as the man who had attacked him, then he would be able to circulate him on the PNC as wanted.

Ten minutes passed slowly by as Danny paced up and down in his office. He heard a quiet tap on the door, turned and saw Chief Superintendent Wainwright standing there.

'Good morning Danny, I think you and I need to have a conversation.'

'Don't tell me sir, Maurice Dennington's been on the phone.'

Bill Wainwright smiled a wry smile and gestured for Danny to take a seat, both men sat down.

'Oh, yes Danny, Dennington's been on the phone alright. He's spitting feathers, he was raging when he called me first thing this morning. What the fuck is all this about a surveillance on him, detectives sitting outside his own house, watching his every move?'

'It was for his own good sir, but the idiot has just forced the two detectives to back off. I've got them on standby at Ranby nick.'

'Explain to me what's going on Danny, for Christ's sake.'

'Right sir, the theory we're currently pursuing is that Maurice Dennington was possibly one of four men, involved in a serious sexual assault on a young woman at Nottingham University back in 1977. Two of the four men believed to have been involved, were Cavalie Naylor and Edward Hall, the third man of the group is believed to be Frank Reece who we think has been abducted by the same man who assaulted Pc Moreton and left him for dead. The victim of the sexual assault in 1977 was a young woman called Jean Mackay, she committed suicide a short time ago after seeing a photograph in the local paper of Maurice Dennington and Cavalie Naylor at the opening of the Sexual Offence Investigation Team's new offices. Her father's a man called Ben Mackay, who's an ex Special Boat Service operative, who now works for the Royal Family at Balmoral as a ghillie. Literally, just before you came in, I was on the telephone to the Secretary of the Royal Household, Sir Jarvis Eccles. He has confirmed that Mackay is somewhere in the East Midlands on compassionate leave. He has access to transport as he's borrowed one of the Land Rovers used on the Balmoral Estate.'

'Bloody hell Danny! This is a right fucking mess.'

The telephone began to ring again, Danny grabbed the phone on the second ring, 'Chief Inspector Flint.'

'Boss it's Rachel, I've just broken every speed limit getting to Kings Mill Hospital. I'm on the ward with Pc Moreton now, he's just positively identified Ben Mackay as the man who attacked him.'

'Great work Rachel, get him statemented, then go back to Gateford Road and pick up Tina.'

Danny put the phone down

'Well that's it sir, Pc Moreton has just positively identified Ben Mackay as the man who attacked him at gunpoint.'

'Where exactly is your surveillance team now Danny?'

'They're at Ranby Police Station, sir.'

'Get on the phone, tell them to get their arses over to Carlton in Lindrick. I want surveillance on Dennington immediately, if he whines about it again, put him onto me.'

'Yes sir.'

Danny picked up the phone, dialled the number for Ranby and ordered the two detectives to travel to Carlton in Lindrick immediately and resume surveillance on Dennington.

Chief Superintendent Wainwright stood up and said, 'I'll go back to my office and give Dennington a call. I'll tell him what the situation is, if he doesn't like it he can take it up with the Chief Constable.'

CHAPTER 64

7.50am Monday 27th March 1986
Sexual Offences Investigation Team, Carlton
in Lindrick, Nottinghamshire

Superintendent Maurice Dennington was still seething as he
drove his Mercedes through the open gates and into the car
park of the SOIT car park. It was still early, there were only
two other vehicles in the car park.

He grabbed his document holder from the front seat and
got out of the car. He walked purposefully towards the stone
steps, that led up to the front doors of the building. He paid
no attention to the man with steel grey hair, who walked
down the steps straight towards him.

As they drew level, the man with the grey hair stopped
and said quietly, 'Superintendent Dennington?'

'Yes, that's me. Do I know you?'

'You'll know who I am soon enough; do as I tell you, or
I'll kill you right here.'

For the first time, Dennington saw the black handgun the
man was holding, the weapon was then firmly pressed into
his ribcage.

Dennington spluttered, 'I don't know who you are, or
what the fuck you think you're doing, but you won't get
away with this.'

'Shut your mouth Dennington! Speak again and I'll
spread your guts all over this car park. Now walk towards
the Land Rover.'

He nodded his head in the direction of the Land Rover.

As realisation dawned on Dennington that the man wasn't bluffing, the colour drained from his face, he obeyed the instruction and walked slowly towards the scruffy green Land Rover parked in the very corner of the car park.

Once they were at the vehicle, the Watcher kept the handgun pressed into the ribs of Dennington, then he reached forward and opened the back door.

'Get in Dennington', he whispered through gritted teeth.

Dennington dropped the document holder, he was carrying, then said in a voice edged with panic, 'You're totally mad, you won't get away with this. Look around you man, there are fucking security cameras everywhere!'

The Watcher smashed the barrel of the gun into Dennington's mouth, then delivered a more concussive blow to the back of his head, using the heavy grip of the pistol. As Dennington slumped forward, stunned by the two blows, the Watcher grabbed him and bundled him into the back of the Land Rover. He climbed in after Dennington, bound his hands and feet with cable ties, then gagged his mouth with Gaffer tape.

He climbed back out of the vehicle, quietly closed the back door and looked around the car park. There wasn't a soul about, there had been no witnesses to the abduction. He wasn't concerned about the CCTV cameras; by the time they were checked it would be too late for Dennington.

The Watcher got into the driver's seat, started the engine and slowly drove out of the car park.

The abduction of Superintendent Maurice Dennington had only taken two and a half minutes, from start to finish.

CHAPTER 65

9.00am Monday 27th March 1986
Major Crime Investigation Unit, Mansfield

Rob sat with Danny in his office, they were discussing possible locations where Frederick Reece could be imprisoned. Now that Pc Moreton had positively identified Ben Mackay as the person who had assaulted him, it was almost certainly Mackay that had been responsible for the abduction of Frederick Reece. If Reece wasn't dead already, he had to be hidden somewhere near the abduction point.

'It's an impossible task Danny, it literally is like looking for a needle in a haystack.'

'I know it's difficult Rob, but we now know that Mackay's using a green Land Rover. I can't help thinking we missed a trick there, Rob. Do you remember the old lady who lived across the road from Edward Hall, she mentioned seeing an old Land Rover?'

'You mean Mrs Hughes, I remember that sighting, but we checked all the available CCTV cameras. At the time there was no sign of any similar vehicle and the house to house didn't reveal anybody else who'd seen a Land Rover.'

'You're right Rob, hindsight's always twenty-twenty vision.'

'At the time, her sighting of that particular vehicle couldn't be connected to what had happened.'

'Anyway, I want you to start at the Co-op in Farnsfield, where the Range Rover was found, then work your way out checking any CCTV you can find. You never know, we might get lucky and pick up a sighting of the green Land Rover.'

There was a knock on the office door and a very worried looking Chief Superintendent Wainwright walked in.

Rob stood up to leave.

'It's alright Inspector, this won't take a minute. Danny, is the surveillance back on Dennington?'

'Yes sir, the team arrived at Carlton in Lindrick just after eight o'clock this morning. The Superintendent was already there, his car was parked in the car park. Is there a problem?'

'I'm not sure. I've been trying to call him and he's not picking up the phone. I'm worried Danny, if his car's there, why isn't he answering my call?'

Danny picked up the phone and called the control room, 'Hello, it's Chief Inspector Flint, I want you to contact Dc Glen Lorimar, call sign MQ73, tell him, from me, to go inside the SOIT offices and make sure that Superintendent Dennington is at his desk. Call me straight back, once they've responded.'

After five tense minutes the phone rang. Danny answered it immediately, 'Chief Inspector Flint.'

'It's the control room sir, MQ73 have just called in, no sign of Superintendent Dennington in his office, they're saying that none of the staff working there have seen him today. On the way into the offices, they have found what appears to be the Superintendent's document case in a corner of the car park. They're awaiting your instructions sir.'

'Tell them to start checking the CCTV in the building, the place is surrounded by cameras. If they see anything at all suspicious on those cameras, they're to call me back immediately.'

'Yes sir.'

Danny replaced the telephone and turned towards Bill Wainwright, 'Dennington's not there, not in his office, not in the building. His car's in the car park but no one has seen him there this morning. There's every likelihood that Mackay has now got Maurice Dennington and Frederick Reece.'

'Right Danny, get back onto the control room, I want an armed team travelling immediately to the Carlton in Lindrick area. I want them on standby. I take it the description of Mackay and the details of the Land Rover have already been circulated.'

Danny nodded, 'Yes sir.'

'As soon as we get a sighting of Ben Mackay or the Land Rover, I want the armed police units deployed. I think we could be running out of time on this Danny.'

'I'll get it organised, sir'.

Wainwright left the office and once again Danny reached for the telephone on his desk.

As soon as he'd arranged the armed response units to be deployed, Danny turned to Rob and said, 'Get a vehicle Rob, I want to be out there on the ground. We're going up to Carlton in Lindrick, tell Brian to man the telephones here, I want to know the minute anything comes through. Make sure the vehicle you get is fitted with a VHF radio, so we can monitor the control room radio traffic.'

'Will do Danny.'

CHAPTER 66

9.30am, Monday 27th March 1986
Rampton Hospital, Nottinghamshire

Breakfast in the large hall had been the same as usual, cornflakes and toast with a mug of strong, sweet tea. Jimmy Wade had eaten his food almost automatically. If today went as planned, it would be his last meal inside this dreadful place. He felt calm and in control, he knew exactly what he needed to do to get out of there.

Clive Winstanley sat opposite him, loudly chewing a slice of toast, his mouth was wide open as he chewed. Jimmy could see the masticated toast being hurled around the huge mouth, before it was swallowed with an equally loud gulp. The toast was washed down noisily with a mouthful of tea.

'For fuck's sake Clive, is everything you do loud?'

The huge West Indian grinned, showing his teeth that were covered in the remnants of the toast.

'Jimmy man, you should hear me when I'm with a woman, I make the bitches squeal man, believe me.'

Jimmy shook his head in disgust, he normally wouldn't tolerate being in the same vicinity as Winstanley, but he knew that for his plan to succeed he would need to stay on the right side of the giant paedophile.

Today, they were both on the roster to work at the concrete slab making facility.

The facility was located near to the perimeter fence of the high security hospital.

Three men were down to work on the concrete slabs that day, the third man was the serial arsonist Lester Silwell. An effeminate man, Silwell was considered a grass by every other inmate, so Jimmy hadn't mentioned any of his plans to him. He'd also ensured Winstanley didn't breathe a word of the plan to Silwell, by making a promise to the big West Indian, that he would ensure he got out too.

It didn't bother Wade that Clive Winstanley was considered a nonce by other inmates at the hospital.

Wade knew Winstanley had been imprisoned ten years ago, for the vicious abduction and rape of three schoolgirls in Northampton. He was now almost fifty-five years of age, but was still extremely strong and powerful. He'd been sentenced to be detained indefinitely; realistically, there was no chance of Clive Winstanley ever being released from Rampton Hospital. He truly was criminally insane. Over recent years, he had portrayed a placid image to the social workers and nurses, that was the main reason he had managed to get himself on the concrete working party on a regular basis. He was also selected on a regular basis because he was such a naturally strong man, his work was second to none, he could manhandle the heavy slabs with ease.

Wade leaned forward and said, 'How many nurses will be watching us today, Clive?'

'Normally, it's two nurses for every one of us, so cos Silwell's coming too, I reckon there'll be six nurses with us.'

'Are you going to do exactly what I tell you to do?'

Winstanley roared with laughter, 'Yeah man, of course I am! I'll be drinking beer tonight in the pub with some girlies.'

Jimmy leaned forward and hissed, 'For fuck's sake Clive, keep it down. I've told you we've got to be all meek and mild, until it's time to act. If you're serious about wanting to get out, you've got to do exactly what I tell you, when I tell you! Have you got that?'

'Yeah man, I got it. You eating that toast Jimmy?'

Jimmy pushed the plate containing the last slice of toast, towards Clive and grinned, 'It's all yours mate, it's all yours.'

He reached down, slipped his fingers inside his boot, felt for the sharpened crochet hook in his boot lining and grinned when he felt the hard steel.

CHAPTER 67

9.30am, Monday 27th March 1986
Worksop, Nottinghamshire

The Watcher parked the Land Rover near to the entrance of Farriers Wood.

The last time he'd been to this woodland, was on the day he'd buried his daughter, he had wanted to see for himself the very spot where his precious daughter had taken her own life.

He and Maggie Fraser had come to the wood alone, after the funeral. They had held each other and wept beneath the oak tree where Maggie had found Jean, lying dead, two weeks before.

The Watcher wiped a tear from his cheek and zipped up his jacket. He got out of the Land Rover and glanced up and down the street. There was a row of four terrace houses on the other side of the road, that were fifty yards from the entrance to the wood.

Farriers Wood was located on the very edge of Worksop, directly opposite the entrance there was nothing but open fields.

Satisfied there were no prying eyes watching his every move, he walked to the rear of the vehicle. He opened the rear door and was immediately met with grunts of protest, from a bound and gagged Dennington.

He reached past Dennington, grabbed a black grip bag and a large axe that was wrapped in a black bin liner. Just the head of the axe protruded from the bin liner.

The Watcher placed the two articles at the rear of the vehicle, then leaned back inside and whispered to Dennington, 'I'm going to remove the cable ties from your ankles and the gag from your mouth. If you try to run or shout for help, I'll kill you on the spot. You and I are going to go for a walk into the woods, where we can talk in peace, without being disturbed. Is that clear, Superintendent?'

The thought that all was not lost, flashed through Dennington's brain. If they were going to talk, he felt sure he could make this lunatic listen, he suddenly felt confident that he would be able to get out of this predicament.

He quickly nodded that he understood.

The Watcher took a large bladed knife from a scabbard attached to his belt and sliced through the cable ties that bound his captive's feet.

He replaced the knife into its scabbard, then removed the handgun from his camouflage jacket pocket.

He shoved the pistol into Dennington's face and said through gritted teeth, 'If you try anything I won't hesitate to put a bullet through your eye, do you understand me?'

Dennington nodded.

The Watcher removed the gag from his prisoner and dragged him from the back of the vehicle.

Dennington didn't protest, he just asked quietly, 'Who are you?'

'Never mind who I am, just walk slowly, two paces in front of me. Go through the entrance, then walk along the path to the woods.'

The superintendent looked wide eyed, at the black handgun in the Watcher's right hand. He was so transfixed by the handgun, he never noticed the large axe that was now resting on top of the grip bag being held in the Watcher's left hand.

'Start walking, Dennington', was the whispered order.

Having closed the doors of the Land Rover, the Watcher walked behind Dennington, the two men moved along the path and deeper into Farriers Wood.

After ten minutes walking the Watcher suddenly said, 'Stop there. Turn left off the path, then start walking again.'

Dennington did as he was instructed.

After a distance of fifty yards he heard the Watcher's voice again, 'Stop there Dennington.'

Having put down the black grip bag and the axe, the Watcher stepped in close behind the terrified policeman, using the razor-sharp knife to slice through the cable ties that bound his wrists.

'Strip. Get your clothes off, now!'

He started to protest, but immediately felt the blade of the skinning knife, slice across his cheek.

'This isn't a fucking debate, do what I tell you!'

Dennington's hand shot up to his cheek, he felt the warm blood on his fingers then felt it start to trickle slowly down his face, slowly he started to undress and said, 'I thought we were going to talk?'

'Oh, we're going to talk alright, but only when I'm ready, hurry up!'

Finally, Dennington stood there naked, instantly he felt vulnerable and cold. His police uniform lay in a crumpled heap at his feet.

His voice flat and devoid of all emotion, the Watcher ordered, 'Lie on the floor and put your hands behind your back.'

Dennington could still feel the blood on his cheek from the first protest, so he did as he was told.

Quickly the Watcher moved in, once again he bound Dennington's hands and feet with cable ties. As soon as the cable ties were tightly secured he grabbed a length of strong blue nylon cord from his bag, he tied the cord very tightly around his captive's knees.

Having effectively immobilised his captive the Watcher lifted Dennington up and dragged him over to the base of a large oak tree. He sat him upright, so his back leaned against the gnarled trunk of the old tree.

He then returned silently to the discarded black bags.

First, he took out the large axe from the bin liner and stuffed the empty plastic bag into the leather grip bag.

Dennington couldn't take his eyes off the wooden handled axe, now propped against a fallen tree, that lay five yards in front of him.

He knew he had to try and talk his way out of the situation, there was nothing he could do physically.

'You said we were going to talk, are you going to tell me what this is all about?'

The Watcher grinned malevolently, 'You still don't know, do you?'

'I've no fucking idea, I don't even know who you are!'

Reaching into the breast pocket of his camouflage jacket the Watcher removed a small photograph. He stepped over to Dennington and said with a snarl, 'But you know her, don't you, Superintendent Dennington?'

He held the photograph right in the face of the now cold and shivering Dennington.

'I don't know her, who is she? This is ridiculous, I've never seen that woman before in my life. Why don't you untie me, then we can work this out? I know I'm a police officer, but I'm prepared to turn a blind eye to your actions so far.'

'That's funny because your friend, Cavalie Naylor, was also prepared to turn a blind eye. Which was convenient for me, I now have both his eyes in a ziplock bag. I pulled them from his face while he was still drawing breath, just as the scriptures demanded. Then I slit his throat and let him bleed to death.'

'What are you talking about, how could you even imagine something as disgusting as that?'

As he spoke, the shock was evident both on Dennington's face and in his voice.

The Watcher continued, 'Before your friend Naylor died, he told me everything that happened on that night, all those years ago, at Nottingham University. He told me the names of the others involved, he told me who's idea it was, he even told me who did what. Has your memory allowed you to remember who the beautiful young woman on the photograph is yet, Dennington?'

Dennington had known exactly who the girl was, just as he had known instantly what incident the maniac was referring to, but he continued to act as though he had no idea.

Trying to maintain an even voice he said, 'I've no idea what Naylor told you, but I wasn't there that night. I do remember her face, but I don't recall ever having a conversation with her.'

'I've already visited your friends, Cavalie Naylor, Stephen Hall and Frederick Reece. They're all dead now. None of them refused to repent their sins. What about you Dennington, are you going to seek forgiveness from the Lord?'

Dennington was trying to think fast, 'You've got to help me understand why you've brought me here, what did those three men do to that poor woman?'

'We both know it wasn't just those three, Dennington. You and your friends accosted her, raped her, sodomised her and then left her naked in the middle of a field to die. You and those other three pigs treated her worse than an animal. You debased her in every way possible, for no other reason than because you could. That beautiful, innocent young woman was my daughter and the time has now come for you to pay for your sins.'

Dennington could no longer hold his own arrogance in check, he laughed out loud and sneered, 'So that's what this is all about, your precious daughter, the Scottish tart. She loved every second of it, it was obvious she'd never received so much male attention in her small, drab life. I don't see what your problem is, all we did was have a little fun with her, nobody died, we didn't kill anybody.'

The Watcher felt bile rise in his throat as he listened to Dennington mocking his dead daughter, he wanted to kill him there and then but the scriptures demanded that he control his rage. He had to give the demon one chance to atone for his sin before he was dispatched back to the Hell he had crawled out of.

Through gritted teeth he said to Dennington, 'The sight of you, dressed in your fancy police uniform, the head of a Sex Crimes Unit, was too much for her to take. My beautiful daughter went against the teachings of the old testament, she crumbled and took her own life. Be under no illusion Dennington, you and your three friends killed my daughter, just as surely as if you had each taken a gun to her head and pulled the trigger.'

The Watcher shook his head, carefully he replaced the photograph in his breast pocket.

He sat down on the fallen tree, opposite Dennington, closed his eyes and said softly, 'Lighten our darkness, we beseech thee O Lord; and by thy great mercy defend us from all perils and dangers of this night; for the love of thine only son our saviour, Jesus Christ. Amen.'

Suddenly, Dennington shouted at the top of his voice, 'Help me!', the plaintive cry echoed around the trees.

Quickly, the Watcher removed the razor sharp Sumunugashi skinning knife from it's scabbard, he stepped over to Dennington and dragged the blade slowly across the man's chest.

There was an agonised howl of pain, which was quickly stifled as the Watcher wrapped Gaffer tape around the naked man's head. There would be no more cries of help from Dennington, nor would anybody hear his screams of agony. The brown tape was wrapped tightly around his head, completely covering his mouth.

The Watcher had heard enough vile words spew from Dennington's mouth, he knew he would never repent for his sins. It was now clear that the others had told the truth before they died, Dennington had been the leader of their group. He had indeed been the one urging them all on to commit atrocity after atrocity upon his beautiful daughter.

He walked over to the now terrified policeman, leaned in close to him, until his mouth was only inches from his ear.

He shouted into his ear, 'Devil can you hear me?'

Dennington nodded and moved his head away from the shout.

'My daughter's name was Jean Mackay; my name is Ben Mackay. I want those two names, to be the last names you hear, before I dispatch you from this earth and back down into Hell. In the name of the Lord God Almighty, this day I shall complete the work demanded by the scriptures, you will join your fellow demons in eternal damnation. As it demands in the Book of Exodus, so shall it be; Eye for eye, tooth for tooth, hand for hand, foot for foot.'

Ben Mackay walked back to the large axe and lifted it from the fallen tree.

CHAPTER 68

10.00am, Monday 27th March 1986
Worksop, Nottinghamshire

Pc Phillip Trenchard was on foot patrol in Worksop, he had covered the shopping area of his beat and was now doing a check on the very perimeter.

He was just out of his two-year probationary period and enjoyed being on foot patrol, working his beat. He had worked this same beat for almost six months, he relished the fact that he now knew it like the back of his hand.

People had got used to seeing his face and he would spend most of every day shift, exchanging pleasantries with the residents on his beat.

He turned the corner, that led onto Farriers Row, a small terrace of four Victorian houses. These four houses were the last on his beat and the last in Worksop, after this there was nothing but open fields one side of the road and the public park, Farriers Wood, on the other.

As he strolled around the bend in the road his eye was immediately drawn to the mud covered, dark green Land Rover, parked directly outside the entrance to the public park.

He stepped back around the corner, but kept the vehicle in his line of sight. He quickly took out his pocket note book from the breast pocket of his tunic and scanned the last scribbled note he'd made.

There it was in black and white, FJH 591, dark green Land Rover.

The radio message he'd received from his control room earlier, was very clear. Under no circumstances was he to approach this particular vehicle, the occupant was believed to be armed and dangerous.

The young policeman strained his eyes as he tried to make out if anyone was still with the vehicle. From his position he couldn't tell, it looked empty, but he just wasn't sure.

He stayed out of sight, took out his personal radio and said, 'Three three five to Worksop control, over.'

'Go ahead three three five, control over.'

'I'm on Farriers Row, near to the entrance of Farriers Wood. I've found that dark green Land Rover, FJH 591. It's parked up, directly outside the entrance to the wood. I can't tell if anyone's still with the vehicle, it looks abandoned, but I can't be sure, over.'

'Control to three three five, maintain a visual on the vehicle only, under no circumstances approach the vehicle or any of its occupants. Armed units are travelling to your location, eta fifteen minutes, control over.'

CHAPTER 69

10.00am, Monday 27th March 1986
Cuckney Crossroads, Nottinghamshire

Danny and Rob were driving towards Worksop along the A60, when they heard the message of the Land Rover's sighting being passed over the VHF radio. The force control room had contacted the armed units that were on standby at Carlton in Lindrick and ordered them to travel to Farriers Wood at Worksop to check on the reported sighting of the dark green Land Rover FJH 591.

Danny said, 'Farriers Wood. That's where Jean Mackay committed suicide.'

Rob gunned the engine and sped through the crossroads at Cuckney village.

'I know Farriers Wood, boss, we can be there in fifteen minutes.'

Danny grabbed the radio handset, 'Det Chief Inspector Flint to control.'

'Go ahead, control out.'

'Show myself and DI Buxton also attending Farriers Wood, eta fifteen minutes. Who's in charge of the Special Ops units that are travelling?'

'Inspector Powell sir, there are two sections of the Special Operations Unit attending, their eta is roughly the same as yours.'

'I'll liaise with Inspector Powell, on our arrival, over.'

'There's another message for you sir, we've been asked by Dc Lorimar to inform you that the CCTV at Carlton in Lindrick has been checked, it clearly shows that Superintendent Dennington has been forced into the back of a Land Rover at gunpoint. The vehicle used in the abduction was the green Land Rover, Foxtrot Juliet Hotel 591. Control out.'

'Received, thanks. Chief Inspector Flint, over.'

Danny gripped the dashboard and said, 'Put your foot down Rob, I've got a nasty feeling this isn't going to end well.'

CHAPTER 70

10.10am, Monday 27th March 1986
Rampton Hospital, Nottinghamshire

'Right, Wade and Winstanley, I want you two, to move this pile of concrete slabs from the stack near the fence, to the main store. We've got all day, so take your time, there's no rush.'

The order had come from Staff Nurse Pete Timmons, he was in overall charge of the working party.

'Right you are boss', said Clive Winstanley before smirking at Jimmy Wade.

'Silwell, I need you to make sure you keep a record of how many slabs we've got in the main store, okay?'

'Yeth both', replied Silwell in his lisping voice, as he clutched the clipboard close to his scrawny chest.

Wade looked at Winstanley, that hadn't been factored into his planning. He couldn't afford to have Lester Silwell watching their every move. As he mulled over the problem of Silwell, he had a flash of inspiration.

He suddenly knew how he could deal with Silwell and reduce the number of nurses supervising them, all at the same time.

He grinned as he picked up one of the heavy concrete slabs.

Wade and Winstanley worked at a steady pace, lifting and carrying the heavy slabs. The six nurses that had been detailed to watch them as they worked, were bored. They smoked cigarettes and chatted amongst themselves, paying little attention to the three men in their charge.

Near the main store, Jimmy turned to Silwell and said quietly, 'Lester, do me a favour mate, can you tell me the colour of this slab? Its covered in dust and I want to make sure I put it on the right pile.'

'Of courthe Jimmy, it'th a beige one. It needth to go over there.'

'Thanks Lester.'

Jimmy turned to walk towards the pile Lester had indicated, then he slammed the heavy slab directly down onto the top of Silwell's foot.

Silwell howled in pain and dropped to the floor clutching his now broken foot.

As he hadn't been tasked with doing any lifting, he wasn't wearing steel toe cap boots. All the toes on his right foot were now crushed.

Jimmy shouted, 'Over here boss, there's been an accident, Lester's hurt his foot.'

Two of the nurses quickly made their way over to the two men.

Silwell rolled around the floor, clutching his foot. He was obviously in a great deal of pain.

Wade looked suitably horrified and said, 'It was an accident boss, I turned around, Lester was right behind me, I bumped into him and lost my grip on the slab, I think it landed on his foot.'

'I can see where it landed Wade, for fuck's sake. Come on Silwell, I think you're going to have to see the doctor, that looks bad.'

'Sorry Lester', said Wade.

'Fuck off Wade! You did that on purpoth!' snarled Silwell.

'Get back to work Wade, I want all them slabs moved by the time we get back.'

Two of the nurses grabbed hold of Silwell by the arms and hoisted him up, they supported him as he hopped away with them.

Now there were only four nurses watching Wade and Winstanley.

The pile of slabs they were moving had been previously stacked directly adjacent to the perimeter fence, very cleverly the two men had moved the slabs in such a way that they had left a series of slabs that acted like steps up towards the fence.

It was nearly time for Wade to make his move.

The perimeter fence at this location, was chain link and only seven feet high. It was topped with three strands of barbed wire and beyond the fence, it was open countryside. The only thing that now stood between himself and freedom, were the four male nurses supervising them.

Jimmy Wade looked at Clive Winstanley and nodded almost imperceptibly.

Winstanley grinned, then walked over to two of the nurses, at the same time Wade sidled his way behind one of the others.

Without warning, Winstanley suddenly punched one of the nurses full in the face, the force of the blow knocked the unsuspecting nurse to the floor. The other nurse immediately grabbed the giant West Indian, around the neck.

Winstanley easily threw the second nurse over his shoulder, before disabling him with a karate chop across the windpipe. Before the other two nurses had time to react to

Winstanley's actions, Wade plunged the home made chiv deep into the first man's eye.

The nurse dropped to the floor, he went into spasm as he clutched his face.

The sharpened point of the crochet hook had gone straight through the eyeball and plunged deep into the brain of the nurse.

Wade then leapt at the last nurse. He held the chiv against the terrified man's throat and growled, 'Take off your coat.'

The nurse quickly removed his heavy coat and dropped it on the floor.

Winstanley picked up the coat, then scaled the slabs to the top of the chain link fence. He draped the jacket across the barbed wire at the top of the fence, climbed over and dropped down the other side.

'Come on Jimmy man, we need to get going, the other two nurses will be back soon.'

Wade grinned, then slowly pushed the sharpened crochet hook deep into the throat of the nurse he was holding. He twisted the chiv in the wound, then let the man drop to the floor. Desperately the nurse grabbed at his gashed throat in a futile bid to stop the bleeding. Jimmy ran up the slabs to the fence, then jumped over the final hurdle to freedom.

Both men were wearing the navy-blue overalls they had been issued with, for the working party.

As they ran from the fence across the open fields, Winstanley shouted, 'We need to find somewhere to ditch these clothes man.'

They reached the first drainage ditch and both men waded through the knee-high water.

Wade turned to Winstanley and said aggressively, 'Fuck off Clive, you're not staying with me. You're going to stand out like a sore thumb around here, whatever you're wearing. How many six foot six Rastas do you think they've got around here? Now fuck off and don't follow me. Got it?'

'Fuck off yourself Wade! I don't need you man.'

'Course you don't Clive. Good luck mate, you're going to need it.'

'Fuck off Wade!'

Winstanley then turned and sprinted away.

Jimmy marvelled at his pace, he was very fast for such a big man. It was just a pity that he was now running back towards the hospital entrance.

Wade grinned, then jogged steadily along the bottom of the next ditch, heading away from the hospital. He knew exactly which direction he needed to go, he'd replayed this moment, over and over again in his mind, in the weeks and days leading up to the escape.

He knew it would only be a matter of time before Winstanley was recaptured, but he was determined that he would not suffer the same fate.

He looked down at his blood-stained hands and the bloody chiv. He stopped jogging, then bent down, he washed the blood from his hands in the little brook that ran along the bottom of the ditch. The palm of his hand had an inch-long gash in it, caused by the base of the crochet hook. It had dug into his hand, as he plunged the makeshift weapon through the eye of the first nurse. The wound had then been made worse, as he pushed the chiv into the second nurse's throat.

He took a handkerchief from his pocket and wrapped it around his injured hand. He slipped the chiv into his pocket and resumed a steady pace as he jogged away from Rampton Hospital.

The mournful wail of an air raid siren rose to a crescendo in the distance.

The siren was only ever sounded in the event of an escape from the maximum-security hospital, it served as a warning to the surrounding villages and farms that an inmate or inmates were on the loose and appropriate precautions should be taken.

It meant parents busied themselves making sure their children were accounted for and indoors.

Local farmers checked and secured their outhouses and barns.

For Jimmy Wade, it meant he had to quicken his pace, he had a rendezvous to keep.

CHAPTER 71

10.15am, Monday 27th March 1986
Worksop, Nottinghamshire

The young constable stood in the middle of the road and raised his right arm.

Rob braked hard and came to a stop, just in front of the officer's knees. Exasperated, Rob wound the window down and said, 'What do you think you're doing? I almost knocked you flying!'

'Just pull in here please sir, this is the designated RV point. The Special Ops vans are over there and Inspector Powell instructed me not to let anyone get any closer.'

Danny got out of the car, his warrant card in hand, 'You're doing a great job son, I'm Detective Chief Inspector Flint and this is Detective Inspector Buxton, we need to liaise with Inspector Powell urgently. Where is he?'

'He's over there, near the first van, sir.'

'Thanks, come on Rob.'

The detectives walked over to the two white Transit vans, where a dozen, stern faced men donned Kevlar body armour, checked their Mp5 semi-automatic weapons and Smith and Wesson .38 revolvers. Three of the men lifted the heavy ballistic shields from the rear of the van.

Inspector Scott Powell was in his late thirties, but still incredibly fit, he maintained his fitness by running and regular gym sessions. He too, was fully kitted up in the black overalls and body armour. He made the final checks of his personal weapons. He was very much a lead from the front man, who wouldn't ask his men to do anything he wouldn't do himself.

Danny had met him on a couple of occasions and had the utmost respect for him.

Inspector Powell saw the two detectives approaching and walked over to them.

'You're going to have to wait here sir, just until we clear the Land Rover. I can't get a visual on it to see if anyone's still in the back of the vehicle. We've got to clear that, before we even think about going through the woodland. I'll be honest with you boss, it's a bit of a nightmare, I was given the background on this guy Mackay, this morning. Being tasked with searching woodland for a man like that, with his undoubted skill set, is just about our worst nightmare, and I personally think is asking for trouble. To compound matters there isn't a dog handler available to assist us, they've all been rushed up to Rampton for an urgent shout up there.'

'Scott, it's just been confirmed that he's got Superintendent Dennington, it's on CCTV at Carlton In Lindrick, he's been abducted at gunpoint by Mackay', said Danny.

'Right sir, that forces our hand a little. Let's get this Land Rover cleared first, then see where we're at shall we. There's some spare body armour in the back of the van, put it on.'

It wasn't a request and both detectives quickly donned the protective clothing.

Danny and Rob then watched from distance, as a group of four men approached the Land Rover behind the cover of ballistic shields.

While two men covered the doors and windows of the vehicle, with their semi-automatic weapons, the other two men tried the doors. All the doors of the vehicle were unlocked and very quickly the vehicle was cleared.

There was no sign of Superintendent Dennington or Ben Mackay.

After clearing the vehicle, every member of the Special Operations Unit team advanced to the Land Rover.

Inspector Powell conducted a quick briefing with his men, then waved Danny and Rob over.

'Chief Inspector Flint, we're going to start advancing through the woodland, I've got to insist that you remain at least twenty yards behind us. My personal advice would be to remain here, but I know you're not going to want to do that.'

'Scott, I believe our suspect Ben Mackay has returned here specifically because it's the place where his daughter committed suicide, pass me that map of the woodland, I can show you exactly where she was found.'

'That's all very well and good sir, but it's only a theory. We will still have to advance towards that point tactically, using cover as we go. Normally, we'd never advance like this towards a loaded gun, but as you say one of our own's in serious danger, so we're left with little or no choice on this occasion. I'm going to put Sergeant Rodgers with you, to look after you. I know you've both completed a basic handgun course, but I don't want you getting too close. Do exactly what the sergeant tells you to do, without argument Chief Inspector, rank doesn't count here, got it?'

'I understand Scott, we'll be guided by Sergeant Rodgers.'

Inspector Powell then turned to his men, 'Right, you've been briefed, move tactically and carefully, use whatever cover you can find and watch out for each other. The first sign of movement, don't be shy I want to hear a shout of contact. Understood?'

There was a chorus of approval before the men made their way into Farriers Wood with Sergeant Rodgers, Danny and Rob bringing up the rear.

CHAPTER 72

10.15am, Monday 27th March 1986
Worksop, Nottinghamshire

Ben Mackay stood in front of the cowering, naked Dennington. He slowly swung the axe back and forth, like a lethal pendulum counting down the seconds of Maurice Dennington's life.

He paused for a moment, deep in thought and replaced the axe against the fallen tree.

Reaching for his skinning knife, he sliced off the Gaffer tape.

Dennington was crying, 'Don't do this to me, I never meant it to go as far as it did, I'm truly sorry. We were all young and stupid, it was only meant to be a bit of a fun.'

'Do you truly repent for your sins, Dennington?'

'Of course, I do, just let me go, please.'

Mackay shook his head, he recognised platitudes when he heard them. The demon was tormenting him.

Well enough was enough.

He walked back over to the fallen tree and picked up the axe.

Striding back towards the whimpering Dennington, he raised the axe high above his head before bringing it down, hard. There was the sound of bone splintering, then the still air was shattered by the piercing scream that erupted from

Dennington's mouth. His right foot had been completely severed with one blow of the axe.

Without pausing Mackay raised the axe again, this time he brought it down onto the left leg just above the ankle. The axe failed to sever the leg in one blow, so for a third time the axe was raised. This time the axe did its work and the left foot was severed.

Mackay threw the axe down behind him, then picked up the two severed feet, holding them above his head.

He looked down at Dennington and said, 'You are dying, your life blood is leaving your body, this is your last chance to repent.'

Dennington's eyes had glazed over, his whole body had lapsed into massive shock, caused by the trauma and huge blood loss. He tried to mouth a word, but it only emerged as an inaudible rasp.

'Then descend into Hell', said Mackay.

Suddenly, he could hear movement, somebody was approaching through the trees.

Instinctively, he ducked low and moved into cover behind the tree that supported Dennington's dying body.

CHAPTER 73

10.20am, Monday 27th March 1986
Worksop, Nottinghamshire

The black clad figures of the Special Operations Unit were weaving their way through the woodland. Their pace had quickened after they heard the blood curdling scream from deeper in the wood. Danny and Rob struggled to keep pace with Sergeant Rodgers as the men moved with urgency and purpose led by Inspector Powell.

Suddenly, there was a shout from the men leading the way into the wood, 'Contact!'

Almost immediately after the shout there was the sound of a single gunshot.

The bullet slammed into the trunk of the tree immediately adjacent to the officer who had shouted the contact. Every man in the team instantly dropped to the floor and rolled into cover.

The next shout was from Inspector Powell, 'Report contact!'

The reply came back, 'I can see Superintendent Dennington boss, he's badly injured. We've come under fire, there's no sign where the shot came from.'

A third voice then broke the silence, this voice had a distinctive Scottish brogue, 'All of you stay down and don't move! I could have killed you with that shot, but I didn't. I have no quarrel with any of you and I don't want to have to hurt any of you. Dennington isn't quite ready to die yet, so I can't let you approach him. I will shoot dead the first man who tries, trust me when I say, I will not miss.'

Scott Powell was in cover behind a fallen tree, he crawled slowly forward until he could see the stricken Dennington. He could see the catastrophic injuries to his legs and the huge blood loss.'

Guided by Sergeant Rodgers, Danny Flint crawled forward until he was at the side of Powell, he too could now see the obviously dying, Dennington.

He whispered to Powell, 'Scott, let me see if I can talk to Mackay.'

'Okay Danny, but if any of my men get the opportunity for a shot, they'll take it.'

'We can't get near Dennington anyway, it's got to be worth a go.'

Danny shouted, 'Ben Mackay, my name's Daniel Flint, it's not too late to stop this, let me help you out of this mess. Put your weapon down and allow my men to administer some first aid to that wounded man.'

'Daniel, is it? And here you are in the middle of the lion's den, how very appropriate. I can't allow any of your men to come any closer. This demon and his friends were all responsible for the assault, rape, sodomy and subsequent death of my beautiful daughter. Now, as the scriptures dictated they have all paid the price. The third demon is already dead, you'll find him where I killed him, at the disused maggot farm.'

'Ben, I promise you, I'll make this man pay for his crimes, police officer or not. Let justice deliver his punishment. Don't let him ruin your life as well.'

'Don't you understand Daniel? My life was ruined on the day my daughter took her own life. Do you think I care to remain in a world, where evil men like Maurice Dennington, can rise to positions of power, where hypocrisy is rife? How could this rapist scum be placed in charge of a Sexual Offences Investigation Team? Anyway, it's all academic now, your Superintendent has bled out, he's finished, as we talk he's descending into hellfire. I know my beautiful daughter and my lovely wife are waiting for me, the Lord will forgive me for what I have to do now.'

Danny shouted, 'No Ben!'

The loud crack of a single gunshot, echoed around the dark forest.

Then total silence.

Inspector Powell turned to Sergeant Rodgers and whispered, 'On me Terry, let's move forward and see what's happened, take it real slow.'

The two men inched forward, their weapons trained on the tree where they had last heard Mackay's voice.

Eventually, Scott Powell found Ben Mackay lying at the base of the tree, he had blown the top of his head off with a single shot through the roof of his mouth.

Powell recovered the black handgun that had fallen to the side of the body, he made the weapon safe, handed it to Sergeant Rodgers and shouted, 'Chief Inspector Flint, you can come forward now, Dennington and Mackay are both dead, you'd better start calling in the circus, this is a murder scene now.'

Danny walked forward and looked at the two bodies, he turned to Rob and said, 'This was only ever going to end one way, I'm just glad Ben Mackay didn't decide to take a few of these men with him. It would have been so easy for him to do that.'

'You're right Danny, this was always only ever about revenge though. His quarrel was with the four men who defiled his daughter, nobody else. Talking about four men, we know where three of them are, what did Mackay say about a maggot farm?'

'He said that the third demon, presumably Frederick Reece, was at a disused maggot farm.'

'Well there can't be too many of those knocking about, can there?'

'Come on Rob, let's get back to the car and start getting things organised for the murder scene.'

Danny walked over to Scott Powell, 'Thanks Scott, you and your men did a fantastic job today, I'm just glad nobody else got hurt.'

'You and me both Danny, that really was the nightmare scenario, he could have taken out as many of us as he wanted to. That was bloody scary shit, boss.'

CHAPTER 74

5.00pm, Monday 27th March 1986
Major Crime Investigation Unit, Mansfield

Danny sat opposite Bill Wainwright in the Chief Superintendent's office, the two men were discussing what had been a very eventful day.

Danny leaned back in the chair and said, 'We've now recovered the body of Frederick Reece from a disused maggot farm just outside Newark. He'd been left in an outbuilding, both his hands had been severed and were missing from the scene, his throat had been cut and he'd bled to death. The stumps of his arms had been cauterised, to stop the bleeding, after his hands had been hacked off. God knows how long the poor bastard was alive before he had his throat cut. The same bible reference had been painted on the wall using his blood.'

'Jesus Christ Danny, what a fucking mess.'

'When we searched the Land Rover, we found a key and documentation for a caravan site in Clumber Park. I've had a forensic team examining the caravan the key fitted, all afternoon. They've recovered, what are probably going to be, Naylor's eyes and Hall's teeth in individual zip lock bags. The hands hacked from Frederick Reece were found in a bin liner in the back of the Land Rover.'

'So, the severed feet of Dennington would have completed the demands of the Old Testament bible reference, is that it?'

'That's it sir, I think Ben Mackay was so devoutly religious, that the rage and madness, brought on by the suicide of his daughter, manifested itself through the demands of the Old Testament, in particular the Book of Exodus. He didn't see his conduct as brutal, cold blooded murder, he thought he was ridding the world of four evil men.'

'From what your enquiries have revealed so far Danny, he probably wasn't far from the truth.'

'Unfortunately, with the skills Mackay possessed, once he'd set this train of events in motion, those four were always dead men walking.'

'And Superintendent Dennington? How could we have allowed this to happen?'

'Are you asking me about his acceptance into the police, his accelerated promotion at Bramshill, his appointment to head the new Sexual Offences Investigation Team or his murder, sir?'

'His murder Danny, the Chief's the one who's going to have to find an answer for all the other questions.'

'In my honest opinion, I believe Maurice Dennington was the architect of his own demise. If he'd allowed the surveillance to continue, he would probably still be alive. If he'd told us the truth about the assault on the woman when he was at university, he would still be alive. If he hadn't been a misogynistic, raping bastard, he would still be alive.'

'Point taken Danny. I know the Chief's already having cold sweats about tomorrow's press conference. They're going to want to know how one of our superintendents became the final victim in the last of the Exodus Murders. Talk about egg on face for him and the force, the man he appointed to be in charge of the Sexual Offences Investigation Team, was nothing more than an unconvicted rapist!'

'With the greatest of respect sir, that's the Chief's problem, I'm glad it's not mine. Don't forget we still owe the editor of the Daily Mirror, first disclosure on this story.'

'Bloody hell, I'd forgotten about that Danny. You'll be pleased to hear that I've already dealt with that snide bastard, Dave Mitchell. Suffice to say, he won't be working on any crime scenes for the foreseeable future.'

'Quite right too sir, we can do without those kinds of problems. To be perfectly honest, I'm more concerned about all the people left behind, who are now suffering because of this mess. I think about Vanessa Hall and her kids, her husband and their father gone. Geoff Parkin and Christopher Baker, they both loved Cav Naylor in their own way. The elderly Mrs Reece, a Parkinson's sufferer, who'll never get another visit from her son. Then there's Liz Dennington, I've just got back from seeing her at the family home, to say she's stunned would be the biggest understatement ever, the poor woman couldn't speak. The fall out and devastation caused by those four men, committing that despicable act, all those years ago, has been simply horrendous.'

'Who was it once said, for every action expect a reaction?'

'I couldn't tell you sir, but it's very true.'

'Talking of reaction, I've also spoken to Sir Jarvis Eccles, the Royals secretary up at Balmoral. Apparently, somebody's, "not amused", that the press has already got wind of the fact that the Royal Household recently employed a serial killer, who was regularly left alone with possible heirs to the throne whilst in possession of loaded firearms. Talk about a shitstorm, Danny.'

'I suppose that's the Chief's knighthood up the creek for the foreseeable future then?'

Both men smiled, before Wainwright again turned serious.

'I wouldn't have wished this to happen Danny, but we needed a case like this to test our capabilities. I've been very impressed how the unit functioned Danny; you and your team pulled the case together very quickly. Unfortunately, due to the skills possessed by the man you were pursuing, the outcome was inevitable. I don't think there was anything you could have done quicker or differently, that would have led to an alternative outcome.'

'That's very true sir, we were always playing catch up, trying to piece everything together and like you said, somebody with the skills of Ben Mackay will always take some stopping.'

'Changing the subject Danny, I hear your wedding day's getting pretty close now?'

'Yes sir, only a few more weeks to wait now. The wedding's set for the 7th of May, put it in your diary, you'll be getting a proper written invitation, when I can get around to sitting down with Sue and writing them all out.'

'Well rest assured Danny, when you return from your honeymoon, your desk will still be here. The MCIU is here to stay, please pass on my thanks to the team for all their hard work.

'Will do sir, and thanks.'

Just as Danny stood to leave, there was an urgent knocking on the office door.

'Come in!' shouted Bill Wainwright.

The door opened and a breathless Rob Buxton walked in.

Rob said to the Chief Superintendent, 'Sorry to interrupt your meeting sir.'

He then turned to Danny and said, 'Boss, you remember how there were no police dogs available this morning because they were all on a shout at Rampton? Well, we've just had a notification stemming from that breakout at Rampton Hospital. Four guards, sorry nurses were injured during the escape. One of the nurses, who received a stab wound through the eye is still on the critical list, the prognosis is that he is not expected to survive his injuries. Apparently, the weapon used to stab him went through the eye and into the brain, causing a massive haemorrhage. The escape could well become a murder enquiry, that's why we've been notified.'

'Are Brian Hopkirk's team travelling to Rampton to start the enquiries?' asked Danny.

'They are sir, the thing is, one of the inmates who escaped was Jimmy Wade.'

EPILOGUE

7.00pm, Monday 27th March 1986
Ranby Village, Nottinghamshire

Liz Dennington stood in the shower and allowed the torrent of hot water to cascade down her naked body. She had stood, motionless, under the hot water for twenty minutes. She closed her eyes, allowed the water to hit her face and tried to lose herself in the steamy heat.

Finally, she reached for the chrome control unit and switched the shower off, she stood in silence, listening to the water drip from her body onto the shower tray.

She opened the glass door and took the soft white towelling robe from the hook. As she dried herself, her thoughts became a little clearer.

It had been a crazy day, first there had been the assault by her husband. Then later in the day, there had been the visit by the senior ranking detective and the police woman. They had come to the house and informed her that her husband had been abducted and murdered, and that the man responsible for his death had then taken his own life. At the time they were there, she had been unable to process the information they had given her.

Liz had been unable to speak, unable to respond in anyway.

When the detective left, the policewoman had stayed with her, until at six o'clock that evening Liz had finally asked her to leave the house. She had lied to the officer, telling her that a relation was coming to stay with her, that she would be fine and just needed a little time on her own.

It didn't bother her that she'd lied to the police woman, and it was true she did need to be on her own now.

Liz wrapped a towel around her wet hair, put it up into a turban and began to walk around the beautifully decorated rooms of her palatial home.

As she walked through the house, she collected boxes of Paracetamol tablets that had been hidden, stashed away in secret places.

Finally, she walked into the bedroom and from her bedside cabinet she took out a half litre bottle of Smirnoff vodka. She threw all the boxes of tablets onto the double bed, unscrewed the cap from the bottle and took a sip of the fiery vodka.

She replaced the bottle on the bedside cabinet, then used the towel to rub her hair dry before throwing it onto the wash basket in the corner of the room.

Liz stood in front of the full-length mirror and discarded her robe.

She studied her reflection in the mirror, her body was still curvaceous and firm. Her face scrubbed clean and slightly flushed from the hot shower and the vodka, was still very pretty, her tousled auburn hair was long and framed her face beautifully.

Staring at herself in the mirror, Liz Dennington knew she was still a very fine looking woman.

But was it enough?

She slipped on a nightie, then sat on the bed amongst the pill boxes.

Very slowly and methodically, she began to puncture each blister pack, popping each white tablet into the empty glass at the side of the bed.

When she had removed the last tablet from the last blister pack, she stared in silence at the huge quantity of tablets in the glass. She had collected them for months, carefully hiding them where he wouldn't find them, waiting for the day when she would finally be ready to set herself free from her living hell.

Liz took another sip of the warming vodka and very slowly a smile spread across her lips. It was almost imperceptible at first, but gradually the subtle grin became a beaming smile.

She stood and picked up the glass, that was now almost full of Paracetamol tablets. Striding purposefully into the bathroom she flushed the toilet at the same time as she poured the tablets from the glass down the pan.

Laughing out loud, she walked back into the bedroom and said, 'I've never met you Ben Mackay, but you must have been sent to me from God. Today was going to be the day I ended my life, but now because of you, today will be the first day of the rest of my life. Thank you so much Ben, you truly were an angel sent by the Lord.'

About the author

Trevor Negus is a retired Police Officer who spent 30 years working with Nottinghamshire Police.

He worked both inner city and rural beats in uniform and spent the entire duration of the Miners' Strike of 1984 on a Police Support Unit.

He then spent six years as an authorised firearms officer and was a sniper on the Force's Special Operations Unit. The last eleven years of his Police career were spent as a detective on the CID, where he was involved in numerous murder enquiries. During his time on the CID he was trained as a specialist interviewer, involved in the planning and interviews of murder suspects.

✳✳ Coming Soon also by Trevor Negus ✳✳

A Different Kind of Evil

The body of an eleven year old boy is discovered at a secluded beauty spot in Nottinghamshire. The post mortem reveals that the boy has been sexually assaulted and strangled.

Chief Inspector Flint and the MCIU begin an enquiry to find the killer or killers.

As their investigation takes them into a murky world of child exploitation at Children's Homes across the county they are also tasked with investigating the escape of psychopath, Jimmy Wade from Rampton High security hospital. Wade was assisted in his escape by an obsessed but troubled young woman and has remained in hiding at the woman's remote woodland cottage. He is fixated on revenge and will stop at nothing to get even with the people who ill-treated him at Rampton and the team of detectives who tracked him down in the first place.

The two investigations set Danny Flint and his team their toughest test yet and stretch their resources and nerves to the limits.

As the detectives close in on their quarry the story races to a thrilling and breathtaking climax.